One Night
PROMISED

Also by Jodi Ellen Malpas

This Man
Beneath This Man
This Man Confessed

One Night
PROMISED

JODI ELLEN MALPAS

FOREVER

NEW YORK   BOSTON

Forever
Hachette Book Group
1290 Avenue of the Americas
New York, NY 10104

www.HachetteBookGroup.com

Printed in the United States of America

RRD-C

First Edition: August 2014
10   9   8   7   6   5

Forever is an imprint of Grand Central Publishing.
The Forever name and logo are trademarks of Hachette Book Group, Inc.

The Hachette Speakers Bureau provides a wide range of authors for speaking events. To find out more, go to www.hachettespeakersbureau.com or call (866) 376-6591.

The publisher is not responsible for websites (or their content) that are not owned by the publisher.

Library of Congress Cataloging-in-Publication Data

Malpas, Jodi Ellen.
    One night : promised / Jodi Ellen Malpas. — First edition.
        pages cm. — (One night trilogy)
    ISBN 978-1-4555-5931-2 (trade pbk.) — ISBN 978-1-4555-5932-9 (ebook) —
ISBN 978-1-4789-3056-3 (audiobook) — ISBN 978-1-4789-2979-6 (audio download)
I. Title.
    PR6113.A47P76 2014
    823'.92—dc23

                                    2014016034

For my assistant, Siobhan. You all know her as The Keeper of All Things Important. I know her as my little sister.

Acknowledgments

It's been a year since I last wrote an acknowledgment. It was for *This Man Confessed*, the final book of my This Man Trilogy, and I remember feeling a great sense of pressure to bring Jesse and Ava's story to an explosive but satisfying end. I also had one constant thought running through my mind . . .

What the hell do I write next?

One Night came to me fast and furiously. Livy and M were born, and while writing their story, the mixture of excitement and worry played havoc on me. Jesse "The Lord" Ward had big boots to fill, yet as my new story progressed, I couldn't help but think I might have equaled all of the qualities I strived to achieve in *This Man*. Then my agent, Andrea Barzvi, read the first book and mirrored my thoughts, followed by Beth de Guzman of Grand Central Publishing and Genevieve Pegg of Orion Books.

The excitement for my new tale began there.

A massive thank you to my wonderful attorney, Matthew Savare, who is a consistent support in my new world. He insists I shouldn't like him. All clients hate their lawyer. I love you too much to dislike you!

My fabulous agent, Andrea Barzvi of Empire Literary: You go

way beyond the call of duty for an agent/client relationship. I'm so grateful for everything you do, professionally *and* on so many other levels.

Beth de Guzman, Leah Hultenschmidt, and the amazing team at Grand Central Publishing, I'm so happy I get to do this all over again with you! Thank you for your faith in my work and for supporting my new adventure.

To Genevieve Pegg, Laura Gerrard, and every wonderful person at Orion Books. I love belonging to such an easygoing, attentive British publishing house. Bottoms up!

I could go on and on. I have a wonderful team working with me, here in Britain and across the Atlantic, and each person is invaluable to me. Every single one.

But there's a bigger thank you, and that goes to my mum and sister. Mum came out of retirement to manage JEM, and my sister gave up her regular job and threw herself into organizing my chaotic life. I treasure our Monday morning meetings at "JEM HQ," and I treasure both of you, too. Thank you for embracing and supporting my new career.

And an even bigger thank you than that goes to my dad—a regular bloke who's sent his three girls off into the big wide world with his support and blessing. Ask anyone and they'll tell you, he's one of the nicest men you'll ever meet. They're right. Big Pat is one of a kind and there are only two people in this world who are lucky enough to call him "Dad." I'm grateful every day that I am one of those two people.

I've created another world of fierce passion, blinding intensity, and consuming love. It's had me crying, laughing, and shouting. I love it as much as *This Man*. I hope you do, too.

Jodi

xxx

One Night
PROMISED

PROLOGUE

He had summoned her. She'd known he would find out— he had eyes and ears everywhere, but it never stopped her from disobeying him. It was all part of the plan to get what she wanted.

Stumbling down the dark corridor of the underground London club toward his office, she barely registered her stupidity. Determination and too much alcohol were getting in the way. She had a loving family at home, people who treasured and loved her, made her feel wanted and valued. She knew deep down that there was no good reason to be exposing her body and mind to this sordid, seedy underworld. Yet she did it again tonight. And she'd do it again tomorrow night.

Her stomach turned as she approached the door to his office, her alcohol-drenched brain only barely functioning enough to make her hand lift and take the handle of the door. On a little hiccup and another stagger in her ridiculous stilettos, she fell into William's office.

He was a handsome man in his late thirties, with a head of thick hair that was beginning to gray at his temples, giving him a distinguished salt-and-pepper fleck that matched his distinguished suits. His square jaw was harsh, but his smile friendly when he chose to flash it, which wasn't very often. His male clients never saw that smile. William chose to maintain the hard front that made all men quiver when in his presence. But for his girls, his eyes always sparkled and his face was always soft and reassuring. She didn't understand it and she didn't try to. She just knew that she needed him. And she knew that William had developed a fondness for her, too. She used that weakness against him. The hard businessman's heart was soft for all his girls, but for her, it was complete mush.

William looked to the door as she stumbled through, raising his hand and halting the serious talk coming from a tall mean-type standing over his desk. One of his rules was to always knock and await instruction to enter, but she never did and William never reprimanded her. "We'll continue this soon," he said, dismissing his associate, who left without delay or protest, shutting the door quietly behind him.

William stood, straightening his jacket while stepping out from behind his huge desk. Even through her alcohol-induced fog, she could see the concern on his face with perfect clarity. She could also see a hint of irritation. He approached her carefully, cautiously, as if he was worried she'd bolt, and gently took her arm. He placed her in one of the quilted leather chairs opposite his desk, then poured himself a scotch and handed her some ice water before taking a seat.

She didn't feel scared in the presence of this powerful man, even in such a vulnerable state. Bizarrely, she always felt safe. He'd do anything for his girls, including castrate any man who overstepped the mark. He had specific rules, and no man in his right mind dared break those rules. It was more than their life was worth. She'd seen the result and it wasn't pretty.

"I told you no more," William said, trying to sound cross, but he only achieved a tone drenched with sympathy.

"If you don't set them up for me, I'll find them myself,"

she slurred, her drunkenness injecting some spunk into her small frame. She threw her purse onto his desk in front of him, but William ignored her lack of respect and pushed it back toward her.

"Do you need money? I'll give you money. I don't want you in this world anymore."

"That's not your decision," she countered fearlessly, knowing damn well what she was doing. His straight lips and the darkening of his gray eyes told her she was succeeding. She was forcing his hand.

"You're seventeen years old. You have your whole life ahead of you." He stood and made his way around his desk, sitting on the edge in front of her. "You lied to me about your age, you've broken endless rules, and now you refuse to let me put your life back together." He took her chin and lifted her defiant face to his. "You've disrespected me and, worst of all, yourself."

She had no answer to that. She'd misled him, tricked him, just to get close to him. "I'm sorry," she mumbled quietly, breaking free of his hold to take a long swig of her water. She didn't know what else to say and even if she could find the words, it would never be good enough. She knew William's compassion for her could tarnish the respect he'd earned in this underworld business, and her refusal to let him fix her situation—a situation he felt responsible for—was only risking that reputation further.

He knelt in front of her, his big palms resting on her bare legs. "Which one of my clients broke my rules this time?"

She shrugged, not willing to share the name of the man she'd tempted into bed. She knew William had warned them all to stay away from her. She had misled him as much as William. "It doesn't matter." She wanted William to be angry at her continued disrespect, but he remained calm.

* * *

"You won't find what you're looking for." William felt like a bastard delivering such harsh words. He knew what she was looking for. "I can't look after you," he said quietly, pulling down the hem of her short dress.

"I know," she whispered.

William took a long, tired breath. He knew she didn't belong in his world. He didn't even know if *he* belonged anymore. He'd never let compassion interfere with business, never put himself in situations that could ruin his well-respected standing, yet this young female had stamped all over that claim. It was those sapphire eyes. He never let sentiment get in the way of business—he couldn't afford to—but this time he'd failed.

His big hand lifted to stroke her soft, porcelain cheek and the desperation in her eyes pierced his hard heart. "Help me do what's right. You don't belong here with me," he said.

She nodded, and William exhaled a breath of relief. This girl was too beautiful and too reckless—a dangerous combination. This girl was going to find herself in trouble. He was furious with himself for letting this happen, despite her deception.

He looked after his girls, respected them, made sure his clients respected them, and he always kept his eagle eyes open for anything that might put them at risk, mentally *and* physically. He knew what they would do before they did it. Yet this one he'd let slip. This one had fooled him. He couldn't blame her, though. He blamed himself. He was too distracted by this young woman's beauty—a beauty that would forever be etched in his mind's eye. He would send her away again and this time he'd make sure she stayed away. He cared about this one too much to keep her. And it seared painfully on his dark soul.

CHAPTER ONE

There's something to be said about making the perfect cup of coffee. There's even more to be said about making the perfect cup of coffee from one of the spaceship-like machines I'm staring at. I've spent days watching my fellow waitress, Sylvie, complete the task with ease, while chatting, grabbing down another mug, and tapping the order through the till. But all I seem to be achieving is a royal mess, of both the coffee *and* the area surrounding the machine.

I force the jammed filter contraption on a quiet curse and it slips, scattering the coffee grains everywhere. "No, no, no," I mutter under my breath, grabbing my cloth from the front pocket of my apron. The damp rag is brown, a dead giveaway to the millions of other times I've wiped up my mess today.

"You want me to take over?" Sylvie's amused voice creeps over my shoulders and makes them sag. It's no use. No matter how many times I try, I always end up in the same pickle. This spaceship and I are not friends.

I sigh dramatically and turn, handing Sylvie the big metal handle thingy. "I'm sorry. The machine hates me."

Her bright pink lips break out in a fond smile, and her black shiny bob swishes as she shakes her head. Her patience is commendable. "It'll come. Why don't you go clear table seven?"

I move fast, grabbing a tray and making my way over to the recently vacated area in the hope of redeeming myself. "He'll sack me," I muse, loading the tray. I've only been working here for four days, but on hiring me, Del said it would only take me a few hours of training on my first day to get the hang of the machine that dominates the back counter of the bistro. That day was hideous, and I think Del shares my thoughts.

"No he won't." Sylvie fires the machine up, and the sound of steam rushing from the froth pipe fills the bistro. "He likes you!" she calls louder, grabbing a mug, then a tray, then a spoon, a napkin, and the chocolate sprinkles, all while rotating the metal jug of milk with ease.

I smile down at the table as I wipe it before collecting the tray and making my way back to the kitchen. Del's only known me for a week, and he's already said that I haven't a bad bone in my body. My grandmother has said the very same thing but added that I'd better grow some soon because the world and the people in it are not always nice or gentle.

I dump the tray on the side and start loading up the dishwasher.

"You okay, Livy?"

I turn toward the gruff voice of Paul, the cook. "Great. You?"

"Top of the world." He continues cleaning out the pots, whistling as he does.

Resuming stacking plates in the dishwasher, I think to myself that I should be just fine as long as I'm not let loose on that machine. "Is there anything else you'd like me to do before I get off?" I ask Sylvie as she pushes her way through the swing door of the kitchen. I envy the way she carries out all tasks with such ease and speed, from dealing with that damn machine to stacking mugs on top of each other without looking.

"No." She turns and wipes her hands on the front of her apron. "You get off. I'll see you tomorrow."

"Thank you." I remove my apron and hang it up. "Bye, Paul."

"Have a good evening, Livy," he calls, waving a ladle above his head.

After weaving my way through the tables of the bistro, I push my way out the door and onto the narrow back street, getting immediately pelted by rain. "Wonderful." I smile, shielding my head with my denim jacket and making a run for it.

I hop between the puddles, my Converse doing nothing to keep my feet dry, squelching with each hurried stride as I make my way to the bus stop.

*　*　*

Taking the steps up to our town house, I barge through the door and rest my back against it, catching my breath.

"Livy?" Nan's husky voice instantly lightens my wet mood. "Livy, is that you?"

"It's me!" I hang my soaked jacket on the coat hook and kick off my sodden Converse before making my way down the long hallway to the back kitchen. I find Nan stooped over the cooker, stirring a huge pot of something—soup, undoubtedly.

"There you are!" She drops the wooden spoon and wobbles toward me. At eighty-one, she is really quite remarkable and still so on the ball. "You're drenched!"

"I'm not so bad," I assure her, ruffling my hair as she assesses me from top to bottom, settling on my flat stomach as my T-shirt rides up.

"You need fattening up."

I roll my eyes but humor her. "I'm starving."

The smile that graces her wrinkled face makes me smile, too, as she embraces me and rubs my back.

"What have you done today, Nan?" I ask.

She releases me and points to the dinner table. "Sit."

I do as I'm told immediately, picking up the spoon she's set down for me. "So?"

She turns a frown on me. "So what?"

"Today. What did you do?" I prompt.

"Oh!" She flaps a tea towel at me. "Nothing exciting. A bit of shopping, and I baked your favorite carrot cake." She points across to the other worktop, where a cake is sitting on a cooling rack. But it isn't carrot cake.

"You made me carrot cake?" I ask, watching as she returns to serving up two bowls of soup.

"Yes. Like I said, Livy. I made your favorite."

"But my favorite's lemon cake, Nan. You know that."

She doesn't falter in her serving, bringing the two bowls to the table and setting them down. "Yes, I do. That is why I made you lemon cake."

I flick a glance across the kitchen again, just to check I'm not mistaken. "Nan, that looks like pineapple upside-down cake."

Her rump hits the chair, and she looks at me like *I'm* the one losing my mind. "That's because it *is* pineapple upside-down cake." She plunges her spoon into the bowl and slurps off some coriander soup before reaching for some freshly baked bread. "I made your favorite."

She's confused, and so am I. After that last few seconds' exchange, I have no clue what sort of cake she's made, and I don't care. I look across at my dear grandmother, studying her feeding herself. She seems okay and doesn't look confused. Is this the beginning? I lean forward. "Nan, are you feeling okay?" I'm worried.

She starts laughing. "I'm pulling your leg, Livy!"

"Nan!" I scorn her, feeling immediately better. "You shouldn't do that."

"I'm not losing my marbles yet." She waves her spoon at my bowl. "Eat your supper and tell me how you got on today."

My shoulders sag dramatically on a sigh as I stir my soup. "I can't get on with that coffee machine, which is a problem when ninety percent of customers order some kind of coffee."

"You'll get to grips with it," she says confidently, like she's an expert on the damn thing.

"I'm not so sure. Del won't keep me just for clearing tables."

"Well, apart from the coffee machine, are you enjoying it?"

I smile. "Yes, I really am."

"Good. You can't look after me forever. A young thing like you should be out enjoying herself, not tending to her grandmother." She eyes me cautiously. "And I don't need tending to, anyway."

"I liked looking after you," I argue quietly, bracing myself for the usual lecture. We could argue about this until we're blue in the face and still be in disagreement. She's fragile, not physically but mentally, no matter how much she insists she's okay. She draws breath. I fear the worst. "Livy, I will not be leaving God's green pastures until I see you pull things together, and that's not going to happen if you spend all your time henpecking me. I'm running out of time, so get your skinny little arse in gear."

I wince. "I've told you. I'm happy."

"Happy hiding from a world that has so much to offer?" she asks seriously. "Start living, Olivia. Trust me, time soon passes you by. Before you know it, you're being measured for false teeth and you won't dare cough or sneeze through fear of pissing yourself."

"Nan!" I choke on a piece of bread, but she's not amused at all. She's deadly serious, as she always is during these types of conversations.

"True story," she says on a sigh. "Get out there. Take whatever life throws your way. You're not your mother, Oliv—"

"Nan," I warn slowly.

She visibly slumps in her chair. I know I frustrate her, but I'm quite happy as I am. I'm twenty-four, I've lived with my nan since I was born, and as soon as I left college, I made my excuses to stay at home and keep an eye on her. But while I was quite happy look-ing after my nan, she was not. "Olivia, I've moved forward. You need to, too. I should never have held you back."

I smile, not knowing what to say. She doesn't realize it, but I needed holding back. I'm my mother's daughter, after all.

"Livy, make your nan happy. Put some heels on and go out and enjoy yourself."

It's me slumping now. She just can't stop herself. "Nan, you'd have to pin me down to get me in heels." My feet ache at the very thought.

"How many pairs of those canvas things do you have?" she asks, buttering me yet more bread and passing it over.

"Twelve," I answer, completely unashamed. "All in different colors." I plan on buying them in yellow on Saturday, too. I take the bread and sink my teeth in, smiling around my bite when she huffs her displeasure.

"Well at least go out and have fun. Gregory's always offering. Why don't you take him up on his constant offers?"

"I don't drink." I wish she'd stop with this. "And Gregory will only drag me around all the gay bars," I tell her, raising my eye-brows. My best friend sleeps with enough men for both of us.

"Any bar is better than no bar. You might like it." She reaches over and brushes some crumbs from my lips, then strokes my cheek softly. I know what she's going to say. "It's frightening how similar you are."

"I know." I rest my hand over hers and hold it in place while she silently reflects. I don't remember my mother very well, but I've seen the proof; I'm a carbon copy of her. Even my blond hair falls strangely similarly into waves that cascade over my shoulders, almost making it seem like too much hair for my tiny body to carry. It's incredibly heavy and only behaves if rough dried and left to do as it pleases. And my big, navy blue eyes that match my grandmother's *and* my mother's have a glassy reflecting quality.

Sapphire-like, people have said. I don't see that part. Makeup is a pleasure, not a necessity, but it's always minimal on my fair skin.

Once I've given her enough time to reminisce, I take her hand and place it by her bowl. "Eat up, Nan," I say quietly, continuing with my own soup.

Dragging herself back to the here and now, she carries on with her supper, but she's quiet. She's never gotten over my mother's reckless lifestyle—a lifestyle that stole Nan's daughter from her. It's been eighteen years and she still misses my mother terribly. I don't. How can you miss someone you hardly knew? But watching my nan slip into these sad thoughts every now and then makes it just as painful for me.

*   *   *

Yes, there's definitely something to be said about making the perfect cup of coffee. I'm staring at the machine again, but today I'm smiling. I've done it—the correct amount of foam, the smoothness like silk, and the little dusting of chocolate, forming a perfect heart on the top. It's just a shame that it's me who's drinking it, not an appreciative customer.

"Good?" Sylvie asks, watching with anticipation.

I hum and gasp, setting the cup down. "The coffee machine and I are now friends."

"Yay!" she squeals, throwing her arms around me. I laugh and match her enthusiasm, looking over her shoulder as the door to the bistro swings open.

"I think the lunchtime rush is about to start," I say, breaking free from her grip. "I'll get this one."

"Oh, she's full of confidence," Sylvie laughs, moving to give me access to the serving counter. She beams at me as I make my way over to the man who's just arrived.

"What can I get you?" I ask, getting ready to jot down his

order, but when he doesn't answer, I look up and find him watching me closely. I start shifting nervously, not liking the scrutiny. I find my voice. "Sir?"

His eyes widen a little. "Urhh, cappuccino, please. To go."

"Sure." I snap into action, leaving Mr. Wide Eyes gathering himself, and take myself to my new best friend, loading the handle thingy and securing it successfully into the holder—so far so good.

"That is why Del won't sack you," Sylvie whispers over my shoulder, making me jump slightly.

"Stop it," I say, retrieving a takeout cup from the shelf and placing it under the filter before pressing the correct button.

"He's watching you."

"Sylvie, stop it!"

"Give him your number."

"No!" I blurt too loudly, quickly checking over my shoulder. He's staring at me. "I'm not interested."

"He's cute," Sylvie concludes, and I have to agree. He's very cute, but I'm very uninterested.

"I don't have time for a relationship." That's not strictly true. This is my first job and before this I spent most of my adult life caring for Nan. Now I'm not sure whether she really does still need the care, or whether it's just my excuse.

Sylvie shrugs and leaves me to finish my second round with the machine. I finish up, smiling as I pour the milk into the cup before releasing a drop of dust on the foam and securing a lid. I'm far too proud of myself and it's obvious on my smiling face as I turn to deliver the cappuccino to Mr. Wide Eyes. "Two pounds eighty, please." I go to place it down, but he intercepts me and takes the cup from my hand, ensuring contact as he does.

"Thank you," he says, pulling my eyes up to his with his soft words.

"You're welcome." I slowly take my hand away from his, accepting the tenner he hands me. "I'll get your change."

"Don't worry." He shakes his head mildly, running his eyes all over my face. "But I wouldn't mind your phone number."

I hear Sylvie chuckling from the table she's clearing. "I'm sorry, I'm in a relationship." I punch his order through the till and quickly collect his change, handing it over to him and ignoring Sylvie's snort of disgust.

"Of course you are." He laughs lightly, looking embarrassed. "How stupid of me."

I smile, trying to ease his awkwardness. "It's okay."

"I don't usually just ask any woman I meet for their number," he explains. "I'm not a creep."

"Honestly, it's okay." I'm feeling embarrassed myself now, and I'm silently wishing he'd leave before I throw a coffee cup at Sylvie's head. I can feel her staring at me in shock. I start to rearrange the napkins, anything to take me away from the uncomfortable situation. I could kiss the man who walks in behind, looking like he's in a hurry. "I'd better get this." I indicate over Mr. Wide Eyes's shoulder to the harassed-looking businessman.

"Oh, yes! Sorry." He backs away, holding up his cup in thanks. "See ya."

"Bye." I lift my hand before looking to my next customer. "What would you like, sir?"

"Latté, no sugar, and make it quick." He barely even looks at me before he answers his phone and walks away from the counter, dumping his briefcase on a chair.

I'm only semi-aware of Mr. Wide Eyes leaving, but I'm more than aware of Sylvie's biker boots marching up to me, where I'm tackling the coffee machine again. "I can't believe you declined!" she whispers harshly. "He was lovely."

I make quick work of my third perfect coffee, not giving her shock the attention it deserves. "He was okay," I reply nonchalantly.

" 'Okay'?"

"Yes, he was okay."

I'm not looking at her, but I know she's just rolled her eyes. "Unbelievable," she mutters, stomping off, her voluptuous rump matching the side-to-side sway of her black bob.

I'm smiling in triumph again as I deliver my third perfect coffee, and my grin doesn't even fall away when the harassed businessman thrusts three pounds into my hand before snatching his cup and marching out, without so much as a thank you.

My feet didn't touch the ground for the rest of the day. I flew in and out of the kitchen, cleaned endless tables, and made dozens of perfect coffees. On my breaks, I managed to check up on Nan, being told off each time for being a whittle arse.

As five o'clock approaches, I sink into one of the brown leather couches and open a can of Coke, hoping the caffeine and sugar might snap me back to life. I'm beat.

"Livy, I'm just going to take the rubbish out," Sylvie calls over, yanking the black sack from one of the bins. "You good?"

"Fabulous." I hold my can up and rest my head back on the sofa, resisting the temptation to close my eyes, instead focusing on the spotlights in the ceiling. I can't wait to fall into bed. My feet are aching, and I desperately need a shower.

"Is anyone working or is it self-service?"

I jump up from the couch at the sound of the impatient but smooth voice, and swing around to tend to my customer. "Sorry!" I rush to the counter, smacking my hip on the corner of the worktop and resisting the urge to curse out loud. "What can I get you?" I ask, rubbing my hip as I look up.

I stagger back. And I definitely gasp. His piercing blue eyes are burning into me. Deep, deep into me. My gaze drifts and takes in his open suit jacket, a waistcoat and pale blue shirt and tie, his dark stubbled jaw, and the way his lips are parted just so. Then I find those eyes again. They're the sharpest blue I've ever seen, and they're cutting right through me with an edge of curiosity. The definition of perfection is standing before me and it has me staring in wonder.

"Do you often examine customers so thoroughly?" His head cocks to the side, his perfect eyebrow arching expectantly.

"What can I get you?" I breathe, waving my pad at him.

"Americano, four shots, two sugars, topped up halfway." The words roll from his mouth, but I don't hear them. I see them. I lip-read every word, writing them down while keeping my eyes on his mouth. Before I know what's happened, my pen has drifted from my pad and I'm scribbling on my fingers. I glance down with a frown.

"Hello?" He sounds impatient again, prompting my eyes to snap up. I allow myself to step back and take in all of his face. I'm shocked, not because of how incredibly stunning he is, but because I've lost all of my bodily functions, except my eyes. They're working just fine, and they can't seem to disconnect from his flawlessness. I don't even lose my concentration when he rests his palms on the counter and leans forward, encouraging a wave from his tousled dark hair to fall onto his forehead. "Am I making you feel uncomfortable?" he asks. I lip-read that, too.

"What can I get you?" I breathe once more, waving my pad at him again.

He nods down to my pen. "You've already asked me. My order's on your hand."

I look down, seeing ink strewn all over my fingers, but it doesn't make a bit of sense, not even when I try to match up the pad to where the pen has trailed off.

Slowly lifting my eyes, I meet his. There's an element of know-ing in them.

He looks smug. It's thrown me completely.

I scan the information stored in my mind from the last few minutes, but I find no order for coffee, just saved images of this face. "Cappuccino?" I ask hopefully.

"Americano," he counters smoothly on a whisper. "Four shots, two sugars, and topped up halfway."

"Right!" I snap myself from my pathetic awestruck state and move to the coffee machine, my hands shaking, my heart thudding. I bash the filter on the wooden drawer to rid it of the used beans, hoping the loud smacking will knock some sense back into me. It doesn't. I still feel . . . strange.

Pulling the lever on the grinder, I load the filter up. He's staring at me. I can feel those piercing blues penetrating my back as I faff and fiddle with the machine that I've grown to love. It's not loving me right now, though. It's not doing anything I tell it to. I can't secure the filter in the holder; my shaking hands are not helping in the slightest.

Taking a deep, calming breath, I start again, successfully loading the filter and placing the cup underneath. I press the button and wait for it to work its magic, keeping my back to the stranger behind me. In the whole week I've worked at Del's Bistro, I've never known the machine to take this long to filter some coffee. I'm silently willing it to hurry the hell up.

When an eternity has passed, I take the cup and slip in two sugars, ready to top it up with water.

"Four shots." He breaks the uncomfortable silence with that soft rasp.

"Pardon?" I don't turn around.

"I ordered four shots."

I look down at the cup, containing just one shot, and close my eyes, praying for the coffee gods to help me out. I don't know how long it takes me to add three more shots, but when I finally turn to deliver his coffee, he's sitting on a sofa, relaxed back, his lean physique stretched out, his fingers tapping the arm. His face doesn't show a hint of emotion, but I detect he's not happy, and for some strange reason, that makes me *really* unhappy. I've handled that damn machine perfectly all day, and now when I really want to look like I know what I'm doing, I'm coming off as an incompetent fool. I feel stupid as I hold up the takeout cup before placing it neatly on the counter.

He looks at it, then back to me. "I want to drink in." His face is serious, his tone flat but sharp, and I stare at him, trying to figure out if he's being difficult or genuine. I don't remember him asking for a takeout; I just assumed. He doesn't look like the type to sit around in backstreet bistros. He looks more like a champagne bar, mingle-with-the-money type.

Grabbing a coffee cup and saucer, I simply transfer the coffee and shove a teaspoon on the side before taking steady steps over to him. No matter how hard I try, I can't stop the chinking of the cup on the saucer. I place it down on the low table and watch as he swivels the saucer before lifting the cup, but I don't hang around to watch him drink, pivoting quickly on my Converse and escaping.

I virtually burst through the swing door of the kitchen, finding Paul putting his coat on. "All right, Livy?" he asks, his rounded face scanning me.

"Yep." I dive into the large metal sink to wash my sweaty hands as the bistro phone starts ringing from the wall. Paul takes the initiative to answer, obviously concluding that I'm dead set on scrubbing my hands until they disappear.

"For you, Livy. I'm outta here."

"Have a great weekend, Paul," I say, drying my hands before I take the phone. "Hello?"

"Livy, honey, are you busy tonight?" Del asks.

"Tonight?"

"Yes, I have a catering contract for a charity gala and I've been let down. Could you be a doll and help me out?"

"Oh, Del, I'd love to, but..." I have no idea why I said I'd love to, because I really wouldn't, and I can't finish that sentence because I can't find a "but." I have nothing to do this evening except faff around my grandmother and get told off for it.

"Arh, Livy, I'll pay you well. I'm desperate."

"What are the hours?" I sigh, leaning against the wall.

"You star! Seven to midnight. It's not hard, honey. Just walk around with trays of canapés and glasses of champagne. Piece of cake."

A piece of cake? It's still walking, and my feet are still killing me. "I need to go home to check on my nan and change. What should I wear?"

"Black, and be at the staff entrance of the Hilton on Park Lane at seven, okay?"

"Sure."

He hangs up, and I hang my head, but my attention is soon pulled to the swing door when Sylvie bursts through, her brown eyes wide. "Have you seen it?"

Her question quickly reminds me of the stunning creature who's sitting drinking coffee in the bistro. I almost laugh as I place the receiver of the phone back in its cradle. "Yes, I've seen him."

"Holy fucking shit, Livy! Men like that should carry a warning." She glimpses back into the bistro and starts fanning her face. "Oh God, he's blowing the steam off his coffee."

I don't need a visual. I can imagine it. "Are you working tonight?" I ask, trying to divert her dribbling into the kitchen.

"Yes!" She swings back toward me. "Did Del ask you?"

"He did." I unhook my keys and lock the doors that lead to the alley.

"He tried to get me to ask you, but I know you're not mad about night work, what with your nan at home. Are you doing it?"

"Well, I agreed." I give her a tired look.

Her serious face grins. "It's closing time. Would you like to let him know that it's time to go?"

Stupidly, I'm battling off the shakes again at the thought of looking at him, and I chastise myself for it. "Yes, I'll tell him," I declare with all the confidence I'm not feeling. Rolling my shoulders back, I walk with sureness, past Sylvie and into the bistro, coming to an abrupt halt when I see he's gone. The strangest sensation comes over me as I scan the area, feeling a bizarre sense of desertion mixed with disappointment.

"Oh. Where's he gone?" Sylvie whines, pushing past me.

"I don't know," I whisper, slowly walking to the abandoned sofa and picking up a half-drunk coffee and three pound coins. I separate the napkin that's stuck to the bottom of the saucer and start to screw it up, but some black lines catch my attention and I'm quickly unraveling it with one hand and flattening it on the table.

I gasp. Then I get a little mad.

Probably the worst Americano that I've ever insulted my mouth with.

M.

My face screws up in disgust, along with the napkin, as I ball it and stuff it in the cup. The arrogant arsehole. Nothing makes me mad, and I know it exasperates my grandmother and Gregory, but I'm really heated with annoyance now. And it really is over something quite silly. But then I'm not sure if it's because I failed to make good coffee when I've been doing so well, or simply because the perfect man didn't approve of it. And what does M stand for, anyway?

After disposing of the cup, the saucer, and the offending napkin, then locking up with Sylvie, I finally reach the conclusion that it's the former and M stands for *Moron*.

CHAPTER TWO

Del leads us through the staff entrance of the hotel, dishing out instructions, pointing to the serving area and ensuring that we're aware of the type of clientele.

Bottom line: posh.

I can deal with that. Once I'd checked on Nan, she virtually pushed me out the front door and chucked my black Converse out after me before she went to get ready for bingo with George at the local oldies group.

"Never leave anyone with an empty glass," Del calls over his shoulder, leading on, "and ensure all empties are delivered back to the kitchen so they can be washed and refilled."

I follow Sylvie, who's following Del, listening intently as I pile my heavy hair up and secure it with a hair tie. It sounds easy enough, and I absolutely love people watching so tonight could be fun.

"Here." Del stops and thrusts a round silver tray at both of us, looking down at my feet. "You didn't have any black flats?"

Following his line of sight, I look down and pull my black trousers up a little. "These are black." I wriggle my toes within my Converse, thinking how much more my feet would hurt if I were wearing anything else.

He doesn't say any more; he just rolls his eyes and leads on until we're in a chaotic kitchen space, where dozens of hotel staff are flying around, shouting and barking orders at each other. I move closer to Sylvie as we continue walking. "Is it just us?" I ask, suddenly a little alarmed. All of the frantic activity suggests a lot of guests.

"No, there will be the agency staff he uses, too. We're backups."

"Does he do this a lot, then?"

"It's his main income. I don't know why he keeps the bistro."

I nod thoughtfully to myself. "Doesn't the hotel provide a catering service?"

"Oh yes, but the type of people you're about to feed and water call the shots, and if they want Del, they'll have Del. He's notorious in this game. You *have* to try his canapés." She kisses her fingertips, making me laugh.

My boss shows us around the room where the function is being held and introduces us to the many other waiters and waitresses, all looking bored and inconvenienced. This is obviously a regular thing for them, but not me. I'm looking forward to it.

"Ready?" Sylvie places a final glass of champagne onto my tray. "Now, the trick is to hold it on your palm." She picks up her own tray, her palm underneath in the center. "Then swing it up onto your shoulder, like this." In one fluid movement, the tray glides through the air and lands on her shoulder, without even a chink from glasses touching. I'm fascinated. "See?" The tray glides back down from her shoulder until it's at waist level again. "When offering, hold it here, and when you're moving around, keep it up here." The tray swishes through the air, landing on her shoulder perfectly again. "Remember to relax when you're on the move. Don't be stiff. You try."

I slide my full tray from the counter and position my palm in the center. "It's not heavy," I muse, surprised.

"Yes, but remember when empty glasses start replacing full

glasses it'll get even lighter, so bear that in mind when you're transferring it up and down."

"Okay." I swivel my wrist, taking the tray up to my shoulder with ease. I smile brightly, taking it back down again.

"You're a natural." Sylvie laughs. "Let's go."

Transferring the tray back to my shoulder, I swivel on my Converse and head toward the increasing sound of chatting and laughing that's coming from the function room.

On entering, my navy eyes widen, taking in the wealth, the gowns, and the tuxedos. But I don't feel nervous. I feel stupidly excited. This is people watching at its best.

Without waiting for any prompt from Sylvie, I lose myself in the growing crowds, presenting my tray to groups of people and smiling, whether they thank me or not. Most don't, but it doesn't dampen my mood. I'm in my element, and I'm surprised by it. The tray glides up and down with ease, my body shifts effortlessly through the masses of wealth, and I dance back and forth to the kitchen time and time again to restock and redeliver.

"You're doing good, Livy," Del tells me, just as I'm leaving with another trayload of champagne flutes.

"Thank you!" I sing, keen to get myself back to my thirsty crowd. I catch Sylvie across the room, and she smiles, encouraging a further beam from me. "Champagne?" I ask, presenting my tray to a group of six middle-aged men, all kitted out in tuxedos and bow ties.

"Arh! Bloody marvelous!" a stout man gushes, taking a glass and handing it to one of his companions. He does this a further four times before taking one for himself. "You're doing a fine job, young lady." His free hand moves toward me and slips into my pocket as he winks. "Treat yourself."

"Oh no!" I shake my head. I won't take money from a man. "Sir, I get paid by my boss. You really mustn't." I try to retrieve the note from my pocket while holding the tray steady on my palm. "We don't expect tips."

"I won't hear of it," he insists, pulling my hand from my pocket. "And it's not a tip. It's for the pleasure of seeing such beautiful eyes."

I immediately blush bright red, stumped for anything to say. He must be sixty, if a day! "Sir, really, I can't accept it."

"Nonsense!" He dismisses me with a snort and a wave of his chubby hand, before returning to the chatter of his group, leaving me wondering what the hell to do.

I scan the room, but I can't see Sylvie to ask, and Del is nowhere in sight, so I quickly off-load the remaining glasses before heading back to the kitchens, finding Del tweaking canapés.

"Del, someone gave me this." I slap the note on the counter, feeling better already for confessing, but my eyes bug when I see it's a fifty. A fifty? What's he thinking?

I'm even more stunned when Del starts laughing. "Livy, you star. Keep it."

"I can't!"

"Yes, you can. These people have more money than sense. Take it as a compliment." He pushes the fifty toward me and continues arranging the tiny flatbreads.

I don't feel any better. "I've only served him a glass of champagne," I say quietly. "It hardly justifies a fifty-pound tip."

"No, it doesn't, but like I said, take it as a compliment. Put it back in your pocket and get serving." He nods at my empty tray, reminding me that it is, in fact, empty.

"Oh! Yes, sure." I fly into action, stuffing the obscene tip in my pocket, ready to dispose of it later, and reload my tray before quickly making my way back into the crowd. I avoid the gent who's just thrown away fifty pounds and circle in the other direction, halting at the back of a red satin gown. "Champagne, madam?" I ask, flicking a gaze across to Sylvie. She nods her reassurance once more, smiling, but I don't need it. I'm nailing this.

I turn my attention back to the satin-adorned woman, who has glossy black, poker-straight hair falling to her pert bum. I smile as she turns toward me, revealing her companion.

A man.

Him.

M.

I don't know how I prevent the tray of freshly filled champagne glasses from falling to the floor, but I do. I don't, however, prevent my smile from falling. His lips are parted again, his eyes stabbing at my flesh, but there's no emotion on his exquisite face. His dark stubble is absent, leaving nothing but perfect tanned skin beneath, and his dark hair is a little less tousled, instead falling in perfect waves to the tops of his ears.

"Thank you," the woman says slowly, taking a glass and pulling my eyes away from the strange man. A huge, sparkling, diamond-encrusted cross is suspended from her delicate neck, the brilliant stones nestling just north of her breasts. I've no doubt it's real. "Would you like?" She turns to him, holding up the glass.

He doesn't say anything. He just takes the glass from her perfectly manicured hand, all the time keeping his shocking blue eyes on me.

He's not at all receptive, and far from warm, but there's something strange burning inside me as I gaze at his face. It's something I've never experienced before—something that makes me feel uncomfortable and vulnerable . . . but not frightened.

The woman helps herself to another glass, and I know it's time for me to leave, but I can't move. I feel like I should smile, anything to break the staring deadlock, but what usually comes so naturally to me is completely failing me now. Nothing is working, except my eyes and they're refusing to break from his.

"That will be all," the woman prompts harshly, making me jump. Her delicate features are screwed up in annoyance and her dark eyes have darkened further. She has a stunning face, even if it's scowling at me right now. "I said, that is all." She steps between me and M.

M? I decide right here and now that M is for *mystery*, because he really is. I say nothing as I finally swing my tray back onto my shoulder and slowly turn, walking away, feeling compelled to glance over my shoulder because I know he's still staring at me and I'm wondering how that might be going down with his girlfriend. So I look, and it's as I suspected—steely blues burning holes into my back.

"Hey!"

I jump out of my skin, the tray tumbling from my hands, and I can do nothing to stop it. The glasses seem to float down to the marble, champagne trickling slowly from the flutes, the tray spinning in midair until it all comes together in a collective crash on the hard floor, silencing the room. I'm frozen on the spot as broken glass dances around my feet, seeming to take forever to settle, the piercing, drawn-out noise ringing through the quiet space around me. My eyes are cast downward, my body tense, and I know all attention is pointed at me.

Just me.

Everyone is looking at me.

And I don't know what to do.

"Livy!" Sylvie's panicked voice snaps my despairing head up, and I see her hurrying toward me, her brown eyes concerned. "Are you okay?"

I nod and kneel to start collecting the broken glass, wincing as a sharp pain shoots through my knee, slicing the material of my trousers. "Shit!" I pull in a sharp breath, tears immediately pinching the backs of my eyes. They're a combination of pain and pure embarrassment. I don't like any attention on me, and I do a good job to avoid and repel it, but I can't escape this. I've brought a room full of hundreds of people to an eerie quiet. I want to run away.

"Don't touch it, Livy!" Sylvie pulls me up, giving me an all-over assessment. She must conclude that I look ready to break down because I'm quickly dragged to the kitchen, removing me from my audience. "Jump up." She pats the counter, and I lift myself, still fighting back tears. She takes the hem of my trousers and lifts the leg until my wound is exposed. "Youch!" She flinches at the clean slice and steps back, looking up at me. "I'm shit with blood, Livy. Was that the guy from the bistro?"

"Yes," I whisper, shrinking when I see Del approaching, but he doesn't look annoyed.

"Livy, are you okay?" He hunkers down and performs his own little grimace at my leaking kneecap.

"I'm sorry," I whisper. "I don't know what happened." He'll probably sack me on the spot for causing such a spectacle.

"Hey, hey." He straightens his body, his narrow face softening completely. "Accidents happen, honey."

"I've caused such a drama."

"That's enough," he says sternly, turning to the wall and unhooking the first aid case. "It's not the end of the world." He opens up the box and fishes around until he lays his hands on an antiseptic wipe and tears it open. My teeth grit as he gently swipes it across my knee, the stinging making me hiss and stiffen. "Sorry, but it needs cleaning."

I hold my breath as he undertakes my cleanup operation, finishing by taping square gauze to my knee and lifting me down from the worktop. "Can you walk okay?"

"Sure." I flex my knee and smile my thanks before collecting a new tray.

"What do you think you're doing?" he asks, frowning.

"I…"

"Oh no," he laughs. "God bless you, Livy. Go to the loo and sort yourself out." He points to the exit across the kitchen.

"But I'm fine," I insist, even though I don't feel it, not because my knee's sore but because I'm not looking forward to facing my spectators or M. I'll just have to keep my head down, avoid a certain steel stare, and see my shift through with no further mishaps.

"Toilet!" Del orders, taking the tray and placing it on the counter. "Now." He rests his hands on my shoulders and guides me to the door, not giving me the opportunity to protest further. "Go."

I force a smile through my lingering embarrassment and leave behind the chaos of the kitchen, stepping into the huge room and striving to hurry through unnoticed. I know I've failed—the feeling of sharp blue eyes prickling my skin everywhere confirming it. I feel like a letdown. I feel incompetent, foolish, and fragile. But most of all, I feel exposed.

I navigate the plush carpeted corridor until I push my way through two doors and land in the ridiculously extravagant washroom, kitted out in cream marble and shiny gold at every turn. I almost don't want to use the facilities. The first thing I do is take the fifty from my pocket and gaze at it for a few moments. Then I screw it up and throw it in the bin. I'm not taking money from a man. I wash my hands before presenting myself to the gigantic gold framed mirror to retie my hair, sighing when I'm confronted by haunted sapphire eyes. Curious eyes.

I don't pay much attention when the door opens, and continue to tuck some wayward strands of hair behind my ears. But then there's someone behind me, casting a shadow over my face as I lean into the mirror. M. I gasp and jump back, straight into the body that's just as hard and lean as I'd imagined.

"You're in the ladies'," I breathe, swinging around to face him. I try to put some distance between us, but I don't get very far with the sink behind me. Through my shock, I allow myself to drink in his closeness—his three-piece suit, his clean-shaven face. He smells out of this world, all manly with a touch of earthy wood. It's an intoxicating cocktail. Everything about him sends my sensible being into a tailspin.

He steps forward, closing the already narrow space between us, and then shocks me by kneeling and gently lifting the leg of my trouser. I'm pushing myself back against the sink unit, holding my breath, just watching him run his thumb softly over the gauze hiding my cut. "Does it hurt?" he asks quietly, lifting those incredible blue eyes to mine. I can't talk, so I shake my head a little and watch as he slowly stands back up to his full height. He's thoughtful for a few moments before he speaks again. "I need to force myself to stay away from you."

I don't point out that he's doing a terrible job of that. I can't take my eyes off those lips. "Why do you need to force yourself?"

His hand meets my forearm, and it takes every ounce of my strength not to flinch at the heat radiating through me from his touch. "Because you seem like a sweet girl who should get more from a man than the best fuck of your life."

My lack of astonishment shocks me. Instead, I feel relieved, even if he's just promised to fuck me and nothing more. He's taken by me, too, and that confirmation pulls my eyes up to meet his. "Maybe I want that." I'm goading him, encouraging him, when I should be running in the other direction.

He seems to drift into thought as he concentrates on the soft trail of his fingertip traveling up my arm. "You want more than that."

He's telling me, not asking. I don't know what I want. I've never stopped and considered my future, either professionally or personally. I'm drifting, that's all, but I do know one thing. I'm on dangerous ground, not just because this unidentified man seems to be forward, dark, and way too stunning, but because he's just said that he'll do nothing more than fuck me. I don't know him.

I'd be inconceivably stupid to dive into bed with him, just for sex. It goes against all of my morals. But I can't seem to locate the reasons to stop me. I should be uncomfortable with what he's provoking from me, but I'm not. For the first time in my life, I feel alive. I'm buzzing, unfamiliar feelings attacking my senses, and an even more demanding buzz attacking me between my clenched thighs. I'm pulsing.

"What's your name?" I ask.

"I don't want to tell you, Livy."

Before I can ask him how he knows my name, Sylvie's cry across the party room plays on repeat in my head. I want to touch him, but as I lift my hand to rest it on his chest, he backs up slightly, his eyes nailed to my floating palm between our bodies. I pause for a second to see if he withdraws further. He doesn't. My hand falls down and comes to lie on his suit jacket, coaxing a sharp pull of his breath, but he doesn't stop me; he just watches as I gently feel his torso over his clothing, marveling at the solidness beneath.

Then his eyes flick up to mine, and his head slowly falls forward, his breath heating my face as he nears until I finally close my eyes and brace myself for those lips. He's getting closer. His scent is intensifying and my face is scorching from his hot breath.

But the happy chatter of women breaks the moment, and I'm suddenly being hauled down the row of cubicles and shoved in the very last one. The door slams and I'm whirled around, pinned to the back of the door with his palm over my mouth, his face close to mine. My whole body is heaving as we stare at each other, listening to the women preen in the mirror, reapplying lipsticks and refreshing perfume. I'm mentally yelling at them to hurry the hell up so we can pick up where we left off. I could very nearly feel his lips brushing over mine, and it's just increased my desire for him tenfold.

It seems like an age, but the chatter eventually fades. My heavy breathing doesn't, though, not even when he allows air into my mouth by removing his hand.

His forehead meets mine and his eyes clench shut. "You're too sweet. I can't do it." He lifts me and removes me from the doorway before hastily exiting, leaving me a stupid bag of pent-up lust. I'm too sweet? I let out a sardonic snap of laughter. I'm angry again—pissed off and ready to track him down to tell him who gets to decide what I want. And it's not him.

Letting myself out of the cubicle, I run a quick check over my face and body in the mirror, concluding I look harassed, before exiting the bathroom and making my way to the kitchen.

I spot Sylvie appearing from the kitchen entrance. "There you are! We were just going to send a search party." She hurries toward me, her face turning from amused concern to concerned concern. "You okay?"

"Fine." I brush her off, concluding that I must look as shook up as I feel. I don't hang around for Sylvie to press further, instead grabbing a bottle of champagne and ignoring her inquisitive stare. It's empty. "Are there any more bottles?" I ask, dumping it down a little too harshly. I'm shaking.

"Yeah," she replies slowly, passing me a freshly opened replacement.

"Thank you." I smile. It's strained, and she knows it, but I can't shake my grievance *or* my irritation.

"Are you sure—"

"Sylvie." I pause from pouring and take a deep breath, turning and fixing a sincere smile on my harassed face. "Honestly, I'm okay."

She nods, unconvinced, but she helps me pour rather than digging further. "I guess we should get serving, then."

"We should," I agree, sliding my tray from the counter and swinging it up to my shoulder. "I'm out of here." I leave Sylvie and brave the crowds of people, but I'm not as attentive to the guests as I was before. I don't smile half as much when offering out the champagne, and I'm constantly scanning the room for him. I'm quick to restock in the kitchen so I can return to the masses of crowds, I'm not paying a bit of attention to my surroundings, and I'm at risk of making a complete fool of myself for a second time if my lack of attention causes me to bump into something and drop my tray again.

But I don't care.

I have an unreasonable need to see him again...and then something makes me turn, an invisible power pulling my body toward the source.

He's there.

I'm frozen in place, tray hovering between my shoulder and my waist, and he's studying me, a tumbler of dark liquid hovering at his mouth. It draws my eyes to his lips—the lips I nearly tasted.

My senses heighten when he slowly raises the glass and tips the contents down his throat before wiping his mouth with the back of his hand and placing the empty on Sylvie's tray as she passes. Sylvie does a double take, and then swings around, clearly looking for me. Her wide browns land on me briefly before she starts flicking eyes full of intrigue, mixed with a little worry, back and forth between me and this confounding man.

He's staring—really staring, and his companion must get curious, because she turns, following his line of vision until she's looking at me. She smiles slyly, lifting her empty champagne flute. Panic sets in.

Sylvie's gone, leaving it down to me to fulfill her request. The woman wiggles the glass in midair, a prompt to get my arse in gear, and my curiosity, coupled with my lack of bad manners, prevents me from ignoring her. So I make my way toward them—her still smiling, him still staring—until I'm standing before them, offering the tray to them. Her attempt to make me feel inferior is obvious, but I'm too intrigued to care.

"Take your time, sweetheart," she purrs, taking a glass and extending it to him. "Miller?"

"Thank you," he says quietly, accepting the drink.

Miller? His name's Miller? I cock my head at him, and for the first time, his lips tip knowingly. I'm sure that if he really let go, he'd probably knock me out with his smile.

"Run along now," the woman says, turning her back on me and pulling a reluctant Miller with her, but her rudeness doesn't dampen down my inner delight. I turn on my Converse, happy to leave with the knowledge of his name. I don't turn back, either.

Sylvie's on me like a wolf when I enter the kitchen, just as I knew she would be. "Holy, shitting hell!" I wince at her burst of bad language and set my tray down. "He's staring at you, Livy. I mean proper burning eyes."

"I know." You'd have to be blind or utterly stupid not to notice.

"He's with a woman."

"Yes." I might be pleased to have learned his name, but I'm not so pleased about that part. Not that I have any right to feel jealous. Jealous? Is that what I am? It's an emotion I've never experienced before.

"Oohh, I'm feeling something," Sylvie chants, laughing as she sashays out of the kitchen.

"Yes. Me too," I muse to myself, turning to look back at the entrance, knowing he watched my every step back here.

*   *   *

I avoid him for the rest of the evening, but definitely feel his eyes on me as I weave through the crowds. I feel a constant pull in his direction and struggle to keep my eyes from drifting over, but I'm proud of myself for resisting. While it's an unfamiliar pleasure to lose myself in his steely gaze, I could risk ruining it by seeing him with another woman.

After saying my good-byes to Del and Sylvie, I push my way out of the staff entrance into the midnight air and head for the Tube, looking forward to curling up in bed and having a morning lie-in.

"She's just a business associate." His soft voice from behind halts me, stroking my skin, but I don't turn around. "I know you're wondering."

"You don't need to explain yourself to me." I continue walking, knowing exactly what I'm doing. He's taken by me, and I may not be familiar with the chasing game, but I do know that I shouldn't appear desperate, even if, annoyingly, I am. I'm sensible; I know a bad thing when I see it, and standing behind me is a man who could crush my logic.

My arm is seized, halting my escape, and I'm swung around to face him. If I were strong enough, I'd close my eyes so I don't have to soak up his exquisite face. I'm not strong enough, though.

"No, I don't have to explain myself, yet here I am doing exactly that."

"Why?" I don't pull my arm from his grip because the heat of his touch is working its way through my denim jacket and warming my chilly skin, setting my blood alight. I've never felt anything like it.

"You really don't want to get involved with me." He doesn't sound convinced of that himself, so he's kidding himself if he expects me to buy it. I want to buy it. I want to walk away and wipe my encounters with him from my mind and return to being stable and sensible.

"Then let me leave," I say quietly, meeting the intensity of his stare with my own. The long silence that falls and lingers between us is an indication that he really doesn't want to, but I decide for him and remove my arm from his grasp. "Good night, Miller." I take a few backward steps before turning and walking away. It's probably one of the most sensible decisions I've ever made, even if the majority of my scrambled mind is willing me to pursue it. Whatever *it* is.

CHAPTER THREE

The lingering strangeness of Friday evening was soon hijacked by Nan on Saturday morning when she said my three favorite words: "Let's go sightseeing."

We roamed, we sat, we drank good coffee, we roamed some more, we had lunch, we drank more good coffee, and we roamed again, finally falling through the front door late Saturday evening with a fish and chip supper from the local chippy. Then on Sunday, I helped Nan stitch together the patchwork quilt that she's been making for a soldier based in Afghanistan. She has no idea who he is, but the local oldies group all have pen pals out there, and Nan thought it'd be nice if hers had something to keep him warm...in the desert.

"Have you got the sun tucked away in your socks, Livy?" Nan asks as I walk into the kitchen ready for work on Monday morning.

I look down at my new canary yellow Converse and smile. "Don't you love them?"

"Wonderful!" she laughs, placing my bowl of cornflakes on the breakfast table. "How's your knee?"

Sitting down, I tap my leg and pick up my spoon. "Perfect. What are you doing today, Nan?"

"George and I are going to the market to buy lemons for your cake." She places a pot of tea on the table and loads my mug with two sugars.

"Nan, I don't take sugar!" I try to swipe the mug from the table, but my grandmother's old hands work way too fast.

"You need fattening up," she insists, pouring the tea and pushing it across the table to me. "Don't argue with me, Livy. I'll put you over my knee."

I smile at her threat. She's promised it for twenty-four years and never followed through. "You can get lemons at the local store," I point out casually, plunging my spoon into my mouth to stop me from saying more. I could say so much more.

"You're right." Her old navy eyes flick to me briefly before she slurps her tea. "But I want to go to the market and George said he'd take me. We'll speak no more of it."

I'm desperately holding back my grin, but I know when to shut up. Old George is so fond of Nan, but she's really quite short with him. I don't know why he sticks around to be bossed about. She plays all hard-hearted and uninterested, but I know George's fondness for Nan is quietly returned. Gramps has been gone for seven years and George could never replace him, but a little companionship is good for Nan. Losing her daughter sent her into a dark depression, but Granddad took care of her, suffering in silence for years, silently coming to terms with his own loss and hiding his own grief until his body gave in. Then there was just me—a teenager left to hold it together...which I didn't do a very good job of in the early days.

She starts to top up my bowl with more flakes. "I'm going to Monday club at six, so I won't be home when you get in from work. Can you sort your supper out?"

"Of course," I say, holding my hand over my bowl to stop the flow of cornflakes. "Is George going, too?"

"Livy," she warns sternly.

"Sorry." I smile as I'm attacked by annoyed eyes, and she shakes her head, her gray curls swishing around her ears.

"It's a very sad situation when I socialize more than my granddaughter."

Her words kill my smile. I'm not getting into this. "I need to go to work." I stand and dip to kiss her cheek, ignoring her sigh.

*   *   *

I jump down from the bus, dodging people as I hurry through the chaos of rush hour pedestrian traffic. My mood reflects the color of my Converse—bright and sunny, as does the weather.

After navigating through the backstreets of Mayfair, I push my way into the bistro, finding it jam-packed already, just like it was last Monday when I started working for Del. I don't have time to chat with Sylvie or apologize to Del again for the fiasco on Friday. My apron is thrown at me, and I swing into action, immediately clearing four tables of empty cups before the vacated seating is snapped up by more arriving customers. I smile, deliver quickly, and clear the tables even faster. I really am a natural at this service-with-a-smile business.

Come five o'clock, my yellow Converse aren't feeling so bright anymore. My feet are aching, my calves are aching, and my head is aching. But I still smile when Sylvie slaps my backside as she passes me. "You've only been here a week and I already don't know what I'd do without you."

My smile widens as I watch her push through the swing door into the kitchen, but it soon falls away when I turn and come face-to-face with him again. I'm not particularly big on fate or things happening for a reason. I believe that you're the master of your own destiny—your own decisions and actions are what influence your life course. But unfortunately, the decisions and actions of others impact this course, too, and sometimes you're powerless to prevent it. Maybe that's why I've closed myself off from the world—shut myself away and rejected any person, potential situation, or possibility that may take the control away from me. I'm perfectly happy admitting it to myself. Someone else's poor, selfish choices have already affected my life too much. What I'm not happy about is my sudden inability to continue with my sensible strategy, probably when it's most important that I do.

And the reason for this lapse in strength is standing in front of me.

The familiar feeling of my heartbeat increasing should tell me all I need to know, and it does. I'm attracted to him—really attracted to him. But what's he doing here? He hated my coffee, and while I've been making endless perfect cups of the stuff all day long, I suspect that may change now.

He's just staring at me again. I should be annoyed, but I'm in no position to ask him what the hell he's looking at because I'm staring at him, too. He's displaying his usual impassive expression. Can he smile? Does he have bad teeth? He looks like he has perfect teeth. Everything I can see is perfect, and I know that everything I can't will be, too. He's dressed in a three-piece suit again, this one navy, making his blue eyes brighter. He looks as perfect and as expensive as ever.

I need to speak. This is silly, but it takes Sylvie to swing the kitchen door into my back to knock me out of my trance. "Oh!" she exclaims, steadying me by clenching my arm. She scans my startled face, worried when I don't respond or make any effort to move. Then her gaze shifts and her mouth gapes a little. "Oh...," she whispers, releasing her grip, her eyes flicking from me to him. "I'll just...urm...empty the bins." She deserts me, leaving me to serve him. I want to yell for her to come back, but once again, my tongue is tied and I'm bloody staring.

He braces his hands on the counter, leaning forward, and that lock of hair falls onto his forehead, diverting my eyes just north of his. "You're watching me very closely," he murmurs.

"You're watching me, too," I point out, finding my tongue. He's *really* watching me. "You're not doing very well at keeping away."

He doesn't entertain my observation. "How old are you?" His gaze drags slowly down my body before returning to my eyes. I don't answer, but I *do* frown as his eyebrow arches expectantly. "I asked you a question."

"Twenty-four," I answer quickly, when I really wanted to tell him to mind his own damn business.

"Are you involved with anyone?"

"No." I stun myself with my willing answer. I always claim to be in a relationship when any man shows his interest. It's like I'm under a spell.

He nods thoughtfully. "Are you going to ask me what I'd like?"

By that I'm *hoping* he means what he'd like to drink. Or am I? Does he want to pick up where we left off? I start twisting the antique sapphire eternity ring that Granddad bought for Nan, an obvious sign of my nerves. It's been in the exact spot for three years after Nan gave it to me for my twenty-first birthday and has been a source of twiddling ever since. "What would you like?" My confidence of Friday night is nowhere to be found. I'm a wreck.

His piercing blues seem to darken slightly. "An Americano, four shots, two sugars, and topped up halfway."

I'm stabbed by disappointment, which is ridiculous. What's also ridiculous is that he's returned after claiming my coffee was the worst he'd ever tasted. "I thought you didn't like my coffee."

"I didn't." He pushes himself away from the counter. "But I'd like to give you the chance to redeem yourself, Livy."

My cheeks heat.

"Would you like to try to redeem yourself?" He's completely poker-faced, totally serious.

I should search deep to find that bad bone that Nan keeps

telling me about and tell him where to go, but I don't search very hard. "Okay," I say instead, turning toward the wretched coffee machine that I know is going to let me down. I would undoubtedly do a better job if I wasn't under such close scrutiny.

Sending a little mental prayer to the coffee gods, I start with the first of four shots, working hard to regulate my broken breathing. I undertake my task slowly and accurately, not caring if it takes me all night. Stupidly, I want him to enjoy this one.

In my peripheral vision, I see Sylvie's curious head pop through the swing door, and I know she's desperate to know what's going on. I can feel her grinning, even if I can't see it. I'd like her to come out and break the awkward silence, give me someone comfortable to speak to, but I also *don't* want her to. I want to be alone with him. I'm drawn to him, and I absolutely cannot help it.

When I'm done, I top up his takeout cup and secure a lid before turning to deliver it to him. He's sitting down again, and I immediately realize my error. He's not even tasted it and I've already cocked up.

He focuses his blues on the cardboard cup, but I speak before he does. "Would you like a proper cup?"

"I'll take the takeout." His eyes lift to mine. "It might taste better." He's not smiling, but I get the feeling he wants to.

Walking carefully, even though the risk of spilling is minimal with a lid, I approach him and hold out the cup. "I hope you enjoy."

"So do I," he says, taking it and nodding at the sofa opposite. "Join me." He removes the lid and slowly blows the steam from his coffee, his already kissable lips seeming to invite me in. Everything he does with that mouth is slow—from talking to blowing steam from hot coffee. It's all so very deliberate, and it makes me wonder what else would be. He's beyond beautiful, if a little standoffish. He must turn heads everywhere he goes.

He cocks a brow and indicates the sofa opposite again. My legs move forward of their own volition to take a seat. "How is the coffee?" I ask.

He takes a slow sip of his Americano, and I find myself tensing, bracing for him to spit it out. He doesn't. He nods in approval, taking another sip, and I relax, stupidly relieved that he doesn't seem disgusted. His eyes lift. "You may have noticed that I'm quite fascinated by you as well."

"As well?" I ask, confused.

"It's rather obvious you're fascinated by me."

What an arrogant prick. "I suppose lots of women must be fascinated by you," I retort. "Do you invite them all for coffee?"

"No, just you." He leans closer and the look in his eyes practically takes my breath away. I've never been the subject of such intense focus. It's too much.

I break the eye contact and find myself looking away, but then I remember something and force myself to confront his intensity. "Who was that woman at the party?" I ask, not the least bit embarrassed to inquire. He came right out and asked me what my relationship status is, so I have every right to know his. She looked far too familiar to be a business associate. I'm not holding my breath, but I'm hoping he says single. The idea that this man is available is ridiculous, and so is the fact that I want him be—I want him to be available . . . for me.

"Business," he replies, watching me carefully, his smooth tone stroking my heated skin.

"You're single?" I ask, wanting complete clarification, but for what purpose I don't know. I'm actually wondering what my subconscious is planning, because I haven't a clue . . . nor am I concerned, and that should *really* concern me.

"I am."

"Okay," is all I say, still watching him, feeling quietly delighted. Now I want to know how old he is. He seems mature and his clothes have been of the highest quality every time I've seen him, screaming money.

"Okay," he counters, taking more coffee slowly as I look on. He's like a giant mass of intensity, enticing me into...something. "I enjoyed my coffee," he says, placing his cup down and swiveling it, before slowly rising from the couch. My gaze follows him up until I feel small under his potent, piercing blues, looking down at me.

"You're leaving?" I blurt, shocked. What was all this about? What was his point?

He shifts uncomfortably and puts his hand out to me. "It was a pleasure to meet you."

"We already met," I point out. "You nearly kissed me but walked away."

His hand drops a little at my sharp words before he gathers himself and raises it again. "And then you walked away from me."

So it's a game? He's unhappy because I was the one who walked away, so now he's returning the favor, having the final say? His hand comes closer and I recoil, too scared to touch him.

"Do you think there will be sparks?" he asks quietly.

My eyes widen. I know there will be sparks because I've felt them already. His mocking injects some bravery into me and my petite hand lifts to meet his. And there they are again. Sparks. Not electricity firing off all over the bistro, causing us both to gasp or jump back in shock, but there's something there, and instead of firing outward, it's shooting inward, ricocheting all over my body, making my heart beat faster and my lips part. I don't want to let go, but he flexes his palm, prompting me to release him.

Then he turns and strides out, without another word or look to suggest that he felt something, too. Did he? What was that? Who is he? My palms rise to my cheeks and I rub furiously, trying to scrub some sensibility into me. I'm way too intrigued by him, and no amount of sightseeing or quilting with my grandmother is going to distract me from where my thoughts are wandering to, not after that brief but enlightening conversation. I'm wandering into unknown territory—dangerous territory. After my years of avoiding all men, even the decent ones, I'm finding myself encouraging one who looks like he should definitely be left alone.

There's a pull, though—a very powerful pull.

*　　*　　*

I've been away with the fairies all week. Every time the bistro door swings open, I look for him. But he's never there. A dozen men over the last four days have asked me my name, my number, or they've told me what stunning eyes I have. And each one I've wished could be Miller.

I've been busy churning out perfect coffee after perfect coffee, and I even waitressed at another posh function for Del on Tuesday, hoping he'd be there. He wasn't.

I've always tried to keep my life simple, but now I'm craving a complication—a tall, dark-haired, mysterious complication.

It's Saturday, and Gregory has humored me, tagging along for a walk through the Royal Parks. He knows there is something on my mind. He kicks a pile of leaves as we traipse down the middle of The Green Park, toward Buckingham Palace. He wants to ask, and I know he won't hold out for much longer. He's made all of the conversation, while I've returned one-word answers. I'm not going to get away with it for much longer. I'm clearly absent in mind, and I could probably muster up the energy to feign my normal self but I don't think I want to. I think I *want* Gregory to press me so I can share Miller with him.

"I've met someone." The words fall from my mouth, breaking the comfortable silence between us. He looks shocked, which is okay because I'm quite shocked, too.

"Who?" he asks, pulling me to a stop.

"I don't know." I shrug, lowering my bum to the grass and picking at some of the blades. "He turned up at the bistro a few times and also at a gala ball where I waitressed."

Gregory joins me, his handsome face morphing into a big grin. "Olivia Taylor has been affected by a man?"

"Yes, Olivia Taylor has most definitely been affected by a man." It feels like such a relief to share my burden. "I can't stop thinking about him," I admit.

"Ah!" Gregory throws his arms in the air. "Is he hot?"

"Stupidly." I smile. "He has the most amazing eyes. As blue as the sky."

"I want to know everything," Gregory declares.

"There's nothing more to tell."

"Well, what did he say?"

"He asked if I was involved with anyone." I try to sound casual, but I know what's coming.

His eyes widen as he leans forward. "And you said?"

"No."

"It's happened!" he sings. "Thank the fucking Lord, it's finally happened!"

"Gregory!" I scold him, but I can't help laughing, too. He's right; it *has* happened, and it's happened hard.

"Oh, Livy." He sits up straight, looking all serious. "You don't know how long I've been waiting for this. I need to see him."

I scoff, pushing my hair over my shoulder. "Well, that's unlikely. He appears quickly and disappears faster."

"How old?" The excitement on Gregory's face is like nothing I've ever seen before. I've made his day—probably his month, or even his year. He's tried relentlessly to drag me out to the bars, even willing to make them straight bars if it means I'll tag along. Gregory has been in my life for eight years, just eight, although it could be forever. The "it" boy at school, all of the girls swooned over him and he dated them all, but he had a little secret—a secret that saw him ostracized once it was discovered. The cool kid was gay. Or eighty-percent gay, as Gregory has always claimed. Finding him behind the bike sheds, beaten to a pulp by some of the college kids, was the beginning of our friendship.

"I'm guessing late twenties, but he seems older. You know, very mature. He always wears very expensive-looking suits."

"Perfect." He rubs his hands together. "Name?"

"M," I say quietly.

"'M'?" Gregory's face screws up into a disapproving frown. "Who is he? James Bond's boss?"

A burst of laughter flies from my mouth, and I giggle to myself while my friend looks on, waiting for confirmation that my muse has a name beyond one letter of the alphabet. "He signed with an M."

"Signed?" His confusion deepens, as does his scowl. I'm not sure if I should divulge this part.

"He didn't like my coffee and chose to let me know by writing it on a napkin. He signed it *M*, but I've since found out that his name is Miller."

"Ooooh h, sexy! But the cheek!" He's shocked, displaying a similar reaction to what I did, but then his face straightens and he narrows his eyes on me. "And how did that make you feel?"

"Inadequate." I say the word without thought, and I don't stop there. "Stupid, angry, irritated."

Gregory's smiling now. "He drew a reaction?" he asks. "You got a little mad?"

"Yes!" I breathe, completely exasperated. "I was really pissed off."

"Oh my God! I already love him." He stands and puts his hand out to pull me up. "I bet he's completely taken by you, like most men on God's green earth."

Accepting his offering, I let him pull me to my feet. "They're not." I sigh, reflecting on the brief words that we exchanged; on one line in particular: *I'm quite fascinated by you, as well.* Does fascinated equal attracted?

"Trust me, they are."

I'm suddenly eager to spit it all out and see what Gregory makes of all this. "I was a millimeter away from his lips."

Gregory inhales sharply. "What do you mean?" His back straightens, and he narrows his eyes on me. "Did you bottle it?"

"No, I was the one pushing it." I'm not even ashamed. "He said he couldn't and left me in the ladies' feeling like a desperate idiot."

"Were you mad?"

"Furious."

"Yes!" His hands slap together, and I'm yanked into his embrace. "This is good. Tell me more."

I spill the whole thing—the dropped champagne, Miller's "business associate," the way he approached me afterward just to warn me off.

When I'm done, Gregory hums thoughtfully. It's not the reaction I was expecting or that I wanted. "He's a player. Not the right man for you, Livy. Forget about him."

I'm shocked, and the quick removal of my body from his, coupled with the reproachful look on my face, tells him so. "Forget? Are you mad? The way he looks at me, Gregory—it makes me want to be looked at like that forever." I pause briefly. "By him."

"Oh dear, baby girl."

I sigh. "I know."

"Distraction," he declares, looking down at my orange Converse. "What color shall we buy today?"

My eyes light up. "I've seen some in sky blue down on Carnaby Street."

"Sky blue, eh?" His arm slips around my shoulder and we start toward the Tube station. "Fancy that."

Chapter Four

Sylvie and I are the last to leave the bistro. While Sylvie locks up, I cart the rubbish into the alley and dump it in the wheelie bin.

"I'm going to have a long soak in the bath," Sylvie says, linking arms with me as we start wandering down the road. "With candles."

"You're not going out tonight?" I ask.

"Nope. Mondays are shite, but Wednesday nights are bombing. You should come." Her brown eyes twinkle suggestively, but dull straight down when she clocks me shaking my head. "Why not?"

"I don't drink." We cross the road, dodging the evening rush hour traffic, getting honked at for not using the pedestrian crossing.

"Oh, fuck you!" Sylvie shouts, drawing a million looks in our direction.

"Sylvie!" I yank her from the road, mortified.

She laughs and flips the driver a finger. "Why don't you drink?"

"I don't trust myself." The words just fall from my lips, shocking me and clearly shocking Sylvie, because startled brown eyes swing to me . . . then she grins.

"I think I might like drunken Livy."

I scoff in disagreement. "That's me." I point to the bus stop as I step into the road, ready to cross again.

"See you tomorrow." She leans in to kiss my cheek, and we both jump when we're honked at again. I ignore the impatient idiot, but Sylvie doesn't.

"For fuck's sake! What is wrong with these people?" she shouts. "We're not even in the way of your fancy AMG, you Mercedes-driving ponce!" She steps toward the car just as the passenger window starts to slip down. I feel road rage brewing. She leans in. "Learn to fucking dr—" She halts her rant, her back straightening as she pulls away from the black Mercedes.

Curious, I lean down to find out what's shut her up, my heart skipping too many beats when I register the driver.

"Livy." Sylvie's voice is barely heard over the rush of traffic and blurting of horns. She steps away from the roadside. "I think he may have been honking at you."

I'm still partially bent as my eyes trail from Sylvie back to the car, where he's sitting back, relaxed, with one hand draped casually on the steering wheel. "Get in," he orders shortly.

I know I'm getting in this car, so I don't know why I look to Sylvie for guidance. She shakes her head. "Livy, I wouldn't. You don't know him."

I return to vertical and my mouth opens to speak, but no words form. She's right and I'm torn, my eyes swinging from the car to my new friend. I'm not careless or stupid—haven't been for a long time—although every thought running through my mind right now is flooring that claim. I don't know how long I stand there deliberating, but I'm distracted when the driver's door of the Mercedes swings open and he strides around the car, clasping my elbow and opening the passenger door.

"Hey!" Sylvie tries to reclaim me. "What the hell do you think you're doing?"

I'm pushed into the seat before he turns toward a stunned

Sylvie. "I'm just going to talk to her." He takes a pen and paper from his inside pocket and scribbles something down before handing it to Sylvie. "That's me. Ring the number."

"What?" Sylvie snatches the paper from his hand and runs her eyes over it.

"Ring the number."

Landing him with a reproachful glare, she drags her phone from her bag and dials the number. A mobile starts screeching, and he pulls an iPhone from his inside pocket before handing it to me.

"She has my phone. Ring it and she'll answer."

"I could ring hers," Sylvie points out, ending the call. "What the hell does that prove? You could take it off her the second you drive away."

"Then I guess you'll just have to take my word for it." He shuts the door and strides around the car, leaving Sylvie on the pavement, her mouth agape.

I should jump out, but I don't. I should protest and curse at him, but I don't. Instead, I look to my friend on the pavement and hold up the iPhone that Miller's just handed me. She's right; this proves nothing, but it doesn't deter me from doing something incredibly stupid—I'm not frightened of him, though. He's no danger to me, except, maybe, to my heart.

More car horns start screeching around us as he slides into the car before pulling hastily away from the curb without a word. I don't feel nervous. I've practically been abducted on a busy London street and my stomach isn't even turning in panic. It is, however, fluttering with something else. I discreetly look across to him, noting his dark suit and stunning profile. I've never seen anything like him. It's silent in the enclosed space surrounding us, but something is speaking and it's neither Miller nor I. It's desire. And it's telling me that I'm about to experience something life-altering. I want to know where he's taking me, I want to know what he wants to talk about, but my desire for this knowledge doesn't prompt me to ask, and he doesn't seem like he's going to offer the information up right now, so I relax back into the soft leather of my seat and remain quiet. Then the stereo kicks in and I'm suddenly listening in wonder to Green Day's "Boulevard of Broken Dreams," a track I would never have paired with this mysterious man.

We're in the car for a long half hour, stopping and starting with the rush hour traffic, until he pulls into an underground car park. He seems to be thinking hard as he shuts off the engine and taps his hand on the wheel a few times before letting himself out and making his way around to me. Opening the door, he finds my eyes, and I can see reassurance in them as he holds his hand out to me. "Give me your hand."

My response is automatic, my hand lifting to take his as I remove myself from the car while savoring that familiar feeling of internal lightning bolts attacking me. It's more incredible each time I experience it.

"There it is again," he murmurs, repositioning his hand to get a better grip on me. He feels it, too. "Give me your bag."

I hand him my bag immediately, involuntarily, not even thinking about it. I'm on autopilot.

"Do you have my phone?" he asks, lightly kicking the door of his car shut and pulling me toward a stairwell.

"Yes." I hold it up.

"Ring your friend and tell her you're at my place." He pushes through the door. "And call anyone else who might be worried about you."

I can do nothing more than follow him as he takes the stairs slowly, still clasping my hand, leaving me to make the calls he's demanded. "I should use my phone," I say, fiddling with his iPhone. My clued-up nan will soon clock the strange number on the caller display and start asking questions—questions I don't want to answer or even know how to.

"Your decision." His lean shoulders shrug as he continues pulling me along behind him. When we pass floor three, my calves begin to burn and my lips part to try and get some air into my tiring lungs.

"What floor are you?" I ask on a little wheeze, ashamed of my fitness level. I walk a lot, but I don't climb this many stairs on a regular basis.

"Ten," he flips over his shoulder casually. The knowledge of six more floors deflates my lungs altogether and makes my legs seize up.

"Are there no lifts?"

"Yes."

"Then why..." I only have air capacity for a gasp and I let one out when he quickly scoops me up and pushes onward. I have no option but to cling on to his shoulders, my hold feeling right, my nose and eyes enjoying the closeness.

When we reach floor ten and he pushes his way through the doorway into an empty corridor, he drops me to my feet and puts the key into the lock of a shiny black door. "After you." He steps to the side and gestures for me to step in, which I do—without thought, protest, or asking why he's brought me here.

I feel his palm on the base of my neck, warm and comforting, as I slowly make my way down the hallway, circling a huge round table, until the hallway opens up into a massive, marble-infested space with vaulted ceilings and colossal pieces of art at every turn, all paintings of London architecture. It's not the grandness of the apartment or the sea of cream marble that holds me rapt. It's those paintings—six of them, all carefully hung in selected spaces where they can be appreciated the most. They're not typical or traditional; they're abstract, making it so you need to squint to see exactly what each is. But I know these buildings and landmarks too well, and as I gaze around me I identify them all—no squinting required.

I'm gently guided toward the biggest cream-colored leather couch I've ever seen. "Sit." He pushes me down and places my bag next to me. "Call your friend," he says, leaving me to find my phone while he strides over to a large walnut cabinet and retrieves a tumbler, topping it up with a dark liquid.

I dial Sylvie, and it rings only once before her fretful voice is piercing my ears. "Livy?"

"It's me," I say quietly, watching as he turns and leans against the cabinet, taking a slow mouthful of his drink.

"Where are you?" It sounds like she's jogging. Her voice is slightly breathless.

"At his place. I'm okay." I feel awkward explaining myself while he's watching so intently, but there's no escaping his steel gaze.

"Who the fuck does he think he is?" she asks incredulously. "And you're beyond stupid for going, Livy. What were you thinking?"

"I don't know." I answer honestly, because I really don't. I've allowed him to take me, bundle me in his car, and bring me to a strange apartment. I really am beyond stupid, but even now, when I'm listening to my friend rant and rave down the phone and he's staring expressionless at me, I'm not frightened.

"Jesus," she huffs. "What are you doing? What's he saying? What does he want?"

"I don't know." I watch him watching me as he takes another slow sip of his drink.

"You don't know a fucking lot, do you?" she fires, her heavy breathing settling down.

"No," I admit. "I'll call you when I get home."

"You'd better." Her tone is threatening. "If I don't get a call by midnight, then I'll be ringing the police. I took his registration."

I smile to myself, appreciative of her concern, but knowing deep down that it's not required. He's not going to hurt me. "I'll call you," I assure her.

"Make sure you do." She's still agitated. "And be careful," she adds more gently.

"Okay." I hang up and immediately dial my nan, keen to finish up and find out why he's brought me here. It doesn't take much explaining to Nan. She's delighted when I tell her that I'm joining a few work friends for a coffee, as I knew she would be.

I finish up and place both my phone and his on the gigantic low glass table in front of me; then I commence twiddling the ring on my finger, wondering what to say. We're just staring at each other, him taking frequent sips of his drink, me losing myself in that potent gaze.

"Would you like a drink?" he asks. "Wine, brandy?"

I shake my head.

"Vodka?"

"No." Alcohol is a weakness he doesn't need to know about, although I don't think that I need alcohol to send me into reckless mode with this man. "Why am I here?" I finally ask the operative question. I think I know, but I want him to say the words.

His fingers tap the side of his glass thoughtfully, and he pushes his tall body away from the cabinet, slowly walking toward me. He undoes his jacket button and lowers himself until he's sitting on the table in front of me, placing his drink carefully and breaking our eye contact to see where his glass has landed before tweaking it slightly and repositioning our mobile phones. My heart rate is speeding up, even more so when he faces me and clasps me under my knees, encouraging me to shift forward on the couch until there's only a few inches between our faces. He doesn't say anything, and neither do I. Our breathy gasps colliding between our close mouths are saying all that needs to be said. We're both bursting at the seams with desire.

His face moves forward, that lock of hair falling onto his forehead, but he's not aiming for my lips. He homes in on my cheek, breathing heavy, controlled breaths into my ear. My face pushing into his is involuntary, as is the heaviness settling between my thighs.

"I can't stop thinking about you," he whispers, his grasp of my knees increasing. "I've tried my hardest, but you're a constant vision wherever I look."

I inhale deeply and find my hands rising and seeking out his thick waves, my fingers threading through them, my eyes closing. "You said you couldn't be with me," I remind him, stupidly or not. I shouldn't point out his reluctance because if he withdraws now, I think I'll lose my mind.

"I still can't." His face slides across mine until his perfect forehead is resting against my confused one. He can't have brought me here just to reinforce his previous declaration. He can't hold me like this, speak to me like this, and then do nothing.

"I don't understand," I murmur, praying to every god that he doesn't halt this.

His forehead rolls across mine slowly, carefully. "I have a proposition." He must sense my confusion because he pulls away and scans my face. Taking a deep breath, I brace myself. "All I can offer you is one night."

I don't need to ask what he's talking about. The dull ache in my stomach tells me exactly what he means. "Why?"

"I'm emotionally unavailable, Livy." He reaches up to cup my cheek, his thumb stroking smooth circles on my temple. "But I have to have you."

"You want me for one night and nothing else?" I ask, the ache transforming into a dull pain now. Just one night? It's obscene for me to be thinking further than that, though. The best fuck of my life. That's what he said. Nothing more.

"One night," he affirms. "And I'm praying that you'll give it to me."

I'm lost in his blues, desperately hoping he'll say something else—something that'll make me feel better, because right now

I'm feeling cheated, which is ridiculous. I hardly know him, but the thought of only being permitted one night with this man is soul destroying.

"I don't think I can." My eyes fall, as does my heart. "It's not fair for you to ask that of me."

"I've never claimed to be fair, Livy." He clasps my chin and brings my face up to his. "I've seen something and I want it. I usually take what I want, but I'm giving you a choice."

"What's in it for me?" I ask. "What will I get out of this?"

"You get to be worshipped by me for twenty-four hours." His lips part and his tongue sweeps across his full bottom lip, like he's attempting to make me see what those twenty-four hours may be like. He's wasting energy. I have a very good idea what those twenty-four hours will be like.

"You said you could only offer me one night."

"Twenty-four hours, Livy."

I want to say yes, but my head starts shaking, my integrity taking over. If I'm going to get involved with a man, it can't be like this. Every method I've adopted to protect myself from following in my mother's footsteps will be quashed if I do this, and I can't let myself down like that. "I'm sorry. I can't." I shouldn't be apologizing for my decline of his unreasonable request, but I *am* sorry. I want to be worshipped by him, yet not enough to set myself up for certain devastation because that's exactly what this will result in. I already feel like I'm in way above my head and he hasn't even kissed me.

He visibly sags and shifts back, breaking all contact between us. I feel a little lost, which should strengthen my decision to decline his offer. One night will never be enough. "I'm disappointed," he sighs. "But I respect your decision."

I'm disappointed that he respects my decision. I want him to fight harder, convince me to say yes. I'm not thinking straight. "I know nothing about you."

He picks up his drink and takes a sip, drawing my eyes to his lips. "If you knew more, would you reconsider?"

"I don't know." I feel frustrated and annoyed—annoyed that he's put me in this position. It should be an easy decision, declining a stranger on such a proposition, but the longer I spend with him, even if it's bizarre and far-fetched, the more I want to retract my answer and take the twenty-four hours he's offering.

"Well, you know my name now." His lips are tipping a little, but it's nowhere near a smile.

"That's *all* I know," I fire back. "I don't know your surname, your age, your job."

"And you need to know all of that to spend the night with me?" His dark eyebrows rise, his lips tipping further. If he would only smile properly, I'd feel like I know him more. But should I be increasing my fascination with him if it means I'll only get more attached?

I don't know, so I shrug noncommittally and drop my head, my hair falling into my lap.

"My name is Miller Hart," he starts, pulling my eyes back to his. "I'm twenty-nine—"

"Stop!" I hold my hand up, halting his flow. "Don't tell me. I don't need to know."

He cocks his head, slightly amused, even if he's still not demonstrating it with his mouth. "Don't need to or don't want to?"

"Both," I spit shortly, feeling the rarity of anger simmering inside of me again. He made me feel irritated before he suggested something so ridiculous, but now I'm *really* feeling it. I stand, prompting him to shift back on the table and gaze up at me. "Thank you for the offer, but the answer is no." I pick up my bag and phone and make for the door, getting no farther than the end of the couch before I'm taken gently and pushed front forward to the wall, my bag dropping to the marble, my eyes clenching shut.

His chin is on my shoulder, his mouth at my ear. "You don't

sound convinced," he whispers, raising his knee between my thighs to spread them.

"I'm not," I confess, cursing myself for my weakness. His body molded to my back feels too right, when I desperately want it to feel all wrong. Everything suggests that this is wrong, but the crazy rightness is making it hard to ignore the warning signs.

"And that's exactly why I'm not letting you leave until you agree. You want me." He turns me around and pushes his palms into the wall on either side of my head. "And I want you."

"But just for twenty-four hours." My voice is a panting wheeze as I fight to rein in my erratic breathing.

He nods and lazily lowers his mouth to mine. He's unsure, hesitant; I can see it in his eyes. But then he braves nibbling at my bottom lip, pecking cautiously and whispering what seems like encouraging words to himself before pushing into my mouth with his tongue until I relax and accept his soft invasion. Nothing would prevent me from moaning, relaxing into his kiss and clasping his shoulders. It's heavenly, just like I knew it would be, but this isn't assisting with my sensibility. Nevertheless, I push my doubts to the back of my mind and lose myself in him. He's worshipping me, and the thought of twenty-four hours of this nearly makes me break our kiss, just so I can scream *"yes!"* But I don't. Despite my enjoyment and mounting desire, I concentrate on enjoying the only kiss I'm ever going to receive from Miller Hart. And it's one I'll remember for the rest of my life.

He groans, pushing his groin into my tummy. His hardness throbs against me. "Jesus, you taste divine. Say yes," he mumbles into my mouth, biting at my lip. "Please say yes."

I want to hold back my answer, just to drag out this exquisite kiss, but I'm rapidly falling deeper with each second he spends seducing my mouth. "I can't," I gasp, turning my face to the side to break our mouth contact. "I'd want more." I know I'll want more, as crazy as it might seem. I've never looked for that connection, but if I had, then this would be it—something painfully good, all-consuming... something special and out of my control—something that will put my previous conclusions about intimacy to shame. I've stumbled across it by accident, when I least expected it, but it's happened and I can't fall further knowing there is no hope and nothing but heartbreak waiting for me at the end of that twenty-four hours.

He releases a frustrated growl and pushes himself away from the wall. "Shit," he curses, striding away, looking up at the ceiling. "I shouldn't have brought you here."

I gather my muddled mind and straighten myself out, all the time leaning against the wall to hold myself steady. "No, you shouldn't have," I agree, proud for sounding certain of that. "I should go." I gather my bag from the floor and head quickly to the door, not looking back.

When I'm in the safety of the stairwell, I collapse against the wall, my breathing labored, my body shaking. I'm being sensible. I need to keep reminding myself of that. Nothing good could come of this, except memories of an incredible day and night that I'll never get to relive. It would be torture, and I refuse to tease myself, give myself a taste of something amazing—because I know it will be—just to have it robbed from me. Never. I refuse to become my mother. Resolute and satisfied with my decision, I take the stairs and find my way to a Tube station. For the first time in many years, I need an alcoholic drink.

CHAPTER FIVE

I've not been myself all week. It's been noticed and mentioned, but my despondent state has halted further interrogation, except from Gregory, who I'm sure is reporting back to Nan, because she went from curious and pushy to concerned and sympathetic. She's also made me lemon cake every single day.

I'm clearing the last table, absentmindedly swishing my cloth from side to side when the door to the bistro swings open and I'm confronted with Mr. Wide Eyes.

He smiles awkwardly, shutting the door quietly behind him. "Am I too late for a takeout?" he asks.

"Not at all." I grab my tray and dump it on the counter before loading up the filter. "Cappuccino?"

"Please," he says politely, his footsteps getting closer.

I busy myself, ignoring Sylvie when she passes with the bins and pauses, clearly after clocking my customer. "Cute," she says simply, before continuing on her way. She's right; he *is* cute, but it's too much like hard work trying to fight another man from my mind to appreciate it. Mr. Wide Eyes is the type of man I should pay more attention to—if I'm going to give my attention to any man—not moody, dark, enigmatic ones, who only want twenty-four hours and nothing else.

Firing up the steam pipe, I start heating the milk, swirling the jug and making a rushing hissing of noise in time to my racing mind. I pour, sprinkle, and secure the lid, then turn to deliver my perfect coffee. "Two-eighty, please." I hold my hand out.

Three pound coins are placed carefully in my palm as I stab the order through the till with my free hand. "I'm Luke," he says slowly. "Can I ask your name?"

"Livy," I flip, tossing the coins into the drawer carelessly.

"And you're involved with someone?" he asks cautiously, drawing a frown from me.

"I've already told you that." For the first time, I allow his charming looks to push past my mental protective wall and the images of Miller. His mousy hair is floppy, but lies just right, and his brown eyes are warm and friendly. "So why are you aski—" I halt mid-sentence and cast my eyes over to Sylvie, who's just pushed her way back through the bistro door, minus two rubbish bags. I hit her with a reproachful look, knowing damn well she's told Mr. Wide Eyes here that I'm perfectly available.

She doesn't hang around to soak up my animosity, instead skulking off to the kitchen where she's safe. Mr. Wide Eyes, or Luke as I now know him, is shifting nervously, blatantly ignoring my guilty friend as she disappears from sight.

"My friend has a big mouth." I hand him his change. "Enjoy your coffee."

"Why did you fob me off?"

"Because I'm not available," I repeat myself, because it's still true, even if it's for a totally different reason now. I might have refused Miller's offer, but it hasn't made forgetting him any easier. My fingers reach up and rest on my lips, feeling his soft, full ones still there, lingering, tickling, biting. I sigh. "It's closing time."

Luke slides a card across the counter, and taps it lightly before releasing it. "I'd love to take you out sometime, so if you decide you're available it would be great to hear from you." I look up and he winks, a cheeky smile spreading across his face.

I return his small smile and watch him leave the bistro, whistling happily as he goes.

"Is it safe?" Sylvie's apprehensive voice drifts in from the kitchen, and I turn to see her black-haired head popping up over the swing door.

"You told him, you traitor!" I start yanking at my apron string.

"It might have slipped." She still doesn't venture into the bistro, choosing to remain protected behind the swing door. "Come on, Livy. Cut him a break." Her attention is firmly set on Luke now, after I followed through on her request to call before midnight the night Miller snatched me from the roadside. I didn't tell her the details, but my despondent state down the line told her all she needed to know—no enlightenment of shocking propositions required.

"Sylvie, I'm not interested," I argue idly, shaking my apron out and hanging it on the coat pegs.

"You didn't say that about the rude fucker in the posh AMG." She knows she shouldn't be mentioning him, but she has a point and every right to make it. "I'm just saying, that's all."

I shake my head in complete exasperation and push past her, heading into the kitchen to grab my jacket and satchel. All of these emotions—the annoyance, the irritation, the heavy heart, and the uncertainty, are all a result of one thing . . .

A man.

"I'll see you in the morning," I call, letting Sylvie lock up on her own.

My peaceful stroll toward the bus stop is short-lived when I hear Gregory calling me. Most uncharitably, I sigh, pivoting slowly and not even bothering to plaster an insincere smile on my tired face.

He's in his gardening clothes, looking all grubby with blades of grass in his mussed-up hair. As soon as he reaches me, his arm drapes over my shoulder and he pulls me into his side. "Going home?"

"Yeah. What are you doing?"

"I've come to give you a lift." He sounds genuine, but I know different.

"Come to take me home or come to squeeze me for information?" I retort dryly, earning myself a flick of his hip into my waist.

"How are you feeling?"

I think carefully about what word to use in an attempt to prevent further interrogation. He knows enough and has filled Nan in, too. I won't be enlightening him on the twenty-four-hour proposition, either, which I'm now in two minds over. I said no and I feel like crap, so perhaps I should just dive right in and feel like crap, anyway. But at least I'll have an experience to remember while I'm feeling like crap—something to relive.

"Good," I answer eventually, letting Gregory lead the way to his van.

"If he's said he's emotionally unavailable, Livy, it can't be a good sign. You've made the right decision not to see him again."

"I know," I agree. "So why can't I stop thinking about him?"

"Because we always fall for the wrong men." He leans in and kisses my forehead. "The ones who will mess us around and stamp all over our heart. I've been there, done that, and I'm glad you've held back before falling too far. I'm proud of you. You deserve better."

I smile, remembering many times when I've held Gregory's hand after he's fallen victim to a man's charm, except Miller isn't charming—not in the least bit. It's difficult to nail exactly what it is about him, except for his spectacular looks, but that feeling . . . oh God that feeling. And what Gregory has just said is perfectly accurate. There's a lack of a mother in my life because of her poor decisions when it came to men. That alone should have me running in the other direction from him, but instead I'm being drawn in. His lips are still soft on mine, my flesh is still warm from his touch, and I've lain in bed every night replaying that kiss. Nothing will ever measure up to those feelings.

*   *   *

I let us in the house and head with Gregory to the back kitchen. I can hear Nan and George chatting and the sounds of a wooden spoon colliding with the side of a huge metal pot—a stew pot. It's stew and dumplings tonight. I screw my face up and contemplate escaping to the local chippy. I can't stand my grandmother's stew, but it's George's favorite and George is here for supper, so it looks like I'm having stew.

"Gregory!" Nan dives on my gay friend and smothers his face with her marshmallow lips. "You must stay for supper." She points to a chair before moving on to me, assaulting me with her squidgy lips, too, and then placing me on a chair next to George. "I do love it when we're all here," she declares happily. "Stew?"

Everyone raises their hands, including me, even though I don't want stew.

"Sit down, Gregory," Nan orders.

Gregory wisely sits, looking at me and George with pursed lips when he sees us both smirking at his wary move. "You say no to her," he whispers.

"Pardon?" Nan swings round, and we all straighten our faces and backs, like good little children.

"Nothing," we chant in unison, earning each one of us a few seconds of narrowed eyes from my dear grandmother.

"Hmm." She places the stew pot on the table. "Tuck in."

George virtually dives into the pot, while I just pick at some bread, breaking off tiny bits and chewing quietly while everyone chats happily.

Miller flashes into my mind, making me blink my eyes shut. I smell him, making me hold my breath. I feel his heated touch, making me shift in my chair. I'm having a mental row with myself as I try to bat away images of him, memories of him and the sound of his smooth voice.

I'm failing on every level. Falling for this man could be a disaster. Everything suggests it will be, and that should be good enough, but it's not. I feel weak and vulnerable, and I hate it. Nor do I like the thought of not seeing him again.

"Livy, you've hardly touched your supper." Nan snaps me from my daydream, tapping her spoon on the side of my bowl.

"I'm not hungry." I push the bowl away and stand. "Excuse me. I'm going to bed." I feel three sets of concerned eyes on me as I leave the kitchen, but I'm past caring. Yes, Livy I-don't-ever-need-a-man Taylor has fallen, and she's fallen stupidly hard. And worst of all, she's fallen for someone she can't, and probably shouldn't, have.

I drag my heavy body up the stairs and flop into bed, not bothering to undress and not bothering to remove my makeup. It's not even dark, but burying myself under my thick quilt soon remedies that. I want silence and darkness so I can torture myself some more.

*　　*　　*

Friday drags painfully. I avoided Nan, choosing to skip breakfast and face the worried call that I knew I'd get on my way to work. She wasn't happy, but she can't shove cornflakes down my throat from a mile away. Del, Paul, and Sylvie have all tried and failed to coax a genuine smile from me, and Luke dropped in for a coffee again, just to see if I've changed my mind on my relationship status. He's persistent, I'll give him that, and he is cute and quite funny, too, but I'm still not interested.

I've been thinking of something all day long, and I keep going to ask, but then I bottle it, knowing what reaction I'll get. And I can hardly blame her. But Sylvie has his number, and I want it. We're closing up the bistro. I'm running out of time. "Sylvie?" I say slowly, twirling my cloth innocently. It's a silly attempt to look sweet, given what I'm about to ask.

"Livy," she mimics my careful tone, full of suspicion.

"Do you still have Miller's number?"

"No!" She shakes her head furiously, rushing into the kitchen. "I threw it away."

I make chase, not willing to give up. "But you dialed him from your phone," I remind her, smacking into her back when she halts.

"I deleted it," she spits unconvincingly. She's going to make me beg or pin her down and steal her phone.

"Please, Sylvie. I'm going out of my mind." My hands meet in front of my pleading face, forming praying hands.

"No." She breaks my hands apart and pushes them to my sides. "I heard your voice when you left his apartment, and I also saw your face the next day. Livy, a sweet thing like you doesn't need to be getting involved with a man like that."

"I can't stop thinking about him." My teeth are clenched, like I'm mad for admitting it. I am mad. I'm mad for appearing so desperate, and I'm even madder for actually being desperate.

Sylvie sidesteps me and pushes her way back into the bistro, her black bob swishing from side to side. "No no no, Livy. Things happen for a reason, and if you were meant to be with—"

I collide with her back again when she trails off and stops dead in her tracks. "Stop stopping!" I yell, feeling the building frustration getting the better of me. "What's the—" It's me who trails off now, as I look past Sylvie and see Miller standing by the bistro entrance, looking smooth in a gray three-piece suit, his hair a mess of dark waves, his blue eyes crystal clear and sinking into me.

He steps forward, completely ignoring my work friend, and keeps his eyes on me. "Have you finished work?"

"No!" Sylvie blurts, stepping back, pushing me with her. "No, she hasn't."

"Sylvie!" I muscle my way past her with some determined effort until it's me pushing *her* back into the kitchen. "I know what I'm doing," I say on a hushed whisper. That's not true at all. I have no idea what I'm doing.

She grabs my arm and leans in. "How can someone go from being so sensible to so damned insane in such a short space of time?" she asks, glancing over my shoulder. "You're going to get yourself in trouble, Livy."

"Just leave me."

I can see she's torn, but she eventually relents, though not before tossing a warning look in Miller's direction. "You're mad," she huffs, turning on her biker boots and stomping off, leaving us alone.

Taking a deep breath, I turn and face the man who's invaded every second of thinking space since Monday. "Would you like a coffee?" I ask, indicating the giant machine behind me.

"No," he answers quietly, walking forward until he's standing mere feet away from me. "Take a walk with me."

A walk? "Why?"

He flicks his eyes to the kitchen entrance, clearly uncomfortable. "Get your bag and jacket."

I do as he tells me, without much thought. I ignore Sylvie's stunned face as I enter the kitchen and grab my bag and jacket. "I'm off now," I say before hastily leaving her ranting at Del and Paul. I hear her call me stupid and I hear Del call me a grown-up. They are both right.

Throwing my satchel across my body, I approach him and my eyes close when he clasps his palm around the base of my neck to guide me out of the bistro. I'm directed across the road into the small square where he sits me on a bench and takes a seat next to me, turning his body to face mine. "Have you thought about me?" he asks.

"Constantly," I admit. I'm not beating around the bush. I have, and I want him to know it.

"So will you spend the night with me?"

"Still just twenty-four hours?" I clarify, and he nods. My heart falls, not that it'll stop me from agreeing. I can't possibly feel any worse than I already do.

His hand rests on my knee, squeezing gently. "Twenty-four hours, no strings, no commitment, and no feelings, except pleasure." Releasing my knee, he shifts his hand to my chin and pulls my face close to his. "And it *will* be pleasurable, Livy. I promise."

I don't doubt him for a second. "Why do you want this?" I ask. I know women are notoriously deeper than men, but he's asking me to disregard something that I simply can't. This isn't just lust I'm feeling—at least I don't think it is. I'm confused. I don't even know what I'm feeling.

For the first time since I've met him, he smiles. It's a proper smile—a beautiful smile . . . and I fall a little bit more. "Because I simply *have* to kiss you again." Leaning in, he gently rests his lips on mine. "It's new to me. I need to taste you some more."

New? It's new to him? What, like different from his usual polished, diamond-adorned women?

"And because what we can create together shouldn't be passed up, Livy."

"The best fuck of my life?" I ask against his lips, feeling him smile again.

"And a whole lot more." He pulls away, leaving me feeling bereft. It might be a feeling that I should get used to. "Where do you live?"

"I live with my elderly grandmother." I don't know why I say *elderly*, maybe to justify my living arrangement. "Camden."

A look of surprise flits across his perfect brow. "I'll pick you up at seven. Tell your grandmother you'll be back tomorrow night. What's the address?"

"What will I say?" I ask, suddenly panicked. I've never stayed out for a whole night, and no plausible reason to do so now is coming to me.

"I'm sure you'll think of something." He stands, putting his hand out to me, and I take it, letting him pull me to my feet.

"No, you don't understand." This will be impossible to pull off. "I don't stay out at night. She'll never believe me if I try to fob her off with anything other than the truth, and I can't tell her about you." I'll kill her off with shock. Or maybe I won't. Maybe she'll dance around the kitchen, clapping her hands and thanking the Lord. Knowing Nan, it'll be the latter.

"You never go out?" He frowns.

"No." I fake nonchalance to within an inch of my life.

"And you've never stayed out overnight? Not even at a girlfriend's?"

I've never been embarrassed by my lifestyle . . . until now. I suddenly feel young, naïve, and inexperienced, which is ridiculous. I need to locate my long-lost sass. While he's promised me mind-blowing sex, what does he get out of it, because I'm certainly no sex kitten who'll rock his bed. A man like this must have women forming a queue at his front door, all kitted out in satin or lace, all in stilettos and all ready to send him wild with desire.

I shake my head, looking down to the ground. "Remind me why you want to do this again."

"If you're speaking to me, isn't it polite to look at me?" He tips my chin up. "You don't seem like a self-doubter."

"I'm not usually."

"What's changed?"

"You."

That one word makes him shift uncomfortably, and I immediately regret saying it. "Me?"

My head drops again. "I didn't mean to make you uncomfortable."

"I'm not uncomfortable," he argues quietly, "but now I'm wondering whether this is a good idea."

My head snaps up, panicked that he might withdraw his offer. "No, I want to do this." I don't know what I'm saying, but it doesn't stop me from babbling on some more. "I want twenty-four hours with you." I step into his chest and look up to his eyes—the ones I'm going to lose myself in very soon, if I haven't already. "I need this."

"Why do you need it, Livy?"

"I need it to show myself that I've been doing things wrong for too long." I brave a kiss and reach up on my tiptoes to push my lips to his, hoping I'll remind him of what it felt like last time, hoping he experienced the surge of energy, too. Before I can even think to engage my tongue, I'm wrapped in his arms and being pulled up to his chest, our mouths fused, our bodies bonded, my heart falling further. His lips on mine and his hard body coating me feels...right.

"Are you sure?" He removes me from his embrace, holding me at arm's length and hunkering down to ensure he's got my eyes *and* my attention. "I've made it clear how it'll be, Livy. If you can deal with that, then for the next twenty-four hours, it's just us— my body and your body doing incredible things."

I nod my head convincingly, even though I'm not at all sure. I can see doubt lingering on his stunning face, which pushes me to force a smile, worried that he might pull on our deal. I might not know what I'm doing, but I certainly don't know what I'll do if he walks away from me now.

"Okay," he says, sliding his hand around my nape and pulling me into him. "I'll take you home." He starts to guide me from the square, his palm secured firmly on my nape as he pushes me onward. I glance up to him, just to check he's there—to check that I'm not dreaming.

He's there, and he's gazing down at me, assessing me, probably analyzing my mental state. Should I ask him his conclusion because I haven't the foggiest? All I know is that he's mine for the next twenty-four hours, and I am his. I just hope that I don't find myself in further desolation once my time is up. I'm ignoring the voice in my head, currently screaming at me to stop this right now. I know how this'll turn out, and it's likely to be messy.

But I just can't refuse him. Or myself.

CHAPTER SIX

I'll wait here for you." He pulls up outside my house and takes his phone from his pocket, waving it at me. "I have a few calls to make."

He's going to wait? And he's going to wait outside my house? No, no, he can't. Bloody hell, Nan's probably sniffed him out already. I look up to the bay window at the front of our house, watching for twitching curtains. "I can get a cab to your place," I try, making a mental list of things I need to do once I get inside— shower, shave . . . everywhere, moisturize, spritz, makeup . . . tell the fattest lie I ever will.

"No." He dismisses my offer without even looking at me. "I'll wait. Go get your things."

I wince, letting myself out of his car and walking slowly, cautiously, up the path to my house, like Nan might hear me if I go any faster. I insert my key slowly. I turn it slowly. I push the door open slowly. I lift my foot slowly, ready to step inside, clenching my teeth when the door creaks.

Damn.

Nan's standing three feet away, her arms folded, her foot tapping the patterned carpet. "Who's that man?" she asks, her gray eyebrows rising. "And why are you behaving like a cat burglar, hmmm?"

"He's my boss." I blurt the words fast, and so begins the fattest lie I'll ever tell. "I'm working tonight. He's brought me home to change."

I definitely see a wave of disappointment travel across her age-worn face. "Oh, well…" She turns, losing immediate interest of the man outside. "I won't bother with supper then."

"Okay." I take the stairs two at a time and burst into the bathroom, cranking the shower on and stripping down at lightning speed. Then I dive in before it's warmed up. "Oh shit!" I pin myself to the side, goose bumps invading me, my body shivering uncontrollably. "Shit, shit shit! Warm up!" My hand hovers under the spray, and I'm frantically egging the hot water on. "Come on, come on."

After far too long, it's just warm enough to bear, and I step under, making super-fast work of washing my hair, soaping everywhere and shaving…everywhere. By the time I've sprinted across the landing in my towel and made it into the safety of my room, I'm out of breath. Under normal circumstances, it usually takes me ten minutes flat to throw some clothes on, give my face a quick brush over with some powder, and rough dry my hair. But now I care; now I *want* to look nice. And I haven't got bloody time to do it.

"Underwear," I prompt myself, hurrying over to my drawers and yanking the top one open, instantly grimacing at the piles of cotton knickers and bras. I must have something—anything other than cotton, please!

After five minutes of assessing each and every piece of underwear I own, I find that I am, in fact, a cotton girl, with no lace, satin, or leather in sight. I knew that, but maybe I thought a sexy pair of something might magic their way into my drawer to save me from underwear humiliation. I was wrong, but with little else to do, I pull on my white cotton knickers and matching boring bra before blasting my hair, brushing some powder across my face, and pinching my cheeks.

And now I'm staring at my satchel and wondering what I need to pack. I have no lingerie or stilettos, or anything remotely sexy. What was I thinking? What was *he* thinking? I drop my backside on the edge of the bed and drop my head in my hands, my heavy hair falling forward and forming a waterfall to my knees. I should stay here and hope he gets fed up of waiting and leaves, because all of a sudden, this doesn't seem like such a good idea. In fact, it's the dumbest idea I've ever had, and happy with that conclusion I crawl under the covers of my bed and hide my face in a pillow.

He's rich, he's stunning, he's refined, if a bit standoffish, and he wants me for twenty-four hours? He needs his head tested. These thoughts plague my mind as I hide from the world, until I reach a perfectly solid conclusion; he must have arm candy throwing themselves at his feet daily—hell, I've seen one already—and they must all be dripping in diamonds, designer handbags, and shoes that cost more than my monthly wage, so maybe he wants to try something a little different, something like me—an average waitress, who buggers up coffee and throws trays of expensive champagne everywhere. I push my face farther into the pillow and groan. "Stupid, stupid, stupid woman."

"No, you're not."

I bolt upright and see him sitting in the armchair in the corner of my room, legs crossed at the ankles, his elbow resting on the arm, his chin in his palm. "What the hell?" I jump up and run to my bedroom door, swinging it open to check for old ears pushed up against the wood. Nothing, but I don't feel any better. Nan must have let him in. "How did you get up here?" I slam the door and flinch when it reverberates through the house.

He doesn't. He's perfectly collected, not in the least bit affected by my flustered state. "Your grandmother should take security a little more seriously." He rubs his index finger slowly across his stubbled chin, his eyes taking a leisurely jaunt down my body.

It's only now I realize that I'm standing in my underwear, and my arms instinctively cross over my chest, attempting in vain to conceal my modesty from his roving eye. I'm horrified, even more so when his lips tip at the edge and his eyes sparkle as they land on mine.

"You'd better lose your bashfulness, Livy." He stands, casually strolling over to me, sliding his hands in his gray trouser pockets. His chest meets mine, and he looks down at me, not touching with his hands, but touching with absolutely everything else. "Then again, I quite like your shyness."

I'm shaking—physically shaking, and no amount of pep-talking is halting it. I want to appear confident, nonchalant and carefree, but I don't know where to start. Decent underwear might be a good place.

He hunkers down, getting his face in the line of my dropped sight, and pulls my falling hair from my shoulders, holding it from my face. Lifting my gaze, only very slightly, I quickly find his. "My twenty-four hours don't start until I get you in my bed."

I feel my brow completely furrow. "You're really going to time it?" I ask, wondering if he'll produce a stopwatch.

"Well." One of his hands drops my hair, and he looks down at his expensive watch. "It's six thirty now. By the time I get you uptown in rush hour, it'll be approximately seven thirty. I have a charity ball tomorrow evening around seven thirty, so I've timed this just perfect."

Yes, he *has* timed it perfect. So when the clock strikes seven thirty, do I get tossed out on my arse? Do I turn into a pumpkin? I feel jilted already and we haven't even started, so what am I going to feel like come seven thirty tomorrow evening? Like shit, that's what—rejected, unworthy, depressed, and abandoned. I open my mouth to call a stop on the whole diabolical arrangement, but then I hear the sound of old footsteps clumping up the stairs.

"Oh shit, my nan's coming!" My palms meet his suit-covered chest and push into him, guiding his back toward a built-in cupboard. I'm panicking, but I'm still appreciating the solidness beneath my flat palms. It makes my steps falter and my heart jump wildly. I glance up at him.

"Feel good?" he asks, sliding his palms around my back and circling my waist. I hold my breath; then I hear the creaking again. It snaps me right out of my lustful state.

"You need to hide."

He snorts his disgust and moves his grip to my wrists, detaching me from his chest. "I'm not hiding anywhere."

"Miller, please, she'll have heart failure if she catches you in here." I feel beyond stupid for making him do this, but I can't let my grandmother barge into my room and see him. I know she'll go into seizure, and I know it'll be in shock, but it won't be shock of the ordinary kind. No, Nan will pass out for a few seconds; then she'll throw a bloody party. I release a frustrated, supressed yell, forgetting all embarrassment with regards to my lack of attire, and give him pleading eyes. "She'll get excited," I explain. "She prays to the Lord Almighty every day for my self-discovery." I'm running out of time. I can hear floorboards creaking as she gets closer to the door of my room. "Please." My naked shoulders sag, defeated. I can barely do this to myself, let alone to my elderly grandmother. It would be cruel to build her hopes up with a complete nonstarter. "I won't ask for anything else, just please don't let her see you."

His lips form a straight line and his head drops forward a little, the wayward lock of dark hair falling onto his brow, and without a word, he releases me and moves across my room, but he doesn't step into the cupboard; he goes behind my floor-length curtains. I can't see him, so I don't argue.

"Olivia Taylor!"

I swing around and find Nan in the doorway, her eyes roaming all over my room, like she knows I'm hiding something. "What's up?" I ask, silently scolding myself for my poor choice of words.

What's up? I would never say that, and her suspicious face notes this, too.

Her eyes narrow, making me feel even more conspicuous. "That man—"

"What man?" I need to shut up and let her spit it out, not intercept her and make her even more suspicious.

"That man in the car outside," she continues, resting her hand on the doorknob. "Your boss."

I must visibly relax because she runs her navy eyes over my semi-naked form, knowing plastered all over her face. She still thinks he's out there, which is just perfect. "What about him?" I pull my skinny jeans from my drawer and hop in, shimmying them up my legs and fastening the fly before snatching a white oversized T-shirt from the back of my dressing table chair.

"He's gone."

I freeze with my T-shirt halfway over my head, one arm fed through a sleeve and my hair caught in the neck. "Where?" I ask, no other words springing to mind.

"I don't know, but one second he's there, and I know because I could see the top of his head through the slightly open window; then I turn to tell George that he has one of those fancy Mercedes things, and when I look back . . . poof, he's gone. But that swanky car is still there"—her foot starts tapping—"and parked illegally, I might add."

I'm immobilized by guilt. She's like Miss bloody Marple. "He's probably nipped to the shop," I say, untangling myself from my T-shirt and pulling it down my body. I make quick work of shoving my feet in my hot-pink Converse. Christ, I've got to get him out yet, and with Ironside on the case, it's looking like a job and a half.

"The shop?" She laughs. "The nearest is a mile away. He'd drive."

I fight to prevent an irritated screech escaping. "What does it matter where he's gone?" I ask, then dive right in with the building of my greatest lie. "Oh, and I'm staying at Sylvie's tonight. She's a work friend."

My shoulders rise in anticipation for her gasp of shock, but it doesn't come, and that has me turning to see if she's still in my room. She is, and she's grinning. "Really?" she asks, her eyes twinkling in delight as she runs them down my static form. "You're not dressed for work."

"I'll change when I get there." My voice is high and squeaky as I busy myself, collecting toiletries and packing what I'll need for twenty-four hours with Miller Hart, which isn't a lot, I expect. "The event I'm working at tonight doesn't finish until midnight, and Sylvie lives close by so I may as well just crash there." I'm a fool and completely wasting my breath. It's only now, when I'm zipping up my bag and chucking it onto my shoulder, that I remember he's in my room. What must he be thinking? I won't blame him if he walks out this very instant. This performance by my nan has nothing to do with her disapproving of a man in my life. She just doesn't like the fact that she doesn't know about it, that's all. And she isn't going to know, not officially, anyway. The silence spreading between us is a mutual understanding of that. Gregory has told her I'm taken by someone, and she can't bear that I've not confided in her. It would be hard enough spilling if I were to get involved with a regular guy, under regular circumstances, but Miller? And with our twenty-four-hour agreement? No, it goes against everything I know, and I'm ashamed of myself because of it. While Nan has been begging me to sow my wild oats, I don't think she quite meant as wild as my mother.

She gazes at me, her old navy eyes thoughtful. "I'm glad," she says softly. "You can't hide from your mother's history forever."

I shrink a little, but not wanting to extend this line of conversation, especially with Miller hiding behind the curtains, I just nod my head at her, my silent way of saying yes. She nods in return and slowly backs out of my room, all cool and casual, but I know she'll be rushing back to the lounge window to see if the man has returned to his swanky car. My bedroom door shuts and Miller appears from behind the curtain. I've never been so embarrassed, and the interested look on his face only enhances it, even if it's nice to see him display a facial expression other than the completely serious one that I've become used to.

"Your grandmother is a busybody, yes?" He's really amused by her interrogation performance, yet I can also see curiosity lingering on that perfect face.

Straightening myself out, just for something to do other than feed his amusement *and* his curiosity, I shrug, feeling smaller than ever. "She's entertaining," I flip, my eyes darting across the floor. I want the ground to swallow me whole right now.

He's pushed up against me in a second. "I felt like a teenager."

"Did you hide behind a lot of curtains back then?" I step away to gain some breathing space, but my attempted escape is in complete vain.

He moves forward. "Are you ready, Olivia Taylor?"

I get the feeling he doesn't just mean to leave. Am I ready? And for what? "Yes," I say, decidedly staunch, not quite knowing where the word spoken with such confidence comes from. I stare at him, unwilling to be the first to look away. I don't know where I'm going or what I'll experience while I'm there, but I know that I want to go...with him.

His lovely lips give an almost undetectable smile, telling me he knows I'm feigning confidence, but I keep my eyes on his, unwavering. He leans down, getting us nose to nose, then blinks slowly, parts his lips slowly, drops his eyes to my mouth slowly, and then he increases my heart rate further by singeing my bare arm with his delicate touch. Nothing extraordinary, but the feeling is beyond extraordinary, like nothing I've felt before...until I met him.

He dips his head, coming so close I can't help closing my eyes. I'm dizzy and exhilarated all at once, feeling his tongue trace my bottom lip.

"If I start, I won't stop," he murmurs, pulling away. "I need to get you in my bed." He grasps my nape and twists his hand slightly, forcing me to turn away from him and walk forward.

"My nan." I barely splutter the words out in my wanton state. "She can't see you." I'm led across the landing and down the stairs—me cautious, him hasty.

"I'll wait in the car." He releases me from his grasp and strides to the front door, opening it and shutting it with no regard for my peeking grandmother.

"Nan!" I shout, panicked, knowing she'll have her face squished against the glass of the window looking for him. "Nan!" I need to get her away before Miller appears from the recess of the front door. "*Nan!*"

"Bloody hell, girl!" She appears in the doorway with George in tow, looking at my frozen form with worried eyes. "What's the matter?"

With a blank mind and blank face, I step forward and kiss her cheek. "Nothing. See you tomorrow." I don't hang around. I leave my nan frowning and George muttering something about a strange woman, and run down the pathway to the shiny black Mercedes, diving in and sinking into my seat. "Go," I press impatiently.

But he doesn't. The car remains idle at the curb, and he remains idle in his seat, showing no sign of rushing away from my house as I've demanded. His tall, suited frame is relaxed in the seat, one hand draped casually on the wheel as he looks at me, completely serious, his steely blues giving nothing away. What's he thinking? I break the eye connection, but only because I want to confirm what I already know. I look up to the front window of my house and see the curtains twitching. I sag farther in my seat.

"What's the matter, Livy?" Miller asks, reaching over to rest his hand on my thigh. "Tell me."

My eyes are on his big, manly hand, my flesh burning beneath it. "You shouldn't have come in," I say quietly. "You may have found it amusing, but you've just made this even harder."

"Livy, it's polite to look at someone when you're speaking to them." He clasps my chin and pulls, making me face him. "I apologize."

"It's done now."

"Nothing about the next twenty-four hours is going to be difficult, Livy." His hand slides across my cheek tenderly, pushing me to nuzzle into it. "I know being with you will be the easiest thing that I've ever done."

It might very well be easy, but I can't see the aftermath being easy. No, I foresee a mountain of hurt on my part and easiness on his. I'm not myself around him. The sensible woman I've molded myself into has gone from one extreme to the other. Nan's at that window, Miller's hand is stroking my cheek sweetly, and I can't even muster up the energy to stop him.

"The windows are tinted," he whispers, slowly moving forward and resting his soft lips on mine.

That may be so; however, he's not my boss, and my cute nan knows that very well. But I'll deal with the interrogation when I get home tomorrow. I'm suddenly not so concerned. I've been distracted from my sensible self again.

"Are you ready?" He asks the question again, but this time I just nod against him. I'm not ready to be heartbroken at all.

* * *

The drive back to Miller's apartment is quiet. The only sound in the air surrounding us is Gary Jules singing about a mad world. I don't know much about Miller, but I've figured out that he must come from good stock. His speech is refined, his clothing of the highest quality, and he lives in Belgravia. He pulls up outside the building and is out of the car and on my side without delay, opening my door and ushering me out.

"Have it cleaned," he orders, detaching his car key from the key ring and handing it to the green-suited valet.

"Sir." The valet tips his hat, then climbs into Miller's car, immediately pressing a button that brings him closer to the wheel.

"Walk." He takes my bag and settles his hand on the base of my neck again as he guides me through the giant glass revolving door and into a mirror-invested lobby. Everywhere I look, we're there, me being guided, looking petite and apprehensive, and him pushing me onward, looking tall and powerful.

We bypass the rows of mirrored elevators, heading for the stairwell. "Are the lifts broken?" I ask as I'm steered through the doors and pushed up the stairs.

"No."

"Then why—"

"Because I'm not lazy." He cuts me off, leaving no room for further questioning, and continues to hold my nape as we take the stairs.

He might not be lazy, but he's seriously crazy. Four flights of stairs in and my calf muscles are burning again. I'm struggling to keep up. I battle on for one more flight, and I'm just about to call for a break when he turns and picks me up, obviously aware of my breathlessness. My arms around his neck feel right, as comforting as they did before, as he continues with me draped across his arms like it's the most natural thing in the world. Our faces are close, his smell manly, and he keeps his eyes set firmly forward until we're outside his shiny black front door.

Miller drops me to my feet, hands me my bag, and takes hold of my nape, using his free hand to get the door open, but as the view inside his apartment hits me, I suddenly want to run away. I see the art, the wall where he restrained me, and the couch where he sat me. The images are all vivid, and so are my feelings of help-lessness. If I cross this threshold, I'll be at Miller Hart's mercy and I don't even think my long-lost sass will assist me . . . if I manage to find it.

"I'm not sure I—" I start backing away from the door, uncer-tainty abruptly plaguing me, sensibility worming its way into my confused brain. But the fiery determination in his clear eyes is telling me that I'm going nowhere and so does the increased grip of his hand on my nape.

"Livy, I'm not going to jump you as soon as I get you inside." His hand shifts down to my upper arm, but he doesn't restrain me now. "Calm down."

I'm trying to, but my heart won't let up, and neither will the shakes. "I'm sorry."

"Don't be." He steps away from me, giving me access to the entrance of his apartment. "I'd like you to go inside, but only if you want to spend the night with me," he says slowly, pulling my gaze to his. "And I want you to turn and leave if you're not sure because I can't do this unless I know you're one hundred percent with me." His face is straight, but I detect an element of pleading behind the impassive blue gaze of his eyes.

"I just don't understand why you want me," I admit, feeling insecure and vulnerable.

I know what I look like; I'm reminded every time someone stares at me or comments on my unique eyes, but I also know that I have very little to offer a man, apart from something pleasant to look at. My mother's beauty was her downfall, and I never want it to be mine. I'm at risk of losing my self-respect, just like she did. I've made it so there's nothing to know. Who would want to give any attention to a girl who offers no intrigue or interest beyond her looks? I know exactly who: men who want nothing more than a pretty woman in their bed, which is exactly why I deprive myself of the potential of being loved. Not lusted after, but loved. I never want to be my mother, yet here I am, tinkering too close for comfort on the edge of debasement.

I can tell that he's thinking hard about how to answer my question, like he knows it'll influence my decision to stay or leave. I'm willing him to make his next words count. "I've told you, Livy." He gestures me inside. "You fascinate me."

I don't know whether that's the right answer, but I slowly walk into his apartment, and I definitely hear a quiet, relieved exhale of breath from behind me. I circle the round table in his entrance hall, placing my bag on the white marble as I pass, before coming to a stop, not knowing whether to sit myself on the couch or go into the kitchen. There's an air of awkwardness surrounding us and despite his words in the car, it's difficult.

He walks ahead of me and shrugs off his suit jacket, laying it neatly over the back of a chair before making his way to the drinks cabinet. "Would you like a drink?" he asks, pouring some dark liquid into a tumbler.

"No." I shake my head, even though he's not facing me.

"Water?"

"No, thank you."

"Sit down, Livy," he orders, turning and gesturing toward the couch.

I follow his pointed hand and take my reluctant body to the large, cream-colored leather couch while he leans against the cabinet, slowly sipping his drink. No matter what he does with those lips, whether it's speaking or simply taking a sip of a drink, it's distracting. They move so slowly, almost sensuously... deliberately.

I'm desperately concentrating on regulating my thundering heartbeat, but I lose the battle completely when he moves toward me and sits on the coffee table in front of me, his elbows braced on his knees, his drink suspended in front of his lips, his eyes simmering with all sorts of promises. "I need to ask you something," he says quietly.

"What?" I blurt the word quickly, worriedly.

His glass lifts slowly, but those eyes stay on mine. "Are you a virgin?" he asks before tipping the tumbler to his lips.

"No!" I recoil, mortified that he's taken my reluctance as an indication of *that*. But in truth, I wish I was.

"Why are you so offended by my question?"

"I'm twenty-four years old." I shift uncomfortably in my seated position, diverting my eyes away from his inquisitive stare. I can feel my face heating, and I want to grab one of his fancy silk cushions to cover it.

"When was the last time you had sex, Livy?"

I'm dying on the spot. What does it matter when I last slept with someone? Running seems like the best option for me, but my reason for escaping has changed.

"Livy," he prompts, placing his drink down, the chink of glass on glass making me jump slightly. "Will you please look at me when I'm speaking to you?"

His sternness irritates me, and that's the only reason I do as I'm told and look at him. "My history has nothing to do with you," I say quietly, resisting the temptation to snatch his drink and down it.

"I simply asked you a question." His surprise at my sudden spunk is clear. "It's usually polite to answer a question when you're asked one."

"No, it's down to my discretion whether I answer any questions that I'm asked, and I don't see what relevance your question has."

"My question has plenty of relevance, Livy, as will your answer."

"And what's that?"

He looks down at his glass and swivels it on the table for a few moments before slowly returning his eyes to mine. They cut straight through me. "It will determine whether I fuck you hard immediately, or break you in first."

I gasp, my eyes widening at his obnoxiousness, not that he's affected by my shock or reaction to his crass words. He simply takes his tumbler and has another slow sip of the dark liquid, keeping his unrevealing eyes on me.

"I don't like repeating myself, but I'll make an exception," he states. "When was the last time you had sex?"

My tongue is knotted in my mouth as I remain under his watchful eyes. I don't want to tell him. I don't want him to think that I'm even more pathetic than he must think already.

"I'll take your reluctance to answer as an indication that it's been a while." He cocks his head, and that lock of hair falls onto his forehead, momentarily distracting me from my humiliation. "Well?"

"Seven years," I whisper. "Happy?"

"Yes." His response is swift and genuine, yet the stunned eyes are evident. "I have no idea how that's possible, but it pleases me immensely." He grabs my chin and lifts. "And I'm talking to you, Livy, so look at me." I follow through on his instruction until our eye contact is restored. "I guess that means I'll be breaking you in."

I don't gasp this time, but my blood instantly heats, sending my pulse rate through the roof, replacing embarrassment with want. I want him more than I know I should.

Meeting his intoxicating stare with my own driven gaze, I send instructions to the muscles in my arms to lift and feel him, but before I can engage them, my phone starts squealing from my bag.

"You should answer it." He sits back, giving me space to leave the intimacy of his closeness. "Let her know that you're still alive." There's no amusement on his face, but I hear it in his tone.

I stand quickly, keen to reassure my inquisitive grandmother that all is well. I don't look at the screen before I answer, but I should've. "Hi!" I greet, way too chirpy, given my circumstances.

"Livy?" The voice on the end of the line prompts me to pull my phone from my ear and look at the screen, even though I know damn well who it is.

I sigh, picturing Nan frantically dialing Gregory to inform him of the events earlier this evening. "Hi."

"That man. Who is he?"

"My boss." I squeeze my eyes shut, hoping he buys it, but he scoffs disbelievingly, which quickly tells me I've failed to fool him.

"Livy, give me a break! Who is he?"

I'm stuttering all over my words, frantically searching my mind for some rubbish to feed him. "Just...he's...it doesn't matter!" I snap, starting to pace. Gregory won't be happy, not after our conversations about Miller Hart.

"It's the coffee hater, isn't it?" His tone is accusing, spiking my irritation.

"Maybe," I retort. "Maybe not." Why I've added that is a mystery. Of course it's the coffee hater. Who else would it be?

I'm so busy trying to fob off my friend, I don't notice the coffee hater looming behind me until his chin is on my shoulder, his breath heavy in my ear. I gasp as I turn around and, stupidly or not, I hang up on Gregory.

Miller's brow is a knot of confusion. "That was a man."

"It's rude to eavesdrop." I stab at the reject button of my phone when it starts ringing again.

"That may be so." He holds his drink up, one finger detached from the glass and pointing at me. "But like I said, that was a man. Who is he?"

"That's none of your business," I say, fidgeting and diverting my eyes from his accusing blues.

"If I'm taking you to my bed, then it is my business, Livy," he points out. "Will you please look at me when I'm speaking to you?"

I don't. I keep my eyes on the floor, silently wondering why I don't just tell him who it was. It's not who he thinks it is, so what does it matter? I've got nothing to hide, but his demand for the information is unearthing a childish rebelliousness in me. Or it could be my sass. I don't need to find it because it seems to come out to play willingly around this man, which is undoubtedly a good job.

"Livy." He hunkers down and captures my eyes, his brow raised in authority. "If there's an obstruction, then I'll happily eliminate it."

"He's a friend."

"What did he want?"

"To know where I am."

"Why?"

"Because my grandmother has obviously told him that you were at the house and he has put two and two together and come up with Miller." My mortification is growing by the second.

"He knows about me?" he asks, those dark brows showing no sign of lowering.

"Yes, he knows about you." This is getting stupid. "Can I use your bathroom?" I ask, wanting to escape and gather myself.

"You may." His glass extends from his body and points toward a corridor leading off the lounge. "Third door on the right."

I don't waste time absorbing his questioning look. I follow his pointed glass, turning my phone off when it rings again, and let myself into the third door on the right, immediately collapsing against the back. But my exasperation is interrupted as I take in the colossal space in front of me. It's not a bathroom. It's a bedroom.

CHAPTER SEVEN

I straighten up and scan the space, noting the obscene leather-framed bed, the gigantic chandelier suspended from the ceiling, and the floor-to-ceiling windows, with the most amazing view across the city. I shouldn't be so stunned. I knew his place was palatial, but this is something else. I see two doors across the room, and deciding that one should be a bathroom, I make my way across the squidgy cream carpet and open the first one I come to, forcing my eyes to avoid the huge bed. It's not a bathroom, but it *is* a wardrobe, if such a vast space could be classed as a wardrobe. The square room has floor-to-ceiling mahogany cupboards and shelves circling the three walls with a freestanding cabinet in the center and a couch backing onto it. The surface of the cabinet displays dozens of small jewelry boxes, all open and exhibiting an array of cuff links, watches, and tie pins. I get the feeling that if I moved one of those boxes, he'd know. I quickly shut the door and hurry to the next one, pushing my way into the most ridiculously regal bathroom I've ever seen. I gasp, my eyes bugging. A giant claw-foot tub sits proudly by the massive window, with intricate gold taps and steps leading up to it, and the shower walls are adorned in a mosaic of cream and gold tiles. I try to take it all in. I can't. It's too much. It's like a show home. After washing my hands, I wipe up carefully and straighten the towels, not wanting to leave anything out of place.

As I exit his bedroom, I freeze, coming face-to-face with Miller. He's frowning again. "Snooping?" he asks.

"No! I was using the bathroom."

"That's not the bathroom; that's my bedroom."

I look down the corridor, counting two doors before the one I'm standing outside of. "You said third door on my right."

"Yes, and that would be the next door." He points to the next door, and I look, completely confused.

"No." I turn and point in the other direction. "One, two, three." I indicate the door behind me. "Third door on my right."

"The first door is a cupboard."

I can feel that irritation rising again. "It's still a door," I point out. "And I wasn't snooping."

"Okay." He shrugs his perfect shoulders and slowly blinks those perfect eyes, before taking his perfection in its entirety and strolling down the corridor. "This way," he calls over his shoulder.

Irritation flares. Who does he think he is? My Converse start a moody march down the corridor in pursuit of him, but when I arrive in the lounge, he's not there. I gaze around to the various doorways, leading to God only knows where, but he's nowhere to be seen. All of these unfamiliar emotions are driving me insane.

Irritation, confusion . . . desire, want, lust.

I stomp across to the hallway, yank my bag from the table, and head for the door.

"Where are you going?" His smooth tone tickles my skin, and I turn to see him with a refilled glass.

"I'm leaving. This was a stupid idea."

He walks forward, a little surprised. "You made a silly mistake by taking the wrong door and that's a cause to leave?"

"No, *you* make me want to leave," I counter. "The door has nothing to do with it."

"I make you uncomfortable?" he asks. I can detect a little concern in his voice.

"Yes, you do," I confirm. He makes me very uncomfortable, and on so many levels, which begs the question why I'm here.

He walks forward and takes my hand, tugging gently until I allow him to pull me back into the lounge. "Sit," he orders, pushing me down onto the couch. He takes my bag and phone and places them neatly on the table before squatting in front of me. He has me with those eyes again. "I apologize for making you feel uncomfortable."

"Okay," I whisper, my eyes dropping to his parted lips.

"I'm going to make you feel less uncomfortable."

I nod because I'm too rapt by the slow motions of his lips as he speaks, but my vision is broken when he rises and puts his glass on the table, tweaking it slightly before collecting his jacket and leaving the room. I follow his back, frowning, and hear a door open and close. What's he doing? My puzzled face flicks around the room, admiring the art briefly and thinking his apartment is too neat and perfect to actually live in, before I'm back to wondering again. Then I hear the door open and close, and I nearly choke on my own tongue when he strolls back into the room, wearing a pair of black, loose sports shorts—nothing else, just some shorts. Yes, his suit-adorned perfection is a little intimidating, but bloody hell, this won't help. Now I just feel even more inadequate and even more lustful, my hands mentally exploring the sharpness of his chest and stomach, my lips meeting the tanned smoothness of his defined shoulders, and my arms snaking around his tight waist.

He's back in front of me, lowering himself to the table and picking up his drink. "Better?" he asks.

I'm sure if I could manage to rip my enthralled eyes off his torso I would find a look of superiority, but I can't knock him for it. He is by far superior. "No." I drag my eyes up his body until I see him tipping his drink to those lips. Slowly. "How would this make me feel comfortable?" I ask.

"Because I'm casual."

"No, you're half naked." I take another glimpse, my eyes greedy for him.

"I'm still making you feel uncomfortable?"

"Yes."

He sighs and gets up, striding from the room again, but he doesn't head toward his bedroom. He goes in the direction of the kitchen. I hear doors opening and closing for a few moments before he's back with me, sitting on the table in front of me with a tray in his hand. He places it down next to him, and I note that it's full of rocks and ice.

"What are they?" I ask, leaning forward to watch him. He swivels the tray, selects a rock, and repositions his body forward, holding it out to me.

"Let's see if we can loosen you up, Livy."

"How? What are they?" I nod to the rock in his hand, now noticing that it's concave on one side and has some sort of jelly shimmering in the pearlescent shell.

"Oysters. Open up." He inches forward and I inch back, my face screwing up in disgust.

"No, thank you," I say politely. I don't know much about the shellfish, but I do know they're obscenely expensive and, supposedly, an aphrodisiac. I don't plan on finding out, though, because they look repulsive.

"Have you tried them before?" he asks.

"No."

"Then you must." He moves in closer, not giving me much more retreating space. "Open."

"You try first," I suggest, trying to buy myself some time.

He shakes his head, a little exasperated. "As you wish."

"I do."

He watches me as he slowly tips the oyster to his mouth, his head falling back, but his eyes holding mine. His neck lengthens and his throat is taut and totally kissable. Then he swallows painfully slowly and an unfamiliar bang lands between my thighs, making me shift. Oh fuck, he looks too sexy. I feel hot.

He dumps the rock, grabs the front of my T-shirt in his fist, and yanks me forward onto his mouth, catching me by complete surprise, but there is nothing I can or want to do to stop him. His hungry invasion is met with equal intent from me. I find his naked shoulders and relish in my first experience of his bare flesh under my palms. It's better than I imagined. His tongue is working through my mouth fervently, and I can do nothing more than accept, tasting the saltiness of the oyster, until he breaks our kiss and removes my hands from his shoulders, him panting, me gasping.

"That wasn't a result of the oyster," he heaves, wiping his mouth with the back of his hand, pulling me forward, his nose meeting mine. "That was a result of you sitting here in front of me with a look of pure desire in your exquisite eyes."

I want to tell him that he has that look, too, but I quickly stop myself, considering, perhaps, that he may just look at all women like that, or maybe it's just the way he looks, period. I don't know what to say, so I say nothing, instead choosing to continue with my fitful breaths as he holds me in place.

"I've just paid you a compliment."

"Thank you," I murmur.

"You're welcome. Are you ready to let me worship you, Olivia Taylor?"

I nod as he slowly moves forward, his blues flicking from my mouth to my eyes constantly until his lips are lightly brushing over mine, but this time he's relaxed and tender with his taking, gently seducing my mouth as he rises, encouraging me to stand with him, before he holds my nape over my hair and starts walking forward, forcing me to step back. I let him guide me until we're entering his bedroom and I'm feeling his bed at the back of my knees, and the whole time he holds our mouths together. He's an extraordinary kisser, overwhelmingly good, like nothing I've ever experienced before. If this is a sign of things to come, then I hope the next twenty-four hours last forever. I'm bursting at the seams with desire, matching him. Sensibility has vanished again.

His hand leaves my neck and grasps the hem of my T-shirt, lifting it and breaking our mouth contact to get it past my head so I'm forced to release his shoulders and lift my arms. My lingering concern for my lack of sexy underwear is long forgotten. I can't seem to focus on anything except him, his passion and his energy. It's all-consuming, leaving no room for anxiousness or hesitation. Or, more importantly, that sensible gene that seems to have disappeared into thin air under his attention.

"Do you feel better?" he asks, breathing down on me, his groin pressing into my stomach.

"Yes," I gasp, clenching my eyes shut, trying to comprehend what's happening.

"Don't deprive me of your eyes, Livy." His hands encase my cheeks. "Open."

I do. I open my eyes, my line of sight leading me straight to shimmering blues.

Leaning in, he kisses me sweetly. "I have to keep reminding myself that I need to take this slowly."

"I'm fine," I assure him, reaching up and resting the flats of my hands on his torso. He's being a gentleman, and I'm grateful, but I'm not sure that I want him to take it slowly. The desire ripping through me is getting hard to control.

He pulls away and smiles, and I fall some more. "I'm looking forward to indulging in you slowly." He reaches down and starts to unbutton the fly of my jeans. "Really slowly."

"Why?" I ask, stupidly or not.

"Because something as beautiful as this should be savored, not rushed. Kick your shoes off."

I do as I'm bid and watch as he drops to his knees and peels the denim from my legs, tossing my jeans to the side before he hooks his fingers in the top of my knickers. I'm looking down at him as he draws them from my legs slowly, prompting me to lift a leg in turn so he can rid me of my white cotton. Reaching forward with his mouth, he kisses me softly, just north of the apex of my thighs, and I noticeably tense, but not because I'm nervous. I don't feel any worries. He's being so careful with me, but the heavy ache, low in my stomach, is intensifying with every second that passes.

He rises to his feet and reaches around my back, finding the clasp of my bra, his mouth resting by my ear. "Are you on birth control?"

I shake my head no, hoping it won't deter him. My periods are regular and light and I've not exactly been sexually active.

"Okay," he whispers, pulling my bra from my body. "Take my shorts off."

His instruction makes me hesitate, the potential of him fully naked unearthing a little bit of nervousness, which is crazy when I'm completely nude myself.

His hands are suddenly on mine and guiding them to the waistband of his shorts. "Stay with me, Livy." His words drive me into action and I slowly, carefully, push his shorts down his muscled thighs, not daring to look down. I keep my eyes on his superb face, finding it comforting. I can't, however, avoid the feel of him when he's free from his shorts and skimming my stomach. I quietly gasp, involuntarily stepping back from him, but he moves with me, his hand sliding around my waist and cupping my bum. "Easy," he whispers. "Relax, Livy."

"I'm sorry." I drop my head, feeling stupid and frustrated with myself. Those doubts are creeping in again, and he must sense it, too, because I'm lifted to his chest and walked to the bed, then laid down carefully before he takes something from the top drawer of the bedside table and positions himself over me, astride my waist, his hard, hot penis directly in my line of sight. I'm fixated, even more so when he rises to his knees and clasps himself. I flick my eyes briefly to his face, seeing him looking down, his lips parted and that wave loose on his forehead. It's a pleasurable sight, but watching him rip the packet of the condom open with his teeth and slowly roll it down his shaft with ease is a light-year past pleasurable, which only leaves me wondering what's to come.

"Are you okay?" he asks, planting his palms on either side of my head and nudging my thighs open with his knee.

"Yes." I nod as I speak, not quite certain what to do with my hands, which are redundant by my sides, but then I feel him at my opening and they fly up to his chest on a gasp.

He's staring at me, and my eyes refuse to leave him, even though I desperately want to clench them shut and hold my breath. "Ready?"

I nod again, and he pushes forward gently, slowly breaching my entrance and sliding into me on a loud exhale of air. Pain sears through me, making me quietly whimper and dig my short nails into his shoulders. I know my face is etched with discomfort, and there's nothing that I can do to stop it. It hurts.

"Jesus," he gasps. "Jesus, Livy, you're tight." The strained expression on his face tells me he's in pain, too. "Am I hurting you?"

"No!" I yelp.

"Livy, tell me so I can fix it. I don't want to hurt you." He's braced on his arms, holding still, waiting for me to respond.

"It hurts a little," I admit on a despairing rush of breath.

"I can tell." He eases back gently but doesn't pull out completely. "I have puncture wounds in my shoulders to prove it."

"I'm sorry." I immediately release him from my vicious grip, and he pushes forward again, only halfway this time.

"Don't be. Save your biting and scratching for when I fuck

you." He smirks, and my eyes widen. "Come on, Livy." He retreats slowly and rocks gently back in. "Don't be bashful. We're sharing the most intimate act together."

I find my hips lifting, wanting him to plunge deeper, now that the pain has subsided a little.

"You're egging me on." He drops to his elbows and gets mouth to mouth with me, easing back and pushing in a little farther, circling his groin. "Tell me how it feels."

"Good!" I breathe, inviting him to increase his pace with another tip of my hips.

"I concur." He rests his lips over mine and teases my mouth with a brief dash of his tongue. It's too much. I attempt to capture his lips, but he pulls away. "Slowly," he murmurs, swaying in and out perfectly, gazing down at me and blinking lazily to match his gentle thrusting. This really is intimate, and he's breaking me in, just like he promised. The quietness surrounding us is only slightly pierced by our matching, quiet, irregular puffs of air. Right now, I'm wondering why I've deprived myself of this feeling. This is nothing like I remember. This is how sex should be—two people sharing in each other's pleasure, not sprinting to the finish line with no consideration for the other person, which is just how I remember my drunken encounters to be. This is worlds away. This is special. This is what I want. I know I shouldn't be thinking that, especially since I've agreed to twenty-four hours and nothing more, but if I'll have this to remember—him staring down at me, him feeling me, him worshipping me, then I think that I can cope with the aftermath.

I feel internal muscles that I never knew existed contract around him, sensitizing me to each delicious drive, pushing me onward to . . . something. I don't know what, but I know it's going to be good.

He leans down and kisses my nose, then moves to my lips. "You're tensing inside. Are you going to come?"

"I don't know."

"You don't know?" he gasps. "You've never come?"

I shake my head under his mouth, not feeling in the slightest bit embarrassed. I'm too distracted by the lush heaviness weighing down between my thighs, getting heavier with each gentle thrust of his hips. I've never climaxed when I've slept with a man. Each encounter disgusted me, made me wonder what my mother found so hard to resist. I couldn't see what pleasure could come of it—I never realized it could be like this. I feel like all rationality is being stripped away.

"Oh, fucking hell!" His face pulls away from mine, his hips jerking forward, a little less controlled. "You've never had an orgasm?"

"No!" I grapple at his shoulders, my head shaking despairingly. The pain has completely gone now. Oh God, it's gone and in its place is something else—something . . . "Miller!"

"Oh, you sweet thing." His drives are controlled again, but slightly firmer—more precise and consistent. "Livy, you've just made me a very happy man."

My nails dig in again. I can't help it. I'm being bombarded with hot sparks stabbing at my epicenter. "Oh!"

He drops his face to mine and kisses me softly. I'm not soft, though. I'm hungry, and my frantic mouth action is proof of it. "Slow down," he mumbles, sounding desperate, trying to guide me by kissing me purposely slow.

I'm turning light-headed; my eyes are rolling and my hands are now grasping his mass of dark waves. But I don't slow down. I can't. I feel a sense of urgency as the pressure builds and builds with every wonderful push of his hips.

"Here it comes." He breaks away from my mouth and rebraces himself on his arms, pumping firmly, leaving me with no mouth to devour and no hair to knot my fingers in. "How does it feel, Livy? Tell me." His jaw is tense, his eyes suddenly deadly serious.

"Good!"

"How good?" He pleasures me with more and more and more.

"Too good!"

"Are you ready to come?"

"I don't know!" Is that what this is? I feel out of control, almost out of my mind.

"Oh, sweet girl, you've not lived." His pace picks up and so does the pressure down below. My hands brace on his forearms and push, taking me farther up the bed, and my head starts to urgently shake from side to side.

"Oh God!" I yelp. "Oh shit!"

"That's it, Livy!" It's becoming frantic—our breathing, the shouting, the sweating and tensing and bracing. But he still maintains that steady, easy pace. "Let it go."

I have no idea what happens. The room starts spinning, a nuclear bomb goes off between my thighs, and I scream. I can't stop it. My arms flop behind my head and Miller lowers himself on top of me, barking his climax into my hair, panting and slipping over my wet skin. The throb, him inside of me and me around him is comforting and so is his fitful breathing in my ear.

"Thank you," I gasp, not even feeling stupid for showing my appreciation. He's the one who keeps reminding me of my manners and what he's just done to me deserves some gratitude. Bloody hell, that was past even my highest expectations.

"No, thank *you*," he breathes, biting at my ear. "The pleasure was all mine."

"Trust me, it was mine," I insist, smiling when I feel him grinning against my ear. I'm desperate to see it, so I turn my face into him, finding the most amazing sight—a full blown, boyish grin, making his eyes sparkle like crazy and revealing a dimple that I've never noticed before. What I'm seeing right now is a million miles away from the coffee-hating, clipped, refined, powerful man who has utterly captivated me. "You look cute when you grin."

It disappears from his face immediately, a heavy frown replacing it. "Cute?"

That probably wasn't the best choice of a word for such a manly man, but he *did* look cute. Not now, because he's not grinning anymore, but that tip of his lips, the revealing of that dimple, and the sparkling of his blue eyes showed me a completely different man, a man who I can tell doesn't appear very often. "You don't smile very much," I say, feeling a little brave. "You should make the effort. You look less intimidating when you smile."

"So I've gone from being cute to being intimidating?" He shifts onto his forearms and brings his face to mine, nose to nose, forehead to forehead.

I nod my head, making his nod, too. "You're a little intimidating."

"Or maybe you're too sweet."

"No, you're too intimidating," I affirm, feeling him throbbing inside of me. All edginess has left me, leaving me feeling calm and serene. It's a lovely sensation, and he made it.

"We'll agree to disagree." He's back to intimidating, but my serenity is still intact. It'll take a lot to pull me from this relaxed state of mind.

Easing out of me, he looks down between my thighs and pulls the condom off. "Consider yourself broken in, Livy."

My face screws up at his lack of tact. "Thank you."

"You're welcome." He shifts down the bed and nestles between my thighs, looking up at me. "How are you feeling?"

"Okay," I answer hesitantly. "Why?"

"I'm just checking if you need a break. Say the word and I'll stop, okay?" He rests his lips over the apex of my thighs, encouraging my receding orgasm to resurrect. I start twitching. I need more recovery time.

"Okay," I whisper, dropping my head back to the pillow and gazing up to the high ceiling. I don't think I'd ever tell him to stop. "Shit!" I blurt when I feel something hot and wet meet the tip of my buzzing clit. My head flies up, my stomach muscles tense, and my hands fist in the sheets by my side. My outburst is ignored and he sits up, taking my leg and bending it before lifting so he can kiss the sole of my foot. I want to throw my head back, curse and shout, but I'm immobilized by those damn clear eyes as he watches me struggling to cope with his tongue running up my ankle and onto my lower leg. "That feels nice," I confess as he inches his way upward until he finds my tummy and starts trailing his lips across my navel and then back down the other side.

"Would you like me to continue?"

"Yes," I wheeze, my leg twitching, my muscles firming up.

"Then I shall." He nibbles the inside of my thigh. "Soon, my mouth will be here," he says quietly, pushing a finger into me, just a little. "Would you like that?"

I nod my answer and he circles, enticing a long, low moan from me. "Oh God," I breathe, pulling at the covers, yanking one side up and letting it float down over my face.

He almost laughs as he pulls the sheets from my face, but my eyes remain firmly shut, even when I feel him moving up the bed until he's settled half on me, his finger still submerged. "Open."

My head shakes adamantly, my brain focused only on the sensation of his finger inside of me. He's not moving, yet I'm still pulsing incessantly around him, but then I feel his lips on the side of my mouth and my face turns toward the source of the heat, opening up to him, my thighs spreading wider, invitingly. I hum. It's low and broken, a clear sign of my pleasure, but I want him to know. I want him to hear how I feel.

"I love that sound," he whispers, withdrawing his finger and slowly thrusting forward with two. I whimper. "There it is again."

"It's good," I tell him quietly against his lips. "Really good."

"We'll agree on that one." His lips leave my mouth and start trailing down between my modest breasts and onto my stomach, his fingers still pushing forward and pulling away neatly, carefully. "It would've been a crime if you had declined this, Livy."

"I know!" I gasp, my stomach curling and knotting, my body movements becoming erratic.

"To think I could've missed out on this." His fingers are suddenly gone and he's moving fast.

"Oh!" My upper body flies up when he separates my folds and skims my clitoris with a light dash of his tongue. "Ohhhhhhh." I fall back to the bed, my palms covering my face, my legs shifting around him.

He nestles farther into me, the hotness of his mouth completely encasing me and sucking gently. I recognize the signs now. I recognize the heaviness in my groin, the regular heartbeat in my clitoris, and the need to tense everywhere. I'm going to climax again. "Miller!" I cry, my hands finding my hair and gripping hard.

He releases me from his mouth and strokes a wickedly firm trail with his tongue, right up the center of my cleft. "Good?"

"Yes!"

He's suddenly on his knees and his hands slide underneath me, his palms cupping my bum, and with one pull, the whole of my lower body is raised from the bed. "Get your legs over my shoulders," he demands, helping me shift them until they're draped over his body. He holds me with ease and pulls me forward until I'm held to his lips. "You taste incredible." His mouth starts a torturous dance across my sensitive lips, plunging into my center and sucking on my clitoris. "Exquisite, Livy."

I can't acknowledge that. I've been tossed into sensory excess, my body struggling to deal with the onslaught of pleasure. This is unknown territory. This is beyond any stretch of my imagination. I feel like I'm having an out-of-body experience.

My calves push into his back, pulling him closer, and his hands slide all over me, stroking and massaging me softly. I rip my eyes open and look up at him in his knelt position, holding me to his mouth, his blues pointing down at me. That look shoves me over the edge. My back bows and my fists slam into the mattress on either side of me. I want to scream.

"Let it go, Livy," he mumbles against my flesh. And I do.

I stop trying to suppress the pressure in my lungs and let it all out on a loud scream of his name, my thighs tensing around his face, my head thrown back. "Oh God, oh God, oh God!" I pant, trying to think clearly. It's no good. Nothing can get past the wall of shock as my body goes lax and my mind goes blank. I've lost control of everything. My mind. My body. My heart. He's hijacking every part of me. I'm at his mercy. And I like it.

I'm eased back down to the bed, and I do nothing to help as he positions me on my side and lies behind me, pulling me into the hardness of his chest. "What about you?" I breathe, feeling him hard against my back.

"I'll let you recover first. I could be a while. Let's just cuddle."

"Oh," I whisper, wondering how long a while is. "You want to cuddle?" I never in a million years expected cuddling to be included in my twenty-four hours.

"Cuddling's my thing with you, Olivia Taylor. I just want to hold you. Close your eyes and enjoy the silence." He gathers my masses of honey hair and pulls it out of his way so he can access my back; then he starts a hypnotizing, slow routine of lazy kisses over my skin. It makes my eyes heavier, finding immense comfort from the attention and his warmth coating every part of my back as he gives me his *thing*.

It makes me realize that I've existed in solitary.

CHAPTER EIGHT

I come to in a dusky darkness, completely naked and completely disorientated. It takes me a few moments to gather my bearings and when I do, I smile. I feel relaxed. I feel at peace. I feel sated and comfortable, but when I roll onto my side, he's not there.

I sit up and gaze around his bedroom, wondering what to do. Should I look for him? Should I stay put and wait for him to return? What should I do? I have just enough time for a trip to the bathroom, ensuring I leave everything exactly how I found it, before the door opens and Miller appears. He has his black shorts on again, and his seminaked perfection attacks my sleepy eyes, making me blink repeatedly just to ensure I'm not dreaming. He looks at me standing and fidgeting, a sheet wrapped around me and my hair probably resembling a bird's nest.

"Are you okay?" he asks, walking forward. His hair looks adorable, the dark waves wild and messy, and that lock sitting perfectly in place on his forehead.

"Yes." I pull the sheet in tighter, thinking maybe I should've gotten dressed.

"I've been waiting for you." He takes the sheet and wrestles it from my grip until he's holding a corner in each hand and opening it, exposing my naked body to shimmering blue eyes. His lips don't smile, but his eyes do. He moves into the sheet and drapes the ends over his shoulders so we're both enclosed in white cotton. "How do you feel?"

I smile. "Good." I feel more than good, but I won't admit it to him. I know why I'm here and it's searing painfully on my conscience and morality each time I think about it. So I simply won't.

"Just good?"

I shrug. What does he want? A thousand-word essay on my current state of mind and state of body? I could probably write ten thousand words. "Really good."

His hands slide around to my bottom and squeeze. "Are you hungry?"

"Not for oysters," I blurt on a shudder.

He removes himself from the confines of the sheets and wraps me back up with the utmost care. "No, not for oysters," he agrees, pecking my lips lightly. "I'll feed you something else." His hand finds the nape of my neck over my hair, and then turns me away from him, leading me from the room.

"I should get dressed," I say, not attempting to stop him, but wanting him to know that I'm not entirely comfortable with a sheet of cotton covering my modesty.

"No, we'll eat, then bathe."

"Together?"

"Yes, together." He doesn't give my concerned tone the attention it deserves. I can shower or bathe myself. I don't need him to worship me to that extent.

I'm taken into his kitchen and placed on a chair at a huge dining table, and I thank the cotton gods for the bedsheets separating my backside from the cold seat beneath me. "What time is it?" I ask, silently hoping that I've not wasted too much of my twenty-four hours sleeping.

"Eleven o'clock." He opens the mirrored door of the huge double fridge and starts shifting things aside and placing things on the counter next to him. "I was allowing you two hours sleep; then I was going to poke you." He places a bottle of champagne on the side and turns to face me. "You came round just in time."

I smile, pulling my sheet in, thinking how much nicer it would've been to wake up to those eyes glistening down at me. "Do you mind if I get dressed?" I ask.

His head cocks to the side, his eyes slightly narrowed. "Are you not comfortable in your skin?"

"Yes." I answer confidently, although I've never found myself asking that question before now. I know that I'm a little on the slender side, Nan reminds me daily, but am I really comfortable? Because the way I'm holding the sheet to me would indicate otherwise.

"Good." He turns back toward the fridge. "Then that's settled." A glass bowl appears, piled high with big, juicy strawberries, and then he opens a cupboard that reveals row after row of precisely placed champagne flutes. He grabs two and places them in front of me, then the bowl of strawberries—all washed and hulled—before he's in another cupboard pulling down a cooling bucket and loading it with ice from the dispenser on the front of the fridge. The bucket gets placed in front of me, the champagne nestled into the ice, and then he's at the stove, putting on an oven mitt. I watch in fascination as he moves around the kitchen at complete ease, every motion precise and neat, and all done so very carefully. Nothing that he moves or puts down stays in the same position for very long. It gets turned a fraction or repositioned before he's happy and continuing with something else.

Right now he's walking toward me, holding a metal pan that is billowing steam from the glass bowl that's resting on the rim. "Would you please pass me that saucepan grid?"

I look in the direction of his pointed finger and get up as quickly as the sheet covering me will allow, retrieving the metal pan stand and placing it next to the bowl of strawberries, champagne, and glass flutes. "There," I say, taking my seat again and watching as he shifts the stand a few millimeters to the right before easing the hot pan onto it. I crane my neck over the pan and spy a deep puddle of melted chocolate. "That looks delicious."

He's next to me now, pulling a chair near and resting his backside on the seat. "It tastes delicious, too."

"Can I dip?" I ask, getting my finger ready to plunge.

"Your finger?"

"Yes." I look to him, finding dark, raised, disapproving eyebrows.

"It'll be too warm." He grabs the champagne and starts peeling away the foil. "And that's why we have strawberries, anyway."

His frowning face and abrupt words make me feel childlike. "So I can dip a strawberry, but not my finger?" I see him look at me out of the corner of his eye while he works the cork.

"I guess so." He brushes off my sarcasm and pours the champagne, but not before neatly placing the rubbish that he's just accumulated into a tidy little pile on a small plate.

He passes me a glass, and I start shaking my head. "No, thank you."

His gasp is barely contained. "Livy, this is Dom Pérignon Vintage 2003. You don't say no to *that*. Take it." He thrusts it forward, and I pull back.

"I don't want it, but thank you."

The look of shock morphs into thoughtfulness. "You don't want this particular drink or *any* drink?"

"Water would be good, please." I'm not going into this. "I appreciate what you've done with the strawberries and champagne, but I'd rather have some water, if you don't mind."

He's clearly stunned by my refusal to drink the expensive liquid, but he doesn't push it, and I'm grateful. "As you wish."

"Thank you." I smile as he leaves me to replace the champagne with water.

"Tell me you like strawberries," he pleads, fetching a bottle of Evian and joining me again.

"I love strawberries."

"That's a relief." He unscrews the lid and pours my water into the other flute. "Humor me," he says when he catches sight of my furrowed brow. I accept the drink and watch as he takes his time selecting a strawberry before he dips it in the bowl and swirls carefully, coating the ripe fruit with dark chocolate. "Open." He clasps the seat of my chair with his spare hand and drags me closer so I'm snugly fit between his thighs. His bare chest is slightly distracting.

My jaw loosens automatically, mainly because I'm gaping at his close beauty, and he holds my eyes as he brings the fruit to my mouth until I feel it skimming my lip. My mouth closes around it and my teeth sink in, biting a small piece from its plump flesh. "Hmmm," I hum happily, and reach up to catch a trail of strawberry juice on my chin, but my wrist is seized before I get to wipe it away.

"Allow me," he whispers, edging farther into me, his lips homing in on my chin and slowly licking away the juice before he slips the remaining piece past his lips. My chewing has slowed right down, matching the precise motions of his mouth. He swallows. "Good?"

My mouth is full, so I nod—knowing Miller's compulsion for manners—and hold my finger up to indicate a second as I chew quickly. I lick my lips and lean toward the bowl again. "You need to feed me another."

His eyes twinkle as he selects another strawberry and dips and swirls again. "It would be even better with champagne," he muses, flicking his eyes to mine.

I ignore him and place my water on the table. "What chocolate is that?"

"Ah." He brings the strawberry to my mouth, but this time he brushes the runny chocolate across my bottom lip, and my tongue instantly leaves my mouth to clear it up. "No." He shakes his head and slides his palm around my neck, pulling me in. "I get to do that," he whispers in my face, moving in.

I don't fight him off. I let him clean up the mess that he's made and take the opportunity to rest my palms on his thighs, on either side of my knees. I smooth across the dark hairs of his legs, enjoying the feel of him, while he finishes up at my mouth, kissing the corner of my lips, the center, and then the other corner.

"What chocolate is it?" I repeat quietly, wanting to forget all sweet-tasting things and taste Miller instead.

"Green and Black's." He offers me the strawberry and I take it, holding it between my teeth. "It has to be a minimum of eighty percent cocoa." The strawberry that I'm holding is preventing me from asking why, so I frown instead, prompting him to go on. "The bitterness of the chocolate coupled with the sweetness of the strawberry is what makes it so special. Add champagne and you have a perfect combination. And the strawberries simply *have* to be British." He leans in and bites the strawberry that's wedged between my teeth and juice explodes between us.

I don't care about the juice all over my chin, or that my mouth is full. "Why?"

He finishes chewing and swallows. "Because they're the sweetest you can buy." He slips his hands under my thighs and lifts, pulling me forward so I'm astride him on the chair. He takes excruciatingly long to clean me up. It makes my skin heat and my breath catch constantly in my throat as I try to contain the urge to pounce on him. The sheet is yanked away, exposing my full nakedness to him. "Bath time."

"You don't need to bathe me," I object, wondering how far he'll take this worshipping business. I'm feeling extremely special, but I can wash myself.

He takes my hands and rests them on his shoulders, then

gathers the masses of honey locks framing my face. "I absolutely *do* need to bathe you, Livy."

"Why?"

He stands, holding my bum cheeks, and takes me to the mirrored fridge. I'm placed on my feet and turned away from him so my front is facing the mirror. I'm staring at myself. I feel uncomfortable, especially when I flick my eyes to Miller behind me and see his gaze journeying the length of my body. My eyes fall to the floor, but quickly snap up again when his chest is pressed against me and I feel his hard length pressed into my lower back—hot and moist. His shorts are gone.

"Feeling better?" he asks, holding my eyes in the mirror and reaching around to gently cup my breast.

I nod, when I really mean to say no. He intimidates me on every level, but it's all very addictive.

He molds my breast gently. "Mouthwatering," he whispers, his lips moving slowly. "Perfectly plump." He tweaks my nipple lightly and kisses my ear. "And incredibly tasty."

My eyes close and I lean back onto him, but my blissful state is interrupted when I'm lightly pushed forward and pressed against the cold mirror of the fridge, my modest boobs squished to the glass and my face turning in to rest my cheek on the cool surface.

"Don't move." He disappears from behind me, but is back within a few seconds, his knee pushing between my thighs and spreading them before he takes my hands, one at a time, and lifts them, flattening my palms on the mirror above my head. I'm spread-eagled against the front of the fridge, pushed up to the glass, and I can only just see him in my peripheral vision. He's holding the bowl of chocolate, and before I can even stop to consider his next move, he tips the whole contents across my shoulders, the warm chocolate making my shoulders jump up in shock, the sensation of it trickling down my back, over my bottom, and down my legs, making me pray for help. It's going to take time to lick all that away, and I've had his tongue on me before. I'll never make it through without screaming or turning to devour him. I start to tremble.

I hear the bowl being placed on the worktop behind me, and I also definitely hear the drag of glass on marble, indicating the repositioning of it. He's just tipped a bowl of melted chocolate all over me, and now he's worried about the positioning of a bowl?

Lifting my face from the mirror, I look for him in the reflection, finding him approaching me. His penis is solid and bouncing freely as he paces, and he has a foil packet in his hand. I gulp and rest my forehead against the glass, mentally preparing myself for the sweet torture that I'm about to endure.

"See? Now I really do need to bathe you." The warmth of his palms lands on the outside of my thighs and skate over my hips, my waist, my ribs—until his hands are sitting on my shoulders, massaging me, his big hands slipping over the chocolate. My head rolls back, a moan rolls from my lips, and my stomach rolls in anticipation.

Gliding his touch down the column of my spine, his finger slips over the cheeks of my bum and to the top of my thigh, down, down, down, until he's kneeling on the floor behind me and reaching up to stroke down my body once more. I'm on high alert. I'm docile, but aware—calm but frenzied . . . alive but fading.

"Livy, I'm not sure twenty-four hours is going to be enough," he whispers, his fingertip circling my anklebone. My eyes close and I try to divert my mind from sending the words that I want to say to my mouth. It won't help. He's turned on, that's all—caught up in the moment.

The tip of that damn finger burns a trail up the side of my lower leg until it's at the back of my knee. My legs wobble.

"Miller," I breathe, my palms sliding over the mirrored glass.

"Hmmm," he hums, replacing his finger with his tongue, licking a wickedly teasing stroke up the back of my thigh and onto my bum. He bites down on my cheek, his teeth sinking into my flesh and sucking...hard.

"Please." I'm begging. I'm doing what I swore I'd never resort to. "Please, please, please."

"Please, what?" He's on my back now, working up the center of my spine, licking, sucking, and biting as he makes his journey. "Tell me what you want."

"You," I pant. "I want you." I'm shameless, but that luscious heaviness is building again, heat racing through my veins, leaving no room for shyness.

"As I want you."

"You can have me." I turn my head when he clasps my nape and twists his grip, finding clear eyes that could rival the bluest of tropical waters.

"I don't understand how something so beautiful can be so pure." His eyes skate all over my face, wonder gushing from the heat of his stare. "Thank you." He kisses me so delicately, his hands roaming everywhere, until they're spreading chocolate up my arms and encasing my balled fists with his palms.

I know the answer to his question, but he's not directly asked, so I should avoid enlightening him. That's not what this is about. For him, it's fulfilling his fascination. For me, it's about remedying a problem that I've inflicted on myself—I have to keep telling myself that.

"Turn around so I can see you," he says against my lips, helping me swivel. When my chocolate-drenched back is pushed up against the fridge, slipping and sliding, he steps back and gives me an all-over visual assessment. I'm not shy because I'm too busy absorbing the mountain of chocolate-covered perfection before me—wide shoulders, tight hips, and strong thighs...a thick, long column protruding from his groin. My mouth waters up, my eyes fixed on that one area, despite the copious amounts of other hard perfection for my eyes to feast on. I want to taste him.

My eyes shoot to his when he steps forward, seeing a straight face, as usual, giving nothing away. "Where is that mind wandering to?" he asks, reaching down and taking a firm grip of his cock, pulling my eyes downward and my breath backward. I choke on a gasp.

Now I'm nervous, and my lack of response is a clear sign of this. Stupidly, I don't want to disappoint him. I'm sure he'll have had plenty of sweet lips wrapped around him, but I bet they all knew what they were doing. "I'm...can...it's..." I stutter and stammer all over the place, prompting him to relieve me of my awkwardness by burying his face under my neck and pushing up until my head's forced back and I'm looking up at the ceiling.

"You need to loosen up some more. I thought we were getting somewhere."

"We are."

He drops me, leaving me weak and wobbly while he rips open the condom and makes quick work of rolling it on. I don't like it. I feel like it's a crime for him to be covering his beauty. "I really wish we could do this flesh on flesh," he muses, glancing up at me. "But I wouldn't be much of a gentleman if I knocked you up, would I?"

No, he wouldn't, but whatever's gentlemanly about keeping me as a sex toy for a day? Or telling me that I'll get the best fuck of my life? He's contradicted that promise. There has been nothing close to fucking since I arrived. He's been a gentleman through and through—a caring, attentive, considerate lover.

I'm falling fast—too fast. And his gentlemanly approach is not helping.

"Livy?" His soft rasp pulls my eyes open. I hadn't realized they were shut. "Are you okay?" He moves in and gets his face level with mine, stroking my cheek.

"Yes." I shake my head mildly, offering a small smile.

"I'll stop. We don't have..." He pauses and slips into thought for a few moments. "I'll have to accept it if you've had enough."

"No!" I blurt, a little panicked. I'm fighting off unwanted hesitance. I'm having flashes of reluctance, despite my craving for this man. But he's too tempting. He's forbidden fruit. I've experienced him worshipping me, and even though I know it'll be bad for me, I want more. "I don't want you to accept it." Did I just say that out loud?

The wave of confusion on his dark stubbled face, mixed with a little relief, tells me I did. "You want to go on?"

"Yes," I confirm, more calmly, more controlled, even if I'm not feeling it. I'm still sizzling with heat and want, and it's all for this beautiful, respectful man before me. I gather some confidence, my hesitancy irritating me, and lift my chocolate-coated arms to place my hands on his smooth chest. "I want you again." I take a deep breath and drop my mouth to the flesh between my palms. "I want you to make me feel alive."

That's exactly what he does.

"Thank God," he exhales, grasping me under my thighs and lifting me to his hips where my legs seem to automatically curl around his tight waist. "I would've accepted it, but I wouldn't have been particularly happy about it." He gently pushes me up against the fridge and takes his hand between our bodies. "I can't seem to get enough of you, Olivia Taylor."

My back straightens, my arms finding the back of his neck when I feel the blunt head of his impressive manhood push against my entrance. "You can have as much as you like," I whisper quietly.

"And I will while you're here." The words kill me, but only very briefly because I'm distracted from his sobering declaration when he pushes into me on a hiss. "Oh Jesus, you've molded to me already." His face falls into my hair while he gathers himself and I adjust to him inside of me. He's right. Every muscle and void seems to shape around him like liquid. There's absolutely no pain, just crippling pleasure, more so when he draws back and pushes forward slowly, keeping his face buried in my neck. "You feel too fucking good."

My heart is in my mouth. I can't speak. My body seems to react mechanically to him, creating feelings, sensations, and thoughts, none of which I can prevent. "Please, just fuck me," I beg, hoping a lack of sentiment and intimacy might cure my building problem. "You've broken me in."

"Savored, not rushed." He reveals his face to me, and I notice chocolate coating his chin. "I've already explained that to you." His words are reinforced with a slow, continuous, meticulous pumping of his hips, over and over and over. "This is good, yes?"

I nod.

"I concur." His grip on my thighs increases, and he lowers his mouth to mine. "I'm dragging this out for as long as possible."

I accept his kiss, falling into the steady flow of his tongue's delicate sweeps. This is easy. I have no reluctance. Following him is the easiest thing that I've ever done. Our mouths are moving like we've practiced this kiss over and over, like this is the most natural thing in the world. It feels like it is. He feels so right to me, despite the fact that we're worlds apart in every element of our lives—him, the powerful, confident, abrupt businessman, and me, the boring, unsure, sweet waitress. Opposites attract has never been so appropriate. My direction of thought is valid and should probably be of concern, but not now, not when he's making me feel like this. My blood is heated, I'm crippled by pleasure, and I feel more alive than ever before.

He's patient, thorough. His gyrating hips are going to be the death of me. My hands are wildly feeling him everywhere they can reach, my legs are aching and heavy, but I don't care. "Miller," I say into his mouth, "it's coming."

He bites my lip and sucks, throwing me into sensation overload. "I can feel it."

"Hmmm..." I attack his mouth forcefully, my hands moving

to his hair and pulling. I need to loosen my iron grip of his hips, but with the pulsations between my thighs hammering violently, I can't concentrate on anything else. My body movements are spontaneous. No instructions are filtering through. Everything is happening, but I'm not telling it to. "Please, please, please," I beg. "Faster." The need for him to tip me over the edge has lowered me to more shameless begging—that and the desperate need to make this something other than tender lovemaking. He's holding me in limbo. I need to let go.

"No, Livy." He pacifies me softy but adamantly. "I'm not ready yet."

"No!" This is torture. Pure, evil torture.

"Yes," he counters, pushing into me, upholding his balanced rhythm. "This is too good. You don't call the shots."

My temper surfaces and I brazenly tighten my fists in his hair and yank his head from my lips. I'm panting, and so is he, but it doesn't hamper those hip movements. His hair is wet, his lips parted, and the usual stray wave has been joined by a few more. I want him to slam me into the fridge. I want him to swear and curse at me for my viciousness. I want him to fuck me.

"Livy, this isn't stopping anytime soon, so rein it in."

I gasp at those words and silently will him to follow them up with a powerful smash of his body into mine, but he doesn't, damn him; he keeps his control. I yank his hair again, attempting to pull some fierceness from him, but he just smiles his full-on beautiful beam . . . so I pull some more.

"Vicious," he mouths, still not giving me what I want, still easing gently into me.

I throw my head back and yell in frustration, ensuring I keep my fist clenched in his hair.

"Livy, you can mistreat me all you like. We're doing this my way."

"I can't take any more," I cry.

"Would you like me to stop?"

"No!"

"Does it hurt?"

"No!"

"So I'm just driving you crazy?"

I drop my head, accepting his careful pumping, still bubbling, and now sweating. I find his eyes, noting that familiar degree of arrogance. "Yes," I grate.

"Is it wrong for me to be delighted by that?"

"Yes." My teeth are clenching now.

His faint smile transforms into a sly smirk, and his eyes glisten. "I'm not going to apologize, but lucky for you, now I'm ready."

And with that, he lifts me, gains more leverage, and eases back before gliding smoothly into me and holding himself deep and high on a strained groan, shaking against me.

It does the job.

I convulse in his arms, my body becoming limp, my mind spacing out, and my hands finally freeing their hold of his hair. I'm not trying to, but my internal wall is grabbing on to him with every pulse he delivers, elongating the waves of pleasure riding through me.

While I'm quite happy being held against the fridge, limp and useless, Miller decides he's not so happy to hold me there. He folds down to the floor until I'm splattered on his chest, and then rolls over to get me beneath him. He watches me fighting to gain control of my short breath, then takes his mouth to my nipple and sucks hard, biting down and squeezing the surrounding flesh with his hand. "Glad you took me up on my offer?" he asks, sounding confident of the answer I'll give.

"Yes," I exhale, drawing my knee up and willing some strength into my arm to lift and stroke the back of his head.

"Of course you are." He kisses his way up my body until he's at my lips, nibbling tenderly. "Shower time."

"Leave me here," I puff, my arms flopping to my sides. "I don't have the energy."

"So I'll do all the hard work. I said I'd worship you."

"You also said you'd fuck me," I remind him.

He releases my lip from his grip and pulls back, thinking hard. "I also said I'd break you in first."

Surprisingly to me, I don't even blush. "I think we can safely say you can tick that item off your list, so now you can fuck me." What the hell has gotten into me?

Obviously, Miller is wondering the very same thing because his eyebrows have just jumped up in shock, but he doesn't say anything. Perhaps I've stunned him into silence. His brow furrows slightly as he starts to climb off me, and after disposing of the condom and wiping the bottoms of his feet, he quickly pulls me up and takes his customary hold of my nape. Then he starts guiding me toward his bedroom. "Trust me, you don't want me to fuck you."

"Why?"

"Because what we just shared was far more enjoyable."

He's right, and though I know it's stupid of me, I don't want to add Miller to my list of meaningless encounters. "Your kitchen is wrecked." I point to the chocolate-coated floor and fridge, but he doesn't follow my indication to look, pushing me onward instead.

"I can't look." His eyes turn dark, and he shakes his head. "I won't sleep."

I can't help smiling, even though I know it won't be appreciated. He's a clean freak. He has odd ways, with the constant repositioning of things, but after being here and seeing that immaculate wardrobe, I think he might even be a little obsessive about it.

Just as we breach the entrance to his bedroom, I'm swiftly scooped up and carried across the room. I'm a little shocked, but the rightness of it prevents me from saying anything. He's so strong and impeccably formed, a true masterpiece of a man, and he feels as good as he looks. When I'm placed on my feet just inside the bathroom doorway, I glance back into his bedroom and quickly reach a swift conclusion. The soles of my feet are covered in chocolate. His are not. He didn't want to mess up his carpet. He's pottering around the bathroom, all particular about where he puts things—the towels, the toiletries—and he doesn't give me a second glance as he passes me, going back into the bedroom, leaving me feeling small and awkward. I frown to myself and wrap my arms around my naked body, while I stand silently gazing around the immense bathroom until he's eventually back. He turns the shower on and tests the water. He has no problem with nudity, and it's hardly surprising. There's absolutely nothing for him to be shy about.

"After you." He sweeps his arm out, gesturing toward the mega shower space.

I'm hesitant; however, I manage to find direction and shuffle forward, naked and coated in chocolate. I glace up at an impassive face as I pass him. He's all formal and cold, a complete about-turn from five minutes ago.

"Thank you," I murmur, stepping under the hot spray and immediately looking down, seeing chocolate water pooling at my feet. I'm alone for a few moments, keeping my eyes down until his feet appear in my field of vision. Even they are perfect. My eyes start a slow climb up his body, studying every perfect, hard inch, until I'm watching him squirt soap onto his palm. Those palms are going to be on me any second, but judging by the look on his face, this isn't going to be a steamy shower scene. He's concentrating too hard on the massaging of suds between his hands.

Without a word, he crouches in front of me and starts rubbing the shower cream into my thighs, slowly washing away the chocolate. I can do no more than watch quietly, but the lack of speaking is making me feel uncomfortable. "What do you do for a living?" I ask, trying to break the awkward silence.

He pauses, but quickly picks up his pace again. "I don't think we should get into personal chitchat given our arrangement, Livy." He doesn't look at me, choosing to remain focused on my cleanup. I wish I had kept quiet because those words haven't relieved my unease; I just feel even more awkward. I'm compelled to know more about him, but he's right. The knowledge will serve no purpose and will only make this cozier than it's supposed to be.

He continues to sweep those splendid hands all over my skin, not saying a word or even looking at me. After the intimacy of our night so far, this is difficult and unwelcome. It's like we're strangers. Well, we are, yet the man kneeling before me is the only person on God's earth whom I've shared myself with. Not my past or any troubles, but my sober body and my vulnerability. He's made me question my approach to life *and* men. He's lured me in with a false sense of security, and now he's carrying on like this is business, not pleasure.

I'm perplexed, but I shouldn't be. I knew the deal, yet his tenderness and the fact that he absolutely has not fucked me, perhaps gave me false hope of this being more, which is obscene. He's really a stranger and an unpredictable, moody, intimidating one at that.

My speeding thoughts are interrupted when his hands make it to my shoulders, the firmness of his thumbs working into my flesh deliciously. And he's now looking at me, his face still straight and his hair sopping wet, looking longer with the water weighing down his waves. Lowering his face, he kisses me gently but sweetly before resuming the task of ridding my body of chocolate.

What was that?

A tender display of affection? A caring gesture? Natural instinct? Or was it just a friendly kiss? The heat of our mouths together suggested otherwise, but his face doesn't. I should leave. I'm not sure how I thought this evening would pan out, but I should have thought harder, and then I'm sure that I would've passed his offer up. This shouldn't be me, and I've swiftly been dragged from awe to resentment.

I'm just about to declare my intention to halt our arrangement when he speaks. "Tell me how it's possible that you've not been taken by a man in seven years," he asks, pushing some wet hair from my face.

I sigh, dropping my face until it's quickly forced back to his. "I . . ." Whatever can I say? "It's just that . . ."

"Go on," he pushes soothingly.

I find avoiding his question easy when I suddenly recall his previous statement. "Given our 'arrangement,' I thought we weren't going to do chitchat."

His frown matches mine. He looks embarrassed. "So I did." My neck is gripped by his hand over my wet hair and I'm directed from the shower. "Forgive me."

I'm still frowning as he dries me off with a towel, and then takes my neck again, leading me from the bathroom toward his giant leather bed. It's dressed beautifully, all plush with deep red, crushed velvet and gold scatter cushions placed delicately. I didn't notice it before, but I know it couldn't have been this neat when I got up earlier, so it's been redressed. I don't want to ruin the preciseness of it again, but Miller releases me and starts taking the cushions and placing them neatly in a chest at the end of the bed before he draws back the quilt and nods for me to climb in.

I step forward cautiously, and slowly clamber onto the huge bed, feeling like the princess and the pea. Nestling down, I watch as he slips in beside me and plumps his pillow before resting his head and snaking his arm around my waist, gently tugging me toward his body. I move instinctively into the warmth of his chest, knowing this is wrong. I know it's wrong, even more so when he takes my hand, kisses my knuckles, and then places my palm on his chest and lays his over it, beginning a guided caress of his skin.

It's quiet. I can hear my mind ticking over with endless hopeful thoughts. And I think I might hear his, too, but there's an invisible strain now, and this invisible strain between us is far outweighing the great things that have come before. His heart is beating steadily under my ear, and the odd squeeze of his hand around mine is a gesture of comfort, but I'm never going to be able to sleep, even though my body is exhausted and my brain drained.

Miller suddenly shifts, and I'm removed from his chest and positioned neatly to the side. "Stay here," he whispers, kissing my forehead before removing his naked body from the bed and slipping his shorts on. He leaves the room, and I prop myself up on my elbows and watch as the door closes quietly behind him. It has to be the early hours of the morning. What is he doing? The absence of the awkward silence should be making me feel better. But it doesn't. I'm nude, sore between the thighs, and I'm tucked up neatly in a stranger's bed, but I can do no more than lie back and stare up at the ceiling with only my unwelcome thoughts to keep me company. He makes me feel wonderful and alive, and in the next breath, awkward and an inconvenience.

I'm not sure how long I'm there, but when I hear a few bangs and definitely a polite curse, I can stay no more. I shuffle toward the edge of the bed, taking the sheet with me, and pad across the bedroom, gingerly letting myself into the corridor and wandering quietly toward the source of the commotion. The noises and muttered curses get clearer and clearer until I'm standing in the doorway of the kitchen looking at Miller wiping down the fridge's mirrored doors.

What should be making me stagger in disbelief is Miller's frantic hand swirling a cloth over the surface, but it's the muscles of his back, all rippling and sharp, that have my breath catching and my hand darting out to the door frame to steady myself. He can't be real. He's a hallucination—a dream or a mirage. I would be sure of this, if I wasn't so . . . broken in.

"Fucking mess!" he hisses to himself, plunging his hand into a bucket of soapy water and wringing the cloth out. "What the fuck was I thinking? Fuck!" He slaps the cloth on the mirrored doors again, continuing to curse and rub frantically.

"Everything okay?" I ask quietly, smiling like crazy on the inside. Miller likes everything just like him: perfect.

He swings round, surprised but scowling. "Why aren't you in bed?" The cloth gets thrown viciously into the bucket. "You should be resting."

My sheet gets pulled in closer, like I'm using it as a protective shield. He's mad, but is he mad with me or with the smeared mirror of the fridge? I start backing away, a little wary.

"Fuck." He hangs his head in shame, shaking it a little and ruffling his dark mop with a frustrated swipe of his hand. "Please, forgive me." His eyes lift and gush with genuine regret. "I shouldn't have spoken to you like that. It was wrong of me."

"Yes, it was," I agree. "I'm not here to be snapped at."

"It's just . . ." He looks at the fridge and clenches his eyes shut, like it hurts him to see the smears. Then he sighs and walks forward, holding his hands out, silently asking my permission to touch me. Stupidly or not, I nod, and he visibly relaxes. He wastes no time and crowds me, pulling me close and sinking his nose into my damp hair. The comfort it gives me can't be ignored. When he said that he wouldn't sleep, he really meant it. He didn't look at the mess when I hinted to it, but clearly it was playing on his mind, tormenting him.

"I'm sorry," he repeats, kissing my hair.

"You don't like mess." I don't ask it as a question because it's painfully clear, and I'm not giving him the opportunity to insult me by denying it.

"I'm house proud," he counters, turning me and pushing me back toward the bedroom.

Every step we take, I'm reminded of my palatial surroundings.

"Don't you have a cleaner?" I ask, thinking a businessman who lives in a place like this, dresses like Miller, and drives a prestigious car would at least have a housekeeper.

"No." I'm unwrapped from the sheet and lifted into bed. "I like doing it myself."

"You like cleaning?" I blurt, shocked. He really can't be real.

His lips tip at the corners, making me feel a whole lot better about the events, words, and feelings that have come after our intimacies. "I wouldn't say I like it." He slips in beside me and pulls me in, tangling our naked legs. "I suppose you could call me a domestic god."

I'm smiling now, too, and my hand is having a field day with free access to his bare chest. "I never would've thought it," I muse.

"You should try to stop thinking too much. People overthink things, making them bigger deals than they actually are." He speaks softly, almost nonchalantly, but there's more meaning to those words; I know there is.

"Like what?"

"Nothing specific." He pecks the top of my head. "I was just being general."

He wasn't being general at all, but I say no more. His reversed mood has calmed my earlier unease, and I'm letting the security of his body encasing me ease me into a peaceful slumber. It's not long before my eyes slowly close and the last sound I hear is Miller humming something hypnotizing and soft in my ear.

*　　*　　*

In a panic, my eyes snap open and I bolt upright in bed. It's completely dark. Brushing my wild hair from my face, I take a few moments to backtrack and it all comes back to me...or was I dreaming?

I pat around on the bed, feeling nothing but soft bedding and a pillow with no head on it. This bed is enormous, but I wouldn't lose a whole man in it. "Miller?" I whisper timidly, then feel down my body, noting no clothing. I always sleep in my knickers. I'm not dreaming, and I don't know whether to be relieved or frightened by that. I stumble out of the bed and feel my way around the wall. "Shit!" I curse, smacking my shin on something hard. I rub away the stab of pain and shift farther, meeting something with my head. The crash pierces the silence, and I fumble with something attacking me. "Bollocks!" I lose the battle to hold whatever has hit me and let it fall, wincing when it smashes, before rubbing my forehead. "Bloody hell."

I expect Miller to appear from wherever he's hiding to investigate the commotion, but after standing in silence forever, hoping he'll flick a switch that'll bless me with light, I'm still blind. I resume my tentative groping of the wall in the darkness until I feel something resembling a switch. I flick it on, blinking back the harsh invasion of artificial light. Of course I'm alone, and I'm also naked. I note the cabinet that I smacked my shin on and the floor standing lamp that I bumped my head on, which is now resting against the cabinet, smashed into a million pieces. I hurry back to the bed and grab the bedding, wrapping it around me as I walk back toward the door. He's probably cleaning the fridge again, but once I've found my way into the kitchen, I find no Miller cleaning. In fact, I find no Miller at all. Nowhere. I circle his apartment twice, opening and closing doors, or all that *will* open. There's one that won't. I jiggle the handle, but it doesn't shift so I gently tap and wait. Nothing. I head back to his bedroom with a completely furrowed brow. Where's he gone?

Sitting on the side of his bed, I wonder what to do, and for the first time, the full force of my stupidity smacks me hard in the face. I'm in a strange apartment, naked in the middle of the night, after having crazy, no-emotions, reckless sex with a stranger.

Sensible, wise Livy has just pulled a stunt worthy of an award. I've let myself down.

I look around for my clothes, but they're nowhere in sight.

"Fucking hell!" I curse to myself. What the hell has he done with them? Logic descends too quickly and I find myself in front of the cabinet, removing the lamp and pulling a drawer open, finding neat piles of men's clothes. It doesn't deter me. I pull the next open, then the next and the next, until I'm on my knees at the bottom drawer, staring at my clothes, all neatly folded, with my Converse positioned deftly next to them, laces tucked into the inner shoe. I laugh to myself, pull my belongings free from the drawer, and quickly dress myself.

As I turn to exit, I notice a piece of paper on the bed. I don't want to believe that he's left me a pillow note, and I should probably leave without reading it, but I'm just too damn curious. Miller makes me curious, and that's a bad thing because everyone knows that curiosity killed the bloody cat. I hate myself for it, but I hurry over and snatch it up, angry before I've even read it.

Livy,

I've had to nip out. I won't be long so please do not leave.
If you need me, call me. I've stored my number in your phone.

Miller
x

Stupidly, I sigh at the sight of a kiss after his name. Then I get mighty irritated. He's had to *nip* out? Who nips out in the middle of the night? I go in search of my phone to establish exactly what time it is. I find my bag and phone on the glass coffee table, and after turning it on and ignoring dozens of missed calls from

Gregory and three text messages advising me that I'm in trouble, the screen tells me it's three o'clock in the morning. Three?

My phone is spun repeatedly in my grasp as I contemplate what could've called him away at this time. An emergency, perhaps? Something could've happened to a member of his family. He could be at a hospital or picking up a drunken sister from a nightclub. Does he have a sister? All sorts of reasons are dancing in my head, but when my phone starts ringing in my hand and I look down and see his name flashing on my screen, I stop wondering because I'm about to find out.

I connect the call. "Hello?"

"You're awake."

"Well, yes, and you're not here." I sit down on the sofa. "Is everything okay?"

"Yes, it's fine." He's speaking quietly. Maybe he *is* in a hospital. "I'll be back soon so just relax in bed, okay?"

Relax in bed? "I was just leaving."

"What?" He's not whispering anymore.

"You're not here, so there's little point in me staying." This isn't being worshipped; this is being abandoned.

"There's a big point!" he argues, and I hear a door slam in the background. "Just stay where you are." He sounds fretful.

"Miller, are you okay?" I ask. "Has something happened?"

"No, nothing."

"Then what's called you out in the middle of the night?"

"Just business, Livy. Go back to bed."

The word "business" spikes unwarranted resentment in me. "Are you with that woman?"

"What makes you say that?"

His question has transformed that resentment into suspicion. "Because you said 'business.'" With all of the mind-blanking worshipping, I'd forgotten about the black-haired beauty.

"No, please. Just get back in bed."

I flop back against the sofa. "I won't sleep. This wasn't part of the deal, Miller. I don't want to be alone in a strange apartment." The absurdity of my words makes me physically kick myself. Yes, because I'm happier in a strange apartment with a strange man, who makes me lose all sensibility.

"The deal was for one night, Olivia. Twenty-four hours, and I'm annoyed enough at having to lose a few of those. If you're not in that bed when I get home, then I'll..."

I sit up. "You'll what?" I ask, hearing his panicked, fitful breaths down the line.

"I'll..."

"Yes?"

"I'll..."

"You'll what?" I hiss impatiently, standing and picking up my bag. Is he threatening me?

"Then I'll find you and put you back in it!" he snaps.

I actually laugh. "Are you listening to yourself?"

"Yes." His tone has calmed. "It's not courteous to break a deal."

"We didn't shake on it."

"No, we fucked on it."

I gasp, scowl, and choke all at once. "I thought you were a gentleman."

"Whatever gave you that idea?"

My mouth snaps shut as I consider his question. Our first meeting never suggested that he's a gentleman, and neither did our following encounters, but his attentiveness and manners since I've been here have. There has been no fucking, not in any sense of the word.

A horrid realization dawns. I really have been very stupid. He's seduced me, and he's done it brilliantly. "I have no idea, but I'm clearly mistaken. Thank you for the countless orgasms." I hear him shouting my name as I pull the phone away from my ear and hang up. I'm stunned by my own brazenness, but Miller Hart spikes my inner spunk. And that's dangerous territory to be falling into, but essential to maintain when dealing with this confounding man. Throwing my satchel over my shoulder, I head for his front door, rejecting the incoming call before turning off my phone.

Chapter Nine

I didn't sleep a wink, despite being in the comfort of my own bed. After sneaking into the house like a professional cat burglar, I tiptoed up the stairs, avoided all of the creaking floorboards, and crossed the landing stealthily until I was in the safety of my own room. Then I lay there in the darkness for the remaining few hours of nighttime, looking blankly and blindly up at the ceiling.

Now the birds are tweeting, I can hear Nan downstairs pottering around in the kitchen, and I have no desire to face the day. My mind is awash with images, thoughts, and conclusions, none of which I want to waste brain space on. But no matter how hard I'm trying, I just can't boot him out of my jumbled head.

Leaning over to my bedside table, I unplug my phone from the charger and brave turning it on. There's another five missed calls from Gregory, one from Miller, and a voice mail. I don't want to hear what either man has to say, but that doesn't stop me from tormenting myself further and listening to the damn message. It's my worried friend, not Miller.

"Olivia Taylor, you and I are going to be having some very strong words when I get hold of you. What are you thinking, baby girl? For crying out loud! I thought you were the sensible

one out of the two of us. You'd better call me, or I'll be paying
a visit to Nan, and I'll be telling her of your transgressions!
He could be a rapist, an axe murderer! Holy shit, you stupid
woman! I'm not a happy bunny!"

He sounds totally exasperated, the drama queen. And I know
he won't spill to Nan because he knows, just as well as I do, that
she'll be rejoicing, not despairing. Empty threats, that's all his
message is. Part true, but over the top and completely knocked
out of perspective.

Kind of.

A little.

Not in the least bit.

He's one hundred percent right, and he doesn't know the half
of it. I *am* an idiot. I call him before he goes into seizure, and he
answers immediately, sounding like he may already be suffering
meltdown. "Livy?"

"I'm alive." I fall back to my pillow. "Take a few deep breaths,
Gregory."

"Don't take the piss! I've been working through the night trying to find out where he lives."

"You're overreacting."

"I don't think I am!"

"You didn't find him, then?" I ask, pulling my quilt up farther
and snuggling down.

"Well, I didn't have much to go on, did I? I googled 'Miller'
but I don't think he grinds crops for a living."

I laugh to myself. "I don't know what he does for a living."

"Well, it doesn't matter because you won't be seeing him again.
What went down? Did you shag him? Where are you? Have you
lost your fucking mind?!"

I'm not laughing anymore. "None of your business, none of
your business, I'm at home, and yes, I have lost my bloody mind."

"None of my business?" he screeches, all high-pitched. "Livy, I've busted my balls for years, trying to pry you from that stupid shell you hide away in. I've introduced you to endless decent men, all of which were mad for you, but you flat-out refused to even entertain the idea of a friendly drink or, at a stretch, dinner. Letting a man wine and dine you doesn't make you your mother."

"Shut up!" I hiss, the mention of my mother spiking too much venom that's evident in my tone.

"I'm sorry, but what is it about this cocksucker that's turned you into an irresponsible, reckless twat?"

"You're the only cocksucker I know," I accuse quietly, because I'm at a loss of what else to say. I have been pretty reckless, just like my moth— "And he's not a criminal or a murderer. He's a gentleman." *Sometimes*, I add to myself.

"What happened? Tell me."

"He worshipped me," I confess. He'll nag me stupid, so I may as well come clean. It's done now. No going back.

" 'Worshipped'?" Gregory's voice is barely a whisper, and I see him in my mind's eye halting whatever he may be doing on the other end of the phone.

"Yes, he's ruined it for all those who will come after." He really has. Nothing will compare. No man will match his skill, attentiveness, and passion. I'm totally buggered.

"Oh Lord." He's still whispering. "That good?"

"Blissful, Gregory. I feel cheated. While he promised twenty-four hours, I only got eight. I annoyingly want the re—"

"Whoa! Rewind! Re-fucking-wind!" he yells, making me jump in my bed. "Back the fuck up! What's this about twenty-four hours? Twenty-four hours for what?"

"To worship me." I turn onto my side, transferring my phone to the other ear. "He offered me that time because it's all he could." I cannot believe that I'm divulging all of this information to

Gregory. This has to get the gold, especially given that it's me who we're juicing it up about.

"I don't even know what to say." I can see the shock on his face when I close my eyes. "I need to see you. I'm on my way."

"No, no!" I sit up urgently. "Nan doesn't know I'm here. I snuck back in."

Gregory laughs. "Baby girl, I hate to be the bearer of bad news, but your nan knows exactly where you are."

"How?"

"Because she's the one who called me to say you were home." There's a degree of smugness in his tone.

I look to the heavens for strength. I should've bloody known. "Then why did you pick my brain about where I am?"

"Because I wanted to see if my soul mate had developed a habit of lying, as well as being a dumb arse. I'm glad to have it confirmed that you're only the latter. I'm on my way." He hangs up, and as soon as I drop my phone to the bed, I hear the familiar sound of creaking floorboards, so I hastily crawl under the covers and hold my breath.

The door opens, but I remain like a statue, out of view, eyes clenched shut and holding my breath—not that I expect it to deter her. I bet she's dying to get the scoop, the nosy old bat.

There's total silence, but I know she's there, and then I feel a light brushing tickle on the sole of my foot and my leg lashes out on an uncontrolled burst of laughter. "Nan!" I shout, throwing the quilt back and finding her plump body at the bottom of my bed, arms crossed, and with a dirty smirk on her old face. "Don't look at me like that," I warn.

"Your boss, my *arse*!"

"He was."

She scoffs and comes to sit on the edge of the bed, putting me on high alert. "Why are you telling me porky pies?" she asks.

"I'm not." My response is feeble and my eyes, diverted from hers, are a sign of my guilt.

"Livy, give your grandmother a break." She slaps my thigh over the quilt. "I might be an old lady, but my eyes and ears work just fine."

I chance a reluctant glance at her, seeing a grin being held back. I'll make her day if I confirm what she already knows. "Yes, and so does your nosy mind."

"I'm not nosy!" she argues. "I'm just being...a concerned grandmother."

I scoff and tug the quilt from under her bum, wrapping it around myself and escaping to the bathroom. "You've nothing to be concerned about."

"I think I have when my sweet granddaughter lives like a recluse, and then suddenly stays out until dawn."

I cringe, quickening my pace as she follows me across the landing. My work excuse won't wash now, so I hold my tongue and make quick work of shutting the bathroom door behind me, just catching a glimpse of her gray eyebrows arched and her thin lips curved.

"Is he your boyfriend?" she calls through the door.

I turn the shower on and drop my quilt. "No."

"Was he your boyfriend?"

"No!"

"Are you courting him?"

"What?"

"Dating. It means dating, dear."

"No!"

"Just having sex, then."

"Nan!" I yell, flashing the door an incredulous look.

"Just asking."

"Well, don't!" I step into the bath and under the hot spray, thankful for the hot water, but not for the flashbacks of my last shower. He's invading every corner of my brain, except the little part that is currently being reserved to answer Nan's unreasonable questions. I squeeze some shampoo into my palms and set about lathering up my hair, hoping I'll physically scrub the memories away as I do.

"Are you in love with him?"

I freeze under the water, my hands sitting idly in the mass of bubbles on my head. "Don't be stupid." I try to sound shocked, but all I achieve is a quiet, thoughtful rush of breath. I'm not sure what my feelings are because they're all over the place at the moment. And they shouldn't be, especially with the knowledge of another woman. I'm not in love with him, though. I'm intrigued by him, that's all. He's fascinating to me.

I wait for Nan's comeback as my body remains still and my mind contemplates what she might say next. It's a long time, but I eventually hear the distant creaking of floorboards. She's gone, and she didn't challenge my unconvincing reply to her final question, which is extremely unusual.

* * *

Gregory is making up for Nan's mild interrogation. He's humored me for a few hours, riding the open-top, hop-on-hop-off tour bus and listened to me remind him of why I love London so much, but when I'm guided to the outside seating area of a café off Oxford Street, I know my time evading him has passed. "Coffee or water?" he asks as the waiter approaches, giving me his roving eye.

"Water." I ignore the waiter and commence a nervous fiddle of the napkin, folding it neatly too many times, until it's no longer foldable.

My friend is looking at the waiter the same way the waiter is looking at me, all bug-eyed and smiley. "Water and an espresso, please, kind sir."

I grin at Gregory, making it a continuous triangle of smiles as the waiter writes down our order and backs away, missing the lady on the next table, who's waving for his attention. It's overcast but muggy, and my tight jeans are sticking to my thighs.

"So," Gregory begins, taking the napkin from my hand, leaving me fiddling with my ring instead. "He promised twenty-four hours and you only got eight." He dives right in, no holding back.

I pout, and I hate myself for it. "That's what I said, isn't it?" I sigh. A few hours being distracted by the grandness of my beloved London did a wonderful job of temporarily washing him from my mind. That's the problem, though; it's just temporary.

"What cut it short?"

"He had to nip out."

"Where?"

"I don't know." I refuse to look at Gregory, like a lack of eye contact might make telling him the truth easier. It must be working because I go on, keen to get his thoughts. "I woke up at three this morning and he was gone. He left a pillow note telling me he'd be back; then he called but wouldn't say where he was, only that it was business. I got a little annoyed and so did he."

"What was he annoyed about?"

"Because I said I was leaving and it's ill-mannered to break a deal." I chance a look at Gregory, finding his brown eyes wide. "We didn't actually shake on it," I finish, not adding the fact that according to Miller we fucked on it.

"He sounds like a knob," he declares spitefully. "An arrogant knob!"

"He's not," I argue quickly. "Well, he can come across a little like that, but not when he had me in his arms. He really did worship me. He said he was going to fuck me, but he—"

"*What?*" Gregory screeches, leaning forward. "He actually said that to you?"

I sink back in my chair, thinking I should've kept that part to myself. I don't want my friend to hate Miller, even if I do a little myself. "Yes, but he didn't follow through on it. He showed me nothing but respect and . . ." I pause, stopping myself from saying such a stupid word in these circumstances.

"What?"

I shake my head. "He was a gentleman."

Our drinks arrive and I immediately pour my water into my glass and take a long swig while I'm ogled by the smiling waiter and Gregory ogles him. "Thank you." My friend beams at the waiter, making his interest known, despite the waiter's obvious sexual preference.

"You're welcome. Enjoy," the waiter says, keeping his eyes on me before he finally takes care of the woman who is again waving for his attention.

Gregory's smiling face soon alters to a scowl when his eyes land back on me. "Livy, you've already said that you saw him with a woman. I know just as well as you do that she's probably no business associate. He sounds nothing like a gentleman."

"I know," I mumble sullenly, the reminder stabbing at my falling heart. That woman is beautiful, elegant, and undoubtedly as cultured and wealthy as Miller. That's his world—posh women, posh hotels, posh events, posh clothes, posh food and drink. Mine is serving that posh food and drink to those posh people. I need to forget about him. I need to remind myself how aggravated he makes me. I need to remind myself that it was meaningless sex. "I won't be seeing him again." I sigh. It wasn't meaningless sex to me.

"I'm glad." Gregory smiles and takes a sip of his espresso. "You deserve the whole package, not just the scraps a man's prepared to throw when he feels like it." He reaches over and gives my hand a comforting squeeze. "I think you know he's no good for you."

I smile, knowing my best friend is talking complete sense. "I do."

Gregory nods and winks, sitting back in his chair, just as my phone starts ringing from my bag. I grab my satchel from the chair next to me and start rummaging through.

"That'll be Nan," I moan. "She's driving me loopy."

Gregory laughs, prompting a snigger from me, too, but I soon halt happy tittering when I note the caller's not Nan. My wide eyes fly to Gregory's.

He soon stops laughing, too. "Is it him?"

I nod, glancing back down to the screen, my thumb hovering over the button that'll connect me to Miller. "I've not returned his call."

"Be wise, baby girl."

Be wise. Be wise. Be wise. I take a deep breath and answer. "Hello."

"Olivia?"

"Miller," I counter coldly and calmly, despite my speeding heart rate. The slow, rounded pronunciation of my name spikes a vivid image of his slow-moving lips.

"We need to pick up where we left off. I have an engagement to keep this evening, but I'll keep tomorrow free." He sounds formal and short, making my heart race that little bit more, but more out of irritation than desire. What am I, a business transaction?

"No, thank you."

"It wasn't a question, Livy. I'm telling you that you'll be spending the day with me tomorrow."

"That's very kind of you, but I'm afraid I have plans." I sound hesitant when I was aiming for sureness. I'm aware that Gregory is watching and listening intently, and I'm glad because I'm certain that if he wasn't here to monitor the conversation, then I'd be agreeing. Hearing his smooth voice, even though there's no element of friendliness to it, is bringing back all of the feelings that came before the anger of being abandoned.

"Cancel them."

"I can't."

"For me, you can."

"No, I can't." I hang up before I cave and quickly turn my phone off. "Done," I declare, shoving it in my bag.

"Good girl. You know it makes sense." Gregory smiles across the table at me. "Drink up and I'll walk you home."

*   *   *

We say good-bye on the corner, Gregory heading off to get ready for a night out, me to go hide in my bedroom from my prying grandmother. As I'm inserting my key quietly into the lock, the door swings open and two pairs of old eyes look at me with interest—Nan trying to read me, George peering over her shoulder with a mild grin on his face. I can only imagine what's gone down in this house since I left this morning and George arrived. He'll do anything for Nan, including listening to her harp on about her boring, withdrawn granddaughter. Except this time I'm not boring. And George's delight at this news is written all over his round face.

"Your phone's off," Nan fires accusingly. "Why?"

My arms drop to my sides on an over-the-top sigh before I push my way past them, heading toward the kitchen. "The battery died."

Her scoff indicates her thoughts on that lie as she tracks me. "Your boss stopped by."

I swing around, horrified, finding straight lips and George still grinning over her shoulder. "My boss?" I ask tentatively, my damn heart pounding against my chest.

"Yes, your *real* boss." She watches for my reaction and she won't be disappointed. I'm trying my hardest not to, but I'm blushing furiously and my body has completely sagged. "Nice cockney man."

"What did he want?" I breathe, gathering myself together.

"He's been trying to call you." She fills the kettle and signals for George to sit, which he does without delay, still grinning at me. "Something about a charity gala this evening."

"He wants me to work?" I ask hopefully, retrieving my phone and quickly turning it on.

"Yes." She continues with tea-making duties, her back to me. "I did point out that it might be too much after your long shift yesterday evening."

I'm scowling hard at her back, and I know George's grin has just widened. "Give it a rest, Nan," I warn, stabbing at the buttons of my phone. She doesn't turn around and she doesn't answer. She's made her point, as have I.

Putting my phone to my ear, I take the stairs to escape to the sanctuary of my room. Del needs me to waitress this evening and I accept eagerly, before I'm told where to be and when. I'll do anything to distract myself.

*   *   *

Pushing my way through the staff entrance of the hotel, I'm immediately greeted by a pacing Sylvie. She's on me like a wolf, like I knew she would be. "Tell me everything!"

I walk past her, heading for the kitchen. "There's nothing to tell." I brush her off, reluctant to confirm that she was right. I take my apron from a smiling Del and start putting it on. "Thank you."

He hands one to Sylvie, too, who snatches it and doesn't thank our boss. "So you told him where to go?"

"Yes," I say very convincingly, probably because it's part truth. I have, in effect, told him where to go. I start loading my round, silver tray with glasses. "So you can quit with the nagging because there's nothing to nag me about."

"Oh," she says placidly, starting to help me. "Well, I'm glad. He's an arrogant bastard."

I neither deny nor confirm it, instead opting to change the subject completely. I'm supposed to be busying my wandering mind, not feeding it. "Did you go out last night?"

"Yes, and I still feel like crap," she admits, pouring the champagne. "My body has craved junk food all day, and I necked something close to two liters of fat Coke."

"That bad?"

"Horrendous. I'm not drinking again . . . until next week."

I laugh. "What makes you bad . . ."

"Don't! The smell of this is turning my stomach." She gags and holds her nose as she continues to fill the flutes. It's only now that I take a good look at her, noticing her usually shiny black bob looks a little dull, as does her usually rosy cheeks. "I know. I look like shit."

I return to the tray. "You really do," I admit.

"And I feel worse than I look."

Del appears, looking his usual happy self. "Girls, we have members of parliament in tonight and a few diplomats. I know I don't have to tell you, but remember your manners." He looks at Sylvie when he speaks, frowning. "You really do look like crap."

"Yes, yes, I know. Don't worry. I won't breathe on them," she quips, breathing onto her palm and smelling. I grimace, watching her face screw up in disgust before she rootles through her pocket and shoves a Polo Mint in her mouth.

"Don't speak unless necessary." Del shakes his head, leaving me and Sylvie to finish up with the champagne and transfer the canapés from the Tupperware to the trays.

"All set?" Sylvie asks, swinging her tray onto her shoulder.

"Lead the way."

"Great. Let's feed and water some elitists," she grumbles, smiling sweetly at Del when he throws her a cautionary look. "Would you prefer snobs?"

He points his finger at her, fighting a fond smile. "No, I'd prefer to have enough staff so I didn't have to resort to drafting *you* in. Get your arse in gear."

"Yes, sir!" She salutes him seriously and marches on, me following behind, laughing.

I don't get very far, though. And my laughing is sucked up in a second.

His face is impassive as he watches me, while I'm frozen on the spot, body shaking, pulse racing. But he seems completely composed, the only clue of his thoughts being how closely he's studying me.

"No," I whisper to myself, trying to gain control of my shaking tray as I reverse my steps, backing up into the kitchen. He's with that woman, and she's adorned in cream silk and dripping with diamonds, her hand glued to his arse, her smiling face beaming at him dreamily. Business? I feel sick—sick with jealousy, sick with pain, and sick with delight at how beautiful he looks in a taupe three-piece suit. His flawlessness defies reality on every level.

"Livy?" Del's concerned voice seeps into my ears and his hands rest gently on my shoulders from behind. "You okay, sweetheart?"

"Pardon?" I rip my eyes away from the painful sight across the room, and turn blankly toward my boss, registering a face to match the concern in his voice.

"Christ, Livy, you're as white as a ghost." He takes the tray from me and feels my forehead. "And you're cold."

I need to leave. I can't work all night in the close proximity of Miller, especially with *her* draped all over him, and definitely not after last night. I'm shifting on the spot, my eyes darting all over the place, my heart showing no sign of letting up. "I think I might have to leave," I whisper pitifully.

"Yes, go home." Del ushers me through the kitchen and shoves my satchel in my arms. "Get in bed and sweat it out."

I nod lamely, just as Sylvie comes steaming into the kitchen with a tray full of empties, her wide eyes looking frantic and worried, even more so when she clocks my pathetic, sweating form. Her mouth opens to speak, but I shake my head, not wanting her to rumble me. What will Del think if he finds out that I'm in this pickle because of a man?

"You'll have to work that little bit harder, Sylvie. I'm sending Livy home. She's feeling ill." Del turns me and pushes my shaking body toward the exit.

I glance over my shoulder, giving Sylvie an apologetic smile, grateful when she brushes off my guilt with a dismissive wave of her hand. "Hope you feel better," she calls.

I'm sent to the mews at the back of the hotel, where deliveries are taken and the staff pop out to smoke. It's dusk and the air is heavy, just like my heart. Finding a step away from the chaos of the loading bays, I lower my backside and slump my head onto my knees, attempting to calm myself down before I drag my feet home. Forgetting my encounters with Miller Hart and the feelings I had during those encounters might be easier if I never have to see him again, but it's going to be impossible if he's around every corner that I turn.

Returning to solitary confinement seems like my best option, but I've been teased, fed something new and appealing, and I want more. The important question, though—the question I should ask and consider seriously—is whether I'm hungry for more with just Miller, or if I can find these tingling, stimulating, alive feelings with someone else, a man who wants me for longer than one night, a man who can maintain these feelings, not spike them, then quickly and cruelly replace them with inadequacy and misery.

I won't hold my breath.

I force my reluctant body to stand, looking up and coming face-to-face with Miller Hart. He's standing just a few feet away, legs spread and hands in his pockets. His expression is still blank, telling me nothing, but his expressionless face takes nothing away from his impossible beauty. There are many things I want to say, but saying them will only prompt conversation, which will almost certainly cast me further under his spell. The only sensible move I should make right now is escaping his presence. And set on doing just that, I start walking away from him.

"Livy!" he shouts, his footsteps trailing me. "Livy, it's simply business."

"You don't have to explain yourself to me," I declare softly. That was no body language of a business associate. "Please don't follow me."

"I'm talking to you, Livy," he warns.

"And I'm choosing not to listen." My nerves are keeping my tone timid and weak when I really want to inject some spunk into it, but the strength required to do so is being used to walk away.

"Livy, you owe me sixteen hours."

His cheek makes me falter midstride, but doesn't stop me completely. "I owe you nothing."

"I beg to differ." His body lands in front of me, blocking my path, so I quickly sidestep him, not allowing my eyes to divert from their focus point: the main road ahead. "Livy." He's grabbing at me now, but I shake him off, silent but firm. "Where are your fucking manners?"

"I don't care for them with you."

"Well you should." He takes hold of me, more forcefully this time, and secures me in place. "You agreed to twenty-four hours."

I refuse to look at him, and I'm also refusing to speak. There's plenty I want to say, but showing my emotions—physically and audibly—would be a grave mistake, so I remain still and silent while he stares down at my nonresponsive form. I'm frustrating him. His overpowering hold on the tops of my arms is confirming it, and so is the rise and fall of his suit-covered chest. I've crawled into a shell, and I don't plan on coming out. I'm safer here—safe from him.

He drops his face into my line of sight, so I drop my gaze farther to the ground to avoid them. Looking into his crystal clear blues will derail me in a split second. "Livy, when I'm talking to you, I'd like you to look at me."

I don't. I ignore his request and concentrate on remaining unreceptive, hoping he'll get bored, decide I'm not worth the effort, and leave me alone. I need him to leave me alone. There's a beautiful woman inside, clearly willing, so why is he wasting time out here on me?

"Livy," he whispers.

My eyes close, picturing those lips speaking my name quietly . . . slowly.

"Please look at me," he orders gently.

My head starts shaking in my own private darkness as I battle to keep my protective shield in place—the Miller shield.

"Let me see you, Olivia Taylor." He stoops farther, pushing his face into my neck. "Let me have my time with you."

I want to stop him. I don't want to stop him. I want to feel alive again, but I don't want to feel lifeless again. I want him more than I know I should.

"I haven't had nearly enough. I need more." His lips find my cheek and his palm feels out the back of my head, his fingers combing through my hair and holding me in place. "I want to drown in you, Livy." His lips reach mine and the feel of them catapults me instantly to the night before. The shield shatters and a suppressed sob slips past my lips, my eyes squeezing shut to prevent the tears from trickling down my cheeks. "Open your mouth," he whispers.

My jaw relaxes at his gentle demand, giving him free rein on my senses, and his tongue slips slowly and softly past my lips, sweeping a sweet circle of my mouth, his body moving in closer to mine. There's not a part of my front that's not touching him. I go lax, my head tilting to give him better access, and my hands lift of their own accord, feeling up his sides until they're on his shoulders. He's set a painfully slow, tender pace, and I'm following, massaging his tongue with mine and failing to do what I know I should.

"See how easy it is?" he asks, slowly pulling away and pecking my lips.

I nod, agreeing, because it really is, but now his lips are off mine, sensibility seems to kick in. "Who's that woman?" I ask, stepping back. "Was this the prior engagement that you were talking about? A date?"

"It's business, Livy. Just business."

I step back again. "And business involves having her hand glued to your backside?" I have no right to sound so accusing. He's played his cards.

His head cocks, a tiny hint of a frown surfacing. "Sometimes I have to accept a bit of familiarity in the name of business."

"What business?"

"We've spoken of this before. I don't think it's a good idea to get personal."

"We've had sex. You don't get more personal than that," I argue.

"I mean emotionally, not physically, Livy."

His words confirm my thoughts. Damn women and their deepness, and damn men for their shallowness. Just sex; I must remember that. These feelings are spiked by lust and nothing more. "I'm not this kind of person, Miller. I don't do things like this." I'm not sure who I'm trying to convince here.

He steps forward and runs his hand behind my neck, taking his signature hold. "Maybe that's what I find so fascinating."

"Or perhaps you're just finding it an entertaining challenge."

"If that's the case"—he drops a soft kiss on my cheek—"then I think we can safely say that I've conquered you."

He's absolutely right. He's conquered me, and he's the only man who has. "I need to go." I start walking back, just as his phone starts ringing from his pocket. He reaches in and glances at the screen, then to me. I can see that he's torn as he watches me backing away. "You should take that call." I nod at his phone, hoping he'll decline and fulfill his promise to put me back in his bed. If I escape now, then that's it. I'm turning my back for good, and I'll find the strength to resist him. But if he stops me, comes with me, then I'm going to be spending the next sixteen hours being worshipped again. I want to do both, but his decision is going to decide for me. Someone else's choice is going to determine my destiny. And I can tell by the look on his face that he knows this, too.

My heart constricts when he answers the call, even though I know that it's undeniably the best outcome for my destiny. "I'm on my way," he says quietly before cutting the call and watching me spreading the distance between us. I smile a little before turning my back on Miller Hart and mentally forming a plan to eradicate him from my mind altogether.

CHAPTER TEN

Monday morning greets me, and I feel no better. I wallowed in self-pity all day yesterday, choosing to stay in bed, with Nan poking her head around my door to check on me every now and then. I've never feigned illness, but I'm making up for that now. My grandmother is super suspicious but keeping her thoughts to herself for once. It's a novelty, and a welcome one. My phone has rung twice, my only two friends in the world calling to check up on me, but I cut off any lengthy conversation. I could tell they're suspicious, too—Sylvie most, having witnessed my meltdown. I'm not much of an actress. In fact, I'm rubbish at it, even cringing myself when I heard my unconvincing voice telling them that I felt rotten with a queasy stomach and cold shivers. Deciding that I need one more day to pull myself together, I call Del to tell him I feel no better.

"Livy?" Nan's wary voice drifts through my door. "I've made breakfast. You'll be late for work."

"I'm not going," I call, trying to croak and failing.

The door opens and she gingerly creeps in, giving my quilt-covered body the once-over. "Are you still feeling ill?" she asks.

"Terrible," I mutter.

She hums thoughtfully, picking up my discarded jeans and folding them neatly. "I'm going shopping. Would you like to come?"

"No."

"Oh, Livy, come on," she sighs. "You can help me pick a pineapple for George's upside-down cake."

"You need help picking a pineapple?"

She huffs her frustration and pulls the quilt back, exposing my semi-naked body to her inquisitive eyes and the cool morning air of my bedroom. "Olivia Taylor, you are getting out of that bed and you're coming to help me pick a pineapple for George's upside-down cake. Get up!"

"I'm ill." I try to retrieve my covers and fail. She looks determined, which means this is a sure losing situation for me.

"I'm not stupid." She waves a wrinkled finger at me. "You need to snap out of this, right now! There's nothing less attractive than a woman wallowing in self-pity, especially over a man. Screw him! Pick yourself up, dust yourself down, and bloody get on with it, my girl!" She grabs my stunned body and physically hoofs me up from the bed. "Get that skinny arse showered. You're coming shopping." She stomps out, slamming the door behind her, leaving me speechless and wide-eyed.

"That was a little harsh," I say to absolutely no one, hearing her stomping feet taking the stairs. She's never spoken to me like that in her life. But I've never given her reason to. It's always me faffing around her, although I'm certainly not as brutal in my pep talks as she was just then. This is hilariously ironic. She's the one who's constantly nagged me about living a little. I did, and look where it's got me. Still stunned and not daring to retreat to the safety of my bed, I walk cautiously across the landing to take a shower.

*　*　*

"We're going to Harrods to buy a pineapple?" I ask, holding Nan's elbow as we cross the road toward the grand, green-canopied building.

Nan raises her hand to a truck driving at us, halting it dead in its tracks, despite it having the right of way. I wave a thank you, while Nan continues across the road, tugging her shopping trolley behind her. "I might buy some double cream, too."

I catch up with her and pull the door open. "Going to town, aren't you?" My eyebrows waggle suggestively, which she completely ignores, instead marching on in the direction of the food hall.

"It's a pineapple."

"That we could've bought from the local Tesco Express," I retort, goading her.

"It wouldn't be the same. Besides, the ones from here are perfectly formed and the skins are shiny."

I'm trying to keep up with her, and everyone's moving out of the way of the elderly, determined woman marching through the store pulling a shopping trolley behind her. "You'll be cutting the skin off!"

"It doesn't matter. Here we are!" She halts at the entrance of the food hall, and I watch as her shoulders rise and drop slowly on a satisfied sigh. "The meat counter!" She's off again. "Get a basket, Livy."

I sag, exasperated, and reach for a shopping basket, then go and join her in front of the glass meat counter. "I thought you wanted a pineapple."

"I do. I'm just browsing."

"Browsing meat?"

"Oh, my girl. This isn't just meat."

I follow her admiring stare to the perfectly displayed lumps of pork, beef, and lamb. "What is it then?"

"Well"—her wrinkled brow furrows—"it's posh meat."

"What, like well-spoken meat?" I'm trying hard not to grin as I point to a steak. "Or did that cow shit in a toilet instead of a field?"

Nan gasps and swings infuriated eyes to me. "You can't use that language in Harrods!" Her eyes shoot around, checking if any attention is on us. It is. The old woman next to Nan is looking at me in disgust. "What's gotten into you?" Nan straightens her floppy hat and hits me with warning eyes.

I'm still fighting a grin. "Where are the pineapples?"

"Over there." She points, and I follow her finger to another glass cabinet, formed in a square and showcasing the best-looking fruit I've ever seen. They're only your standard fruits—apples, pears, and such like, but they are the most beautiful apples and pears I've ever seen—so beautiful, my face is pushed up to the glass counter to check if they're real. The colors are vivid and the skins polished. They literally look way too good to eat.

"Oh, look at that pineapple!" Nan sings, and I do. Her enthusiasm is warranted. It's a stunning pineapple. "Oh, Livy."

"Nan, it's too pretty to hack up and shove in a cake." I join her by the supermodel of pineapples. "And it's fifteen quid!" My palm slaps against my mouth, and Nan's hand slaps my shoulder.

"Will you shut up?" she hisses. "I should've left you at home."

"Sorry, but fifteen pounds, Nan? Surely you're not."

"Yes, I am." She straightens her shoulders and starts to wave the attention of the server, her hand movements rivaling the Queen's wave. "I would like a pineapple," she tells him, all posh and proper.

"Yes, madam."

I stare at her in disbelief. "Does being in Harrods Food Hall put a plum in your mouth?"

She flicks me a sideways glance. "Whatever are you talking about?"

I start laughing. "That. The voice. Come on, Nan!"

She leans in discreetly. "I do not have a plum in my mouth!"

I smile. "Yes, you do. A huge, great big plum, and it's making you sound like the Queen with respiratory problems."

Nan's beautiful pineapple is handed delicately over the counter and she takes it, gently placing it in the basket I'm holding.

"Ooh, be gentle," I whisper, laughing to myself.

"You're not too old to lie over my knee," Nan threatens, increasing my laughter.

"Would you like to do it here?" I make my face serious. "You could polish my arse while you're at it so I match your pretty pineapple." I snort on a supressed laugh.

"Shut up!" she snaps. "And be careful with my pineapple!"

I'm at the point of doubling over as I watch Nan straighten her scowling face before turning back to the gentleman who served her. "Could you remind me where I might find the double cream?"

I start falling all over Harrods Food Hall in hysterics as I watch Nan's hand movements and listen to her fake posh voice. Remind her? She's never bought double cream from Harrods in her bloody life!

"Certainly, madam." He directs us to the back of the hall where the fridges are stocked with posh dairy. Nan's back straightens and she's smiling and nodding politely at everyone we pass, while I titter, shake, and hold my aching stomach from laughing too hard.

I'm still chuckling as I watch her read the back of every pot of cream on the shelf, humming to herself. She shouldn't bother with the ingredients and should maybe pay more attention to the price of the cream. Deciding that I need to calm myself down before my nan swings at me, I start taking deep breaths as I wait for her to pick a pot of cream, but my shoulders won't let up, and I can't help my eyes from looking down at the perfect, shiny pineapple, reminding me of why I'm in stitches.

I jump when I feel hot breath in my ear and turn, still laughing, until I see whose breath it is. "You look incredibly beautiful when you laugh," he says quietly.

I stop immediately and back up, but I should've stayed put

because I've just bumped into Nan, causing her to huff some more and swing around. "What?" she spits before she clocks my company. "Oh my..."

"Hello." Miller closes the distance, getting way too close, and puts his hand out. "You must be Livy's famous nan."

I die on the spot. She's going to lap this up good and proper. "Yes." She still sounds like she has a plum in her mouth. "And you're Livy's boss?" she asks, placing her hand neatly in Miller's, flicking me a questioning look.

"I think you know that I'm not Olivia's boss, Mrs...."

"Taylor!" she practically screeches, delighted that he's confirmed her suspicions.

"I'm Miller Hart. It's a pleasure, Mrs. Taylor." He kisses the back of her hand—he actually kisses the back of her bloody hand!

Nan giggles like a schoolgirl and now that my heart is over the shock, it starts a steady thump in my chest. He's adorned in a three-piece gray suit, white shirt, and silver tie...in Harrods. "Shopping?" I manage to breathe.

He regards me intently as he releases Nan's wrinkled hand and holds up two suit bags. "I was just collecting some new suits and an enchanting laugh caught my attention."

I ignore his compliment. "Because you don't have enough suits?" I ask, remembering the rows and rows of matching jackets, trousers, and waistcoats lining the three walls of his wardrobe. I've never seen him in the same one twice.

"You can never have enough suits, Livy."

"I agree!" Nan trills. "It's so refreshing to see a young man so well turned out. These youngsters who have jeans sagging around their arses, their underwear out for the world to see. I just don't understand it."

Miller's slight amusement is clear. "I concur." He nods thoughtfully, flicking his eyes to mine while I consider how silly it sounds, referring to him as a young man. He is, but his persona hints to a much wiser, more lived-in man. He acts older than his years, even if he looks perfectly gorgeous at twenty-nine. "That's a delicious-looking pineapple." He nods at the basket in my hand.

"My thoughts exactly!" Nan sings delightedly, agreeing with him again. "Worth every penny."

"It is," Miller replies. "The food here is sublime. You must try the caviar." He reaches out to a nearby shelf and takes a jar, showing it to Nan. "It's exceptional."

I can do nothing more than watch in shock as Nan has a good look at the jar, nodding her unknown agreement as they chat away in Harrods Food Hall. I want to curl up in a ball and hide.

"So how are you and my lovely granddaughter acquainted?"

"*Lovely* being the operative word, wouldn't you agree?" Miller asks, placing the jar back and tweaking it so the label is positioned just so. He doesn't stop there. He runs his hand across each jar flanking the one he's just placed, straightening them all up.

"She's a doll." Nan elbows me discreetly while Miller finishes up with the shelf display.

"That she is." He gazes at me, and I feel my face heat under his intense stare. "She makes the best coffee in London."

"Do I?" I blurt. The lying bastard. He's on the charm offensive.

"Yes; I was most disappointed when I dropped in today to find you're off sick."

My redness increases. "I'm feeling better."

"I'm glad. Your colleague isn't as friendly as you." His words carry a double meaning. He's playing games, and it's irritating the hell out of me. Friendly or easy? If Nan wasn't here, I'd be asking that very question, but she is here and I need to remove her *and* myself from this painfully difficult situation.

I take her elbow. "We should get going, Nan."

"Should we?"

"Yes." I try to tug her onward, but she makes herself a dead weight. "It was nice to see you." I smile tightly at Miller, tugging harder. "Come on, Nan."

"Would you like to join me for dinner tonight?" Miller asks with a sense of urgency to his tone that probably only I can detect.

I stop trying to remove my static nan and flash him a questioning look. He's trying to get his remaining time allowance, and he's using my grandmother to his advantage, the conniving twat. "No, thank you." I can feel Nan's shocked stare drilling into me.

"Livy, you must take the gentleman up on his invitation to dinner," Nan claims incredulously. "It's very kind of him to offer."

"I don't often," Miller interjects quietly, like I should be grateful. It only increases my irritation as I fight to recall why I vowed not to see him again. It's hard when my wayward mind is presenting me with a stream of images of our naked bodies entwined and a replay of the comforting words exchanged.

"See!" Nan screeches in my ear, making me wince. The plum has gone and desperation has set in. She plasters a stupid smile on her face as she returns to Miller. "She'd love to."

"No, I wouldn't, but thank you." I try to pull my annoying grandmother away from my heart's annoying nemesis, but the stubborn old bat refuses to budge. "Come on," I plead.

"I would be delighted if you would reconsider." Miller's soft rasp halts my battle with Nan's motionless form, and I hear her sigh dreamily, gazing at the annoyingly handsome man who's cornered me. But then her dreamy gaze turns into slight confusion and I follow her stare to see what's caused her sudden change in expression. There's a well-manicured hand resting on Miller's shoulder with a dusky pink silk tie suspended from it, cascading down Miller's chest.

"This one will go perfectly." The silky smooth voice is familiar. I don't need to see the stunning face to confirm who that hand belongs to, so I lift my gaze from the silk tie to Miller's eyes instead. His jaw is tight, his tall body still. "What do you think?" she asks.

"It's fine," Miller replies quietly, keeping his eyes on me.

Nan is silent, I'm silent, and Miller is saying very little, but then the woman steps out from behind him, stroking the tie and the silence is broken. "What do *you* think?" she asks Nan, who nods, not giving the tie a glance, instead keeping her eyes on this beautiful woman who has appeared from nowhere. "And you?" She directs her question at me, toying with the diamond-encrusted cross that's always suspended from her delicate neck. I can see a threatening look through the layers of expensive makeup. She's marking her territory. She's no business associate.

"It's lovely," I whisper, dropping the basket and deciding to abandon my nan in favor of retreat. I'm not being held to ransom in front of my old grandmother and I'm not being subjected to looks of inferiority by that perfect woman. Every corner I turn, he's there. This is hopeless.

I weave my numb body through the various departments until I break free of the confinements of the colossal store and drag in some fresh air, resting my back against the wall outside. I'm angry, sad, and irritated. I'm a jumbled bag of mixed emotions and confusing thoughts. My heart and my head have never disagreed or battled so furiously.

Until now.

*   *   *

Hyde Park sorts me out. I sit on the grass with a sandwich and a can of Coke and watch the world go by for a few hours. I think about how lucky the people wandering past me are to have such a beautiful place to roam. Then I count at least twenty different breeds of dog in less than twenty minutes and think how lucky they are to have such a wonderful stomping ground. Children are squealing, mothers are chatting and laughing, and runners are prancing by. I feel better, like something familiar and desired has successfully eliminated something unfamiliar and undesired.

Undesired, undesired... completely desired.

I sigh and unfold my seated body from the ground, swinging my satchel onto my shoulder and throwing my rubbish in the litter bin.

Then I take the familiar journey home.

*   *   *

Nan's frantic by the time I fall through the front door. Really frantic. I feel guilty, even if I should actually be feeling rather mad with her. "Oh my goodness!" She dives on me, not giving me the chance to dump my bag by the coat stand in the hall. "Livy, I've been so worried. It's seven o'clock!"

I embrace her hold, the guilt taking a firmer grip. "I'm twenty-four years old," I sigh.

"Don't disappear on me, Olivia. My heart can't take it."

Now guilt is crippling me. "I had a picnic in the park."

"But you just left!" She separates us and holds me at a distance. "It was incredibly rude, Livy." I can see from her sudden annoyance that her earlier panic has completely diminished.

"I didn't want to have dinner with him."

"Why not? He seemed like such a gentleman."

I resist snorting my disgust. She wouldn't think that if she knew the ins and outs. "He was with another woman."

"She's a business associate!" she gushes, almost excited to clear up the misunderstanding. "Nice woman."

I cannot believe she bought that. She's too cute. Business associates don't shop for silk ties together. "Can we leave it there?" I drop my bag and skulk past her, making my way to the kitchen, getting a waft of something delicious as I enter. "What are you cooking?" I ask, finding George at the table. "Hi, George." I sit next to him.

"Don't turn your mobile telephone off, Livy," he scolds quietly. "I've endured hours of Josephine repeatedly dialing and cursing in between cooking supper."

"What is it?" I ask again.

"Beef Wellington," Nan chirps up as she follows in behind me. "With Dauphinoise potatoes and steamed baby carrots."

I throw a confused look at George, but he just shrugs and picks up his paper. "Beef Wellington?" I ask.

"That's right." She doesn't give my questioning tone the attention it deserves. What happened to stew and dumplings or a chicken roast? "Thought I'd try something new. I hope you're hungry."

"A little," I admit. "Is that wine?" I ask, clocking two bottles of red and two bottles of white on the worktop.

"Oh!" She flies across the kitchen and grabs the white bottles, shoving them quickly in the fridge before opening the red. "These need to breathe."

Shifting in my chair, I chance a glance at George, hoping to get something from him, but he's undoubtedly doing what he's been told by sitting still and shutting up. He knows that I'm looking at him. I can tell because his eyes are running too quickly across the text of the paper for him to truly be reading it. I knock his knee with mine, but I'm flat out ignored, Nan's male companion choosing to shift his legs to avoid another purposeful nudge.

"Nan . . ." The doorbell interrupts me, my head swinging toward the hallway.

"Oh, that'll be Gregory." She opens the oven and sticks a long metal stick in the middle of a huge chunk of pastry. "Will you answer it, please, Livy?"

"You invited Gregory?" I ask, pushing my chair away from the table.

"Yes! Look at all of this food." She removes the rod from the meat and purses her lips as she checks the temperature on the dial. "Nearly done," she declares.

I leave Nan and George and jog down the hallway to let Gregory in, hoping Nan hasn't been gossiping with him again. "Am I missing a special occasion?" I ask as I throw the front door open.

My smile falls away immediately.

Chapter Eleven

What the hell are you doing here?" That damn irritation flares dangerously.

"Your grandmother invited me." Miller's arms are filled with flowers and a Harrods bag. "Are you going to invite me in?"

"No, I'm not." I step outside and pull the door shut so Nan can't hear our conversation. "What are you doing?"

He's completely unruffled by my ruffled state. "Being polite and accepting a dinner invitation." There's no humor in his tone. "I have manners."

"No." I step closer, my shock and exasperation crossing the line into anger. My damn conniving grandmother. "You have a nerve, that's what you have. This has to stop. I don't want you for twenty-four hours."

"You want longer?"

I recoil. "No!" *How much longer?*

"Oh..." He looks unsure of himself and it's the first time I've seen this in him. It straightens my back and makes my eyes narrow questioningly.

"Do you?" I whisper the question on a skip of my heartbeat, my mind going into overdrive.

His uncertainty flashes to frustration in a nanosecond, making me wonder if it's directed at me or whether he's frustrated with himself. I'm hoping it's the latter. "We agreed no personal."

"No, you declared that part of the deal."

His eyes fly up, shocked. "I know."

"And does it still stand?" I ask, trying so hard to appear confident and strong, when I'm crumbling on the inside, bracing myself for his answer.

"It still stands." His voice is resolute, but his expression isn't. That's not enough for me to build my hopes on, though.

"Then we're done here." I turn on my Converse and push my defeated body through the door, meeting Nan as I do. "It's a salesman," I say, not letting her pass me. My plan is never going to work, I know that. She invited him, and she knew the second the doorbell chimed who it was.

I put up little resistance when I'm barged from her path, letting her open the front door, where Miller is striding slowly away from the house. "Miller!" she calls. "Wherever are you going?"

He turns and looks at me, and as much as I'm willing a threatening look to materialize on my face, it's just not happening. We just stare at each other for the longest time before he gives Nan a small nod. "It was really very kind of you, Mrs. Taylor, but..."

"Oh no!" Nan doesn't give him the opportunity to make his excuses. She marches down the path, not in the least bit intimidated by his tall, powerful frame, and takes his elbow, leading him into the house. "I've prepared a blinding supper, and you'll stay to eat it." Miller is pushed into the narrow hallway, where with three people, it's all very cozy. "Livy will take your jacket." Nan leaves us and marches back to the kitchen, barking a short instruction at George as she enters.

"I'll leave if you want me to. I don't want to make you feel uncomfortable." He makes no move to drop the things from his hands and remove his jacket. "Your grandmother is quite a woman."

"She is," I answer quietly. "And you always make me feel uncomfortable."

"Come home with me and I'll put some shorts on."

My eyes widen at the thought of Miller bare chested and barefoot. "That didn't make me comfortable," I point out. He knows that.

"What I did to you following the removal of my clothes did, though." That lock of hair slips down on cue, as if backing up his words, making them more suggestive.

I shift on the spot. "That won't happen again."

"Don't say things you don't mean, Livy," he counters softly.

My eyes fly to his, and he moves in, the flowers that he's holding touching the front of my tea dress. "You're using my own grandmother against me," I breathe.

"You leave me no choice." He dips and rests his lips over mine, sending a delicious warmth to my core to match the heat of his mouth on mine.

"You're not playing fair."

"I've never claimed to play by the rules, Livy. And anyway, all of my rules were obliterated the second I laid my hands on you."

"What rules?"

"I've forgotten." He takes my mouth gently, pushing the flowers farther into my chest, the cellophane encasing them crinkling loudly, but I'm too consumed to care whether the noise attracts the attention of my nosy nan. My senses are saturated, my blood is heated, and I'm reminded of the incredible feelings that Miller Hart draws from me. "Feel me," he moans against my mouth.

Without thought, my hand slowly moves down between our bodies, bypassing the flowers and Harrods bag, until I'm brushing my knuckles over the long, hard length of him. His deep groan emboldens me, my hand turning to feel, stroke, and squeeze over the top of his trousers.

"You do that," he growls. "And for as long as you do this to me, you're obliged to remedy it."

"It wouldn't happen if you didn't see me." I gasp, biting at his lip, not bothered by his arrogant declaration.

"Livy, I only have to think of you and I'm solid. Seeing you makes me ache. You're coming home with me tonight, and I'm not taking no for an answer." His lips press harder to mine.

"That woman was with you again."

"How many times do we have to go over this?"

"Do you often go clothes shopping with female business associates?" I ask around his unrelenting lips.

He pulls away, panting, his hair in disarray. Those blue eyes will be the death of me. "Why can't you trust me on this?"

"You're too secretive," I whisper. "I don't want you to have this hold over me."

He leans in and kisses my forehead tenderly, lovingly. His words don't match his actions. It's so confusing to me. "It's not a hold if you accept it, sweet girl."

I'd be inconceivably stupid to trust this man. It's not so much the woman; my conscience seems quite happy to overlook her. It's my destiny. My heart. I'm falling too hard and too fast.

He steps away, glancing down at his groin area before adjusting himself. "I have to face a sweet old lady with this, and it's entirely your fault." He lifts almost mischievous eyes to mine, throwing me off course again. It's another expression from Miller Hart that's alien to me. "Ready?" he asks, sliding his palm around my neck and turning me toward the kitchen.

No, I don't think I *am* ready, but I say yes anyway, knowing what I'm going to find in the kitchen. And I'm right on the money. Nan is smiling smugly and George's eyes have just popped out of his head at the sight of Miller guiding me. I gesture to my nan's long-suffering male companion. "Miller, this is George, my nan's friend."

"Pleasure." Miller off-loads the flowers and bag, rather than letting go of me, and accepts George's hand, giving it a firm, manly shake. "That's a rather dashing shirt you have on there, George." Miller nods at George's striped chest genuinely.

"You know, I think so, too," George agrees, stroking down his front.

I don't know why I didn't notice this before. George is in his Sunday best, usually reserved for bingo or church. Nan really is a conniving old bat. I cast my eyes over to her, noticing her floating, floral, button-up dress, also usually reserved for Sunday best. Looking down at myself, I note that I am far from practically dressed in my creased tea dress and hot pink Converse, and suddenly uncomfortable with that, I pipe up.

"I'm just going to use the bathroom." I'm not going anywhere until Miller releases me from his grasp, but he doesn't seem in much of a hurry to do so.

Instead, he picks up the bouquet, a mass of yellow roses, and hands them to Nan, followed by the Harrods bag. "Just a few things to say thank you for your hospitality."

"Oohh!" Nan shoves her nose into the bouquet, then her face into the bag. "Oh my, caviar! Oh, George, look!" She drops the roses on the table and presents George with the tiniest jar. "Seventy pounds for that little thing," she whispers, but I don't know why because we're standing mere feet away and can hear her perfectly. I'm horrified. The plum is a distant memory and so is her decorum.

"Seventy quid?" George chokes. "For fish eggs? Well, slap me sideways!"

I sag under Miller's hold, and then feel him start to massage my nape over my hair. "I'm going to use the bathroom," I repeat, twisting myself out of Miller's hold.

"Miller, you shouldn't have." Nan removes a bottle of Dom Pérignon and flashes it at George with a gaping mouth.

"It's my pleasure," Miller replies.

"Livy." Nan pulls my attention back to the table. "Have you offered to take Miller's jacket?"

Turning tired eyes onto him, I smile, sickeningly sweetly. "Can I take your jacket, sir?" I resist curtseying, and detect an amused glint in his eyes.

"You may." He shrugs out of his jacket and hands it to me, while I marvel at his shirt and waistcoat-covered chest. He knows that I'm staring at him, picturing his naked chest. He leans in, dropping his mouth to my ear. "Don't look at me like that, Livy," he warns. "I can barely contain myself as it is."

"I can't help it." I'm honest in my quiet reply as I leave the kitchen, fanning my face before neatly draping his jacket over mine on the coat stand. I smooth it down and take the stairs, falling into my bedroom and darting around like a woman possessed, stripping, spraying, redressing, and freshening my makeup. Glancing in the mirror, I think about how far removed I am from Miller's business associate. But this is me. If it goes with my Converse, then it's a contender, and my white shirt dress, scattered with red rosebuds, matches my cherry red Converse perfectly. There's another woman and what's worrying is my ability to ignore the obviousness of the situation. I want him. Not only has he fractured my sensibility, but he's also chased away my conscience.

Giving myself a mental stinger of a slap, I ruffle my mass of blond hair and hurry downstairs, suddenly worried by what Nan and George might be saying to Miller.

They're not in the kitchen. I backtrack, heading for the lounge, but that's empty, too. I hear chatter coming from the dining room—the dining room that's only used on very special occasions. The last time we ate in the dining room was on my twenty-first birthday, over three years ago. That's how special we're talking. I make my way to the oak-stained door and peer in, seeing the huge mahogany table that dominates the room is beautifully laid, using all of Nan's Royal Doulton crockery, cut crystal wineglasses, and silver cutlery.

And she's put my heart's nemesis at the head of the table, where nobody has had the pleasure ever before. That was my grand-dad's place at the table, and not even George has been allowed the honor.

"Here she is." Miller stands and pulls out the empty chair to his left. "Come sit."

I walk slowly and thoughtfully over, ignoring Nan's beaming face, and take my seat. "Thank you," I say as he tucks me under the table before resuming position next to me.

"You've changed," he observes, turning the plate at his setting a few millimeters clockwise.

"I was a little creased."

"You look beautiful." He smiles, nearly making me pass out at the sight of it, that lovely dimple making a rare appearance.

"Thank you," I breathe.

"My pleasure." He doesn't take his eyes off me, and even though mine are firmly set on his, I know Nan and George are watching us.

"Wine?" Nan asks, interrupting our moment and distracting Miller's eyes from mine. I'm instantly resentful.

"Please, allow me." Miller rises and my gaze rises with him, my eyes seeming to lift forever until his body has straightened. He doesn't lean across the table to reach for the wine. No, he steps out and circles, collecting the wine from the ice bucket and standing on my grandmother's right side to pour.

"Thank you very much." Nan flashes George a wide-eyed, excited stare, and then turns her navy blues onto me. She's get-ting way too excited, just like I knew she would, and it's playing heavily on my mind for the brief moments that I'm distracted from Miller. Like right now when Nan is beaming at me, so elated by our guest's presence and impeccable manners.

Miller makes his way around the table, filling George's glass, too, before he reaches me. He doesn't ask me if I'd like some; he just goes right ahead and pours, despite knowing damn well that I've politely declined all alcohol when it's been offered to me previously. I'm not going to pretend that he's ignorant to it. He's too smart—way, way too smart.

"Right." George stands as Miller takes his seat. "I'll do the honors." He takes the carving knife and starts to neatly slice through Nan's masterpiece. "Josephine, this looks spectacular."

"It really does," Miller agrees, taking a sip of his wine and replacing it, his fingers scissoring and resting on the base of the glass, the crystal stem towering from between his middle and index finger. I study his resting hand closely, concentrating hard, waiting for it.

And there it is. It's miniscule, but he shifts the glass a very tiny bit to the right. It's probably barely noticeable to anyone except my scrutinizing stare, and I smile as I raise my eyes, finding him watching me studying him.

He cocks his head, his eyes narrowing but twinkling wildly. "What?" he mouths, drawing my attention to his lips. The bastard licks them, prompting me to make a grab for my glass and take a sip—anything to distract me. It's not until I swallow that I realize what I've done, the unaccustomed taste making me shudder as it slides down my throat. My glass hits the table a bit too harshly, and I know Miller has just glanced at me curiously.

A piece of beef Wellington lands on my plate. "Help yourself to potatoes and carrots, Livy," Nan says, holding her plate up for George to transfer some crumbly pastry to. "Let's fatten you up."

I spoon some carrots and potatoes onto my plate before putting some on Miller's. "I don't need fattening up."

"You could gain a few pounds," Miller declares, pulling my incredulous face back to him as George finishes his plate off with the Wellington. "Just an observation."

"Thank you, Miller," Nan huffs smugly, raising a glass to toast their agreement. "She's always been skinny."

"I'm slender, not skinny," I argue, lobbing Miller a warning look and getting a hint of a smile. In a very juvenile fit of revenge, I discreetly reach over and casually start twisting his wineglass by the stem, pulling it a fraction toward me. "Is that nice?" I ask, nodding at his forkful of beef.

"It's delicious," he confirms, placing his knife perfectly parallel with the edge of the table, and then resting his hand over mine, slowly removing it and repositioning his glass. He picks his knife back up and resumes with his dinner. "The best Wellington I've tasted, Mrs. Taylor."

"Nonsense!" Nan blushes, a rarity, but my heart's nemesis is making my nan's heart flutter, too. "It was very easy."

"It didn't look it," George grumbles. "You were flapping all afternoon, Josephine."

"I was not flapping!"

I start picking at my carrots, chewing slowly as I listen to Nan and George quarrel, leaving one hand free to move Miller's wineglass again. He looks at me out of the corner of his eye, and then places his knife down again before reclaiming his glass and putting it where it needs to be. I'm restraining my grin. He even eats precisely, cutting his food into perfectly sized pieces and ensuring all of the prongs of the fork are pushed into each piece at a right angle before taking the fork to his mouth. He chews slowly, too. Everything he does is with such thought, and it's spellbinding. My hand creeps across the table again. I'm intrigued by this anal need to have things just so, but this time I don't make it to the glass. My hand is seized midway across the table and held between us, looking nothing more than a loving hold of my hand. His hold is firm, though, not that anyone would notice unless they were on the receiving end of the grip. And I am. And it's a very harsh grip—a warning grip. I'm being told off.

"What do you do for a living, Miller?" Nan asks, delighting me. Yes, what does Miller Hart do for a living? I doubt he'll tell my sweet grandmother that he doesn't want to get into personal talk when he's sitting at the head of her dinner table.

"I won't bore you with that, Mrs. Taylor. It's mind-numbing."

I was wrong. He hasn't directly brushed her off, but he's succeeded in a roundabout way. "I'd like to know," I push, feeling brave, even when his grip on my hand tightens by another notch.

He blinks slowly, then raises his eyes slowly. "I like to keep business and pleasure separate, Livy. You know that."

"Very sensible," George mumbles around his food, pointing his fork at Miller. "I've lived by that saying my whole life."

My pluck is being beaten down by Miller's look, and worst of all, by those words. I'm pretty much a business transaction—a deal, an agreement or an arrangement. Call it what you like, it doesn't change the meaning. So, technically, Miller's words are a pile of shit.

I flex my hand in his grip and he eases up, raising his eyebrows as he does. "You should eat," he prompts. "It really is delicious."

Taking my hand out of his, I follow through on his order and resume my meal, but I'm not at all comfortable. Miller shouldn't have accepted my grandmother's dinner invitation. This is personal. He's invading my privacy, my security. He is the one who made his intention to keep things physical clear, yet here he is, immersing himself in my world, albeit a small world, but it's my world, nevertheless. And this is not being physical.

Just as I think that, I feel his leg brush against my knee, snapping me from my wandering mind and bringing me back to the table. I gaze up at him as I try to eat, seeing him looking at Nan, listening intently to her rambling on. I don't know what about because all I can hear are replays of Miller's words.

"For as long as you do this to me, you're obliged to remedy it."
"All of my rules were obliterated the second I laid my hands on you."

What rules, and how long will I do that to him? I want to affect him. I want to make his body respond to me like mine does to him. Once I'm past the moral pull that's trying to yank me away from his potency, it's all very easy—too easy . . . frighteningly easy.

"That was bloody scrumptious, Josephine," George declares, the clatter of his cutlery against his plate breaking the distant hum of chatter. I've been dragged back to the present, where Miller is still here, and Nan is now scowling at her friend for his clumsiness. "Sorry," George says timidly.

"If you'll excuse me." Miller's cutlery gets placed accurately on his empty plate, before he dabs at his mouth with his embroidered napkin. "Would you mind if I use your bathroom?"

"Of course!" Nan sings at him. "It's the door at the top of the stairs."

"Thank you." He stands, folding the napkin and placing it to the side of his plate before tucking his chair under the table and leaving the room.

Nan's eyes follow Miller from the room. "Would you look at the buns on that," she muses, just as his back disappears.

"Nan!" I splutter, mortified.

"Tight, perfectly formed. Livy, you are letting that man take you to dinner."

"Will you behave!" I look down at my plate, noting my barely touched beef. I can't possibly eat. I feel like I'm in a trance. "I'll clear the table," I say, reaching over for Miller's plate.

"I'll help." George makes to stand, but I place my hand on his shoulder and apply a little pressure, encouraging him to remain seated.

"It's fine, George. I'll take care of it."

He doesn't argue, instead topping up the wineglasses.

"Get the pineapple upside-down cake!" Nan calls to my back.

With a handful of stacked plates, I make my way to the kitchen, eager to escape the lingering presence of Miller, even though he's no longer in the room. I didn't refuse when he told me that I'll be going home with him tonight, and I should've. What will I say to Nan? There's no getting away from the fact that he's the cause for my recent mood swings. My mind has never been so jumbled. I'm not in control, nothing is making sense, and I'm not accustomed to any of these feelings. But what is most mystifying to me is the man who's the cause of my derailment. An unfathomable, beautiful man who screams heartache on every level.

Physical.

No feelings.

No emotion.

Just one night.

Twenty-four hours, of which I still owe him sixteen. That's twice as long as what I've already experienced—double the sensations and desires...double the pain when we're done.

"I can hear you think."

I jump and swing around, still with the stack of plates in my hand. "You startled me," I breathe, placing the crockery on the work surface.

"I apologize," he says sincerely, strolling over to me. I don't mean to, but I back up. "Are you overthinking things again?"

"I call it being prudent."

"Prudent?" he asks, standing in front of me now. "I wouldn't call it that."

I'm looking up at his face but desperately trying to avoid those eyes. "No?"

"No." He takes a gentle hold of my chin, encouraging me to look at him. "I call it being foolish."

Our eyes connect and so do our lips, but he only rests them over mine. There would be nothing foolish about avoiding Miller Hart. "I can't read you," I say quietly, but my words don't make him pull away with concern.

"I don't want to be read, Livy. I want to be flooded in the plea-sure you give me."

I liquefy against him, despite the fact that his words have only reinforced what I already know. I want to be flooded in the pleasure that he gives me, too, but I don't want the feelings that come after-ward. I can't cope with them. "You're making this really difficult."

His arm creeps around to my lower back and strokes up until he's on my neck. "No. I'm making it all very simple. Overthink-ing makes it difficult, and you're overthinking." He kisses my cheek and nuzzles into my neck. "Let me take you to bed."

"By doing that, I'll be something I swore I'd never be."

"What's that?" He spreads delicate kisses across my neck, and he's doing it because he knows I'm torn. He's a smart man. He's scrambling my senses, but worst of all, my mind.

"At a man's mercy."

There's definitely a slight falter in the trailing of his lips. I'm not imagining it. He removes himself from the sanctuary of my neck and studies me thoughtfully. So much time passes—enough for my mind to linger on many of the touches he's blessed me with, the kisses we've shared and the passion we've created together. It's like I'm watching it all in his eyes, making me wonder if he's reliv-ing those moments, too. He eventually reaches up and runs his knuckles softly down my cheek. "If there is anyone at the mercy of someone here, Livy, then it is me at yours." His eyes divert to my lips and lazily start moving in. And I do nothing to stop him.

I don't see a man at my mercy. I see a man who wants some-thing and seems prepared to do anything to get it.

"We should get back to the table." I try to break away from him, turning my face away from his.

"Not until you say you're leaving with me." He surprises me by lifting me from my feet and sitting me on the counter. Laying his hands on the tops of my thighs, he leans in and looks at me, wait-ing for my agreement. "Say it."

"I don't want to."

"Yes, you do." He gets nose to nose with me. "You've never wanted anything so much in your life."

He's right, but that doesn't make it wise. "You're very confident."

He shakes his head on a mild curve of his mouth and reaches up to drag his thumb across my bottom lip. "You may be trying to convince both of us with words, but everything else is telling me different." He slips his finger into his mouth and sucks it, then runs a moist trail down my throat, over my breast, and onto my stomach before his hand disappears up my dress and between my legs. My jaw tightens, my back straightens, and my core starts pulsing, willing him to touch me there. My body is betraying me on every level, and he knows it. "I think I'll find warmth." He inches closer to the apex of my thighs, and my head falls forward, meeting his forehead. "I think I'll find wetness," he whispers, his finger slipping into the side of my knickers and spreading that wetness around. "I think if I enter you now, your greedy muscles will grab on and never let go."

"Do it." The words leave my mouth without thought, my hands lifting and grabbing the tops of his arms. "Please do it."

"I'll do anything you want me to, but I'll be doing it in my bed." He kisses me hard on the lips and removes his hand, pulling the hem of my dress down. "I have manners. I'm not about to disrespect your grandmother by taking you here. Can you control yourself while we eat pineapple cake?"

"Can *I* control myself?" I ask on a breathy whisper, looking down to his groin. I don't need to see it to know it's there. He's solid and rubbing against my leg.

"I'm struggling, believe me." He readjusts himself and lifts me down from the counter, then sets about arranging my hair neatly over my shoulders. "Let's see how fast I can eat pineapple cake. Do you want to get an overnight bag?"

No, actually, I don't. I want him to lose his manners. I attempt in vain to compose my pent-up state, but all of the heat from down below is rising to my face at the thought of facing Nan and George. "I'll grab some things after dessert."

"As you wish." He takes my nape and directs me from the kitchen, the warmth of his hold intensifying my want. I want him so badly. I want this enigmatic man, who conducts himself so well, but contradicts every gentlemanly act in the next breath. He's a fraud, that's what he is.

An actor.

A conceited man, cleverly disguised as a gentleman.

Which makes him the worst kind of enemy that my heart could find.

"Here they are!" Nan claps, jumping up. "Where's the pineapple upside-down cake?"

"Oh!" I go to turn but quickly realize that with Miller still holding my neck firmly in his grasp, I'm going nowhere.

"No matter." Nan waves her hand at my empty chair. "Sit down, I'll get it."

Miller practically places me on the chair before tucking me in, almost like he has a compulsion to have *me* just so, as well as everything else that he touches. "Comfortable?"

"Yes, thank you."

"My pleasure." He takes his seat beside me and rearranges everything at his place setting before taking his recently shifted glass of wine and taking a slow sip.

"Oohhh, pineapple upside-down cake!" George rubs his hands together and licks his lips. "My favorite! Miller, you might die of pleasure."

"You know, George, we bought the pineapple from Harrods." I shouldn't be telling him this. Nan will kill me, but she's not the only one who can play matchmaker. "She paid fifteen pounds for it, and that was before she invited Miller for dinner."

He gasps, but then a thoughtful smile spreads across his face. It warms me to the core. "She knows how to spoil a man. Wonderful woman, your grandmother, Livy. Wonderful woman."

"She is," I agree quietly. She's as annoying as hell, but a wonderful woman.

"Pineapple upside-down cake!" Nan calls, walking in proudly with a silver platter in her hands. She places it in the middle of the table and everyone cranes their necks over, admiring the masterpiece. "This is my best to date. Would you like to try some of my pineapple upside-down cake, Miller?" she asks.

"I would love to, Mrs. Taylor."

"It's so good you'll inhale it in a second," I say casually, picking up my spoon and flicking my eyes to Miller. He takes the bowl from Nan when she hands it over the table and places it down before turning it a few millimeters clockwise.

"I've no doubt I will." He doesn't look at me and he doesn't begin eating. He waits politely for Nan to serve everyone else before she takes a seat and picks up her spoon. His manners won't allow him to fulfill his suggestion to eat quickly. He just can't help himself.

His spoon is lifted and sunk into the cake, breaking a piece away. Then he scoops it up with ultimate precision and pops it in his mouth. My eyes make the journey, following his spoon from his bowl to his lips, my own spoon hovering in front of me. His whole being is a ridiculously strong magnet to my eyes, and I'm beginning to give up trying to resist him. It seems my eyes are craving him as much as my body.

"Are you okay?" he asks, studying me staring at him as he takes another bite. Not even his awareness to my shameless gawking deters me.

"Yes, I'm fine. I was just thinking that I've never seen anyone eat one of my grandmother's cakes so slowly." I'm shocked by my suggestive observation and Miller coughing, his hand flying to his mouth, is an indication that he is, too. I'm glad. I have a feeling that I'll need to match his poise if I'm devoting another sixteen hours to him, so I may as well start now.

"Are you okay?" Nan's concerned voice hits my ears. I'm sure her old face will display concern, too, but I won't look to confirm it because seeing Miller flustered is too much of a novelty to miss any of it.

He finishes chewing, sets his spoon down, and wipes his mouth. "I apologize." He picks up his glass and gazes over to me, lifting it to his lips. "Beautiful things should be savored, Livy, not rushed." He sips his wine, and I feel his foot brush up my leg under the table. I shock myself further by flashing him a secret smile and remaining composed.

"It really is beautiful, Nan." I mimic Miller and take a mouthful, chewing slowly, swallowing slowly, then licking my lips slowly. And I know my unabashed string of actions have had the desired effect because my skin is being singed by his blue glare. "Did you enjoy, George?"

"Did I ever!" He leans back in his chair and rubs his belly on a satisfied huff of air. "I may need to undo my top button."

"George!" Nan hisses, reaching over and slapping his arm. "We're at the dinner table."

"Never usually bothers you," he grumbles.

"Yes, well, we have a guest."

"This is your home, Mrs. Taylor," Miller interjects. "And I'm privileged to be welcomed into it. That was the best beef Wellington I've ever had the pleasure of tasting."

"Oh." Nan waves a dismissive hand over the table. "You're too kind, Miller."

He's a brownnoser, that's what he is. "Better than my coffee?" I'm throwing innuendos all over the place, but I simply cannot help it.

"Your coffee was like nothing I've tasted before," he retorts softy, raising his eyebrows at me. "I hope you'll have one ready for me tomorrow around noon when I'm passing."

I shake my head on an amused smile, enjoying our private exchange. "Americano, four shots, two sugars, and topped up halfway."

"I look forward to it." He gives me a hint of the smile I long to see again, the one I've seen only a few times since I've known him. "Mrs. Taylor, would you object if I were to ask Olivia to join me for drinks at my home?"

I'm staggered by his confidence, and why didn't he ask me? My grandmother wouldn't say no, anyway. No, she'll probably try desperately to find a silk negligee in my underwear drawer to stuff into my bag on my way out. She'll be looking in vain.

"I'd love to," I answer, halting the potential of the decision being made for me. I'm a grown woman. I make my own decisions. I'm the master of my own destiny.

"How very chivalrous of you to ask." Nan's excitement is clear but a bit of a gut wrench. She's building hopes on the basis of what very little she knows of the man sitting at her table. The whole story would put her in an early grave. "We'll clear up and you two go have fun!"

My chair is being pulled out from behind me before I can drop my spoon, and I'm on my feet, being directed toward Nan and George's end of the table without delay. "Mrs. Taylor, thank you."

"Not at all!" She stands and lets Miller peck each of her cheeks while she widens her eyes at me. "It's been a wonderful evening."

"I concur," he says, holding his spare hand out to George. "It's been a pleasure to meet you, George."

"Yes." George is on his feet, taking position beside Nan and the opportunity, while she's in such a good mood, to slip his arm around her waist. "Lovely evening." He takes Miller's hand.

I'm silently begging them to hurry with the polite exchanges. Dinner has been a painfully long process of secret, suggestive remarks and sneaky touches. The pent-up lust in me is both unfamiliar and quite unsettling, but the overwhelming need to release it all is blocking any intelligence that I have, and I have lots of intelligence to block. I'm a smart woman...except when Miller is around.

I feel the soothing kneading of his fingers into my nape, completely obliterating that intelligence. I'm not going to try and find it because it's long gone, leaving me vulnerable and desperate.

I kiss Nan and George and allow Miller to guide me from the dining room. He doesn't let his hold of me drop as he takes his jacket from the stand, and then unhooks my denim jacket, too. "Do you want to get some things?"

"No," I answer quickly, not wanting to delay things further.

He doesn't argue, swiftly opening the front door and pushing me onward. He opens the door of his car and places me in the seat, shutting it quickly and pacing around the front to get in. Starting the engine, he pulls smoothly away from the curb, and I look up to my house, seeing the curtains twitching. I can only imagine the conversation going on between George and Nan right now, but that thought trails off when Depeche Mode's "Enjoy the Silence" creeps from the speakers, making my brow knit as I remember him telling me to do exactly that.

"You were extremely naughty during dinner, Livy."

My head swings to face him. Naughty? "You're the one who cornered me in the kitchen," I remind him.

"I was securing my evening's prospects."

"I'm a prospect?"

"No, you're a foregone conclusion." He keeps his eyes on the road, his face straight. Does he realize what he's saying?

"You make me sound like a tart." My jaw is clenched and so are my fists, my lust dissipating in a split second at those words. I may have stamped all over my rules in recent weeks, but I am not, and never will be, a tart. "I'd like you to take me home."

He takes a hard left, prompting me to grab the door, and we're suddenly driving down an alleyway, flanked by loading bays for shops on either side. It's dusk, it's eerie, and it's deserted. "You're *my* foregone conclusion, Livy. No one else's." Skidding to a halt, he unbuckles his seat belt, then mine, and I'm quickly being yanked across the car onto his lap.

"What are you doing?" I ask, shocked, the track making me shudder as it continues to invade my hearing as Miller invades all my other senses.

Eyes.

Nose.

Touch.

And soon taste.

His seat is shifted back, giving him more room to pull my dress up to my waist. "I'm doing what you've been begging me to do throughout dinner."

"I wasn't begging." My voice has dropped to a husky whisper. I don't recognize it.

"Livy, you were most certainly begging. Lift yourself up," he orders, taking my hips, encouraging me.

I put up no resistance, pushing on my knees and rising. "I thought you were waiting to put me back in your bed."

"I would have, had you not teased and tortured me for the past hour. There's only so much I can take." A condom appears from nowhere and he takes it between his teeth before reaching down and unfastening his trousers. "I realize how cheap this is but I really cannot wait." His penis breaks free from his trousers, hard and ready, and he makes fast work of ripping the packet open with his teeth and rolling it on.

I can't find my breath. My hands are holding the seat on either side of his head and I'm completely rapt as I watch him sheathe himself. Fizzles of heat are stabbing at the pit of my belly, working their way down to my groin, and I'm mentally egging him on, wanting him to hurry. I've lost control and my impatience is evident, more so when I gaze up at him and find misty blue eyes and moist, parted lips.

Pulling my cotton knickers aside, he guides himself to my opening, brushing the inside of my thigh, making me pull in a sharp breath. "Lower slowly," he whispers, replacing one hand on my hip.

Trying to rein in the temptation to crash down, I slowly inch my way down, letting the air from my lungs gush from my mouth, my head falling back, my fingers digging into the leather on the seat behind him. "Miller!"

"Good God!" he barks, his hips shaking. "I've never felt anything like it. Stay where you are."

I'm completely impaled on him. I can feel the tip of his arousal in the deepest part of me, and I'm shaking like a leaf. Uncontrollable shakes. My body is alive, desperate to fly into action and instigate further pleasure. "Move." My head drops, finding Miller's head resting back, his eyes low and staring into our laps. His hair is a wavy, damp mess, crying for me to feel it. So I do. I lace my fingers through his waves and play with it, stroking and pulling. "Please move."

"I'll do whatever you want, Livy." He clenches my hips and grinds deeply, spiking a low, alluring moan from me. "Jesus, that damn sound you make."

"I can't help it."

"I don't want you to," he says, circling firmly, making me moan some more. "I could listen to it for the rest of my days."

I'm a fevered mess of longing. He even makes love precisely, each rotation, circle, and grind a perfectly executed move, building me up perfectly. I'll never get enough of this. "Miller," I pant, pushing short, uncontrolled breaths through my lips.

"Tell me what you want." He lifts me and pulls me back down slowly, his eyes clenching shut. "Tell me how you want me, Livy."

I don't care. Each time he's worshipped me it has been perfectly perfect. He can do no wrong. "I want it all," I breathe, meaning so much more than just movement. I want to feel this good forever, and I'm not sure that any other man will do it for me. "Kiss me," I beg as he slides me back up and guides me down, rotating his hips, grinding firmly. I'm losing my mind. My hands are tightening in his hair, my knees on his waist.

His eyes lift, his hand finds its place on my nape, and I'm pulled forward slowly, accurately, with no rush or impatience. I don't know how he's doing it. "You've knocked me sideways, Olivia Taylor," he murmurs, claiming my lips gently. "You're making me question everything I thought I knew."

I want to agree because I feel the same, but my mouth is too busy relishing in the attention of his soft, worshipping lips. I do, however, note that his declaration can only be a good thing. Maybe he won't let me walk away after our time is up. I'm *hoping* he won't let me walk away because I've given myself up to him again, despite my better judgment. But saying no to Miller Hart doesn't seem to be something I can do . . . or I simply won't do.

"Can you feel it, Livy?" he asks between tentative, delicate circles of his tongue. "Doesn't it feel like nothing else?"

"Yes." I bite his lip and plunge my tongue back into his mouth, moaning and pushing my body into him, feeling twinges in the tip of my sex, the hints of an orgasm powering forward. It makes me harden our kiss as the desperation to nail it down derails my determination to follow his leisurely lead.

"Calm," he moans. "Take it easy."

I try, but he's starting to thump inside of me, swelling and throbbing, pushing me on. I start shaking my head against his lips. "You feel too good."

"Hey." He breaks our kiss but maintains the flow of his body into mine, taking over completely to stop me hurrying things along. "Savor it."

My eyes close and my head rolls back on my shoulders as I try to gather the strength required to follow his guidance. I'm amazed by his self-control. Every piece of him is gushing with desperation to match mine—his eyes smoking, his body shaking, his sex throbbing, his face damp with sweat. Yet he seems to find it so easy to tolerate the painful pleasure that he inflicts on us both.

"Shit, I wish I had you in my bed," he moans. "Don't hide your beautiful face from me, Livy. Show me."

My body starts to spasm with an orgasm I couldn't delay even if I wanted to. My hand flies out, my palm slapping against the window, but it instantly starts slipping all over the condensation on the glass, doing nothing to stabilize me.

"Livy!" He grabs my hair and yanks my head forward. Things are frantic, but his rhythm is still slow and exact. "When I ask you to look at me, you look at me!" His hips thrust up, and I gulp back air as my hearing is flooded by the rush of roaring blood to my head, slightly distorting the music surrounding us. "Here it comes."

"Please, faster," I beg. "Make it happen."

"It's happening." His grip tightens and he directs me back to his mouth, kissing me to my peak as I grapple with the sleeves of his shirt. My world implodes and every nerve ending pulses viciously as I groan, low and satisfied into his mouth while Miller throbs within me.

"Another sixteen hours isn't enough for me," I confess quietly, my intense physical feelings only enhancing my emotional state of mind. "You can't do this to me." My overworked lips drag across his stubble until they're glued to his neck, my head heavy, my body limp.

"Have you considered what you're doing to me?" he asks quietly. "You seem to be under the impression that this is all very easy for me."

I remain with my face hiding in the crook of his neck, finding it easier to off-load my thoughts when I don't have to look at him. "I'm surrendering myself to you. I'm doing what you've asked of me." My voice is low and weak, a mixture of exhaustion and timidity.

"Livy, I'm not going to pretend I know what's happening." He pulls me from my hiding place and cups my hot cheeks in his hands. His face is serious and there's unquestionably a hint of confusion. "But it's happening and I think we're both powerless to stop it."

"Are you going to walk away from me?" I feel stupid asking this question of a man I've known for such a short time, but something is pulling us both together, and it's not just his persistence. It's something invisible, powerful and determined.

He takes a long pull of breath and tugs me down to his chest, giving me his *thing*. His strong arms surrounding me easily put me in the safest place that I've ever been. "I'm going to take you home and worship you."

It's not an answer, but it's not a yes either. This is special, I'm sure. I've found it incredibly easy to avoid these feelings for so long, but I'm incapable of stopping myself from falling with Miller Hart, and even though I don't quite understand him, I want to pursue this. I want to discover myself. But most of all, I want to discover him—all of him. The morsels he's fed me so far have mostly irritated me or angered me, but there's more than meets the eye with this part-time gentleman.

And I want to know it all.

Breaking free of his chest, I slowly lift myself from his lap, his semi-erection slipping free as I do. That alone makes me feel half complete. I settle in the passenger seat and gaze out of the window to the murky, litter crowded alleyway while he sorts himself out next to me and the music fades to nothing. A small part of my mind is willing me to walk away now before he has the opportunity to do just that to me, but I find it easy to ignore it. I'm not going to be walking anywhere unless I'm forced to. There's only one thing that I've ever been determined to do, and that's avoid putting myself in this situation. Now I find myself determined to stay here, no matter what the cost to my falling heart.

CHAPTER TWELVE

I have the stamina to get to the seventh floor this time, before Miller carries me up the rest of the stairs. It's no wonder his physique looks like it belongs to a mythical god.

"Would you like a drink?" He's returned to sharp and formal, but his manners are still intact. The door is held open for me, and I slip in, immediately noticing a huge spray of fresh flowers on the round table.

"No, thank you." I circle the table slowly and break the threshold into the lounge, glancing around at the paintings adorning the walls.

"Water?"

"No."

"Please, sit." He indicates the sofa. "I'll just hang these," he says, holding up our jackets.

"Okay." Things are strained, our honest words causing a friction that I want to be rid of. Then soft music is with me and I look around, wondering where it's coming from while absorbing the calmness of the beats and the gentle tones of the male's voice. I recognize it. It's Passenger's "Let Her Go." My mind starts racing.

Miller returns, his waistcoat and tie removed, his collar unbuttoned. He pours some dark liquid into a tumbler, and I notice the label this time. It's scotch. He takes a seat on the coffee table in front of me again and sips slowly, but then he almost frowns at the glass before tipping the neat alcohol down his throat and placing the glass on the table.

As I knew he would, he tweaks the position, then clasps his hands together, looking at me thoughtfully. I'm immediately wary of that look. "Why don't you drink, Livy?"

I was right to be worried. He keeps saying he doesn't want to get personal, yet he has no problem asking me personal questions or invading my personal space, namely my home and my dinner table. I don't say that, though, because what I actually want is for this to get *really* personal. I don't just want to share my body with him. "I don't trust myself."

His eyebrows jump up, surprised. "You don't trust yourself?"

I'm squirming, my eyes darting around the room, despite my desire to share this with him. It's just finding the courage to form the words that I've refused to utter for so long.

"Livy, how many times do we need to go through this? When I'm talking to you, you look at me. When I ask you a question, you answer." He takes my jaw gently and forces me to face him. "Why don't you trust yourself?"

"I'm a different person with alcohol in my system."

"I'm not sure I like the sound of that." He didn't need to tell me that. His eyes are telling me all by themselves.

I feel my face flush, probably heating the tips of his fingers. "It doesn't agree with me."

"Elaborate," he demands harshly, his lips pursed.

"It doesn't matter." I try to pull my face from his grip, suddenly not so keen to share a part of my personal life, his approach to my news the reason for my change of heart. I don't need to feel any more ashamed.

"That was a question, Livy."

"No, that was an order," I snap defensively, managing to break free from his hold. "One that I'm choosing *not* to elaborate on."

"You're being cagey."

"You're being intrusive."

He recoils a little but quickly gathers himself. "I'm being intuitive here, and I'm going to suggest that the only times you've had sex were when you were intoxicated."

My color deepens. "Your instincts are correct," I mutter. "Is that all, or would you like a run-by-run account of who, what, where, and when?"

"There's no need for insolence."

"With you, Miller, there is."

He narrows bright blues on me, but doesn't scold me for my bad manners. "I want a run-by-run account."

"No, you don't."

"Your mother." Those words make me instantly stiffen, and by the look on his face, he's noticed. "When I was forced to hide in your room, your grandmother mentioned your mother's history."

"It doesn't matter."

"Yes, it does."

"She was a prostitute." The words fall from my mouth automatically, taking me by surprise, and I chance a glimpse at Miller to gauge his reaction.

He goes to speak but only achieves a stunned rush of air. I've shocked him, as I knew I would, but I wish he'd at least say something...anything. He doesn't, but I do.

"She abandoned me. She dumped me on my grandparents in favor of a life of sex, alcohol, and expensive gifts."

He's watching me closely. I'm desperate to know what he's thinking. I know it can't be good. "Tell me what happened to her."

"I've told you."

He tweaks his glass again and returns his gaze to me. "All you've told me is that she accepted money in return for...entertainment."

"And that's all there is to know."

"So where is she now?"

"Dead, probably," I spit nastily. "I really don't care."

"Dead?" he gasps, showing more emotion. I'm pulling reactions from him left, right, and center now.

"Probably." I shrug. "She chased a rainbow. Every man who had her fell for her, but no one was ever adequate, not even me."

His face softens, sympathy washing over his features. "What makes you think she's dead?"

I take a deep breath of confidence, ready to explain something that I've avoided explaining to anyone ever. "She fell into the wrong man's hands too many times and I have a bank account loaded with years of *earnings* that hasn't been touched since she's been gone. I was only six, but I remember my grandparents constantly arguing over her." My mind is instantly bombarded by images of my granddad's anguish and my nan crying. "She would disappear for days regularly, but then she didn't come back. My granddad called the police after three days. They investigated, questioned her current beau and the many men before him, but with her history they closed the case. I was a little girl, I didn't understand, but when I was seventeen I found her journal. It told me everything—in vivid detail."

"I . . ." He doesn't know what to say, so I go on. I feel a sense of relief off-loading it all, even if it means he'll walk away from me.

"I don't want to be anything like my mother. I don't want to drink and have sex with no feelings. It's nothing, except degrading and meaningless." I realize what I've said the second it falls from my lips, but I've given Miller no reason to believe there are no feelings from my side. "She chose that lifestyle over her family." I surprise myself by keeping my voice steady and strong, even if hearing it aloud for the first time ever causes me physical pain.

Miller's cheeks puff, letting out a rush of air, and he takes his empty glass and frowns at it.

"Shocked?" I ask, thinking I could do with one of those shorts.

He looks at me like I'm daft, then stands and paces back to the drinks cabinet, pouring more whisky into his tumbler, this time halfway as opposed to the usual two fingers. And then he surprises me by pouring another glass before resuming his position opposite me. He hands me the fresh glass. "Have a drink."

I look a little stunned at the glass being waved under my nose. "I told you—"

"Olivia, you can have a drink without getting mindlessly drunk."

Cautiously reaching forward, I take the glass. "Thank you."

"Welcome," he practically grunts before knocking back his drink. "Your father?"

I have to stop myself from spilling a sardonic laugh and shrug my answer instead, making him exhale over the rim of his glass.

"You don't know?"

I shake my head.

"I hate your mother."

"What?" I ask, shocked, considering I may have just misheard him.

"I hate her," he repeats, venom dripping from his voice.

"So do I."

"Good. Then we both hate your mother. I'm glad we've cleared that up."

Not knowing quite what to say, I sit quietly, watching him drift in and out of thought, taking breaths as if intending to say something, but thinking better of it. There's nothing that he can say. It's ugly, and no reassuring words will pretty it up. That's my history. I can't change who my mother was, what she did, and I can't change how I've allowed it to impact my life.

He eventually speaks, but it's not a question I expected. "So I'm your only sober lover?"

I nod and rest back on the couch, putting space between us but finding it impossible to look away from him.

"And did you enjoy it?"

This is a stupid question. "It scares me."

"I scare you?"

"How you make me feel scares me. I don't know myself around you," I whisper, slowly showing him all my cards.

He places his glass accurately on the table and lowers to his knees in front of me. "I make you feel alive." He slides his hands around my back and pulls me forward until our faces are close, our breaths mingling in the small space between our mouths. "I'm not a tender or gentle kind of man, Olivia," he says, like he's trying to make me feel better by sharing a little piece of him. "Women want me for one thing alone, and that's because I've given them no reason to expect anything more."

A million words dance on my lips, all desperate to form a sentence and spill from my mouth, but I don't want to be hasty. "Expect nothing more than the best fuck of their life," I state quietly.

"Precisely." He rids me of my glass and takes my hands, draping them over his shoulders.

"You promised me that," I remind him.

The lids of his eyes slowly drop. "I don't think I can fulfill that promise."

"What are you saying?" I ask, willing him to confirm that I'm not imagining things, or that he's saying this out of sympathy. His shoulders drop a little with a tired exhale, but he keeps his eyes down, keeping quiet, too. "It's polite to answer someone when they ask you a question," I murmur, making his head lift in surprise. I don't shy away. I want him to confirm what's happening.

"I'm saying I want to worship you." His head tilts and moves forward, capturing my lips as he rises, taking me with him. He's the one being cagey now, but I won't rush an admission from him. I can wait, and in the meantime, he'll worship me.

I'm surprised when he takes us down to the couch and maneuvers until he's on his back, positioning me between his spread thighs so I'm sprawled up the center of his body. Our clothes are all still in place and he doesn't attempt to remove them, seemingly content with just kissing the living daylights out of me. His dark stubble is coarse on my skin, counteracting the subtle movements of his lips, but through my absolute blissful state, I hardly register the scratchy feel. With Miller, things just happen naturally. He leads and I follow. I don't need to think, I just do, which is why I'm now unbuttoning his shirt so I can feel the heat of his flesh under my palms. Moaning around his lips, I get the first spark of his heat mixed with mine as my hands slip across his stomach, rising and falling subtly with the ripples of his abdominals.

"There's that sweet sound again," he says on a murmur, gathering my masses of blond hair that're pouring all around his head. "It's addictive. *You* are addictive."

His pleasure spurs me on, my mouth visiting everywhere on his stunning face until I'm at his neck, taking a hit of that intoxicating, manly scent. "You smell so good." I work my way down to his chest, my movements just happening without thought or instruction. His nipples are tight, and my tongue homes in, circling and licking, making him shift and moan beneath me. His sounds of pleasure only embolden me and his solid length pushing into my stomach reminds me of where I want to be. I want to taste him. I want to feel him in my mouth.

"Oh shit, Livy. Where are you going?" He raises his head and looks down at me, then clasps his head in his hands. "You don't have to do that."

"I want to." I run my palm over his trousers, clasp his zip, and gently tug it down as I watch him watching me.

"No, please, it's okay, Livy."

"I. Want. To."

His eyes are unsure, his hands visibly tightening on his head as he flops back down to the pillow. "Take it easy."

I smile to myself, feeling confident, loving his vulnerability and loving how right this feels. He hasn't run away from my shameful history. I undo his button and tug down his trousers, sitting up on my knees to rid him of them. It leaves him in a fine pair of black boxer shorts that cling everywhere. They look too good to remove, but what's underneath spurs me on. I chuck his trousers on the floor and tuck my fingers into the waistband before slowly drawing them down his muscular thighs, glancing up at his face, and then focusing on his thick, solid cock, resting on his lower stomach. My tongue involuntary leaves my mouth and swipes across my bottom lip as I admire him in all of his magnificent masculinity. I don't feel intimidated by the pulsing, solidness of him. I feel excited.

Throwing his boxers to join his trousers on the floor, I scoot down and make myself comfortable, my hands lying on his hips, my nose practically resting on the underside of his penis. I'm staring down, watching him twitch, my mouth dropping open as I breathe heavily onto him. His hips lift slowly, pushing himself toward me, making me pull in a steady breath of air.

"Livy, sweet Jesus, I can feel the heat of your breath." He lifts his head and hits me with hungry eyes. "Are you okay?"

"I'm sorry, it's just..." I glance back down.

"It's fine." His acceptance is easy. It makes me feel stupid, and with those words, my tongue leaves my mouth and I get my first taste of Miller Hart. I follow my instincts and lick straight up his shaft lightly, climbing onto my knees as I do. I've never tasted anything quite like it.

"Oh, fuuuuck." His head falls back and his palms cover his face, which I take as a good sign, so I take him in my hand and pull him up, noting a pearl of white liquid beading on the very tip. I lick it off, *really* getting a good taste.

I gasp a little, working hard to keep my confidence. He looks so thick and long. I'll never take it all. My earlier poise is slipping, but I'm desperate not to look like a complete idiot. I curse silently to myself, hating my hesitance, and take him into my mouth, plunging until he hits the back of my throat.

"Fuck!" His hips fly up, pushing him farther into me, making me gag and retreat quickly. "Sorry!" he blurts on a suppressed bark. "Shit, Livy, I'm sorry."

Frustrated with myself, I don't delay getting him back into my mouth, this time only taking him halfway before pulling back and working my way down again. The smoothness of him is a surprise. It feels nice—his heat, his hardness beneath the smooth skin.

I'm working up into a comfortable rhythm, his moans of pleasure encouraging me as my hand roams freely, feeling his chest, his thighs, his stomach.

"Livy, stop now." His stomach muscles tense as he rises into a sitting position, his knees rising, too, and dropping outward, leaving me kneeling between his spread legs, my head in his lap. "Stop." His hands are in my hair, gently guiding me up and down slowly, patiently. He's telling me to stop, but seeming to encourage me, too. "Oh, Jesus," he chokes as I feel one hand leave my head, feeling the zip of my dress being slowly drawn down my spine. "Lift up," he says, pulling at the hem of my dress.

Feeling a little cheated, I do as I'm told and drop him from my mouth, lifting my backside from the backs of my feet and my hands into the air. My dress is pulled up as I look down at him, loving the mess of his hair, all falling freely, the waves enhanced from his sexed-up state. He disappears from sight for just a few seconds while he gets my dress past my face before throwing it carelessly on the floor and reaching around my back to unfasten my bra. He slowly drags it down my arms and drops it before taking my hips gently and leaning forward to place his lips on my stomach. Reaching down, I start to push his shirt from his shoulders, keen to get him fully naked and feel all of him, and he obliges, releasing one hand from my body at a time to allow the removal of his remaining clothes, but keeping his mouth on my stomach, nibbling lazily across to my hip.

"Your skin is exquisite, Livy." His voice is rough and low. "*You* are exquisite."

My hands find his hair, and I look down at the back of his head as he takes his time working his mouth all over my navel. As always, it's slow, soft and precise, making my body hum and my eyes close dreamily. Nothing about our intimacies suggests that this is just sex—not one thing. I may not be *au fait* with sexual relationships, but I know this is more than sex. This *has* to be more than sex.

I'm happy enough to kneel in front of his sitting body and let him indulge himself for as long as he likes. His hands are everywhere, cupping my bottom, trailing delicately up my spine and drifting back down to the backs of my thighs. I feel his thumbs slip into the sides of my knickers and tug, pulling them down until they're at my knees, unable to go any farther. Dropping my head and opening my eyes, I find him looking up at me. His eyes are screaming desire as he lazily blinks, like his dark lashes are too heavy and it's an effort to reopen them.

"How about I lock the door and we stay here forever?" he suggests on a low murmur, encouraging me to shift one leg at a time to allow him to remove my knickers. "Forget about the world outside those doors and stay here with me."

I settle back down on my knees, my bum resting on my heels. "Forever would be much longer than one night."

His lips twitch and he extends his hand, rubbing his thumb across my nipple. I look down, reminding myself of my lack of breasts, not that he seems at all bothered. "So it would," he muses, keeping his focus on his thumb circling the dark rim around my hard nub. "It was a stupid deal."

My heart skips too many beats, my spirits lifting to crazy heights. "We didn't shake on it," I remind him. "And we definitely haven't fucked on it."

He sends me dizzy when he smiles at my breast, and then lifts his blue gaze to mine. "I concur." He reaches up and pulls me down so we're nose to nose. I'm powerless to prevent the small smile plaguing my lips as a result of those words and the look on his face. "I don't think you're quite broken in enough yet."

"I concur." My smile widens. We both know that I am more than broken in. This is an implicit, mutual acknowledgment and agreement. He wants me for longer, just as much as I want him. We have both been taken aback by this fascination. "Will you break me in some more now?" I ask innocently, lifting and unfolding my legs, putting myself in his lap.

He helps me, guiding my legs around his back before holding my bum in his palms and pulling me in. "I think I'm under obligation to do so." He pecks my lips. "And I always fulfill my obligations, Olivia Taylor."

"Good," I breathe, homing in on his lips and lacing my fingers together behind his neck.

"Hmmm," he sighs, swinging his legs off the couch and standing, cradling me against his body like I'm nothing more than a feather. He paces toward his bedroom, and when we enter, he takes me straight to his bed and kneels on the end, walking to the top on his knees before turning and resting his back against the headboard, me on his lap.

He leans over and opens the top drawer of his bedside table, pulling out a condom and handing it to me. "Put this on me."

I hate myself for stiffening on his lap. I don't have the first idea of how to go about putting one on. "It's okay, you can do it." I try to look unbothered, rather than scared.

"But I want you to." He pushes me farther down his lap, exposing his rigid length and taking a hold, standing it vertical from his body before handing the foil packet to me. "Take it."

I look at him and he nods reassuringly, so I tentatively reach forward and take it from him.

"Open," he orders. "Rest it on top and roll it down gently."

My hesitance is obvious as I carefully rip the packet open and slide the condom out, fiddling with it in my fingers. Having a silent, stern word with myself, I take a deep breath and follow his instructions, resting the loop over the broad head of his erection.

"Hold the tip," he breathes, lying back and watching intently.

Taking the end between my finger and thumb, I use my other hand to roll the condom down his length until I can roll no more. Again, I'm annoyed at having to conceal him.

"Nothing to it." He smiles up at my concentrating face and pulls me back onto his lap, so far forward that he can raise his knees a little behind me. I'm encouraged to lift up and he takes his arousal to my opening, both of us panting as I lower down. I'm thrown straight into utter ecstasy, immediately holding my breath and pushing my palms into his shoulders.

I whimper as he bucks within me. I'm on top, and I know movement will only happen when I instigate it, but I can't move yet. I'm completely filled, but then his legs straighten out and he goes deeper. "Oh my God!" I gasp, my arms going straight and rigid against him, my chin dropping to my chest.

"You're in control, Livy," he breathes. "If it hurts, ease up."

"It doesn't hurt." I circle my hips to demonstrate. "Holy shit!" I'm bombarded by scorching hot shots of pleasure, the friction rubbing my most sensitive spot just right. It prompts me to circle again. "It feels good." My arms relax and my grip shifts to his face, encasing his cheeks in my palms as I rotate my hips around and around, again and again.

I'm urged forward, our foreheads meeting, the passion from both of our eyes colliding. "This must be heaven," he whispers. "There's no other explanation. Pinch me."

I don't pinch him. I lift up and ease down on a firm grind instead, making damn sure he knows that I'm real. My determination is boosting my confidence. The pressure of him filling me is sending me out of my mind, taking me to pleasurable places that I never realized existed. He does this to me, and judging by the constant moans seeping from those lips, I do it to him, too. I pull back, still circling, still grinding, so I can see his face in its entirety. His hair is everywhere, the wayward locks wet on his forehead, the soft curls on his nape flicking out, defined by the dampness. I love it.

He watches me, his lips slightly parted and sweat trailing his temples. "What are you thinking?" he asks me, shifting his hands to my thighs. "Tell me what you're thinking."

"I'm thinking that you only have thirteen hours left." I undertake a perfect, overly firm grind as I speak. I'm being cunning, but I've lost all of my inhibitions.

His eyes narrow on a slight pout, and then the bastard jolts upward, knocking my cockiness completely off kilter. "You've been here an hour, maximum. I have fifteen hours."

"Dinner was two hours." I groan, my head becoming heavy, but I'm still relentlessly working him. That luscious warmth is spreading over every inch of my skin, telling me I'm on my way.

"Dinner doesn't count." He transfers a hand to my hair, combing through with his fingers and finding my nape under the wild, damp strands. "I couldn't touch you during dinner."

"You're making up rules now!" I blurt. "Miller!"

"Are you going to come, Livy?"

"Yes! Please don't say you're not ready," I beg, my legs squeezing against his sides.

"Fuck, I'm always ready for you." He sits up and heads straight for my neck, latching on with his mouth, kissing and biting. "Let it go."

I do. Every muscle constricts and I yell, my head falling back and dangling freely while I shudder around him, my mind a complete fuzz of jumbled thoughts.

"Jesus!" he shouts, surprising me, even through my numb, blissed-out state. "Livy, you're pulsing around me." He guides my nonresponsive body on him. I'm useless, except for the relentless muscles gripping greedily onto Miller inside of me.

He climaxes with a loud groan and an uncontrolled buck of his hips. I'm just swaying in his hold, relying on him to hold me up. "You do serious things to me, Olivia Taylor. Serious, serious things. Let me see your face." He helps me pull my limp head up, but I don't stay upright for long, my chest falling forward and forcing him back to the headboard. He doesn't complain. He lets me burrow into his neck and leaves me to catch my breath. "Are you okay?" he asks with slight amusement in his tone.

I can't speak, so I nod, my hands stroking down his biceps as he drags his palms all over my back. The only sound is strained breaths, mostly emanating from me. But it's comfortable. It feels right.

"Are you thirsty?"

I shake my head no and burrow deeper, content to remain exactly where I am, grateful for his acceptance of me.

"Have you lost your voice?"

I nod, but then I feel him jerking underneath me. He's laughing and I desperately want to see it, so I spring to life, scrambling from his chest and quickly getting his face in my field of vision. It's straight, and his eyes are wide with shock.

"What's the matter?" he asks, all concerned, scanning my face.

I gather all of the air in my lungs and use it to form a sentence. "You were laughing at me."

"I wasn't laughing *at* you." He's all defensive, clearly thinking that I'm insulted, but I'm not. I'm delighted, but pissed I missed it.

"That's not what I meant. I've never seen or heard you laugh."

He looks uncomfortable all of a sudden. "Maybe that's because there's not much to laugh about."

I feel my brows meet in the middle. I get the impression that Miller Hart doesn't laugh very often. He barely smiles either. "You're too serious," I say, sounding more accusatory than the simple observation that it was meant to be.

"Life is serious."

"Don't you laugh in the pub with your friends?" I ask, trying to imagine Miller drinking a pint in a spit and sawdust pub. I can't see it.

"I don't frequent pubs." He almost looks offended by my question.

"What about friends?" I press, finding it hard to imagine Miller laughing and joking with anyone full stop, with or without a pub added to the mix.

"I believe we may be getting personal." He snubs me completely, making me choke. After everything I've shared?

"You pressured me into sharing something *very* personal, and I told you. When someone asks you a question, it's polite to answer."

"No, it's my prerogative to—"

I cut him off with a dramatic roll of my eyes and fail to halt my mischievous hand from slipping up to his armpit. He watches me suspiciously, his eyes following my hand until I'm tickling him there.

He doesn't even flinch, just raises his eyebrows cockily. "Afraid not." He's straight faced but smug, making me more persistent, so I walk my fingers across his collarbone to his stubbled chin and attack him with wriggling fingers, but still nothing. He shrugs. "I'm not ticklish."

"Everyone's ticklish somewhere."

"Not me."

My eyes narrow and my fingers creep down to his stomach, giving a little dig in the hard, muscled area of his abdomen. He remains impassive and unaffected by my tactics. I sigh. "Feet?" He shakes his head slowly, making me sigh deeper. "I wish you'd express yourself more." I crawl back up his body and settle to his side, propping my head up on a bent elbow as he shifts to mirror me.

"I think that I express myself just fine." His hand reaches over, taking a lock of my blond hair, and he starts twirling it between his fingers. "I love your hair," he muses, watching his slow playing fingers.

"It's unruly and unmanageable."

"It's perfect. Don't ever cut it off." His hand slides around my nape and tugs me closer so there are just a few inches between our faces. My eyes are torn, not knowing whether to focus on his eyes or his lips.

They choose his lips. "I love your mouth," I confess, inching forward and resting mine over his. My bravery is increasing, my ability to express myself with this expressionless man becoming easy.

"My mouth loves your body," he mumbles, pulling me in farther.

"My body loves your hands," I counter, falling into the relaxed movement of his tongue.

"My hands love how you feel under their touch."

I hum as he glides those hands to my stomach, onto my hip, and down my thigh. The smoothness of his palms defies his masculinity. They're clean, soft, and free from rough calluses, hinting to a life free of manual labor. He's always in suits, always impeccably turned out, and his manners are faultless—even with his moody arrogance. Everything about Miller is mystifying, but incredibly enticing, and the invisible pull that's constantly yanking me toward him is confounding and aggravating, but impossible to resist. And in this moment, when he's worshipping me, feeling me, and taking me so tenderly, I conclude that Miller Hart *does* express himself. He's expressing himself right now. He does it like this. He may not laugh or smile much, or give me any facial expressions when we're talking to tell me what he's thinking, but his whole physical being tells me his emotional state. And I don't think I'm mistaking it for feelings, not just fascination.

I'm a little annoyed when he breaks our kiss and pulls away, gazing at me quietly before turning me away from him and pulling me back against his chest. "Get some sleep, sweet girl," he whispers, burying his nose in my wild blond locks.

Falling asleep with a man wrapped around me is not something I'm used to, but with his soft breaths in my ear and him humming that soft melody quietly, I find slumber too easily, smiling to myself when I feel him break away and get out of bed.

He's going to tidy up.

Chapter Thirteen

He's standing in the doorway to his bedroom in his suit trousers and shirt, fixing his tie, while my arms are wrapped protectively around my naked body. I would pull the covers over me, but the side of the bed that he slept on has been made and I don't want to disturb it. His hair is wet and his face unshaved, and though he looks divine, I'm hurt that he's not still in bed with me.

"Will you join me for breakfast?" he asks, undoing his tie and starting again.

"Sure," I answer quietly, hating the awkwardness closing him off from me. I'm surprised to have woken up to daylight. When I dozed off last night, I was certain that I'd only be given a few hours' recovery time before Miller woke me up to recommence worshipping me . . . or, more to the point, I was *hoping* he'd wake me up. I'm disappointed, and I'm trying not to make it obvious.

I don't know why I glance around the room for my clothes because I know they won't be anywhere in sight. "Where are my clothes?"

"Take a shower. I'll prepare breakfast." He strolls over to his wardrobe and appears moments later, buttoning up his waistcoat. "I need to leave in thirty minutes. Your clothes are in the bottom drawer."

I shift uncomfortably, wondering what's changed. He's more closed off than ever before. Has he spent all night thinking, validating exactly what I've told him? "Okay," I confirm, not able to think of anything else to say. He's barely even looking at me. I feel cheap and worthless, something that I've fought to avoid for years.

Not saying another word, he gets his suit jacket from the wardrobe and leaves me in his bedroom, feeling slighted and confused. I desperately want to escape the uneasiness, but I really don't want to, too. I want to stay and loosen him up again, make him see me, not the illegitimate child of a hooker, but it doesn't sound like I have much choice. He needs to leave in thirty minutes, and I need to shower before I join him for breakfast, which is limiting my time further.

Jumping up naked from the bed, I rush into the bathroom to shower. I use his body wash, working it in firmly, like some way to keep him with me. Reluctantly rinsing off, I step out of the shower and pull one of the crisp, perfectly folded towels from the shelf and dry myself in record time before throwing my clothes on.

I traipse through his apartment, finding him in front of the mirror in the hallway, messing with his tie again. "Your tie is fine."

"No, it's askew," he grumbles, yanking it free from his neck. "Fuck it!"

I watch as he stalks past me, into the kitchen. I follow, a little bemused, and I shouldn't be shocked when I find him standing in front of an ironing board, but I am. He lays the tie neatly, then with the utmost concentration, he glides the iron across the blue silk before flicking the switch on the socket and draping the tie around his neck. He sets about putting away the board and iron, then returns to the mirror and starts the meticulous task of fastening his tie again, all as if I'm not even here.

"Better," he affirms, pulling his collar down and looking over to me.

"Your tie is wonky."

He frowns and turns back to the mirror, giving it a little jiggle. "It's perfect."

"Yes, it's perfect, Miller," I mutter, making my way into the kitchen.

I admire the selection of breads, preserves, and fruit. But I'm not hungry. My stomach is a knot of anxiety, and his formality isn't easing my trepidation.

"What would you like?" he asks, taking up his seat.

"I'll just have some melon, please."

He nods and takes a bowl, spooning some of the fruit in and handing me a fork. "Coffee?"

"No, thank you." I take the fork, and then the bowl, setting it down as neatly as I can.

"Orange juice? It's freshly squeezed."

"Yes, thank you."

He pours me some juice and tops his coffee up from the glass pot. "I forgot to thank you for smashing my lamp," he muses, lifting his cup slowly and watching me as he takes a sip.

I feel my face burn up under his accusing stare, my stomach knotting further. "I'm sorry." I shift on my chair, my eyes dropping to my bowl. "It was dark. I couldn't see."

"You're forgiven."

My eyes fly up on a small laugh. "Why, thank you. *You're* forgiven for leaving me in the dark."

"You should've stayed in bed," he retorts, sitting comfortably back on his chair. "You made an incredible mess."

"I'm sorry. The next time you abandon me in the middle of the night, I'll have my night vision goggles at hand."

His eyebrows jump up in surprise, but I know it's not because of my sarcasm. " 'Abandon'?"

I cringe, diverting my eyes away from him. I should think before I speak, especially in the presence of Miller Hart. "That came out wrong."

"I hope so. I left you sleeping. I didn't abandon you." He continues with his French toast, leaving those words lingering unwanted in the awkward air surrounding us—unwanted by me, anyway. "Eat up and I'll take you home."

"Why do you hope so?" I ask, feeling anger flare. "So I don't tarnish you with the same brush as I do my pathetic mother?"

"Pathetic?"

"Yes, spineless. Selfish."

He blinks his shock, twitching in his chair. "We have a deal for twenty-four hours," he fires across the table.

My teeth grit as I lean forward. I can see with one hundred percent clarity that I'm drawing anger from this normally impassive man with my accusation. Yet what's not clear is whether he's angry with me or himself. "What was yesterday? In the car and last night? An act? You're pathetic!"

Miller's eyes darken and a flash of anger crosses his face. "Don't push me, sweet girl. My temper isn't something you should toy with. We had an arrangement and I was ensuring it was fulfilled."

My falling heart splinters painfully, remembering a very different man from last night. An accepting man. A loving man. The man sitting opposite me now is confounding. I've never seen Miller Hart lose his temper. I've seen him get agitated and I've heard him curse—mostly when something isn't Miller-perfect—but the look in his eyes right now tells me I've seen nothing. That coupled with his serious warning also tells me I really don't want to.

I stand abruptly, my body seeming to engage before my brain does, and walk away, letting myself out of his apartment and taking the stairs to the lobby. The doorman nods as I pass through, and when I emerge into the fresh morning air, I let out a heavy sigh. The smell and sound of London doesn't make me feel any better.

"I was talking to you." Miller's annoyed tone hits me from behind, but it doesn't prompt me to find my manners and turn to acknowledge him. "Livy, I said that I was talking to you."

"And what did you say?" I ask.

He appears in my line of sight and stands in front of me, regarding me closely. "I don't like repeating myself."

"I don't like your mood swings."

"I don't have mood swings."

"Yes, you do. I don't know where I am with you. One minute you're sweet and attentive, the next you're cold and short."

He's thinking hard about my words, and it's a good few moments of staring at each other before he finally utters some himself. "We were getting too close to personal."

I pull in a long breath and hold it, desperately trying to stop myself from shouting at him. I knew this was coming from the second I opened my eyes this morning. But it still hurts like hell. "Is this anything to do with your business associate, or is it just me and my sordid history?"

He doesn't answer, choosing to watch me silently instead.

"I should never have given you more of me," I whisper quietly.

"Probably not," he agrees without hesitation. It cuts too deep, and I force myself to walk away before I lose control of the building emotion. I will not cry on him. I plug my earbuds in, select random on my iPod, and have a quiet laugh to myself when Massive Attack's "Unfinished Sympathy" fills my ears, keeping me company all the way home.

*   *   *

"You don't look any better, Livy," Del says, giving me the once-over with concerned eyes. "Perhaps you should go home."

"No." I force a reassuring smile, but struggle terribly. Nan is at home, and I need to be distracted, not interrogated.

She was all smiles when I walked through the front door this morning, until she registered my face. Then the questions started, but I quickly escaped to my bedroom, leaving my grandmother pacing the landing outside my room, tossing the odd question through the door, all of which I brushed off. I shouldn't feel annoyed with Nan; I should reserve it all for Miller, but if she hadn't poked her old nose in and invited Miller to dinner, then last night wouldn't have happened and I wouldn't currently be in turmoil.

"I feel much better, honestly." I escape the kitchen and dodge Sylvie at the till, who's been trying to nail me down all morning. Luckily for me, we're busy, so I can evade all interrogation for the meantime and busy myself clearing tables and serving coffee.

On my break, I accept the tuna mayo sandwich that's handed to me by Paul, but choose to eat it on the go, knowing that taking a time-out will lure Sylvie over to press me for answers. It's cunning, but my head aches with constant thoughts of him and talking will certainly spur tears. I refuse to cry over a man, especially a man who can be so cold.

"Are you enjoying that?" Paul asks on a smile, tossing some wet lettuce leaves in a colander.

"Hmmm." I chew and swallow, then wipe my mouth of any stray mayonnaise. "It's delicious," I say truthfully, looking over the other half that I'm yet to eat. "There's something different about it."

"Yes, but don't ask me what because I'll never tell."

"Secret family recipe?"

"You've got it. Del will never let me leave as long as the Tuna Crunch is his bestseller and I'm the only sucker who knows how to make it." He winks and scatters the lettuce between the prepared mixed seeded bread slices that have been coated with Paul's secret recipe. "Here. These are for table four."

"Sure." I push my back through the swing doors of the kitchen, skulk past Sylvie, and head for table four. "Two Tuna Crunch sand-wiches on seeded," I say, sliding the plates onto the table. "Enjoy."

Both businessmen express their gratitude with a thank you and I leave them to eat, meeting Sylvie in the kitchen when I push my way back through the swing door. She has her hands on her hips. It's not a good sign.

"You don't look better, but you're not ill," she snipes, moving slightly to let me pass. "What gives?"

"Nothing." I sound way too defensive, and I immediately chas-tise myself for it. "I'm okay."

"He followed you out."

"What?" My shoulders tense. I know full well what Sylvie is talking about, but it's not an area of conversation that I want to indulge in. I feel raw, tender, and speaking of him will only enhance that.

"After you nearly passed out and Del sent you home, he fol-lowed you out. I would've come to find you, but I was kind of rushed off my feet. What happened?"

I still don't face her, choosing to take my time loading the dishwasher. I could leave, but that would mean facing her and I won't hold my breath that she'll let me pass. "Nothing happened. I walked away."

"Well, I figured as much when he returned with a face like thunder and turned up at the bistro yesterday."

He was angry? Strangely, that delights me. "There you have it, then," I flip casually, grabbing a tray but delaying my return to the bistro front. She's not finished yet and she's still in my way.

"He was with that woman again."

"I know."

"She was all over him."

I feel a lump forming in my throat. "I know."

"But he was clearly distracted."

Swinging around, I finally face her, discovering the expression that I knew I would: narrowed eyes and bright pink pursed lips. "Why are you telling me this?" I ask.

She shrugs, her short black bob skimming her shoulders. "He's bad news."

"I know that," I mutter. "Why do you think I walked away? I'm not stupid." I should slap myself for my obscenely inaccurate comment. I'm very stupid.

"You're moping." Her questioning eyes are burning holes through me, and quite rightly, too.

"I'm not moping, Sylvie," I argue feebly. "Do you mind if I get back to work?"

She sighs, moving out of my way. "You're too sweet, Livy. A man like that will eat you alive."

I close my eyes and take a deep breath as I move past Sylvie. She doesn't need to know about last night's cozy family dinner, and I wholeheartedly wish that there was nothing to tell.

* * *

My week doesn't improve. Nan has been back to Harrods twice with the excuse that George thought her special pineapple upside-down cake was so delicious, she simply had to make it again...twice. Her secret hopes of bumping into Miller on the off chance that he may be there buying more suits had nothing to do with her compulsion to spend thirty quid on two pineapples. I've avoided Gregory at all costs after receiving a terse voice mail from him advising me that Nan has been blabbering and he thinks I'm stupid. I know all of this.

I skip breakfast and slip out of the front door, eager to avoid Nan and even keener to get my Friday done and dusted. I have plans to lose myself in the grandeur of London this weekend, and I can't wait. It's just what I need.

I pace down the street, my long, black jersey dress swishing around my ankles, my face warm under the morning sunshine. As ever, my hair is doing what it damn well pleases, and today it's wavier than usual as I slept on it wet.

"Livy!"

Without any instruction, my pace quickens, not that I'm going to get very far. He sounds pissed off.

"Baby girl, you'd better stop right now or there will be trouble!"

I halt dead in my tracks, knowing that I'm already in trouble, and wait for him to catch up to me. "Morning!" My overenthusiastic greeting isn't going to wash, and when he lands in front of me, his handsome face distorted with displeasure, I can't help scowling back. "What?" I snap, making him jump back in shock. I feel irritated with my best friend, yet I have absolutely no right to be. It's Friday, but he's in ripped jeans and a tight T-shirt, and he's wearing a baseball cap. Where are his gardening clothes?

"Don't *what* me!" he snaps right back. "What happened to staying away?"

"I tried!" I screech. "I bloody tried, but we bumped into him in Harrods and Nan invited him to bloody dinner!"

Gregory jumps back some more, stunned by my unusual outburst, but his chiseled, scowling face softens. "You didn't have to leave with him, though," he points out softly. "And you definitely didn't have to stay at his place."

"Well I did, and I bloody wish I hadn't."

"Ahh, Livy." He steps forward and wraps me in his arms. "You should have answered my calls."

"So you could just tell me off?" I mumble into his T-shirt. "I already know that I'm an idiot. I don't need it confirmed."

"It near on killed me to see Nan so excited," he says on a sigh. "Shit, Livy, she was ready to go buy a hat."

I laugh because if I didn't, I'd cry. "Please don't. I can't take it much more, Gregory. He only sat at her dinner table for an hour or two. She was gushing all over him, and now she's all confused and wondering why I'm not seeing him."

"Cocksucker."

"I keep telling you, you're the only cocksucker I know." I feel him laugh a little, but when he pulls me from his chest, his face is serious.

"Why did you leave with him?" he asks.

"I can't say no when he's with me," I sigh sullenly. "Things just happen."

"But you've not seen him all week?"

"No."

His blond brows rise. "Why not?"

Damn it, I want to say that I walked away off my own back, but Gregory will rumble me in a nanosecond. "It was wonderful, and then it was awful. He was sweet, and then he was an arsehole." I brace myself. "I told him about my mum."

I can see the surprise on Gregory's face, and there is definitely a bit of hurt mixed in there, too. He knows that I absolutely never speak of her, not even with him, and I know he wishes I did. He collects himself and forces the hurt plaguing his face to morph into contempt. "Cocksucker," he spits. "Complete knob-head. You need to be stronger, baby girl. A sweet thing like you will be walked all over by a man like that."

My nostrils flare and I bite my tongue to prevent my natural reaction to that statement from slipping past my lips. And fail. "Oh bollocks to the lot of you," I grumble, making him recoil in shock. I push past him and stomp off down the street.

"See, that's what I want more of. A little spunk!"

"Fuck off!" I yell, shocking myself with my vulgar language.

"Ooh, yes, carry on, you filthy-mouthed bitch!"

I gasp and swing around, finding him grinning from ear to ear. "Wanker."

"Cow."

"Tosser."

He grins some more. "Dog."

"Shirt lifter," I retort.

"Tart."

I recoil, horrified. "I am not a tart!"

He pales instantly, realizing his mistake. "Shit, Livy, I'm so sorry."

"Don't bother!" I storm off, my blood boiling with rage at his insensitive, careless remark. "And don't follow me, Gregory!"

"Arhhhh, I didn't mean it. I'm sorry." He scoops me up, preventing me from running away. "A stupid word slipped." He walks onward with me draped across his arms, and I reach up and pull his hair. "Twat."

Grinning, he leans down and kisses my cheek. "I had a date last Sunday."

"Another?" I roll my eyes and firm up my grip of his shoulders. "Who's the lucky guy this time?"

"Actually, it was our fourth date. His name's Ben." A thoughtful, dreamy look washes over Gregory's face, making me pay more attention. It's been a few years since he's had this look.

"And...," I push, wondering how he managed to keep four dates with the same man quiet. I can't challenge him on it, though. Not after my lack of sharing.

"He's cute. I might like you to meet him."

"Really?"

"Yes, really. He's a freelance events planner. I've told him all about you, and he'd like to meet you."

"Oh?" I tilt my head, and he gives me a shy smile. "Ohhhh...," I breathe.

"Yes, ohhhhh."

"Benjamin?"

"Nooo." He narrows playful eyes on me, continuing with his

even strides down the street with me still bobbing up and down in his arms. "Just Ben will do."

"Benjamin and Gregory," I muse thoughtfully. "It has a nice ring to it."

"Ben and Greg sounds much better. Why do you insist on calling me Gregory? Even Nan does it. It makes me sound like a poofter," he grumbles.

"You are a poofter!" I laugh, getting a set of teeth sunk into my neck for my trouble. "Stop it!"

"Come on." He sets me on my feet and links arms with me. "Let's get your sweet arse to work."

"Aren't you working today?"

"Nope. I finished my recent project early, and I have a haircut."

"Oh yeah?" I grin up at him. "A whole day off work for a haircut?"

"Shut up. I told you. I finished my project early."

I smile, wondering why I've alienated myself from my treasured Gregory all week. I feel a million times better already.

Chapter Fourteen

No one at work actually asks me if I'm all right because it's obvious that I am. Or are they just stunned into silence by my chirpiness? Am I being over-the-top? I don't even care. Gregory has lifted my spirits. I should've seen him earlier in the week.

"Service!" Paul yells, prompting me to skip over with my tray, ready to be loaded up. "What are you all smiley about?" he laughs, sliding a tuna crunch onto my tray.

Sylvie dumps a load of empties nearby and joins us by the hot plates. "Don't question it, Paul. Just embrace it."

"It's Friday." I shrug, twirling and sashaying out of the kitchen with a smile on my face. As I approach the table, I'm confronted with a huge beam, courtesy of Mr. Wide Eyed Luke. My good mood prevents me from being anything but polite, and I find myself smiling back at him. "Tuna crunch?"

"That's me," he pipes up as I slide it onto the table. "You look especially lovely today."

I roll my eyes, but I'm still smiling. "Thank you. Can I get you another drink?"

"No, I'm good." He sits back in his chair, his warm brown eyes friendly as they regard me. "I'm still after a date."

"You are?" I feel myself blush a little and in an attempt to hide it, I start clearing the next table.

"Can I take you out?"

I'm wiping the table furiously, my hand rotating just as fast as my mind. "Yes." The word falls from my mouth without me realizing, until I hear it with my own ears.

"Really?" He sounds as shocked as I feel.

The table is spotless, but it doesn't stop me from rubbing the cloth over the wood some more. Did I really just accept a date? "Sure," I confirm, shocking myself further.

"Great!"

I try to cool down my burning cheeks before I turn to face my...date. He's really smiling now, and he's scribbling down his number on a napkin. It draws an unwanted memory, which I quickly toss to the back of my mind. I can go on a date with Luke. Actually, I *need* to go on a date with Luke. "When were you thinking?"

"Tonight?" He looks up at me hopefully, handing me the napkin.

I take it, pushing my doubts away. I can't go on like I have, even more so after my encounters with Miller Hart. I need to start living, forget about him, my mother, and start living...sensibly. "Tonight," I confirm. "Time, place?"

"Eight outside Selfridges? There's a little bar down the side street. You'll love it."

"Great. I look forward to it." I collect my tray and leave Luke smiling around the first bite of his tuna crunch.

"Hey, you're not going to stand me up, are you?" he calls, his words muffled by his full mouth. That stupid little thing alone reminds me of manners and...

"I'll be there," I assure him on a smile, his mouthful of sandwich while he talks only spurring me on. He might not be in the same league as Miller Hart, but he's still cute, and his carefree attitude and lack of manners is even more reason to accept his offer.

When I push my way through the swing door, Sylvie's pink lips are smirking at me. "I'm so proud of you!" she sings in my face.

"Oh, stop it!"

"No, really, I am. He's cute and normal." She starts to help me unload the tray, the big smile on her face pulling one from me. "Think of it as new beginnings."

I frown, wondering if I should do exactly that. I've not known Sylvie for very long, although it seems like years. "I'm just going on a date, Sylvie."

"Oh, I know. But I also know that Olivia Taylor doesn't do dating. It's just what you need."

"What I need is for you to stop making such a fuss about it." I laugh. By *need*, she means what I *need* to get over someone, but I'm slowly concluding that I am, in fact, already over someone. Someone doesn't have a name. Someone doesn't even exist. Someone is long forgotten.

"Okay, okay." Sylvie holds her hands up, still grinning, still delighted. "What are you going to wear?"

I feel my face pale as I consider Sylvie's question. "Oh God, what *am* I going to wear?" My wardrobe is full of Converse in every color, piles and piles of jeans and endless tea dresses, but they are floaty and girly, not tight and sexy.

"Don't panic." She holds my shoulders and gives me serious eyes. "We'll go shopping after work. We'll only have an hour, but I think I'll come up with something."

I look down at Sylvie's skin-tight black jeans and chunky, studded boots and wonder if I *should* go shopping with Sylvie. But then I have a thought. "No, don't worry!" I break free of Sylvie's hold and hunt down my satchel, finding my phone. "Gregory is off work today. He'll come." I don't even consider that I may have offended Sylvie until she heaves an exasperated sigh of relief.

"Thank fuck for that!" She flops against the worktop. "I would've endured Topshop for you, Livy, but it would have been pure hell." Her brow puckers. "Gregory? As in a bloke?"

"Yes, my best friend. He's got terrific fashion sense."

She looks suspicious. "He's gay, isn't he?"

"Only eighty percent." I run out the exit door from the kitchen to the back alley and dial Gregory as I pace up and down.

"Baby girl!"

"I have a date tonight!" I blurt. "And I have nothing to wear. You have to help me!"

"With him?" Gregory spits. "I'm doing nothing except pinning you down. You're not going out with that prick!"

"No, no, no! It's Mr. Wide Eyes!"

"Who?"

"Luke. A guy who's been asking for a few weeks. I figured why not." I shrug to myself, and I can practically hear the excitement bubbling down the line before Gregory's even spoken. Then he does speak, confirming my suspicions.

"Oh my God!" he shrieks. "Oh my God, oh my God, oh my God! What time do you finish work?"

"Five. And I'm meeting Luke at eight."

"Buy an outfit and get you ready in three hours?" he gasps. "Bloody hell, it'll be a challenge, but it's doable. I'll meet you at work at five."

"Okay." I hang up and rush back into the kitchen before my absence is noticed by Del. It'll be a rush, but I have every faith in Gregory. He has impeccable taste.

* * *

As soon as Del's gone for the day, I run to grab my satchel and denim jacket, giving Sylvie a kiss on the cheek and throwing a wave at Paul, leaving them laughing in the kitchen.

"Good luck!" Sylvie calls.

"Thank you!" I burst into the fresh air and find Gregory waiting across the road.

He waves his arms frantically, signaling for me to hurry. "We have three hours to dress you, preen you, and deliver you to your date. That's my mission, and I choose to accept it." He grins and throws his arm around me, leading me quickly toward Oxford Street. "You look cheerful."

"I am," I admit. Surprisingly to me, I'm looking forward to going on a date. "Nice hair."

"Thanks." His hand glides over his scalp on a smile, prompting one from me.

"Isn't it sad that I've never actually been on a date?"

"Yes, it's tragic."

I nudge him in the side. "You've been on enough for both of us."

"Yes, that's tragic, too. But I might be a one-man guy soon."

"Aren't you already?" I ask, hoping Gregory isn't about to be crapped all over. He's stupidly good looking, and should probably hold all of the cards when it comes to a relationship, but he's too nice and he's paid for it in the past. He's a player when single but devoted when captured.

"You have to remain open to offers, Livy." He sounds resolute, but that look is there again, and it's screaming *fallen*.

*　　*　　*

I'm utterly exhausted by the time we get home. I've spent practically every penny I've earned since working at Del's, and I have three outfits—all short and not really me—and two pairs of shoes, neither of which are Converse. It's a waste. I'll probably only wear one pair of the shoes this evening, and as for the dresses . . . well, I don't know what I was thinking.

I'm standing in my towel in front of my wardrobe, running my eyes over each of my new outfits.

"It has to be the black one." Gregory skates his hand down the short tight dress on a sigh. "Yes, this one and the black pointed stilettos."

I feel a little overwhelmed as I look at the dress, then down to the shoes. It's been a long, long while since I've worn heels. "I'm scared," I murmur quietly.

"Rubbish!" He dismisses my worry on a snort and heads for the bed, picking up some of the fancy underwear he forced me to buy. We both wasted at least twenty minutes in La Senza arguing over the lacy matching sets, one of which he's currently having a thorough inspection of. He's right, though. I can't wear white cotton under these sorts of dresses. "You know, I might be eighty percent gay, but there's something about a woman in sexy underwear." He chucks the set at me. "Put them on, then."

I keep my mouth shut for fear of objecting and shimmy into the knickers while deftly holding my towel in place. The bra's not so straightforward, and I end up turning away from Gregory, who doesn't seem in the least bit perturbed by the potential of copping a load of my nakedness.

He starts laughing as he watches me battling with the bra, and I grumble to myself, not amused by his amusement as I arrange my poor excuse of a chest into the cups. I look down, surprised to see something close to cleavage.

"See," Gregory says, grabbing the towel and whipping it away. "Push-up bras are the best things ever invented."

"Gregory!" I cross my arms over my chest, feeling shy and exposed, as he moves to stand in front of me.

His eyes are slightly bugged as he drags them down my petite frame. "Fucking hell, Livy!"

"Stop it!" I attempt in vain to steal the towel back, but he's having none of it. "Give me it!"

"You look steaming." His mouth is open, his eyes wide.

"You're supposed to be gay!"

"I still appreciate a woman's form, and you've got form, baby girl." He throws the towel on the bed. "If you can't stand in front of me in your underwear, then who can you?"

"I'm going on a date, nothing more." I escape Gregory's appreciative stare and grab my hair dryer. "Will you stop looking at me?"

"Sorry." He seems to shake himself back to life before plugging in some hair styling device: straighteners, I think. "What are you going to drink?"

The question catches me off guard. I've not thought that far ahead. Accepting a date, getting ready for the date, and getting myself *to* the date has been enough for me to get my head around. What I'm going to drink and talk about while I'm actually *on* the date hasn't entered my head. "Water!" I shout over the roar of my hair dryer.

He recoils, a disgusted look all over his face. "You can't go on a date and drink water!"

I'm scowling across the room at him, not that he's bothered. "I don't need alcohol."

His shoulders drop dramatically, as does his arse to my bed. "Livy, have a glass of wine."

"Listen, the fact that I'm going out with a man should be enough, so don't start pressing me on drinking." I flip my head upside down and blast my blond everywhere. "Baby steps, Gregory," I add, thinking that I need to keep my wits about me, and alcohol won't help me do that. But I didn't need alcohol in the equation to make me lose my mind in the company of Miller Ha...

I throw my head back up in the hope of physically tossing the thought from my mind. It works, but it has nothing to do with head tossing and everything to do with Gregory gawking at me.

"Sorry!" he blurts, immediately busying himself with unpacking my shoes.

I drop my dryer and look dubiously at the straighteners that are steaming on a heat mat on the carpet. They look dangerous. "I think I might leave my hair."

"Oh no," he pouts. "I've always wanted to see your hair straight and sleek."

"He won't recognize me," I complain. "You're sticking me in that dress and these heels, and now you want to iron my hair, too." I start rubbing some E45 into my face. "He asked *me* on a date, not the polished thing that you're trying to create."

"You wouldn't be a polished thing," he objects. "You'd be you, just enhanced. I think you should surrender all decisions to me." He stands and fetches the dress, taking it off the hanger.

"How do you know what a man wants from a woman?"

"I've gone out with women."

"Not for over two years," I point out, remembering each and every time that he has, and it was always after a breakup with a guy.

He shrugs nonchalantly and holds the dress up. "How did this become about me?" he asks. "Shut up and slip that neat little body into this delightful dress." He jiggles his eyebrows cheekily, and I reluctantly drag myself over to him, letting him put the dress over my head and down my body. "There." He steps back and gives me the once-over while I slip my feet into the painfully high shoes.

I look down at myself, seeing the black dress clinging to every curve that I *don't* have and my feet at a stupidly high angle. I feel unsteady. "I'm not sure," I say, feeling far too overdressed. When Gregory doesn't respond to my wavering, I look up, seeing a dumbstruck face. "Do I look stupid?"

He snaps his gaping mouth shut and seems to mentally slap himself. "Urh...no...I..." He starts laughing. "Fucking hell, I have a hard-on."

I huff, flaming red instantly. "Gregory!"

"I'm sorry!" He starts adjusting his groin, prompting me to swing around to escape the view, which subsequently prompts me to stagger in the stupid heels. I hear Gregory gasp. "Livy!"

"Shit!" I go over on my ankle, losing a shoe, then proceed to hop around like a demented kangaroo. "Shit, that hurt!"

"Oh God!" Gregory is clearly in pieces behind me, the bastard. "Are you okay?"

"No!" I snap, kicking the other shoe off. "I'm not wearing them!"

"Oh, don't be like that. I'll control myself."

"You're bloody gay!" I yell, picking up a shoe and waving it around above my head. "I can't walk in these."

"You've hardly tried!"

"You put them on and tell me how easy it is." I chuck the shoe at him, and he laughs as he catches it.

"Livy, that would make me a drag queen."

"Be a drag queen, then!"

Gregory loses control altogether and collapses on my bed in a helpless fit of laughter. "You're making me cry!"

"Bastard," I spit, yanking the dress off. "Where are my Converse?"

"You can't." He dives up, immediately noticing that the dress has been ditched, as well as the shoes. "Oh no! You looked fabulous." His eyes run down my semi-nakedness.

"Yes, but I couldn't walk," I mutter, stomping over to my wardrobe. This irritation is a good enough reason alone to maintain my boring lifestyle. I've been bombarded with new situations recently, and for the most part I've mainly felt angry, pissed off, or useless throughout. Why the hell am I doing this to myself?

I viciously yank down a cream layered dress and shove it on, quickly realizing that my underwear is black and you can see the damn stuff through my dress, so I set about removing everything all over again, telling Gregory to stick his face in the pillow so I can do it all quickly and comfortably. When I'm done, I have my white cotton underwear back on, my cream dress in place, my denim jacket over the top, and my navy Converse gracing my feet. I feel so much better.

"Ready," I declare, quickly brushing over my cheeks with some blusher and putting a pink sheen on my lips.

"What a waste of a shopping trip," Gregory mutters, removing himself from my bed and strolling over. "You looked lovely."

"Don't I now?"

"Well, yes, you always look lovely, but you looked less of a walkover in the black number. It would've empowered you—given you confidence."

"I'm happy the way I am," I counter, wondering if that's strictly true. I don't even know anymore. My head's not my own in recent weeks. It's thinking things I never considered and making my body do things I definitely never considered.

"I just want you to express yourself a little more, like you did just then." He grins at me as he fluffs my hair.

"You want me to be mad?" I ask, because that's exactly how I feel. Moody. Irritable. Pressured.

"No, I want some sass to surface. I know it's there."

"Sass is dangerous." I brush him off and transfer my things from my satchel to a more suitable across-the-body bag. "Let's go before I change my mind," I mutter, ignoring his grumbles of disapproval as I march out onto the landing.

I thank all of the Converse gods as I walk down the stairs in my stable flats, but soon stop smiling when I find Nan pacing restlessly at the bottom of them. George is moving out of her way each time she performs an about-turn, pinning himself against the wall of the hallway to avoid being run down.

"Here she is!" George says, clearly relieved that his body dodging will soon come to an end. "And doesn't she look lovely?"

I halt on the bottom step and watch Nan give me an all-over assessment, then flick her eyes over my shoulders, homing straight in on Gregory. "You said heels," she says in disbelief. "You said a lovely black dress and heels to match."

"I tried," Gregory mumbles grumpily behind me, and I swing around to fire an accusing glare at him. He meets my accusing glare with his own. "You try avoiding a Nan-style interrogation."

I sigh my frustration and take the last step, pushing my way past my grandmother, keen to escape all of the bloody fuss. "Bye."

"Have fun!" Nan calls. "Is this one really better than that Miller?" I hear her ask quietly.

"Much!" Gregory assures her confidently. It just makes me walk faster. How the hell does he know? He's not met either of them.

"See," George laughs. "Now where's my pineapple upside-down cake?"

I march onward, grateful for my flats and looking forward to my date because it gets me out of the house and away from Nan, an uncharitable thought, but Lord, give me strength! A quiet life was an easy life, kind of, except for the odd grumble about my reclusiveness. Now it's a constant stream of questions and brain picking. It's painful.

"Livy!" Gregory catches up to me as I reach the end of the road. "You look dead cute."

"You don't have to try to make me feel better. I feel fine, no thanks to you."

"You're grumpy today."

"No thanks to you." I let out a girly squeal as I'm hoofed from the pavement. "Will you pack it in!"

"Sass," he says simply. "You can have it without being a bitch, you know."

"You deserve it. Put me down."

He places me on my feet, and straightens me out. "I'm headed in the other direction, so I'll love you and leave you." He leans down and pecks my cheek. "Be good."

"That's a really stupid thing to say to me." I jab his shoulder in an attempt to restore our normality.

"Well, yes, it usually would be, but my best friend has developed a stupid gene in recent weeks." He jabs my shoulder right back.

He's right; I have, but I've also lost that gene again, so he has nothing to worry about, and neither do I. "I'm going on a friendly date, that's all."

"And a little kiss wouldn't hurt, but no hanky-panky until I've met him. I need to check him out." He grabs my shoulders and turns me around. "Off you trot."

"I'll call you," I say as I start to leave him behind.

"Only if you're not too busy," he calls back, earning himself a roll of my eyes that he can't see to appreciate.

*   *   *

It's ten minutes to eight when I arrive at Selfridges. Oxford Street is still bustling, even at this hour, so I prop myself up against the shop front and watch the world go by, making my best effort to look casual and at ease. I know I'm failing.

After five minutes of waiting, I decide that fiddling with my phone will make me look much more relaxed, so I rootle through my bag and start a text to Gregory, just to pass the time.

How long do I wait?

I click send, and my phone starts ringing almost immediately, Gregory's name flashing up. "Hi," I answer, grateful he called because actually *being* on the phone is an even better way to appear relaxed.

"He's not there yet?"

"No, but it's not even eight."

"Doesn't matter!" he exclaims. "Damn it, I should've made you late. It's the number one rule of dating."

"What is?" I ask, changing my standing position to lean on my shoulder rather than my back.

"The woman has to be late. Everyone knows that." He doesn't sound happy.

I smile to the crowd of strangers scurrying by. "So what happens when the two people dating are men? Who's the one to be late then?"

"Very funny, baby girl. Very funny."

"It's a perfectly reasonable question."

"Stop diverting the conversation to me. Is he there yet?"

I glance back, my eyes darting around briefly, but find no Luke. "Nope. How long should I wait?"

"I hate him already," Gregory grumbles. "Two pricks in two weeks. You're on fire!"

I laugh to myself, silently agreeing with my aggravated friend, although I'll never tell him so. "Thank you." I roll onto my back against the glass and sigh. "You've still not answered my question. How long should I . . ." My tongue dries up in a second as I watch a car cruise past, my head turning to follow its path down Oxford Street. There must be thousands of black Mercedes driving around London, so why am I so drawn to this one? The tinted windows? The AMG plate on the wing?

"Livy?" Gregory snaps me back to the present. "Livy, you there?"

"Yes," I say, watching as the Mercedes slows and then pulls a highly illegal three-point turn in the road before driving back toward me.

"Is he there?" Gregory asks.

"Yes!" I squeak. "I should go."

"Better late than never," he mutters. "Have fun."

"Will do." I barely push the words past the lump in my throat and quickly hang up, turning to face the other way, like it might look as if I'm unaware. Should I leave? What if Luke turns up and I've gone? You can't park on Oxford Street so he can't stop. If it's even him. It might not be. Shit, I know it is. I push my body away from the glass and quickly weigh up my options, but before my brain makes an informed decision, my feet are in action and carrying me away from my distress. I walk with purpose, taking deep breaths, concentrating hard on maintaining my even pace.

I close my eyes when I see the car pass me slowly, and only reopen them again when I'm barged from the side by an impatient businessman, who proceeds to ridicule me for not looking where I'm going. I can't even find the power to apologize, instead picking up my stride again, but then I notice the car has stopped and I stop, too. I watch as the door to the driver's side opens. His body flows from the car like liquid, rising to his full height before pushing the door shut and buttoning up the jacket of his gray suit. His black shirt and tie complement his dark waves, and his jaw is covered in stubble. He looks magnificent. I feel conquered, and he hasn't even made it to me yet. What does he want? Why has he stopped?

I fight some balanced thoughts into my mind and I'm in action again, turning away from him and walking fast. "Livy!" I can hear his footsteps coming after me, the sound of expensive shoes beating heavily on the concrete behind me, even over the bustling sounds of London surrounding me. "Livy, wait!"

The jolt of surprise that kicked my feet into action turns to irritation as I listen to him shouting my name, like I owe him the time of day. I stop and face him, feeling more determined than irritated when I finally meet his eyes.

He skids to a stop on his fancy shoes and straightens his jacket out, just standing in front of me, making no attempt to speak.

I'm not saying anything, because I have nothing to say, and, in fact, I hope he doesn't speak because then I won't have to encounter those lips moving slowly and listen to the smoothness of that voice. I'm safer when he's silent and unmoving . . . or remotely safer than when he's touching me or talking to me, at least.

I'm not safe at all.

He steps forward, like he knows what I'm thinking. "You're waiting for someone. Who?"

I don't answer, just keeping my eyes glued to his.

"I asked you a question, Livy." He takes another step forward, his growing closeness registering as a danger, yet I stay exactly where I am when I should be moving away. "You know I hate repeating myself. Please answer."

"I have a date." I try for cool detachment, but I'm not certain I've completely succeeded. I'm too pissed off.

"With a man?" he asks, and I can practically see his hackles rise.

"Yes, with a man."

His normally expressionless face is suddenly a wealth of emotion. He's very clearly not happy. The knowledge spurs my self-assurance. I don't want to feel the small pang of hope that's fluttering in my stomach, but there is no denying it's there.

"Is that all?" I ask, my voice stronger.

"So now you're dating?"

"Yes," I say simply, because I am, and like an omen, I hear the not-so-familiar calling of my name.

"Livy?" Luke appears by my side.

"Hi." I lean in and kiss his cheek. "Are you ready?"

He flicks his eyes to Miller, who I notice is rigid and silent as he watches me greet Luke. "Hi." Luke holds his hand out to Miller, and I'm surprised when he takes it, giving Luke a firm shake, his manners never failing him.

"Hello. Miller Hart." He nods, jaw tense, and I see my date

wince before Miller quickly releases Luke's hand, then rearranges his perfectly neat jacket. I'm definitely not imagining the subtle rise and fall of his broad chest or his eyes darkening with anger. I can almost hear something ticking inside of him, like an unexploded bomb. He's mad and his murderous eyes nailed on Luke begin to worry me.

"Luke Mason," Luke replies, shaking his hand. "Nice to meet you. Are you a friend of Livy's?"

"No, just an acquaintance." I jump in quickly, eager to remove Luke from such palpable fury. "Let's go."

"Great." Luke holds his arm out for me to link, and I do, letting him lead me away from the horridly awkward situation. "I thought we'd try The Lion around the corner. It's had a makeover, apparently," Luke tells me, looking over his shoulder.

"Great," I reply, not helping myself from glancing over my shoulder, too, and instantly wishing that I hadn't. He's standing, just watching me walk away with another man, his face cold, his body rigid.

We soon turn a corner, and when I feel Luke look down at me I feel guilt start to take hold. I don't know why. A date, that's all. And is my guilt because of an oblivious Luke or a clearly affected Miller?

"He was a bit of a strange one," Luke muses. I hum my agreement, pulling his gaze down to me. "You look lovely," he says. "I'm sorry I'm a few minutes late. I should've skipped the cab and jumped on the Tube."

"Don't worry. You're here now."

He smiles, and it's a cute smile, one that warms his already friendly face. "It's just up here, look." He indicates up the street. "I'm hearing great things."

"It's new?" I ask.

"No, just refurbished. It's now a wine bar, not a typical London pub." He checks for traffic and quickly guides me across the road. "I do love a good old-fashioned pub, though."

I smile, thinking that I could definitely imagine Luke in a spit and sawdust pub, drinking a pint and laughing with his mates. He's normal, just a regular guy—the type of guy who I should be investing in, now it's become apparent that I am, in fact, investing my time in men.

Luke opens the door, ushering me in, and then leads me to a table at the rear of the bar on a raised mezzanine floor. "What would you like to drink?" he asks, indicating for me to sit.

It's that question, and while I felt perfectly fine about asking for a water when I was with Gregory, I now feel young and stupid. "Wine," I say quickly before I can convince myself that it's a bad idea. Besides, I feel like I need a drink. Damn Miller Hart.

"Red, white, pink?"

"White, thank you." I try to appear unaffected and completely comfortable in my surroundings, but seeing Miller again has nudged me back to unbalanced and unsure. I'm wobbly, thinking of his face when he saw Luke.

"White it is." Luke smiles and heads for the bar, leaving me alone at the table, feeling like a fish out of water. The bar is busy, mostly with men in suits who look like they've come straight from the office. Their loud chatter and laughing is evidence of their length of time here, too, with ties loosened and jackets disappearing.

I appreciate the stylish décor of the place, but not the noise. Shouldn't a first date be something to eat somewhere quiet where you can talk and get to know each other?

"Here." A glass of wine slides toward me, and I instinctively slide back on my chair instead of picking it up and thanking him for it. Luke sits opposite me, pint in hand, and takes his first swig, gasping appreciatively before placing it down. "I'm really glad you agreed to have a drink with me," he says. "I was about to give up."

"I'm glad I came."

He smiles. "So tell me about yourself."

I force my hands to join and rest on the table where I fiddle with my ring and give myself a quick mental kick up the arse. Of course he's going to ask questions. That's what normal people do on dates, not offer unreasonable propositions. So taking a deep breath, I bite the bullet and divulge a piece of me to someone new, something that I've never done, or ever thought I would do.

"I've only recently started working at the bistro. I was looking after my grandmother before that." It's not much, but it's a start.

"Oh, did she die?" he asks, looking uncomfortable.

"No," I laugh. "She's far from dead, trust me."

Luke laughs, too. "That's a relief. For a moment there I thought I'd put my foot in it. Why were you looking after her?"

This question isn't so easy to answer and the truth too complicated. "She was unwell for a while, that's all." I'm ashamed of myself, but at least I've shared a *little* piece of me.

"I'm sorry."

"Don't be. She's fine now," I say, thinking Nan would love to hear me admit that.

"So what do you do for fun?"

My hesitance is obvious. I do nothing, in truth. I don't have an army of girlfriends, I don't socialize, I don't have any hobbies, and because I've never put myself in a situation where someone might want to know, I've never considered how utterly cut off and isolated I actually am. I always knew it—God, I aimed for it, but now, when I want to come across as an interesting person, I'm stumped. I have nothing to offer this conversation. I have nothing to offer a friendship or a relationship.

I panic. "I go to the gym, go out with my friends."

"Oh, I do the gym at least three times a week. Which one do you go to?"

It's getting worse. My lies are leading to further questioning, which means further lies. This is not the best way to start a friendship. I take my wine and raise it to my lips, a desperate tactic to buy me more time while I frantically search my mind for a local gym. I can think of none. "The one in Mayfair."

"Virgin?"

The relief of Luke answering my question for me is obvious. "Yes, Virgin."

"I go there! I've never seen you."

I'm in physical pain. "I tend to go pretty early." I need to divert this conversation quickly before I tell any more lies. "What about you? What do you do?"

He accepts my request for information and dives right in with a detailed report of him and his life. Over the next half hour, I learn so much about Luke. He has a lot to tell, and I don't doubt that all he's saying is the truth and as interesting as it seems, unlike my poor attempt to express me and my life. He's a stockbroker and lives with his mate, Charlie, after splitting with his girlfriend of four years, but he's in the process of buying his own place. He's twenty-five, far closer to me in age, and genuinely a nice, stable, sensible bloke. I like him.

"So no ex-boyfriend I should be wary of?" he asks, finishing his pint.

I'm enjoying listening to him. I'm engrossed, contributing the odd opinion or thought, but it's mainly Luke talking, and I'm happy with that.

Until now.

"No." I shake my head and take a tiny sip of my wine.

"There must be someone," he laughs. "A girl who looks like you."

"I was looking after my grandmother. I didn't have time for dating."

He slumps back in his chair. "Wow! I'm stunned."

My relaxed state has been shifted back to uncomfortable now the conversation has been reverted back to me. "Don't be," I say quietly, fiddling with my glass.

The look on his face tells me he's curious, but he doesn't press further. "Okay." He smiles. "I'll get another drink. Same again?"

"Yes, thanks."

He nods thoughtfully, probably wondering what the hell he's doing wasting his time on a guarded, ambiguous waitress, and makes his way to the bar, shifting through the crowd to get to the front. Letting out an aggravated sigh, I flop back on my chair and twirl my glass, scolding myself for...everything. My life approach, focus, and direction need some serious rethinking. But I don't know where to start.

I jump a mile when I feel hot breath in my ear and a firm grip of my nape. "Come with me."

I stiffen under his hold, my eyes darting toward the bar to see where Luke is. I can't see him, but that's not to say he can't see me.

"Get up, Livy."

"What are you doing?" I ask, ignoring the heat that's being injected into the flesh of my neck from his touch.

He takes a grip of my upper arm with his free hand and pulls me to my feet, then starts pushing me toward the back of the bar. "I haven't a fucking clue what I'm doing, but I can't seem to stop myself from doing it."

"Miller, please."

"Please what?"

"Please stop doing this." I'm begging quietly when I should be fighting him off and slapping his face. "I'm on a date."

"Don't say that." He grinds the words out and I'm sure if I could see his face, it would look pissed off. But I can't see his face because he's behind me and his grip on my nape is preventing me from turning. He pushes on, leaving me no choice but to scuttle to keep up with his long, determined strides.

The fire exit door is pushed open and kicked closed, and I'm spun around and pushed gently up against the wall, his hard body pushing into me. "Are you going to sleep with him?" His lips are straight, his eyes piercing. He's still mad.

Of course I'm not, but that has nothing to do with him. "That's none of your business." I raise my chin in a little act of defiance, fully aware that I'm provoking him. I could've said no, but I'm too curious about what he's going to do. I'm not falling to my knees to please him, to tell him what he wants to hear.

I want to, though.

I want to swear that I'll never look at another man again, as long as he worships me forever. His tall body flush against mine, his clear eyes burning into me, and his parted lips releasing subtle steams of air are all coaxing those inconceivable feelings to the surface. I'm starting to quiver under him.

I want him.

He brings his lips closer to mine. "I asked you a question."

"And I'm choosing not to answer," I breathe, pushing myself farther back. "I've had to endure seeing you on a date more than once."

"I've explained that a hundred times. You know how much I hate repeating myself."

"Then perhaps you should explain yourself better," I retort.

"Why is there a glass of wine on your table?"

"None of your business."

"I'm making it my business." He presses in farther, pushing a breathy gasp from my lips. "You're planning on sleeping with him, and I'm not going to let that happen."

I turn my head away from him, losing the desire and gaining some irritation. "You can't stop me." I don't know what I'm saying.

"You still owe me four hours, Livy."

My head swings back toward him in shock. "You expect me to commit another four hours to you, just so you can turn cold and hard-hearted on me again? I shared something with you. You made me feel safe."

His lips purse and his breathing becomes heavier, more forced, like he's trying to control himself. "You *are* safe with me," he growls. "And yes, I do expect you to give me more. I want the rest of the time that you owe me."

"You're not going to get it," I proclaim confidently, disgusted with his absurd demand. "Do you really think I owe you anything?"

"You're coming home with me."

"No, I'm not." I fight the urge to scream *yes*. "And you didn't answer *my* question."

"I'm choosing not to." He hunkers down and levels his lips with mine. "Let me taste you again."

The desire is fighting its way forward. "No."

"Let me take you to my bed."

I shake my head desperately and clench my eyes shut, wanting to let him, but knowing it would be a gargantuan mistake. "No, not so you can toss me out again." I feel the warmth of his mouth closing in, but I don't turn my head.

I wait.

I let it happen.

And when the moist softness of his lips connects with mine, I go lax and open up to him on a low moan, my hands finding his shoulders, my head tilting to give him full access. I blank out. My intelligence has been blocked again.

"There are sparks," he mumbles, "full-on, electric sparks, and we're creating them." He pecks my lips. "Don't deprive us of this." He kisses his way into my neck and nibbles up to my ear. "Please."

"Just four hours?" I whisper.

"Stop overthinking."

"I'm not overthinking. I can barely think at all when you're near me."

"I like that." He encases my neck with his palms and tilts my face up. His stunning features cripple me. "Let it happen."

"I already did, more than once, and you turned distant on me every time. Will it be like that again?"

"No one knows what's going to happen in the future, Livy." His lips move slowly, holding my attention at his mouth.

"That's a poor answer," I murmur. "And *you* can tell me what will happen because you're in control of it." Annoyingly, I've laid my cards—I've made it perfectly clear that I want more than he's willing to give.

"I really can't." He moves in to kiss me, but I force my face to the side, leaving him hovering over my cheek. "Let me taste you, Livy."

I have to resist him, and his vague answer to my question gives me the strength I need to do it. "You've already had too much." If I fall now, there will be no getting up. By accepting this, I'm giving him the power to turn his back after he's taken what he wants, and I would never have a valid reason to hold it against him, because I allowed it . . . again.

"Have you?" he asks. "Have you had enough of me, Livy?"

"Too much." I push him away. "Way too much, Miller."

He curses and runs his hand through his hair. "I'm not letting you go home with that man."

"And how will you stop me?" I ask quietly. He doesn't want me, but he doesn't want anyone else to have me either. I don't understand him, and I'm not going to let him swallow me up again, just so he can spit me back out.

"He won't make you feel like I can."

"You mean used?" I retort. "You make me feel used. I've never exposed myself emotionally to a man before, and I did you. I've built up a pile of regrets in my life, Miller. And you're at the top of it."

"Don't say things you don't mean." He reaches forward and runs his knuckles across my cheek. "How can you regret something that was so beautiful?"

"Easily." I take his hand from my cheek and drop it gently to his side. "I can regret it easily when I know I'll never have it again." I shuffle past him, ensuring there's no contact, and start my journey home.

"You can have it again," he calls. "We can have that again, Olivia."

"Not just for four hours," I reply, clenching my eyes shut. "I'd rather not have it at all." My feet are moving, but I can't feel them, and I'm vaguely aware that I have a date inside the bar, who's certainly wondering where I've got to. But I can't go back inside and feign a good mood, not when I'm feeling so utterly broken. So I text Luke a feeble excuse about Nan falling ill. Then I drag myself home.

Chapter Fifteen

How did it go?" Gregory asks when I call him the next morning. No "hello" or "how are ya doing?"

"He's nice," I admit, "but I don't think I'll be seeing him again."

"Why aren't I surprised?" he grunts, as I hear shuffling in the background.

"Where are you?"

There's a lengthy silence, then a few more shuffles, and definitely the sound of a door closing. "I caught up with Ben last night," he whispers.

"Oh yeah?" I grin down the phone. "Dirty stop out."

"It wasn't like that. We went out and had coffee back at his place."

"And breakfast."

"Yeah, yeah, and breakfast." He's smiling around his words, making my own grin widen. "Listen. You know I said Ben wanted to meet you?"

"I do recall."

"Well, there's an opening of a nightclub tonight. Ben's been planning it for weeks and he's invited me. He wants you to join us."

"Me?" I blurt. "In a nightclub?"

"Yes, come on. It'll be fun. It's a dead plush place called Ice.

Please say yes." His beseeching voice won't shift me. I can't think of anything worse than subjecting myself to a London nightclub. And anyway, three's a crowd.

"I don't think so, Gregory." I shake my head to myself.

"Oh, baby girl," he groans. If I could see him, I know he'd be pouting. "It'll take your mind off things."

"What makes you think my mind needs taking off things?" I ask. "I'm fine."

He almost growls. "Cut the crap, Livy. I'm not taking no for an answer. You're coming and that's it. And there will be no Converse, either."

"Then I'm definitely not coming," I grumble. "You're not putting me in those heels again."

"Yes, you are. And yes, I am!" he snaps. "You've got so much to offer the world, Livy. I'm not letting you waste any more time. This isn't a practice session, you know. One life, baby girl. Just one. You're coming out tonight, and you're going to make an effort of it, too. Put those heels on and walk around the house in them all day if that's what it takes. I'll be there at eight to pick you up. I expect you to be ready." He hangs up, leaving me with my phone at my ear and my mouth open, ready to object. He's never spoken to me like that before. I'm shocked, but wondering if I've just received the kick up the arse I deserve, and which has been a long time coming.

Too many years have been wasted, too much time spent pretending to be content with my closed off life. Not anymore. Miller Hart may have sent me into unfamiliar emotional turmoil, but he's also made me realize that I have so much more to offer the world. No more closing myself off and hiding away, too afraid to be vulnerable—too afraid to become my mother.

I jump off the bed and slip my feet into the black stilettos and start pacing around my room, concentrating on walking with poise and with my head held high, not looking down at the ridiculous angle that my usually flat feet are at. While I'm doing this, I search Google on my phone for local gyms—not Virgin—and I call to arrange an induction for Tuesday evening. Then I try the stairs, taking them carefully and at a slight angle to maintain my ladylike posture and gracefulness. I'm doing well.

Walking down the hall, I smile when I hit the wooden floor of the kitchen, having gotten here without a stumble, stagger, or slip.

Nan swings around at the sound of heels clicking on the floor, her mouth falling open.

"What do you think?" I ask, taking a little turn to demonstrate my stability, to both my nan and myself. "Obviously with a dress," I add, registering my pajama shorts.

"Oh, Livy." She clutches the tea towel to her chest on a sigh. "I remember the days when I pranced around in high heels like they were flats. I have bunions to prove it."

"I doubt I'll be prancing, Nan."

"Do you have another date with the nice young man?" She looks hopeful as she takes a seat at the kitchen table.

I'm not sure whether she means Miller, who she's met, or Luke, who she hasn't. "I have a date with two men tonight."

"Two?" Her old, navy eyes widen. "Livy, sweetheart, I know I said live a little, but I didn't . . ."

"Relax." I roll my eyes, thinking she should know better, but then again, her boring, introvert granddaughter has been out more times this week than in her whole life. "It's Gregory and his new boyfriend."

"How lovely!" she sings, but then her wrinkled brow puckers some more. "You're not going to one of those gay bars, are you?"

I laugh. "No, it's a new place uptown. Tonight's the opening, and Gregory's new fellow has been organizing it. He's invited me."

I can tell by her face that she's delighted, but she's going to make a fuss, anyway. "Nails!" she screeches, knocking me back a step in my heels.

"What?"

"You must paint your nails."

I look down at my short, tidy, bare nails. "What color?"

"Well, what are you wearing?" she asks, and I wonder if many twenty-four-year-olds seek this kind of advice from their grandmother.

"Gregory made me buy a black dress, but it's a little short and I'm sure I could've done with the next size up. It's tight."

"Nonsense!" She zooms up, all excited and enthusiastic about my night out. "I have pillar box red!"

She disappears from the kitchen and moves up the stairs, faster than I've ever known. It's only moments before she's back, shaking a bottle of red nail polish in her wrinkled hand.

"I save it for special occasions," she says, pushing me down onto a chair and taking one next to me.

I can do no more than watch as she takes her time, neatly coating each of my nails, blowing little streams of air over my fingers when she's done. Sitting back in her chair, she tilts her head and I follow her gaze down to my fingers, wriggling them for a few moments before bringing them closer and running my eyes over them. "They're very . . . red."

"It's very classy. You can't go wrong with red nails and a black dress." Her mind seems to wander, and I smile fondly at my grandmother, childhood memories of her and my gramps flooding my mind.

"Do you remember when Gramps took us to The Dorchester for your birthday, Nan?" I ask. I was ten years old and in complete awe of the affluence. Gramps wore a suit, Nan a floral two-piece skirt and jacket, and I was treated to a navy blue dungaree dress, which was covered in large white polka dots. Gramps always loved it when the women in his life wore navy blue. He said it made our already stunning eyes look like bottomless pits of sapphires.

My grandmother takes a long pull of air and forces a smile,

when I know that she really would like to shed a tear. "That was the first time I painted your nails. Granddad wasn't happy."

I return her smile, remembering all too well the stern word he had in her ear. "He was even less happy when you tinted my lips with your red lipstick."

She laughs. "He was a man of principles and set firmly in his ways. He didn't understand a woman's need to cake her face in makeup, which made it all the more difficult for him to deal with your moth . . ." She trails off and quickly starts screwing on the lid of the polish.

"It's okay." I place my hand over hers and give it a little squeeze. "I remember." I may have only been a small child, but I remember vivid shouting matches, slamming doors, and Gramps with his head in his hands on many occasions. I didn't understand it at the time, but maturity has brought it all home, making everything painfully clear. That and the journal I found.

"She was too beautiful and too easily led."

"I know." I agree, but I don't think she was easily led at all. I've concluded that that's what Nan has told herself over the years to deal with her loss. I'm happy to let her have that.

"Livy." She shifts her hand carefully to avoid smudging my polish, so she's the one gripping mine, and it's a firm grip—a reassuring grip. "Everything about you is your mother, but not this." She taps her temple with her index finger. "You mustn't be afraid of becoming her. It'll just be another life wasted."

"I know," I admit. My own underlying reasons to avoid a repeat of my mother's life are good enough, but remembering my grandparents' devastation has only ever sealed it.

"You've completely shut yourself down, Livy. I know I was, well, a little bit of a handful after your granddad died, but I'm fine now—have been for some time, sweetheart." She raises gray eyebrows at me, desperate for me to acknowledge it. "I'll never get over losing them both, but I can still live. You haven't experienced half of what life has to offer, Olivia. You were such a spirited child and teenager until you found—" She halts, and I know it's because she can't say the words. She's talking about the journal, the frighteningly vivid accounts of my mother's life.

"It was safer that way," I murmur.

"It was unhealthy that way, sweetheart." She lifts my hand and kisses it lovingly.

"I'm beginning to see that." I take a deep breath of confidence. "That man, the one who came for dinner—" I don't know why I don't use his name. "He unearthed something in me, Nan. It'll never go anywhere, but I'm glad I met him because he's made me realize what life could be if I let it."

I don't divulge any more than that, and I also don't confess that given the chance, I would have whatever that is with him, if only he would let me. It's not the sex; it's the connection, the feeling of complete refuge that beats anything I've attempted to achieve on my own. It defies sensibility, really. Miller Hart is irrational, arduous, and temperamental, but the times between those irritating moments are inconceivably blissful and serene. I want to, but I have no faith in finding those feelings with another man.

Nan looks at me thoughtfully, keeping her firm grip of my hand. "Why will it not go anywhere?" she asks.

I'm honest and she must see it for what it is, anyway. She's not stupid. "Because I don't think he's really available," I say quietly.

"Oh, Livy," Nan sighs. "We can't help who we fall for. Come here." She stands up and pulls me into her arms, giving me a big squeeze. The tension and uncertainty seems to drain right out of me under her hold. "In every experience we have in life, we have to find a positive. I can see many positives coming from your encounter with Miller, sweetheart."

I hum my agreement into her shoulder, but wonder if I'll be in any fit state to embrace these supposed opportunities. He's already successfully intercepted one date. If I'm going to continue to resist

Miller Hart, I need to maintain my willpower and grow some resilience. The sass the Taylor girls are renowned for has eluded me, but I'm on a mission to relocate it. It's there. It's popped up now and then recently, but I need to grab on to it and never let go.

*   *   *

I squint as a camera is shoved in my face and Nan blinds me with the flash. "Get a grip, Nan," I moan, pulling down the hem of my ridiculous dress. I've been standing in front of the mirror for twenty minutes deliberating on the dramatic transformation. All day, all bloody day, I've spent waxing, plucking, painting, smoothing, and straightening. I'm exhausted.

"See, George!" Nan snaps a few more shots. "Sassy!"

I roll my eyes at a smiling George and pull my hem down again. "Stop it now." I push the camera from my face, feeling like a teenager going to prom. It was inevitable, but the fuss is just making me feel even more conspicuous.

"You look spectacular, Livy!" George laughs, taking the camera from Nan and ignoring her appalled glare. "Leave the poor woman alone, Josephine."

"Thank you, George," I say, again pulling down my dress.

"Stop tugging at your dress." Nan smacks my hands away. "Walk tall, chin high. Keep fidgeting and you'll look out of place and uncomfortable."

"Oh God, I'm going." I grab my stupidly small purse and make for the door, desperate to escape the over-the-top reactions to my...enhanced look. I slam the door harder than I mean to and click on my heels down the path, hearing Nan shout at George as I do. I smile, pull my shoulders back, and set on my way, shoving my purse under my arm and resisting the urge to pull the hem of my dress down again.

I'm only a few paces into my strut when I see Gregory in the distance, walking toward me. He falters slightly mid-stride, and I know that if I was close enough, I would see him squinting. Strangely, this reaction doesn't make me feel conspicuous; it makes me feel bold, so I raise my chin and make my best attempt of impersonating a model on the catwalk. I don't know if I pull it off, but it makes Gregory grin from ear to ear and wolf whistle from fifty yards away.

"Hot stuff!" He halts and spreads his legs, holding his hands out to me. "Fuck me, I'll be fighting them off!"

I don't even blush. I perform a perfectly executed twirl before throwing my arms around his neck. "I've been practicing all day."

"I can tell." He removes me from his body and runs his eyes up and down me, then smoothes my hair and smiles. "Straight and sleek. You look even more gorgeous than normal. Holy shit, look at those legs!"

I glance down at my legs, seeing curves I've never noticed before. "I feel good," I admit.

His arm falls around me and he pulls me into his side. "Well, you should, because you look amazing. Were you leaving without me?" he asks, starting us toward the main road to get a cab.

"No, I couldn't stand it in there anymore."

"I can imagine."

"You're looking very dapper." I give the sleeve of his pink shirt a little tug. "Trying to impress?" I glance up at him, finding a restrained grin. It makes me smile.

"I don't need to try, Livy." He's cocky. "Promise me something?"

"What?"

"You'll call me Greg tonight."

My smile widens and my arm snakes around his waist. "I'll call you Greg if you call me sassy lady."

He laughs. "Sassy lady?"

"Yes, baby girl, sweet girl, lovely girl—" I realize my error immediately.

"Who calls you sweet girl?"

"It doesn't matter." I put the stoppers on his inquiry immediately, and I also put the stoppers on my trail of thought. "The point is I'm not a girl."

"All righty, then. Sassy lady it is." He leans in and kisses my forehead. "You'll never know how happy I am right now."

"Because you're about to meet Benjamin?"

"It's Ben." He nudges me with his hip. "And no, not because of Ben. Because of you."

I look up at my treasured friend and smile. "I'm happy, too," I reply thoughtfully.

CHAPTER SIXTEEN

I have my first predicament in the short dress. Gregory slides from the cab with ease while I'm deliberating the best way to exit without flashing my fancy black knickers. I hold the hem of my dress with both hands, but my clutch drops from under my arm.

"Shit," I curse, scooping it up.

"You didn't practice this part, did you?" Gregory teases, putting one hand out for my bag and his other for my hand. "To the side. Step out to the side."

I hand over my purse and take his hand, following his instruction and lowering my right foot from the cab, finding it rather easy to exit without bending or giving any passersby an eyeful. "Thank you."

"As graceful as a swan." He winks and tucks my bag under my arm. "Ready?"

I refuel on confidence by taking a long inhalation of air. "Ready," I confirm, looking up at the building, seeing blue lights climbing up the glass front and a red carpet stretched down the side, with piles and piles of people waiting to be granted access.

I'm a little awestruck. Robin Thicke's "Blurred Lines" is pouring from the open glass doors, blue lights are flashing inside of the building, and doormen are keeping guard, marking clipboards before letting people in.

My hand is grasped and I'm pulled toward the front of the queue. I don't miss the filthy looks being thrown in our direction by the waiting clientele. "Gregory, there's a line," I whisper loudly, just as we land in front of a doorman holding a clipboard.

"Greg Macy and Olivia Taylor, guests of Ben White," Gregory states confidently, while I'm wincing under the fierce, stabbing eyes of the queue haters.

The doorman flicks the pages and glides down the list of names, eventually grunting and unhooking the thick rope linking two metal posts together. "Champagne bar's on the first floor at the back to your left. Mr. White is in the VIP area there."

"Thank you." Gregory nods, pulling me forward and pushing me gently through the door. "VIP area," he whispers in my ear. "And you just called me Gregory, sassy lady."

"I can't help it." I glance around, seeing various levels, all accessed by frosted glass stairs with illuminated blue lights guiding the way. Well-dressed people are everywhere, draped over the glass balustrades, not a pint of beer or a bottle in sight . . . except champagne. Behind all of the bars—three I've seen so far—are stacks and stacks of champagne bottles. I've never tasted the stuff, but it looks like I might soon.

"This way." Gregory escorts me up the glass steps, and the practical side of me can't help considering the damage that could be done if someone was to fall down them. My heels chink sweetly, though, and I look down and admire them, smiling and finding my butt swaying a little more. "Are you strutting?" Gregory giggles and smacks my backside. "Work it, baby girl."

I turn and scowl around my grin. "Sassy," I say, sticking my nose in the air, making my friend break out into a proper laugh.

"You most certainly are."

We reach the top of the stairs and head left as directed, reaching the champagne bar, which is ironic because all I saw at the other bars was champagne, too, making all of the bars champagne bars. "What would you like?"

"Coke," I say casually, looking around to avoid meeting my friend's outraged eyes.

He scoffs, but doesn't retaliate, instead leaning over the bar and ordering two glasses of champagne. The club is crammed full already, and there were at least a few hundred people in the line outside. Gregory wasn't kidding when he said it was dead plush, and the name reflects the ambiance. If it wasn't so full with people generating heat, I think I'd feel cold.

"Thank you." I take the glass being handed to me and waft it under my nose, taking a hit of a bitter smell. The strawberry floating on top takes my attention away from the aroma that's invading my nose and switches my mind to a place where I really don't want it to go.

Strawberries—British, for the sweetness.

Chocolate—at least eighty percent cocoa, for the bitterness.

Champagne to round it off.

I jump, a little startled when Gregory nudges me. "You okay?"

"Sure." I bat the thoughts of sweet and bitter away, along with the thought of Miller's hot tongue, slow-moving mouth, and hard, warm body. "Swanky place." I raise my glass a little and take the plunge, sipping my first ever taste of champagne. "Hmmm," I hum as the cool, sparkling liquid slides down my throat like silk.

"I cannot believe you've never tasted it." Gregory shakes his head as he tips the glass to his lips. "Heaven in a glass."

"It is," I agree, swirling it in my hand. "So he put you on the guest list, then?"

"Of course." He doesn't bite to my teasing. "I'm not queuing like cattle."

"You're a snob." I laugh. "Can I eat this strawberry?"

"Yes, but don't be plunging your fingers into the glass. Be a lady about it."

"How do I get it out, then?" I frown down at the narrow glass, wondering if my fingers will even fit in, but not daring to find out.

"Tip it in." Gregory demonstrates, tilting the flute to his lips and catching the strawberry in his mouth when it slides down the glass. "Best to wait until you've finished the champagne," he adds as he munches through the fruit.

"You have a big mouth." I sip more, not prepared to hurry my way through. Not drinking for so long has undoubtedly made me a lightweight.

"Oh, you have no idea, baby girl."

My nose wrinkles in distaste. "And I don't want to, Gregory," I retort, earning myself a grin through a glare.

"It's Greg!"

"Sassy lady!" I bump his thigh with my bum. "Where's Benjamin, anyway?" I ask, intrigued by the man who's captured my Gregory so fully.

"*Ben* is over there." He points discreetly with his glass, and I follow, looking through the crowd and seeing too many men to even begin to work it out. "Which one?"

"In the VIP area. Black suit, fair hair."

I flick my eyes over a crowd of men, all chatting in the closed off section near to the bar, laughing and regularly slapping each other's backs. City boys. Then my eyes land on a well-built man. I can literally see his muscles bulging through his suit. I'm surprised. He's not my best friend's usual taste, but again, it's been a while since I've had the pleasure of meeting one of Gregory's partners.

"He's..." I try to figure out the right words to describe him. Colossal. Pumped. "Large," I finally settle on.

"He's a fitness freak."

I look up and see Gregory with a small smile on his face as he gazes over to Ben. "So are you," I point out. Gregory's physique isn't anything to be ashamed of, not in the least, but Ben's . . . well, he's a mammoth of a fine man, but not to the point of being unattractive. I can see the appeal.

"I'm an amateur in the gym compared to Ben. We're talking every day, sassy lady."

"Are you going to go over?" I ask.

"No." He almost laughs. "I don't do the chasing, Livy."

"But you've been on dates. He invited you and put you on the guest list."

"Yes, he's chasing."

"Playing hard to get?"

"Treat them mean and all that." He places his fingertip on the base of my glass and applies a little pressure. "You'll get that strawberry now."

I look down and find I've sipped my way through my first glass and I can, indeed, get to the strawberry. I tilt and sigh as I sink my teeth into the sweet fruit. "Delicious." Just like the ones . . .

"Another?" He doesn't wait for my answer. He takes my hand and leads me to the bar, which is a giant plank of clear glass, displaying bottles of champagne on ice beneath. "Two more." He signals to the waiter, who swiftly presents Gregory with two full glasses, before our empties are taken and I'm being led away.

"Don't you have to pay?"

"Launch night. It's all free, but don't get too carried away."

"I won't."

"Oh, he's spotted us." Gregory starts to mildly fidget, and I look across the bar, finding Ben on his way over, smiling brightly. "Remember, sassy lady. It's Greg."

"Yes, yes," I say, keeping my eyes on Ben's big frame approaching.

"Greg," Ben says formally when he arrives. "Glad you could make it." He extends his hand and Gregory takes it, shaking firmly.

"Good to see you," my friend replies, dropping Ben's hand and shoving his in his pocket. "This is Livy."

I can't help my brow from wrinkling in confusion. "Hi."

"The famous Livy." He leans in and kisses my cheek. "Thank you for coming." He pulls away, and I get my first proper look at him as I focus on his face and not his formal actions or bulked physique. He's handsome in a rugged kind of way.

"Thank you for inviting me."

"No problem." He slaps Gregory on the shoulder. "I wish I could talk a bit more, mate, but there are a million people here to speak to. Maybe later?"

"Later." Gregory nods.

"Great." Ben smiles warmly at me. "Pleasure to meet you, Livy."

"Sure," I say quietly, flicking my eyes from one man to the other before watching Ben's back disappear into the crowd. "He's not come out!" I swing my body toward Gregory. "No one knows he's gay!"

"Shhhh," Gregory hisses. "He's waiting for the right time."

I'm stunned. Gregory has been up front and honest about his sexuality ever since he came out in high school, and he's ridiculed those who haven't been true to themselves. "These dates: you didn't go out at all, did you?"

Gregory refuses to meet my eyes, his fidgeting becoming less mild. He looks downright uncomfortable. "No," he replies quietly.

My heart squeezes a little for my best friend. This is no different from a woman seeing a married man, who constantly assures her that he'll leave his wife for her. And my role tonight is suddenly too clear. What a shitbag! "How old is he?" I ask.

"Twenty-seven."

"How long has he known himself?" I press, not liking what I'm hearing.

"He says he's always known."

Gregory's answer only cements it for me. If he's always known and he still hasn't revealed his true sexual status, then what makes Gregory think that he will now? I don't say that, though, because judging by the look on my friend's face, he's already asked himself that question. Gregory doesn't act camp or feel the need to display his sexual preference for all to see, but he's not ashamed of it, either. After spending just a minute with Ben, I can tell it's not the case for him, and when I look across the bar and see him making an over-the-top display of greeting a woman, my thoughts are only confirmed.

I glance back to Gregory and see that his line of sight is pointed that way, too, and in an attempt to distract him, I ask for another drink by waving my empty glass under his nose.

"More?"

"It's going down very well." I go to hand my glass over, but quickly notice the strawberry. "Oh, wait." I tilt and catch the fruit, then give up my glass.

While Gregory fetches more drinks, I wander over to the glass-paneled gallery and lean over, observing the masses of well-groomed men and chicly dressed women below. This place is an exclusive, high-end club and reserved only for London's elite. This should make me feel even more uncomfortable, but it doesn't. I'm just glad I came, because with Ben avoiding Gregory in public places, he would've been floating around on his own like a plum.

"Here." A flute appears over my shoulder. "What are you looking at?"

"All of these rich people." I turn around and rest my bum against the glass. "Is it a private club?"

Gregory laughs. "What do *you* think?"

I hum my acknowledgment. "And Ben organized the opening?"

"Yes, he's renowned in his field." He leans his elbows on a tall glass table close by. "Don't you notice it?" he asks.

I look around. "Notice what?"

"The looks." He nods to a group of men close by, all staring over at us, not bothering to hide their interest, even though I have male company. Gregory could be my boyfriend for all they know.

I turn my back on them and find Gregory still looking over at the group, but for a whole different reason. "Stop gawking," I say, taking another sip of champagne.

"Sorry." His eyes land on me. "Shall we go explore?"

"Yes, let's."

"Come on, then." He straightens and places his palm in the small of my back to lead me.

On our way up a flight of glass stairs, I look down to the bottom floor and notice Ben has gone, and I wonder whether that's why we're on the move.

"There's a garden bar," Gregory tells me.

"Then why are we going up?"

"It's on the roof." Gregory directs me to the left and up some more stairs, where a wall of glass comes into view, and beyond, London by night in all of its glory.

"Oh wow!" I breathe. "Look at that!"

"Impressive, ah?"

It's more than impressive. "Would you de-friend me if I took pictures?" I ask, ready to hand him my drink so I can riffle through my purse for my phone.

"Yes, I would. Let's just do what everyone else is doing—drink and enjoy the view."

I feel cheated, wanting to snap away, just in case my memory doesn't store an accurate image of what I'm looking at. I'm used to London, its architecture and its grandeur, but I've never seen it looking quite like this. "So how did you meet Ben?" I ask, tearing my eyes away from the stunning view. Gregory gestures around us with a *how'd-ya-think* look all over his handsome face, and for the first time, I take in the garden where we've landed. I gasp a little. "You did this?"

"I did." His chest swells proudly. "Designed it, created it, and finished it. It's my best project to date."

"It's incredible," I muse, starting to absorb all of the little but significant details—the small touches that really bring it to life. The side walls are nothing more than compacted box plants, the tiny leaves lush and green, with ice blue twinkle lights embedded in the shrubbery. And the topiary trees are all trimmed into neat circles with lights woven through the foliage. "Is the grass real?" I ask, padding my feet and noticing my heels aren't sinking in.

"No, it's imitation, but so authentic you'd never know."

"It is," I agree. "I love the furniture."

"Hmmm. The theme was ice, as you've probably gathered. I wasn't quite sure how I was going to create a lush, functional outside space on that brief, but I'm pretty pleased."

"You should be." I reach up and kiss his cheek. "It's fabulous, just like you."

"Stop it," he laughs. "You're making me blush."

I giggle with him, and then cast my eyes over to take another hit of the outlook, but my eyes don't make it to the open air and view beyond because they find Ben first. And they find him stuck to a woman's mouth. I wince and quickly try to work out my best move, but I can think of nothing except downing my fresh drink and shoving it in Gregory's face.

"Another?" he asks incredulously. "Calm down, Livy."

"I'm fine," I assure him, taking his elbow, but he doesn't shift, and as I glance up, I see that he's found what I'm trying to get him away from. "Greg?" His eyes slowly fall to mine, and I see too much misery to take the softy-softy approach, so I tug at him until he's forced to move. "Let's get a drink."

"Yes, let's." He grinds the words out, shifting his arms from my grip and taking my hand.

I'm led with purpose back down the two flights of stairs and to the bar where Gregory orders two champagnes. In the short time that we've been away, the atmosphere has cranked up a few notches and people are starting to move toward the round dance floor, drinks in hand. The music seems louder, too, and there's definitely a shift in the reserved environment as the champagne flows freely—and for free—and Daft Punk, featuring Pharrell Williams, pumps through the speakers.

"Drink up." Gregory doesn't pass me a flute this time. It's a shot, and my eyes dart to his. "Come on," he pleads.

My reluctance is clear. I've had a few glasses of champagne and I feel okay, but that shouldn't be a green light to start throwing shots down my neck. "Greg—"

"Come on. I won't let anything happen, Livy," he assures me, and stupidly or not, I take the glass and knock it with his before tipping the contents down my throat. The burn is instant and so is the reminder of all the times I've drunk before.

I gasp and slam my shot glass down before taking the flute and downing the more pleasant champagne. "That was nasty."

"That was tequila, but you forgot the salt and lemon." He holds up a salt shaker and a wedge of fresh lemon before carrying out the practice the right way, licking the back of his hand, sprinkling the salt, licking again, downing the liquid, and sinking his teeth into the wedge. "It's much better this way."

"You should've stopped me," I complain, struggling to rid my mouth of the rancid taste.

"You didn't give me a chance," he laughs. "Let's do another." He orders another and this time I see through the sequence correctly, following Greg's lead.

I shudder at the lingering flavor, but then I'm shuddering for a whole other reason when a familiar beat takes over the current track. I instantly look to see Gregory's wide, delighted eyes.

"Carte Blanche," I whisper, my mind bombarded with memories of Gregory creating a disco in my bedroom all of the times I refused to go to an actual club.

"How apt," Gregory confirms, a grin spreading across his face. " 'Veracocha'! Our tune, baby girl! We both down another champagne before my hand is grasped and I'm being dragged to the floor. I don't object. I wouldn't. Gregory's smiling, and after what has just transpired, this is a good thing.

He pushes us through the crowd until we're joining the flurry of other dancers who all appreciate the classic anthem as much as we do. Strobe lighting darts around us, flitting across the faces of people and intensifying my feel-good mood. We both slip into the groove, hands in the air, bodies swaying, twisting and twirling each other around the floor, laughing as we do. It's a novelty and a good one. I'm having fun.

Gregory pulls me into his chest and puts his mouth to my ear so I can hear him over the music and cheering. "I'm giving it three minutes for a bloke to move in on you."

"I'm dancing with a man," I laugh. "He'd have to be pretty cocksure."

"Give me a break," he scoffs. "We're clearly not dating."

I'm about to disagree, but I see Ben approaching behind Gregory, smiling and greeting people as he passes through the dance floor crowd. I want to drag my friend away, but I'm also curious how this will play out. Ben doesn't know that we saw him, and I'm wondering how Gregory will handle it. Breaking away from him, I move back, ensuring I keep my smile and Gregory's attention.

As Ben nears, I watch him studying Gregory's body discreetly, still greeting people, still smiling. There's no mistaking the intended body contact as he passes my friend, his arm sliding around his waist in a subtle gesture made to look like he's trying to pass without bumping into him, but the look on Ben's face is screaming desire and the sudden shift in Gregory from easy, fluid movements to stiff awkwardness is obvious. Will he push him away or give him a dirty look?

No. He loosens up immediately when he sees Ben and falls right back into his previous ease as the track slows momentarily before dramatically cranking up ten gears and blasting the clubbers into complete elation. We're in a triangle, both Ben and Gregory smiling and dancing, but the sexual sparks flying off each man is tangible. They're not touching, nor are they looking at each other all lusty, but it's there and it's obvious. Ben is playing it risky.

Gregory moves toward me, smiling. "There's a man about to take hold of you."

"Is there?" I go to turn, but I'm stopped when Gregory grabs my shoulders.

"Trust me on this. Let him." He fans his face and releases me, and I tense from top to toe, bracing myself. Gregory has great taste in men, but shouldn't I at least get a say in who takes hold of me? Or should I just let this happen—stay in control, but let it happen?

It's his hips I feel first, pushing into my lower back. Then there's his hand sliding around my stomach. My moves fall straight into his set pace without thought, and my hand rests over his on my navel. Gregory is smiling brightly, but I have no compulsion to turn and get a glimpse of my dance partner because—probably due to the alcohol—he feels good...comfortable...right.

My eyes close when I feel hot breath at my ear. "Sweet girl, you've floored me."

CHAPTER SEVENTEEN

I'm very suddenly aware of internal sparks firing off wildly. I gasp, my eyes flying open, and I try to turn, getting absolutely nowhere. His groin pushes into my lower back, his grip of my waist firming up, as is what's beneath his trousers. I've been thrown into panic, all the feelings that he provokes attacking me relentlessly.

"Don't try to escape me," he whispers. "I won't let it happen this time."

"Miller, let me go."

"Over my dead body." He sweeps my hair to one side and wastes no time getting his lips on my neck, injecting fire through my flesh, straight into my bloodstream. "Your dress is very short."

"And?" I breathe, digging my fingernails into his forearm.

"And I like it." His hand slides over my hip, onto my bum, and down to the hem of my dress. "Because it means I can do this." He kisses my neck, skating his hand under my dress and pushing his finger past the seam of my knickers. My bottom flies back on a small cry, colliding with his groin. He bites my neck. "You're drenched."

"Stop it," I beg, feeling all rationality running away from me under his touch.

"No."

"Please, stop it, stop it, stop, it."

"No...," he breathes. "No..." He circles his groin confidently. "No, Livy."

His finger enters me and my face distorts with a mixture of pleasure and desperation, my internal muscles grabbing on to him. My head is drifting to one side, letting him at me, and the fingers of my hand resting over his are squeezing hard, prompting his palm to shift and his fingers to lace through mine, constricting firmly. I know I'm falling, and through my desperate desire, I look for Gregory for help. But he's gone.

And so is Ben.

Fury flames, Gregory's promise to not let anything happen only stoking it further. He's let something happen, and he's let it happen with the worst man. I struggle in Miller's hold, until he's left little option but to release me or manhandle me to the floor, and I swing around, my hair whipping my face. I glare at him, ignoring his impossible beauty. He's in his usual finery, minus the jacket, and the sleeves of his shirt are rolled up in the most casual, unlike-Miller fashion. His waistcoat is still buttoned, though, and his hair is a stunning mop of waves. His piercing blue eyes are stabbing at my flesh accusingly.

"I said no," I say through gritted teeth. "Not now, not for four hours, not ever."

"We'll see," he retorts confidently, stepping forward. "You might be repeatedly saying the word no, Olivia Taylor. But this"—he runs his fingertip over my breast and onto my stomach, forcing me to gulp down air to control my shakes—"this is always telling me yes."

My legs are in motion before my brain sends any instruction, which quickly makes me conclude that this is natural instinct. Escape. Get away before I lose my mind and my integrity and let him cast me aside again. I find myself at the bar before I've even registered what direction I'm headed in. I order a drink, quickly taking it from the barman's hand and turning as I take a swig.

Miller is standing right in front of me. His jaw is tense as he nods over my shoulder to the barman. Then, as if by magic, a tumbler is passed over my shoulder into Miller's waiting hand. My gaze falls to his lips as he takes a slow sip while he watches me, as if he knows what that mouth does to me. I'm mesmerized by it. Totally rapt. Then he licks his lips and not knowing what else to do, but knowing that I'm likely to kiss him if I remain here, I run again, this time up the stairs and around the galleried walkway, looking through the glass for any sign of Gregory. I need to find him, the stupid pain in the arse that he is.

I'm so busy looking for my friend in the space below I don't notice where I'm going and walk straight into a body. The sharp angles of the chest under the shirt and waistcoat are too familiar. "Livy, what are you doing?" he asks, almost tiredly, like I'm fighting a losing battle. I fear I might be.

"Trying to get away from you," I say calmly, making his jaw tense in annoyance. "Please move."

"No, Livy." He mouths the words extra slowly, making it impossible to rip my eyes away from his lips. "How much have you had to drink?"

"That's none of your business."

"It's my business when you're drinking in my club."

My mouth falls open, but he maintains his straight, unhappy expression. "This is your bar?"

"Yes, and it's part of my responsibility to ensure my clients are . . . behaving." He moves in again. "You're not behaving, Livy."

"Throw me out, then," I challenge him. "Have me escorted from the premises. I don't fucking care."

His eyes narrow fiercely. "The only place you're being thrown is in my fucking bed."

It's me who moves in now, getting my face up close to his, like

I'm going to kiss him. It takes every effort not to connect our mouths, like I'm fighting a powerful magnet hauling me in. He's thinking that, too. His lips have parted, and he's looking down at me, his eyes full of desire. "Go to hell," I say evenly and calmly, almost on a murmur.

I'm surprised by my own coolness, not that I let it be known. I meet his shocked eyes with confidence, not backing down, and take another slow, long glug of my drink. But it's quickly snatched from my hand. "I think you've had enough."

"Yes, you're right. I *have* had enough. Of you!" I turn on my stilettos and walk away, on a mission to find Gregory, rescue him from a stupid situation, and leave to escape my own diabolical position.

"Livy!" he calls after me.

I blank him, walking on, venturing down some stairs, around a few corners, into the toilets, and the whole time he's tailing me, just following me as I pace calmly around his club.

"What are you doing?" he shouts over the music. "Livy?"

I ignore him, thinking of where else I can possibly look. I've been everywhere, except...

I don't even think about what I'm doing when I viciously yank the door of the disabled toilet open. Not until I hear the sound of the metal lock hitting the tiled wall and I'm standing staring at Gregory bent over the sink with his jeans around his ankles. Ben, who has a firm hold of my friend's hips, is pounding forward on constant barks. Neither one seems to have noticed me, nor the rise in noise level, both men utterly consumed in each other. My hand flies to my mouth in shock and I walk back, meeting Miller's chest, but he pushes me in and slams the door behind us, snapping Ben and Gregory from their private euphoria. It's not private now, and as both men seem to pull themselves together, fear, embarrassment, shame, discomfiture—it all takes hold, with each of them rushing to make themselves decent.

I turn to Miller. "We should go," I prompt, pushing my hands into his chest. "Miller."

He's just staring at Gregory and Ben, brows heavy, lips straight. "I have a check for your work on the roof terrace in my office, Greg."

"Mr Hart." Gregory nods, his face flushing.

"And I have one for you, too." Miller looks to Ben, who's clearly mortified. I feel for them both, and I hate Miller for making them feel so small. "I would kindly ask you not to use the washrooms of my club as a knocking shop. This is a private, exclusive establishment. Your respect would be greatly appreciated."

I nearly choke. Respect? He's just had his hand up my dress in the middle of the dance floor. I need to leave before I gun for one of these three men. I have a grievance with them all. I let myself out, shocked by so many things in such a short space of time. My head is swimming with alcohol, the feeling of losing control beginning to worry me.

As I stagger down the corridor, I see a man approaching, his roving eye trailing lustfully up and down my body. I know that look. And I don't like it. It's smarmy. He brushes past me and smirks. "I've been watching you," he purrs, eyes burning with want.

I should continue walking, but flashbacks have halted my movements, my brain not prepared to home in on any instructions to make me walk away and is instead making me see things stored at the back of my mind that I've hidden for many years.

He growls and pushes me into the wall. I freeze. Nothing will work. Then he smashes his lips to mine and the bad memories multiply, but before I have a chance to find the mental and physical strength to fight him off, he's absent and I'm left heaving, propped up against the wall, watching Miller physically restrain the struggling man.

"What the fuck?" the guy yells. "Get the fuck off me!"

Miller calmly removes his iPhone from his pocket and presses just one button. "Outer on floor one. Toilets."

The guy continues to struggle, but he's held firmly in place with little effort from Miller, who's staring at me, his face completely impassive. But he's mad. I can see it in the steely gloss of his blue eyes. There's rage—hot rage, and I'm not at all comfortable seeing it. I start an unsteady walk away, moving to the side of the corridor when two huge doormen come barreling toward me. I glance over my shoulder to weigh up my situation and see them take over Miller's hold of the guy, leaving Miller to straighten out his shirt and waistcoat before his eyes lift and find mine. He's fuming, a telling sweat shimmering on his brow. He starts to shake his head slowly as he strides forward, his hair now falling onto his forehead from his exertion. I know I won't get far, but I'll make it to the bar. I need another drink, so I hurry, quickly reaching my intended destination and ordering a champagne, necking it quickly before the empty is snatched from my grasp and his hand is locked on my nape, leading me away, my feet moving fast to keep up with his long strides behind me.

"You're not getting your four hours!" I shout desperately.

"I don't fucking want them," he growls, roughly pushing me on. The declaration pricks at my chest repeatedly.

Many people nod, smile, and speak to Miller as he pushes me through the bar, but he doesn't stop for anyone, not even acknowledging them. I can't see his face to confirm it, but the wary looks on all of the faces we pass tell me all I need to know. His grip of my neck is tight over my hair, and he makes no attempt to ease up, even though he must be aware of the pressure of it. We're heading for the entrance of the bar, the glow of big, glass doors coming into view with people still lining up to gain entry.

Something catches my eye and I do a double take, spotting Miller's business associate. She's staring openmouthed at Miller manhandling me, her drink at her lips ready to sip, clearly shocked by what she's witnessing. Even through my tipsiness, I manage for the first time to wonder what Miller is telling her about *me*.

"Livy!" I hear Gregory from behind and try to turn, to no avail.

"Keep walking," he orders.

"Livy!"

Miller halts and swings around, taking me with him. "She's coming with me."

"No." Gregory shakes his head, moving forward, looking at me. "Coffee hater?" he asks, and I nod, making Gregory's face flame with guilt. He fed me to the lion, and then skulked off to have his *later* with Ben.

"Miller," I answer, confirming he is exactly who Gregory thinks, but wondering how he didn't know that already if he's been working for him.

"You can stay and have a drink," Miller says calmly, "or I can have you removed from my club—your choice." Miller's words, although calm, are threatening, but I have no doubt that he'll follow through on his threat.

"If I'm leaving, then Livy's coming with me."

"Wrong," Miller fires back simply and confidently. "Your lover will probably ask you to do the sensible thing and let me take her." He's playing dirty.

Ben appears from behind Gregory, his face washed out and full of apprehension. "What are you going to do?" he asks Miller.

"That depends on whether you make a big deal of this. I'm going to my office with Olivia, and you two are going back to the bar to enjoy a drink on me."

Gregory and Ben both flick cautious eyes to me and Miller, both clearly in turmoil. It makes me speak up.

"I'm okay," I say quietly. "Go have a drink."

"No." Gregory steps forward. "Not after what you've told me, Livy."

"I'm okay," I repeat slowly before looking up at Miller in a silent indication to lead on. His grip eases instantly, his anger receding, and his fingers start kneading my flesh, working some life back into the stiffness.

"Miller?"

I cast my eyes to the left and see the woman. She's followed us and her cherry red, pursed lips tell me she recognizes me despite the makeover. Then I look up to Miller. He looks totally detached as he stares at her. This is awkward, the tension ricocheting between all five of us tangible, and for very different reasons. I feel like an interloper, but it doesn't stop me from letting Miller guide me away from the awful scene.

He's silent as he leads me down some stairs and through a maze of corridors until we're at a door, where he curses while bashing in a code on the metal keypad before pushing his way through. I expect to be released after he's kicked it shut, but he doesn't let up, instead directing me to a big white desk and spinning me around. He pushes me onto my back, pulls my thighs apart, and lays himself all over me, grabbing my cheeks in his hands and forcing his lips to mine, his tongue pushing past and starting an impossibly smooth rotation in my mouth. I want to ask him what the hell he's doing, but I know I'm going to savor this. I won't, however, savor the heated words that I know will be exchanged following this kiss, so I accept it. I accept him. With this kiss, I'm accepting everything that he has done tonight and before that, when he's played with my heart—filled it, and then quickly drained it again, leaving it a mass of aching muscle in my chest.

He moans, and my hands skate their way up his back until they're resting on the back of his head, pushing him in closer to me. "I'm not letting you do this to me again," I mumble weakly around his lips.

His mouth working mine doesn't let up, and I don't try to stop him, despite my words. "I don't think it's a matter of letting me, Livy." He pushes his groin into my core, putting more friction on my pulsing flesh. I whimper, searching for the willpower to stop this. "This is happening." He bites my lip and sucks it, pulling back and looking down at me. He moves my hair from my face. "We've already accepted this. It can't be stopped."

"I can stop it, just like you have plenty of times," I breathe on a whisper. "I *should* stop it."

"No, you shouldn't. I won't let you, and I should never have stopped it either." His eyes run over my face and he dips, kissing me tenderly. "What has happened to you, my sweet girl?"

"You," I accuse. "You've happened to me." He's made me reckless and irrational. He may make me feel alive, but he makes me feel lifeless just as quickly. I'm playing the devil's advocate with this man disguised as a gentleman, and I hate myself for not being stronger, for not stopping it. How many times can I do this to myself, and how many times will he do this to me?

"I don't like this." He pulls my hand from his back and looks down at my red nail polish. "And I don't like this." He drags his thumb over my red lips as he watches me. "I want my Livy back."

"*Your* Livy?" My brain engages fast, my heartbeat quickening. He wants the old Livy back so he can walk all over her again. Is that it? "I'm not yours."

"Wrong. You are very much mine." He pushes himself up and clasps my hand, pulling me up to a sitting position. "I'm leaving this office to tell your friend that you're coming home with me. He's going to want to speak to you, so you'll answer your phone when he calls."

"I'm coming?" I slip off the desk, and he immediately places me back on it.

"No." He points over my shoulder. "You're going into that bathroom, and you're going to remove that shit from your face."

I recoil, but he's not perturbed. "Are you going to go out there and tell that woman that I'm going home with you?" I grate, anger bubbling as he watches me closely.

"Yes," he answers simply and swiftly. Just yes? I have nothing to say to that, drunkenness blocking all rational thinking, and when he's finished studying my dumbstruck face, he walks out, shutting the door behind him. I know I hear a lock click into place, so I jump down from his desk and run over to the door, jiggling the handle, fully aware that I'm wasting my time. He's locked me in.

I don't go to the bathroom; I go to the glass drinks cabinet, seeing some champagne on ice and two used glasses, neatly placed at just the right angle. That's Miller's doing, but the rim of one glass caked in cherry red lipstick isn't. I start to shake with fury and grab a glass, pouring in some champagne and downing it before refilling my glass and tipping that down quickly, too. I'm drunk enough, I don't need this, but control is slipping rapidly away.

Just as Miller promised, my phone starts bleeping from my purse and I retrieve it from the desk, fishing around and finding Gregory's name on the screen. "Hello." I try to sound cool and collected, when I want to scream down the phone, vent and lash out.

"You're leaving with him?"

"I'm okay." I don't need to be worrying him further, and I definitely won't be leaving with Miller. "You didn't know his name?"

"No," he sighs. "Just Mr. Hart, uptight fucker."

"You told me to let him take me on the dance floor!"

"That's because he's fucking hot!"

"Or so you could have your later with Ben?"

"A little dance, that's all. I wouldn't have let it go further."

"You did!"

"I have no excuse," he mumbles. "I'm pissed, but regardless of that, it's a moot fucking point now, isn't it? He's the fucking coffee hater and you're already in love with the jumped-up twat!"

"He's not a twat!" I don't know what I'm saying. I can think of far harsher words to use and Miller would be all of them right now.

"I don't like this," Gregory grunts.

"I didn't like what I was subjected to earlier, either, Gregory."

There's silence down the line for a few moments before he speaks. "Sassy," he retorts sullenly. "Please hold on to that if you're giving him more of your time, Livy."

"I will," I assure him. "I'll be fine. I'll call you. Is Ben okay?"

"No, he's still not got his color back." He laughs, lightening the mood. "He'll live."

"Okay. I'll speak to you tomorrow."

"You will," he confirms. "Be careful."

I exhale deeply and hang up, slumping my arse on the edge of Miller's desk, where there's no paperwork, pen, computer, or stationery, just a cordless phone set precisely to the side. His chair is tucked under, perfectly straight, and as I gaze around the whole room, the preciseness of everything registers. It's just like his home. Everything has a place.

Except me.

He owns a nightclub?

My head snaps up when the mechanism on the door sounds and he's back, looking satisfied, until he sees my face. "I asked you to do something."

"Will you force me if I don't?" I challenge, the alcohol injecting some bravery into me.

He seems confused by my question. "I would never force you to do anything I know you don't want to, Livy."

"You forced me down here," I point out.

"I didn't force you. You could've battled with me or struggled from my hold if you'd really wanted to." He runs his hand through his hair and takes a deep breath, then brings himself to me and pushes my thighs open, standing between them. His finger slides under my chin and pulls my face to his, but he's a little blurred. I squint, frustrated that I can't fully appreciate his features. "You're drunk," he says softly.

"It's your fault." I'm beginning to slur.

"Then I apologize."

"Did you tell your girlfriend about me?"

"She's not my damn girlfriend, Livy. But yes, I told her about you."

The thought thrills me, but if he's felt the need to tell her, then there's more to it than business.

"Is she an ex?"

"Fuck, no!"

"Why the need to tell her about me, then? What business is it of hers?"

"None!" He's exasperated. I don't care. It's quite satisfying to see something more than a straight face and clipped tone.

"Why do you keep doing this?" I ask, pulling away. "You're tender, sweet, and affectionate, then hard and cruel."

"I'm not ha—"

"Yes, you are," I interrupt him, and I don't care if I get chastised for my lack of manners. It wasn't very polite of him to manhandle me down here, but he still did it, and he's right, I could've tried harder to stop him. But I didn't. "Are you finally going to fuck me?" I ask, barefaced and completely even.

He recoils, repulsion plaguing his face. "You're drunk," he hisses. "I'm not doing anything to you when you're drunk."

"Why?"

He pushes his face to mine, his jaw ticking. "Because I'll never do anything less than worship you, *that* is why." Taking a moment to calm down, his eyes close briefly and reopen lazily. He hits me with a determined gaze. "I'll never be a drunken fumble, Olivia. Every time I take you, you'll remember it. Each and every moment will be etched on that beautiful mind of yours forever." He gently taps my temple. "Every kiss. Every touch. Every word."

My heart rate accelerates. It's too late, but I say it anyway. "I don't want it to be that way." He's already got a permanent residence in my mind.

"Tough luck, because that's how it's going to be."

"It doesn't have to be," I goad, wondering where these confident words and tones are coming from and if I really mean them.

"Yes, it does. It has to be."

"Why?" I'm beginning to sway a little, and he notices because he takes my arm to steady me. "I'm fine!" I slur insolently. "And you haven't answered my question."

He clenches his eyes shut, and then slowly opens them, blasting me back with blue puddles of sincerity. "Because that is how it is for me."

I swallow, hoping my drunkenness isn't making me hear things. I have no reply, not now, perhaps not even when I'm sober. "You want me." My drunken mind still wants him to say the words.

He takes a deep breath and makes a point of burning through my eyes with his gaze. "I. Want. You," he confirms slowly... clearly. "Give me my thing."

I throw my arms around his neck and pull him in, giving him his *thing*.

A cuddle.

My heart is free-falling.

He holds me for the longest time, stroking my back and combing my hair with his fingers. I could fall asleep. He's sighing repeatedly into my neck, constantly kissing me and squeezing me to him.

"Can I take you back to my bed?" he asks quietly.

"For four hours?"

"I think you know that I want a lot longer than four hours, Olivia Taylor." He surrenders his *thing* and palms my bum, sliding me from his desk and up to his body. "I wish you had never covered your face."

"It's makeup. It doesn't cover; it enhances."

"You're a pure, natural beauty, sweet girl." He turns and starts for the door, but detours to the drinks cabinet to rearrange the champagne flutes first. "I'd like it to stay that way."

"You want me to be timid and merciful."

He shakes his head lightly and opens the door to his office, setting me on my feet and taking his signature hold of my nape. "No, I just don't want you behaving so recklessly and giving those lips to another man to taste."

"I didn't mean to." I stagger, prompting Miller to grab my upper arm to steady me.

"You need to be more careful," he warns, and he's right. I realize that, even through my drunkenness. So I prevent my drunken insolence from resurfacing.

As we walk down the corridor and back up the stairs to the main club, I feel my stupid drinking binge really take a hold. People are a wish-wash of blurred, slowed movements and the loud music is a bombardment of pain on my ears. I wobble on my heels, feeling Miller look down at me.

"Livy, are you okay?"

I nod, my head not quite doing what I'm telling it to, making my movement more of a limp roll on my neck. Then I bump into a wall. "I feel . . ." My mouth is suddenly producing far too much saliva, my stomach turning violently.

"Oh shit, Livy!" He scoops me up and charges for his office again, but he's not quick enough. I throw up all over the corridor . . . and Miller. "Bollocks!" he curses.

I retch some more as he gets me into his office. "I feel sick," I mumble.

"What the hell have you had?" he asks, negotiating my floppy body onto the toilet in his bathroom.

"Tequila," I giggle. "But not properly. I forgot the salt and lemon so we had to do it again. Oh!" I slip from the toilet seat and land on my backside. "Ouch!"

"Oh, for crying out loud," he grumbles, picking me up and holding me in place, my head lolling while he tries to remove his sick-splattered waistcoat and shirt. "Livy, how many shots did you have?"

"Two," I answer, my bottom dropping to meet the toilet seat again. "And I helped myself to more champagne," I slur, "but I didn't use the glass with cherry *red* lipstick on it. She wants an association in more than business, you stupid man."

"What's gotten into you?"

I pull my heavy head up and try to focus, finding a bare, smooth, masterpiece of a chest at eye level. "You, Miller Hart." I rest my hands on his pecs and take my time caressing him. I might be stinking drunk, but I can still appreciate what I'm feeling, and it feels good. "You've gotten into me." I lift my eyes with some effort, finding his are dropped, watching me feeling him. "You've worked your way into me and I can't shake you out."

He slowly crouches in front of me and strokes my cheek before sliding his hand around the back of my neck and pulling my face close to his. "I wish you weren't so pissed right now."

"So do I," I admit. There's no way I'll handle him in a drunken stupor. And I wouldn't want to. I *want* to remember every intimate moment, even this one. "If I forget the look on your face right now, or the words you said to me on your desk, promise me you'll remind me."

He smiles.

"And that!" I blurt. "Promise me you'll smile at me like that the next time I see you." His smiles are rare and beautiful, and I hate him for giving me one now, when I'm not likely to remember.

He groans, and I think he closes his eyes. Or did I close mine? I'm not even sure. "Olivia Taylor, when you wake up in the morning, I'm going to be catching up on what you've deprived me of this evening."

"You've deprived yourself," I retort. "But remind me first," I mumble as he pulls me in for his *thing*. "Smile at me."

"Olivia Taylor, if I have you, then I'll be smiling for the rest of my life."

Chapter Eighteen

My brain feels warped, and in my darkness I wonder what year it is. It may have been a long time, but I know exactly how I'm going to feel when I open my eyes. My mouth is dry, my body clammy, and the dull thump in my head is likely to transform into a full-on carnival of relentless bongo drums when I lift my head from the pillow.

Deciding my best option is more sleep, I roll over to find a cool spot and burrow back down into my pillow, sighing happily at my new, comfortable position. The sweet sound of a low, peaceful hum is soothing and distinguishable.

Miller.

I don't bolt upright because my body won't allow it, but I do open my lids, discovering shockingly blue smiling eyes. I frown and drop my eyes to his mouth. Yes, he's smiling, and it's like sunlight bashing its way through gray clouds and making everything just perfect. Bright. Real. But what's he so delighted about, and how did I end up here?

"Have I done something funny?" I croak. My throat is rough and parched.

"No, not funny."

"Then why are you smiling so hard?"

"Because you made me promise that I would," he says, planting a light kiss on my nose. "If I ever make you a promise, Livy, I'll keep it." He pulls me over to his side of the bed and goes about giving me his *thing*, positioning me beneath him and squeezing me tightly, sinking his face into my neck. "I'll never do anything less than worship you," he whispers. "I'm never going to be a drunken fumble, Livy. Every time I take you, you'll remember it. Each and every moment will be etched on that beautiful mind of yours forever." He kisses my neck sweetly and squeezes a little tighter. "Every kiss. Every touch. Every word. Because that's how it is for me."

My breath catches in the back of my throat, his words sending a deep warmth to my very center, pure happiness shining through my fuzziness. But my eyebrows meet in the middle. I feel like he's privy to a one-way, secret conversation.

"It's a good job I keep my promises." He emerges and studies my face closely. "You disappointed me last night."

His light accusation stimulates a blurry memory of me...and another man...and lots of alcohol. "It was your fault," I retort quietly.

His brow wrinkles in surprise. "I don't remember demanding that you let another man taste you."

"I didn't let him, and I don't remember agreeing to you bringing me here."

"I don't expect you to remember a lot." He leans down and bites my nose. "You threw up all over me and my new club; you fell over, more than once; and I had to stop the car twice for you to be sick. And you still managed to vomit in my Mercedes." He kisses my nose while I concentrate on cringing, mortified. "You then decorated the floor in the lobby of my apartment block *and* the floor of my kitchen."

"Sorry," I whisper. I must have sent him into a tailspin with his cleaning habits.

"You're forgiven." He sits up and pulls me onto his lap. "My pure, sweet girl turned into the devil last night."

Another memory is jolted. *My Livy.* "Your fault," I repeat, because there's nothing else I can claim, apart from it being my fault, which it is, partly.

"So you keep saying." He stands and places me on my unstable feet. "Do you want the good news or the bad news?"

I try to focus on him, annoyed my clouded, post-drunken vision isn't allowing me to absorb him all. "I don't know."

"I'll give you the bad news." He gathers my hair and rests it neatly down my back. "You had one dress and you've vomited all over it, so you have no clothes."

I look down, finding I'm completely nude, not even knickers, and I doubt the vomit reached those.

"They were lovely, but I prefer you naked."

I glance up and find a knowing look. "You've washed my clothes, haven't you?"

"Your lovely new knickers, yes. They're in the drawer. Your dress, on the other hand, was rather soiled and needed soaking."

"What's the good news?" I ask, slightly embarrassed by his acknowledgment of my new underwear and reminder of my vomiting episode.

"The good news is that you don't need them because we're broccoli today."

"We're broccoli?"

"Yes, like veg."

I smile my amusement. "We're going to veg like broccoli?"

"No, you've got it all wrong." He shakes his head a little. "We lie like broccoli."

"So we're vegetables?"

"Yes," he sighs, exasperated. "We're going to veg all day, making us broccoli."

"I'd like to be a carrot."

"You can't lie like a carrot."

"Or a turnip. How about a turnip?"

"Livy," he warns.

"No, scrap that. I would definitely like to be a courgette."

He shakes his head on an eye roll. "We're going to slob out all day."

"I want to veg." I grin, but he doesn't give me anything. "Okay, I'll lie like broccoli with you," I relent. "I'll be whatever you'd like me to be."

"How about less irritating?" he asks seriously.

I have a raging hangover, and I'm a little confused by how I came to be here, but he's smiled at me, said some meaningful words, and he's planning a whole day with me. I don't care whether he laughs or smiles anymore, or if he doesn't engage with me when I'm trying to be playful. He's too serious and there's no sign of a sense of humor, but despite his clipped manner, I still find him impossibly captivating. I can't stay away from him. He's alluring and addictive, and as he glances down at his watch, I remember something else...

I think you know that I want more than four hours.

The memory thrills me. How long is more? And will he backtrack on that...again? Another image worms its way into my fuzzy mind—an image of pursed cherry red lips and a stunned face. She's beautiful, well maintained, classy. She's everything I would expect a man like Miller to go for.

"You okay?" Miller's concerned tone pulls me from my thoughts.

I nod. "I'm sorry for vomiting everywhere," I say sincerely, thinking a woman like Miller's business associate wouldn't do something so lowly.

"I've already forgiven you." He takes my neck and guides me

to the bathroom. "I tried to brush your teeth last night, but you refused to hold still."

I'm squirming, thinking it best that I can't remember half of the evening. The things that I can are not making me feel any better about the stuff that I can't—Gregory and Ben, for a start. "I need to call Gregory."

"No, you don't." He hands me a toothbrush. "He knows where you are and that you're okay."

"He took your word for it?" I ask, surprised, their heated words coming back to me.

"I'm not compelled to explain myself to the man who encouraged your reckless behavior." He puts some paste on a brush before putting it back in the cupboard behind the giant mirror that's hanging over the sink. "But I did explain myself to your grandmother."

"You called her?" I ask warily, wondering what he means by *explaining* himself. Explain that he's moody, that he's playing with my heart and sanity?

"I did." He takes my hand and leads it to my mouth, encouraging me to brush. "We had a nice conversation."

I put the brush in my mouth and start circling, just to stop myself from probing him on how that conversation went. But my face must be revealing pure curiosity, even though I have no desire to know what they spoke about.

"She asked me if I'm married," he muses, making my eyes widen. "And once we'd cleared that up, she told me a few things."

My brush slows in my mouth. What has she told him, damn her? "What did she tell you?" The question I really don't want to know the answer to just slips past my paste and brush.

"She mentioned your mother, and I told her you'd already shared that with me." He stares thoughtfully at me, and I tense, feeling exposed. "Then she mentioned that you disappeared for a time."

My heart starts a relentless, nervous beat in my chest. I feel mad. It's not Nan's place to share my history with anyone, least of all with a man that she's met a handful of times. It's *my* story to tell, *if* I want to tell it. And I don't. *That* part I never want to share. I spit my toothpaste out and rinse, dying to escape the intensity of his inquisitive stare.

"Where are you going?" he asks as I leave the bathroom. "Livy, wait a minute."

"Where are my clothes?" I don't bother waiting for his answer, instead heading for the drawers, kneeling and pulling open the bottom one, then finding my purse, knickers, and shoes.

He reaches me and pushes the drawer shut with his foot, then pulls me to my feet. I keep my head lowered, my hair tumbling all over my chest and face, giving me the perfect hiding place, until he removes it and lifts my chin, exposing me to that curious face. "Why are you hiding from me?"

I don't speak because I have no answer. He's looking at me all sorrowful, which I hate. The mention of my mother and my disappearance has brought every second of last night flooding back, every single detail, every drink, every action...everything.

When he realizes that he's going to get nothing, he picks me up and takes me back to his bed, gently easing me down to my back and kneeling to push his shorts down his thighs. "I will never force you to do anything I know you don't want to." He dips and kisses my hip bone, the feel of his slow moving mouth on my sensitive skin immediately chasing away my woes. "Please understand. I'm going nowhere, and neither are you." He's trying to reassure me, but I've already shared enough.

My eyes close and I let him take me to that wonderful place where anguish, self-torture, and histories do not exist. Miller's realm.

I can feel his lips climbing up my body, leaving a scorching trail in their wake. "Please let me take a shower," I plead, not wanting to stop this, but also not relishing the thought of him worshipping my post-drunken body.

"I showered you last night, Livy." He reaches my mouth and pays some attention to my lips before pulling back to look down at me. "I washed you, stripped your face back to the beauty I love, and I savored every moment of it."

My breath hitches at the word "love." He said the word "love," and I'm so disappointed that I missed him doing all of those things. He looked after me, even after my appalling performance last night.

Taking my hair, he lifts it, and I register the absence of straight, glossy locks, my usual wild waves back where they belong. He holds it to his nose and inhales deeply. Then he takes my hand and shows me my bare nails, no red nail polish in sight. "Pure, unspoiled beauty."

"You dried my hair and removed my polish? You keep nail polish remover?"

His lips tip. "I may have detoured to a twenty-four-hour store." He lifts to his knees, reaching over to the bedside cabinet to pick up a condom. "We needed to stock up on these, anyway."

The mental image of Miller scanning the aisles of a shop for nail polish remover makes me smile. "Nail polish remover and condoms?"

He doesn't entertain my amusement. "Shall we?" he asks, ripping it open with his teeth and sliding it out.

"Please," I breathe, not caring if I sound like I'm begging. We don't have a time constraint, there's really no rush, but I desperately want him.

He takes hold of his arousal on a small hiss and rolls on the condom before pushing me onto my front and spreading his body all over me. "From behind," he whispers, guiding one of my legs out and bending it upward, opening me up to him. "Comfortable?"

"Yes."

"Happy?"

"I am."

"How do I make you feel, Livy?" He shifts down my back and bites at my bottom, molding my cheeks as he sucks and licks. "Tell me."

"Alive." I exhale the word on a fast rush of breath, turning my face outward as he climbs back up my body and sinks straight into me, making no noise whatsoever, whereas I cry out. "Miller!"

"Shhhh, let me taste you." He hovers his mouth over mine, keeping his body still. My cheek on the pillow pushes forward to capture his lips, meeting him harder than I intended to. "Savored, Livy. Never rushed." He takes over the speed, calming my frantic mouth with his gentle pace. "See? Slowly."

"I want you." I raise my bum, impatient. "Miller, I want you, please."

"Then you'll have me." He retreats and drives forward slowly on a suppressed moan into my mouth. "Tell me what you want, Livy. Anything you want."

"Faster." I bite down on his lip, knowing there's some ferocity in there somewhere. He always insists on taking it so slow, but I want to experience everything that he has to give. I want his moodiness and arrogance when he takes me. He pushes me to it, makes me crazy with desire, yet always keeps his head and control.

"I've told you before, I like to take my time with you."

"Why?"

"Because you deserve to be worshipped." He pushes himself up and slips out, sitting back on his heels before grasping at my hips and pulling me up. "You want deeper penetration?" I'm on my knees, my back still to him. "Let's see if we can satisfy you this way."

I look over my shoulder to see him holding himself upright, looking down, the sight of his rippling stomach beyond the solid column of muscle he's holding making me pant.

"Rise and move back." He pulls on my hip, guiding me to him, until my kneeling body is straddling his lap. "Lower gently."

My eyes close as I sink down onto him. "Ohhhhh," I groan, feeling him impale me, each fraction I lower pushing him deeper and deeper until I have to hold myself on my knees and take some steadying breaths. "Too deep," I pant. "It's too deep."

"Does it hurt?" His hands slide around my front and cup my breasts.

"A little."

"Take your time, Livy. Give your body time to accept me."

"It does accept you," I object. Every modicum of me accepts him. My mind, my body, my heart . . .

"We have all the time in the world. Don't rush it." He circles my nipples and bites into my shoulder. My legs start to tremble, my muscles objecting to my held position, so I lower a little more, holding my breath and letting the back of my head fall onto his shoulder. One hand leaves my breast, dragging up my chest and onto my throat, his whole palm covering it.

"How are you keeping so still?" I push the words through controlled breaths, wanting to release my leg muscles and take him to the hilt, but I'm wary of the pain it'll cause.

"I don't want to hurt you." He turns his face into my cheek and bites down before kissing it gently. "Trust me, it's taking everything out of me. Down a bit more?"

I nod and drop a fraction farther. "Oh God." I grit my teeth, the persistent stabbing pain making my head heavy, my face turning into his neck and hiding.

"Get past this and we're in a whole new world of pleasure."

"Why does it hurt so much?"

"I don't want to sound self-assured, but . . ." He gasps and starts to shake. "Fucking hell, Livy."

"Miller!" I hold my breath and release the muscles in my legs, falling straight onto his lap on a shocked yelp. "Shit!"

"Are you okay?" he shouts. "Jesus, Livy, tell me you're okay."

I've broken out in a sweat, and I'm still shaking, despite my relaxed body. It's beyond my control. "I'm okay." I nuzzle into his neck some more.

"Am I hurting you?"

"Yes...no!" I pull away from him and delve my hands into my hair in despair. "Just give me a moment!"

"How long is a moment?" he spits.

I grit my teeth and push up from my knees, only a very small way, before dropping down, less controlled than I planned. He barks. I yelp. "Miller, I can't!" I feel utterly defeated by the mixture of pleasure and pain. I want to grab hold of the heaviness in my groin and take it to the next level, but my legs haven't got the strength required to take me there. "I can't do it." I fall back against his chest, my arms falling limply to my sides, my breathing labored from doing hardly anything.

"Shhhh," he soothes me. "Do you want me to take care of it?"

"Please." I feel useless, feeble.

"I don't think I've worked hard enough to break you in, Olivia Taylor." He executes a slow, firm rotation of his groin into my bum, keeping deep but not instigating the sharpness that's causing me discomfort.

"Hmmm."

"Better?" he asks, resting his palms on my hips. I nod my acceptance on a sigh, letting him keep us completely close and connected while he grinds continuously, around and around, over and over. "How does that feel?"

"Perfect," I breathe.

"Can you lift a little bit?"

I don't answer, lifting myself a fraction, feeling him slip slightly from my passage. "You're so patient with me," I murmur, wondering whether he's this attentive with every woman he's slept with.

"You make me appreciate sex, Livy." I feel him rise slightly, too, his hands drifting from my hips to my breasts, then onto my shoulders and down my arms where he holds my hands. Lacing his fingers through mine, he lifts my useless limbs and takes them behind his head and holds them there. He thrusts forward gently, pulls back, and inches forward once more. "Let me taste you."

I turn my head and find his eyes. It's been too long since I've seen them. "Thank you." I don't know why I've said that, but I feel the profound need to voice my gratitude.

"Why are you thanking me?" His eyes twinkle curiously as he maintains the steady flow of his body into mine. It's divine, all tenderness long forgotten, being replaced with pure, beautiful pleasure.

"I don't know," I admit quietly.

"I do." He sounds confident, following up his assured words with a confident kiss, hard but slow, demanding but oh so giving. "You've never felt like this." His hips dip and roll up at an excruciatingly accurate angle, pulling a low, pleasure-filled moan from deep within me. "And neither have I." He pecks my lips. "So I need to thank you, too."

I'm starting to shake. "Oh God!" I sound panicked, desperate.

"Keep your hands in my hair," he orders tenderly, letting his own hands fall to my breasts. He massages them gently and circles his thumbs over the very tips of my nipples, hurling me beyond pleasure.

I'm losing control of my muscles, my entire body giving in to wild shakes, and I'm purring, pulling his head closer to locate his lips. "Let me taste you." I mimic his words, plunging my tongue into his mouth, rolling, retreating, and pushing back in, while he tortures my body with his delicate rhythm, so careful and attentive.

"Do I taste as good as you?" he asks.

"Better."

"I very much doubt that," he claims. "I need you to focus, Livy." He groans and separates our mouths, his hair damp from sweat and dripping down his face. "I'm going to lower you so we can both finish, okay?" I nod my acceptance, and he kisses me as he takes my hands from his head and pushes me down so I'm on all fours. "Comfortable?"

"Yes." I shift my arms, feeling no reluctance or vulnerability at being so exposed. I'm at complete ease, and when he repositions himself, widening his stance and taking a gentle hold of my hips, my blissed-out mind just blisses out more. I take a deep breath as he lazily withdraws, then let it all rush back out when he plunges forward. "Ohhhhhhhhhhh..."

One hand leaves my hip and his fingers walk up my spine, each connection of his fingertips on my skin singeing my flesh. When he reaches my neck, he flattens his palm and strokes his way down until he's at my bottom, rubbing soft, wide circles. "Jesus, Livy, I'm in awe of such perfection."

My legs may have been relieved from holding my weight, but my arms are now shaking in their place. "Miller." I resist collapsing to my front and try to rein in the uncontrollable spasms.

He jerks forward on a curse, and then reaches under my stomach, feeling down until his fingers are slipping across my throbbing flesh. I cry out, my head dropping, my hair pooling the bed beneath me. "You need a little help." His throat sounds sore, his voice like gravel. "Let it take hold." He slips his fingers back and forth over my clit as his hips advance and retreat, and his spare hand finds my breast, his grip compressing gently. I'm in sensory overload, helpless to what my body's striving to find.

Explosion.

Release.

And it comes fast, my bottom flying back on a choked cry, my arms finally giving out.

"Oh Jesus!" he cries, tugging me onto him and grinding deeply. He sighs and holds us connected while he thrusts the remnants of our pleasure away, mumbling confused words quietly.

I don't think I'm quite with it. My mind is a pleasure-induced fuzz, not allowing me to think straight, and my body is totally replete. It's morning. I'll never survive his endurance all day. I let him grind into me lazily, him groaning, me trying to stabilize my pleasure-fueled gasps.

"Come here, sweet girl," he murmurs, pulling at my body impatiently.

"I can't move," I breathe, going limp.

"Yes, for me, you *can* move." He doesn't leave me be, instead becoming more impatient, so I heave my exhausted body up and turn to him, letting him lift me and position my thighs on either side of his lap. His head cocks to the side a little as he runs his eyes down my torso, his hands skating slowly up and down my sides. "I've been desperate to touch you all night."

"You could've felt me."

"No." He shakes his head. "You misunderstand."

"How?" I don't pass up this opportunity to touch his hair, twisting a lock between my fingers.

"Touch you, not feel you." He looks up at me and I frown, not quite fathoming the difference. "Feeling you gives me untold pleasure, Livy." Dipping, he kisses the center of my chest. "But touching you, touching your soul. That's beyond the realms of pleasure." His eyes make a slow blink as he returns them to mine, and it's in this moment that I realize he doesn't do it on purpose. His slow movements are part of this man disguised as a gentleman. This is him. "It's like something powerful happens," he whispers. "And the pleasure of making love to you is just a little bonus."

"I'm still frightened," I admit. Even more so with every hopeful word he says to me.

"I'm a little terrified of you, too." He brings his hand between our chests and rubs feathery circles around my nipple.

Dropping my eyes, I watch his movements. "I'm not scared *of* you. I'm scared of what you can do to me."

"I can make you feel like no other, like you have me," he murmurs. "Take you to pleasure-filled places beyond your imagination, places that you have taken me." Dipping his head, he takes my breast between his teeth and grazes the tip of my nipple, encouraging my head to fall back and my lungs to drain of air. "That's what I can do to you, Olivia Taylor. And it's what you do for me."

"You already have." My voice is unrecognizable, fueled with lust, bursting with desire.

He's suddenly moving, carrying me forward and placing me on my back, his body covering me completely and my arms settling over his shoulders. I'm looking up at him, my eyes spoiled for places to settle—his wet hair falling onto his face, his stubble darkening his jaw, but it's the pull of his glistening eyes that captures mine. Whenever he catches my attention with that gaze, I'm hypnotized...helpless. I'm his.

"You look good in my bed," he declares quietly. "Messy, but good."

"I look a mess?" I ask, injured, thinking he should've let me take the shower I wanted.

"No, you misunderstand." He frowns, clearly frustrated by my misinterpretation of his words, but I heard all too well what he just said. "My bed looks messy. You look gorgeous."

My lips start twitching as I realize his issue. I bet he sleeps deathly still, the covers folded neatly at his waist, whereas I'm a fidget in my sleep, and I know this because of the state of my own bed in the mornings—a bit like Miller's bed is right now. "Would you like me to make your bed?" I ask seriously, hoping the answer is no, because, quite frankly, the thought scares me. I've seen the precision of the fancy cushions and the silk runner across the center. I expect he keeps a ruler in the drawer of his bedside cabinet to measure the exact distance from the headboard to the sheets and from the pillows to the runner.

He knows I'm teasing, despite my success in keeping a straight face and even voice. His thoughtful look confirms it. "As you wish." He kisses my startled face and pushes his naked body from the bed, standing to the side and removing the condom before taking his perfection to the bathroom to dispose of it.

I should've kept my mouth shut. My bedmaking efforts will never come up to scratch. Shifting to the edge of his bed, I stand and stare blankly at the mess of sheets, wondering where to start. The pillows. I should start with the pillows. Grabbing one of the four plump rectangles, I arrange it neatly, then set another by its side before placing the remaining two on top of each, running my palms over the surfaces to smooth the cotton. Happy with the result, I take two corners of the quilt and fling my arms skyward, flapping the sheet into a perfect square that floats gently down to the bed. I'm pleased with myself, it looks tidy, but I know it's not tidy enough, so I set on a journey around the bed, pulling at corners and ironing out the crinkles with my palms. Then I open the lid of the giant chest and begin placing the cushions, trying my hardest to remember the exact positioning from when I was last here. When I'm satisfied with my display, I slide the silk throw across the center and tweak the edges into place.

I smile triumphantly and stand back, admiring my handiwork. He can't possibly turn his nose up at that. It looks spectacular.

"Happy with yourself?"

I swing my naked body around and find Miller, arms folded, leaning up against the door frame of the bathroom. "I think I've done a good job."

He casts his eyes over the bed and pushes himself away from the frame, walking over slowly and thinking hard. He doesn't think it's a good job at all. He wants to start all over again, and the juvenile side of me is willing him to do just that, just so I have ammo to poke fun at him.

"You're dying to pull it all off and start again, aren't you?" I ask, mirroring his folded arms and close studying of his bed.

He shrugs nonchalantly, blatantly feigning acceptance. "It'll do."

I smile. "It's perfect."

He sighs and walks off, leaving me to admire his bed. "Livy, that is far from perfect." He disappears into his wardrobe and I follow behind, discovering Miller pulling some black boxers up his thighs.

It's hard to form words when confronted with such a sight. "Why the need to have everything just so?" I ask, watching as his fluid movements falter at my question.

He doesn't look at me, only continues arranging the waistband of his boxers around his hips. "I appreciate my possessions." His answer is reluctant and curt and clearly not going to be elaborated on. "Breakfast?"

"I have no clothes," I remind him.

He takes a leisurely jaunt down my nakedness with sparkling eyes. "You're fine as you are."

"I'm naked."

His face is completely impassive. "Yes, as I said, fine." He proceeds to pull on some black shorts and a gray T-shirt, and something in this moment makes me wonder if Miller Hart has ever stepped out in anything less than a three-piece suit.

"I'd feel more comfortable if I had some cover," I argue quietly, annoyed with myself for sounding so unsure and timid.

He straightens his T-shirt and regards me closely, making me shift and feel even more uncomfortable, now that he's clothed. "As you wish," he grumbles, and I waste no time seeking out something to throw on.

Flicking through the rails of shirts, I lose a bit of patience at the constant stream of dress shirts and pull down a blue one by the sleeve in exasperation.

"Livy, what are you doing?" He chokes the words out as I feed my arms through the sleeves.

"Covering myself," I reply, my actions slowing as I register the look of pure horror on his face.

He seems to release a calming breath, and then he's on his way over to me and quickly removing the shirt from my body. "Not in a five-hundred-pound shirt."

I'm naked again and watching as he rehangs the shirt and starts brushing down the front, huffing his annoyance when the miniscule crease that I've created doesn't disappear. I can't laugh. He's too aggravated, and it's quite alarming.

After a good few moments of Miller faffing with the shirt and me watching on in shock, he yanks it down, screws it up, and tosses it in a wash basket. "Needs washing," he mutters, stomping over to a drawer and pulling it open. He lifts out a pile of black T-shirts and sets the stack on the cabinet in the center of the room before taking each shirt individually and starting another pile to the side. When he reaches the last, he shakes it out and hands it to me, then goes about lowering the newly rotated pile of T-shirts back into the drawer.

As I watch him, completely fascinated, I steel myself to acknowledge something that's been pretty obvious for quite some time. He's not just tidy. Miller Hart suffers from obsessive-compulsive disorder.

"Are you going to put it on?" he asks, still clearly annoyed.

I don't say anything; I'm not sure what to, so I pull it over my head and down my body, thinking he lives his life to military precision, and I might have thrown him a curveball with my presence, although he keeps putting me here, so I shouldn't be too concerned about it.

"Are you okay?" I inquire nervously, wishing he'd put me back in his bed and resume worshipping me.

"Fine and dandy," he mutters, very un-fine and un-dandy-like. "I'll make us breakfast."

My hand is clasped abruptly and I'm pulled through the bedroom with purpose. It doesn't pass my notice that Miller makes a terrible job of pretending to ignore the bed, his jaw ticking a little as he glances out of the corner of his eye to the neat covers and pillows—neat by my standards, anyway.

"Please, sit," he instructs when we reach his kitchen, leaving me to lower my naked bum to the cool surface of the chair. "What would you like?"

"I'll have what you're having," I say, thinking I should make this as easy as possible for him.

"I'm having fruit and natural yogurt. Would you like that?" He opens the fridge and lifts out a stack of plastic containers, all containing various chopped fruits.

"Please," I answer on a sigh, praying we're not heading down that familiar road of shortness and detachment. It feels like it.

"As you wish." His tone is clipped as he sets about taking bowls down from the cupboard, spoons from the drawer, and yogurt from the fridge.

I'm silent as I watch him. Each object he puts in front of me is nudged to get it just so. Orange juice is squeezed, coffee brewed, and he's sitting opposite me in no time. I'm not touching a thing. I dare not. It's all been placed with utter precision, and I won't risk lowering his mood further by moving anything.

"Help yourself." He nods at my bowl. I gauge the position of the fruit bowl, so I can reposition it exactly right, and start spooning some fruit into my bowl. Then I replace it carefully. I've not even picked up my spoon before he's leaning over the table and nudging the fruit dish to the left. My fascination with Miller Hart just keeps growing, and while these little traits are quite irritating, they're really quite endearing, too. It's becoming quite clear that it is *me* who's sending this gentleman into a tailspin—me and my inability to satisfy his compulsion to keep things just the way he likes them. But I'm not going to take it personally. I don't think there's anyone on the planet who could get this right.

The silence is awfully uncomfortable, and I know exactly why. He's eating, but I can tell that he's fighting the urge to leave the table and restore his bedcovers to their normal perfect glory. I want to tell him to just go and do it, especially if it means he'll relax, which means I'll relax. I don't get a chance to, though. He closes his eyes, takes a deep breath, and rests his spoon across his bowl.

"Excuse me while I use the bathroom." He stands and leaves the room, and my eyes follow his path, wanting to follow and see him in action. But I take the opportunity to study all the items on the table, trying to figure out exactly what it is about their positions that keep him calm. I can't see it.

It's a good five minutes before he returns to the kitchen, visibly more relaxed. I relax, too, and I'm relieved that I've finished my breakfast and drank my juice, so there is absolutely no need for me to move *anything*... except me, and I'm beginning to register an issue with my positioning and movements, too—like in his bed.

He tucks himself under the table and takes his spoon, loading it with a strawberry and popping it in his mouth. The inevitability of my eyes focusing on his slow chews is something that I can't help. His mouth hypnotizes me as much as his eyes do when they're glistening at me. And I know they are now, which leaves me in a predicament. Eyes or mouth?

He decides for me when he speaks. I almost don't hear him, as I'm too rapt by those lips. "I have a request," he declares. The words, when they finally filter into my distracted mind, pull my eyes up to his. I was right. They're glistening.

"What kind of request?" I ask warily.

"I don't want you to see other men." He watches me thoughtfully, clearly trying to gauge my reaction, but I can't be giving him much to go on as my face is blank, not having quite worked out what reaction to give. "I think it's a reasonable request in light of your performance last night."

Now I have a facial expression, and I know it's a little stunned. "*You* are the reason for my performance last night," I retort.

"That may be so, but I'm uncomfortable with the idea of you exposing yourself like that."

"Exposed in general, or exposed to other men?"

"Both. You didn't feel the need to expose yourself before you met me, so I can't see that it would be a difficult request for you to fulfill." He takes another mouthful of his fruit, but I'm not compelled to watch him chew this time. No, I'm still stunned and looking into completely unaffected eyes.

He clearly seems to think it's perfectly reasonable to make these demands. I don't even know what to make of it. He's just worshipped me in his bed, said some pretty touching words, and now he's all businesslike.

"And the dating nonsense," he continues. "That won't be happening again, either."

I have to stop myself from laughing. "Why are you asking this of me?" I probe. Is this his way of saying he wants us to be exclusive?

His shoulders jump up on a shrug. "No man will make you feel like I can, so it's really in your best interest."

I'm staggered by his arrogance. He's right, but I'm not about to fuel his ego. "Miller." My elbows hit the table and my forehead falls into my palms. "Will you please just say exactly what you mean?" I look up at him, finding slight concern etched on his perfect face.

"I don't want anyone else tasting you," he says unapologetically. "It may seem unreasonable, but that's what I want and I'd like you to agree."

"And what about you?" I ask on a whisper. "I know about that woman."

"She's dealt with."

Dealt with? So he had to deal with her? "And she accepted that?"

"Yes."

"Why would it matter if she's just a business associate?"

"Like I said last night, it doesn't, but it does to you so I told her about you and let that be the end of it."

I scowl across the table at him. "I don't know anything about you."

"You know about my club."

"Only because I landed there by accident. I doubt I would've found out if I had waited to be told, and I'm certain you wouldn't have had me there by choice."

"Wrong."

I frown at his one word, assertive counter.

"You were on the guest list, Livy. If I had wanted to keep you away, I would've had you removed from it."

I snap my mouth shut and cast my mind back to what I can remember before the champagne and tequila took hold. "You were watching me all evening, weren't you?"

"Yes."

"I was with Gregory."

"You were."

"Did you think that he was my date?"

"Yes."

"And you didn't like it?"

"No."

Just like he didn't like seeing me with Luke. "You were jealous," I tell him, wondering at what point he figured out that Gregory's gay. Maybe the dance floor. Or maybe the toilet. He's been working at Ice, but my friend isn't obviously camp. He's a strapping bloke, who turns as many women's heads as he does gay men's.

"Frighteningly," he confirms.

I was right and I'm glad, but is he going to give me more than one word? "What's in it for me?" I ask, knowing damn well what he's going to say.

"Pleasure."

I sag at the table. Pleasure delivered by Miller is the ultimate prize . . . nearly. But what I want is his constant loving, like how he is when he has me in his *thing* or in his bed. "You're asking me to make myself exclusive to you?"

"Yes."

I'm absolutely fine with that, but given the circumstances of this conversation and how it's come about, I'm not sure this will mean that Miller is exclusively mine. "And what about you?"

"Me?"

"Will you stop speaking in monosyllables?" I snap.

He leans across the table. "I beg your pardon."

"You can beg all you like," I hiss back, fury burning in my gut. "You won't be getting any pardon from me."

"I beg to differ."

"There you go again!" I push my bowl away from my place setting and it collides with the glass fruit bowl, knocking it out of position. "Begging!" I watch as his eyes focus on the disturbed items on his perfect table, and he starts twitching, a flash of anger flying across his face. It makes me sit up and take notice.

More calmly than I know he's feeling, he spends a few silent moments putting everything back into position; then he stands and my eyes follow him around the table until I can no longer see him. He's behind me, and I tense when his palms rest on my shoulders, delivering a shot of fire through the material of his T-shirt and into my skin.

"It is you who will be begging, sweet girl." His mouth is at my ear, biting at my lobe. "You will accept my request because we both know that you're constantly wondering how you will survive without my attention." His thumbs start massaging delicious, firm circles into my shoulders.

"Don't pretend that this is all about my needs," I breathe, wanting to relax into his touch but refusing to grant my body the further pleasure that it's craving. He said he couldn't have me in the very beginning and in actual fact, he couldn't stay away.

His hands are gone in a moment and I'm being lifted from the chair. "I don't pretend, Livy." He starts a slow walk forward, forcing me to step back until I'm being gently pushed into the wall. "This is just as much for my needs, which is why I'm making this proposition, and it's also why you will accept."

My mind is doing an amazing job of preventing the desire from steaming forward. It's there, but so is the desire for answers. "You're making this sound like a business transaction."

"I work hard. I'm emotionally and physically drained by it. I want to have *you* to worship and indulge in when I'm done."

"I think you might be referring to a relationship," I whisper.

"Call it what you like. I want you to be at my disposal."

I'm horrified, delighted . . . unsure. For a man who's so articulate, he has a pretty strange way with words. "I think I'd like to call it a relationship," I say, just so he knows exactly what page I'm on.

"As you wish." He dips and finds my mouth, wrapping his forearm around the small of my back and lifting me, crushing me to his chest. I fall straight into the tender rhythm of his tongue, cocking my head to the side and sighing into his mouth, but my mind is still mulling over the weird words that have just been exchanged. Is Miller Hart now my boyfriend? Am I his girlfriend? "Stop overthinking," he mumbles into my mouth, turning and carrying me from the kitchen.

"I'm not."

"Yes, you are."

"You confuse me." My legs curl around his waist, my arms around his body.

"Take me as I am, Livy." He releases my lips and squeezes me to him. It's a silent, pleading follow-up to his words.

"Who are you?" I whisper my question into his neck and return his squeeze.

"I'm a man who's found a beautiful, sweet girl who gives me more pleasure than I ever thought possible." He lowers me to the couch and lies beside me, his face close to mine, his palm stroking up the inside of my thigh. "And I don't just mean with sex," he whispers, and I gasp. "I've made my intentions clear." His hand brushes over the hair at the apex of my thighs and his finger slips down my center. My back bows. "She's always ready for me," he murmurs, working the heated moisture over every inch of my flesh. "She's always aroused by me." I push my forehead to his and close my eyes. "And she accepts that she can't stop it. We were made to fit together. We fit perfectly together."

My breath diminishes and my legs stiffen.

"She responds to me without even knowing it." He uses his forehead to push me back from him. "And she knows how I feel when she deprives me of her face."

Forcing my eyes to open and my head to remain still, I start involuntarily thrusting my hips gently back and forth to match his caressing of my damp, throbbing center. He's building me up lazily, watching me come apart. My hands are fisted on the front of his T-shirt, pulling and grappling at the cotton, making a mess of the previously creaseless garment.

"She's going to come," he muses, his eyes drifting down my body to watch his hand work me. My legs start shifting, trying to control the onslaught of pressure surging forward. And then he pushes a finger into me on a hitch of his breath, quickly swapping it for two when I cry out and start to shake. "That's it, Livy."

I lose the battle to hold my eyes open and throw my head back, mumbling senseless words as my climax takes hold.

"Show me your face."

"I can't," I moan.

"You can for me, Livy. Let me see you."

I yell my despair and toss my head forward. "You can't do this to me."

He kisses me, too gently for my current frenzied state. "I can, I am, and I always will. Scream my name." He pushes his thumb onto my clitoris and circles firmly, watching me as I fight to deal with the pleasure that he's inflicting on me.

"Miller!"

"That's the only man's name you'll ever scream, Olivia Taylor." He tackles my mouth, kissing me to orgasm as he moans and pushes his chest into mine, his body absorbing my shocked trembles. "I promise that I'll always make you feel this special." He brings his fingers to my mouth and runs the moisture across my lips. "No one will ever taste that, except me and you." His face is expressionless, but I'm beginning to recognize his emotional frame of mind through his mesmerizing eyes. Right now, he's sanctimonious, satisfied . . . victorious. I've confirmed all of his claims with my low moans and bodily responses to his touch.

Miller Hart rules my body.

And it's fast becoming obvious that he rules my heart, too.

CHAPTER NINETEEN

My legs are cold and my body stiff. Miller isn't on the sofa with me, but I can hear him close by, the sounds of cupboards opening and crockery gently clanking, quickly telling me where he is and what he's doing. Stretching out on a happy groan, I smile as I look up at the ceiling, then sit up to remind myself of the beautiful art that graces the walls of his apartment. After switching my eyes from one to another, and then another a few times, I give up on trying to pick my favorite. I love them all, even though they are distorted and bordering ugly.

My head is only fuzzy with sleep, as opposed to alcohol, and despite my slightly achy muscles, I feel perfect. Getting to my feet, I go in search of Miller, finding him wiping down the countertop with antibacterial spray. "Hi."

He looks up, pushing his hair from his forehead with the back of his hand. "Livy." He folds the cloth and lays it next to the sink. "Are you okay?"

"I'm fine, Miller."

He nods. "Excellent. I've drawn a bath. Would you like to join me?"

We're back to gentleman mode. It makes me smile. "I'd love to join you."

He cocks his head curiously as he walks toward me. "Have I said something amusing?" he asks as he takes hold of my nape and turns me.

"I find your manner amusing." I let him lead me to his bedroom and into the bathroom where the huge, claw-foot bath is full of bubbly water.

"Should I be offended by that?" He grasps the hem of my T-shirt and lifts it over my head, then neatly folds it and places it in the laundry basket.

I shrug. "No, your habits are charming."

"My habits?"

"Yes, your habits." I don't elaborate. He knows what I'm referring to, and it's not just his gentlemanly ways—when he chooses to use them.

"My habits," he muses, pulling off his T-shirt and going about the same folding routine. "I think I *am* offended." He slides his shorts down his thighs, folding and placing them neatly in the laundry basket, too. "After you," he says, gesturing to the bath, his naked perfection sending me dizzy. "Need some support?"

I glance up, finding smugness in his eyes and his hand held out. "Thank you." I tentatively take his offered hand and climb the steps before lowering myself into the tub.

"Is the temperature okay?" he asks, following me in and taking the opposite end so we're facing one another, his legs bent, his knees breaking the surface of the deep water.

"Sure." I lie back, and the soles of my feet slip along the bottom of the tub until they're wedged under his arse. He raises his eyebrows, making me blush. "Sorry, it's slippery."

"No need to apologize." He collects my feet from beneath him and lifts to settle them on his chest. "You have cute feet."

"Cute?" I have to stop myself from laughing. I never know what words or tones are going to fall from Miller Hart's lips, but they affect me in one way or another every time, whether it be amusement, irritation, lust, or confusion.

"Yes, cute." He dips and kisses my little toe. "I have a request."

His declaration makes it very easy to stop the threatening laughter from surfacing. Another request? "What is it?" I ask nervously.

"Don't look so apprehensive, Livy."

Easy for him to say. "I'm not apprehensive. I'm curious."

"So am I."

I frown across the bath at him. "What are you curious about?"

"How it will feel to be inside you without anything between us."

"Oh . . . ," I breathe.

He reaches into the water and locates my hand, pulling me to my knees and leading it to the solid rod resting on his abdomen. "You must be curious, too."

I am now. "You're speaking like this is long-term," I say hesitantly, bracing myself for his reply.

"I've already told you that I want more than our remaining four hours, which I believe have expired now." He positions my grasp around him and lays his hand over mine, then starts guiding me up and down slowly under the water. My whole being relaxes, peace settling over me in response to his words. The movement of his chest visibly changes, the rise and fall increasing dramatically. He feels like velvet, but my view of our combined movements is hampered by the gallons of water surrounding us. I can only see the swollen head of his penis, so I lift my eyes and let them indulge in the subtle parting of his incredible lips.

"I *am* curious," I confess, shifting forward on my knees. "But I'm not on the pill."

"Are you prepared to rectify that so we can both feed our curiosity?"

I nod my agreement as I allow him to control the strokes of my hand over his erection. He feels sublime—smooth, firm, and large.

He looks sublime, too, and breathing some confidence into myself, I flex my hand until he releases on a frown and watches me climb up his body.

"What are you doing, Livy?" he asks warily, but he doesn't stop me from finding my way until I'm sitting on his lap, his arousal resting perfectly beneath me. In fact, he helps me.

"I want to feel you." I lower my face to his, the sensation of him pulsing under me injecting more confidence. I'm losing my mind, my body acting without instruction.

He shakes his head lightly and homes in on my lips, kissing me adoringly. I might be teasing and tormenting him, but he's the one in control. "That can't happen, Livy."

"Please," I breathe, finding his hair. "Let me."

"Oh, Jesus, you're ruining me."

I take his weak, breathless words as defeatism and reach down between our bodies while keeping up our kiss. "It is me who's ruined." I bite his tongue gently. "You've ruined me." My hand finds what it's looking for, and I lift to position him at my opening.

"I haven't ruined you, Livy." I feel his hand wrap around my wrist, halting my reckless intention. "I've awakened a desire in you that only I can satisfy." He pulls my hand away, his lips straight in warning. "And it seems one of us needs to keep our head before we find ourselves in a situation."

I'm pent up on lust, but his cautionary face soon drags me back to reality. "Your fault," I mumble, embarrassed and feeling unreasonably rejected.

"So you keep telling me," he says, rolling his blue eyes. It's a sign of exasperation, a rare show of emotion. In an attempt to restore my slighted state and distract Miller from scorning me further, I start to shift down, keen to taste him again. But I don't get very far.

He halts me, looking almost nervous, and pulls me up,

completely crowding me with his body and falling back against the bath, settling me on his chest. "*Thing.*"

Despite my confusion at his decline, I hum happily and embrace his iron hold, clinging on to him everywhere and relishing in the sound of his breathing as the water around our bodies laps gently. "I have a request, too," I whisper, feeling brave and comfortable asking.

"Hold your thought." He turns his head and kisses my wet cheek. "Let me have my *thing.*"

"I can ask *while* you're having your *thing,*" I counter on a smile.

"Probably, but I like to see you when we're conversing."

"I think cuddling might be my *thing* now, too." I squeeze some more, causing our bodies to slip. The comfort and peace that engulfs me during these moments makes me want to superglue myself to him.

"I hope you mean with me."

"Exclusively," I sigh. "Can I voice my request yet?"

I'm reluctantly released from his chest and pushed up on his lap. "Tell me what you want."

"Information." My bravery diminishes at the sight of his straight lips and tight jaw, but I find the courage to continue. "Your habits."

"My habits?" He raises his eyebrows, almost in warning.

I push on carefully. "You're very . . ." I stop myself to choose my words wisely. "Exact."

"You mean tidy?"

This is more than tidy. This is obsessive, but I'm getting the feeling that he's sensitive about this subject. "Yes, tidy," I relent. "You're very tidy."

"I make sure I take care of what's mine." He reaches forward and pinches my nipple, making me jerk on top of him. "And you are now mine, Olivia Taylor."

"I am?" I sound shocked, but I'm secretly delighted. I want to be possessed by him every moment of every day.

"Yes," he says simply, taking my waist and pulling me down until our foreheads meet. "You are also my habit."

"I'm a habit?"

"You're an addictive habit." He kisses my nose. "A habit that I never plan on giving up."

I don't hesitate to let him know my thoughts on him and his new habit. "Okay."

"Who said you have a choice?"

"You said you'd never make me do anything I don't want to," I remind him.

"I said I'd never make you do anything that I *know* you don't want to do, and I know that you really want to be my habit. So this is a pointless discussion, wouldn't you agree?"

I scowl at him, stumped for any comeback. "You're cocky."

"You're in trouble."

I retreat on his lap. "What do you mean?" I ask. Is he warning me?

"Let's talk about yesterday evening," he suggests, like we might be discussing where to have dinner. I'm instantly on my guard, and my chest falling onto his and my face hiding in his neck is evidence of this.

"We've already talked about it."

"Not at length. I'm none the wiser as to why you behaved so recklessly, Livy, and it makes me uncomfortable." He wrestles me out of his chest and holds me in place. "When I'm talking to you, you look at me."

I keep my head down. "I don't want to talk to you."

"Hard luck." He's moving, making himself more comfortable. "Explain yourself."

"I got drunk, that's all." I don't mean to, but I'm gritting my teeth and looking up at him through pissed off eyes. "And stop talking to me like I'm a delinquent child."

"Then stop behaving like one." He's deadly serious. I'm stunned.

"You know what?" I push up and get out of the bath, and he does nothing to stop me. He just lays back, all relaxed and completely unaffected by my little tantrum. "You might make me feel incredible, say some beautiful things when you make love to me, but when you behave like this, all . . . all . . . all . . ."

"All what, Livy?"

"You're a self-righteous prick!" I spit desperately.

He's not at all fazed. "Tell me why you disappeared. Where did you go?"

His demanding questions only heighten my fury . . . and my desperation. "You said you'd never make me do anything I didn't want to."

"That I *know* you don't want to. I can see a burden weighing down my sweet girl." He reaches for me with his hand. "Let me ease it."

I look at his hand for a few moments, my mind racing with only one worry. He'd leave me again if I ever told him. "You can't." I turn on my bare feet and stalk away. I can't stand this. Miller Hart is a roller-coaster ride, tossing me from untold pleasure to indescribable anger, from confident to timid and nervous, from pure joy to painful hurt. I'm being constantly pulled in two directions and while I know full well how I felt when he abandoned me before, at least the despair was consistent. At least I knew where I was. I'll make the decision this time.

Cold and wet, I pull open the bottom drawer of the chest and take my knickers, purse, and shoes, then hurry into his wardrobe and grab the first shirt that I lay my hands on, tossing it over my shoulders and dropping my shoes to the floor. Once I've slipped my knickers on and my feet into my heels, I make my escape, running across his bedroom, down the corridor, and into the lounge, desperate to hide from his pressing questions and disapproving tones. I know that I was reckless last night. My mistakes are plentiful, but none as big as the man who I've just left in the bath. I don't know what I've been thinking. He won't understand.

Dashing toward the front door of his apartment, I begin to relax when my hand makes contact with the handle. But I can't turn it. It's not locked, I can leave if I want to, but my muscles are ignoring my brain's faint order to open the door. And that is because there's a more powerful command drowning it out, telling me to go back and *make* him understand.

I look down at my hand, mentally willing it to turn the knob. But it doesn't. It won't. My forehead meets the shiny black door, my eyes clamping shut as I battle the conflicting commands and stamp my heel on the floor in pure frustration. I can't leave. My body and mind are not prepared to pass this door and leave behind the only man who I've ever connected with. I didn't allow this to happen. It was unstoppable.

I roll my body around until my back is stuck to the door and I'm staring at Miller. He's standing quietly watching me, completely naked and dripping wet. "You can't leave, can you?"

"No," I sob, my knees becoming as weak as my falling heart and refusing to hold my body up any longer, leaving me sliding down the door until my bottom hits the floor. My anger turns to tears, and I cry silently to myself, the last of my defenses melting away. I let my hopelessness pour into my hands and my barricades completely diminish under the scrutiny of the confounding Miller Hart. It feels like a lifetime, but I know it's only mere seconds, before he's gathering me up and carrying me back to his bed. He doesn't say a word. He sits me on the edge and slips my shoes and knickers off, and then pushes his shirt from my shoulders and down my arms, leaning into me and resting his lips on my cheek as he does. "Don't cry, sweet girl," he whispers, uncharacteristically throwing his shirt to the floor before taking me gently down to the bed. "Please don't cry."

His plea has the opposite effect and more tears flow, his bare chest becoming as sodden as my face as he presses me into him, tenderly kissing the top of my head every now and then, while he hums that peaceful harmony above me. It starts to soothe me and my sobs begin to abate under the hard warmth of his body holding me and the calming hum of his voice seeping into my ears.

"I'm not a sweet girl," I whisper into his chest. "You keep calling me sweet girl, but you shouldn't."

His humming fades out and the tender kissing of my head stops. He's thinking about my declaration. "You are very much a sweet... woman, Livy."

"It's not the reference to 'girl' so much," I whisper. "It's the sweet part that bothers me most." I feel him stiffen a little before he encourages me from his chest. We're conversing, he wants eye contact, and when he finds it, he wipes my damp cheeks with his thumbs and gazes at me, his eyes full of pity. I don't want pity, and I don't deserve it.

"You're *my* sweet girl."

"You're mistaken."

"No, you're mine, Livy," he asserts, almost showing annoyance.

"I don't mean that," I sigh, dropping my eyes, but soon bringing them back up when he shifts his hands from my cheeks to my neck and tilts my head back.

"Elaborate."

"I want to be yours," I murmur, and he smiles. He gives me that rare, beautiful smile, and my heart skips with happiness for a split second, but then I remember the conversation direction. "I really want to be yours," I affirm.

"I'm glad we've cleared that up." He drops his lips to mine and kisses me delicately. "But you really don't have a choice in the matter."

"I know," I agree, aware that it's not just because Miller says that I don't have a choice. I tried to leave, and I couldn't. I really tried.

"Listen to me," he says, sitting up and dragging me onto his lap. "I shouldn't have pressed you. I said that I'd never make you do anything I know you don't want to. That will always stand, but please know that whatever you fear will change my opinion of my sweet girl is wasted anxiety."

"What if it isn't?"

"I'm never going to know unless you choose to tell me, and if you don't, then that's fine, too. Yes, I would prefer it if you confide in me, but not if it's going to make you sad, Livy. I can't see you sad. I want you to trust me that it won't make any difference to how I feel about you. Let me help you."

My chin starts to tremble.

"Your mother," he says quietly.

I nod.

"Livy, you're not like that. Don't let someone else's bad choices affect your life."

"I could have been like that," I whisper, shame beginning to flood me, my head dropping.

My face is grasped and pulled to him, but I keep my eyes low, not wanting to face the contempt he'll be showing. "We're talking, Livy."

"I've said enough."

"No, you haven't. Look at me."

Forcing my eyes up, I meet his, but there's no contempt. There's no anything. Even now, Miller Hart gives nothing away. "I wanted to know where she'd gone."

He frowns. "You've lost me."

"I read her journal. I read about the places she went and who with. I read about a man. A man named William. Her pimp."

He's just staring at me. He knows where I'm heading.

"I put myself in her world, Miller. I lived her life."

"No." He shakes his head. "No, you didn't."

"Yes, I did. What was so amazing about that life that it kept her from being a mother? That it made her abandon me?" I fight to control the tears threatening to break free again. I refuse to shed another tear for that woman. "I found Nan's gin and then I found William. I tricked him into taking me on and he set me up with clients. Her clients. I went through most of the men listed in my mother's journal."

"Stop," he whispers. "Please stop."

I harshly brush at my wet cheeks. "All I found was the humiliation of letting a man slam into me."

He winces. "Don't say that, Livy."

"There was nothing glamorous or appealing about mindless sex."

"Livy, please!" he yells, pushing me from his body and standing, leaving me feeling exposed and lonely on his bed. He starts pacing around his room, clearly agitated, his head falling back on a curse. "I don't understand. You're so pure and beautiful to the core. I love that."

"Alcohol got me through it. I was just there in body. But I couldn't stop. I kept thinking there had to be more, something I was missing."

"*Stop!*" He flies around and hammers me with an enraged glare, making me jump back on the bed in shock. "Any man who's done anything less than worship you should be fucking shot!" He crouches on the floor, his hands in his hair. "Fuck!"

My entire being goes lax—my body, my mind, and my heart. It's all given up, my past very much in my present and forcing me to explain myself. He looks up at me. His blues are boring into me. Then they close and he pulls in a long, calming breath of air, but I don't give him time to start firing his thoughts at me. I have a good idea what they are, anyway.

I've ruined his opinion of his pure, beautiful girl. "I'm sorry," I say evenly as I drag myself off the bed. "I'm sorry for destroying your ideal." I collect his shirt from the floor and calmly start to put it on. I can feel the pain turning in my gut, stirring years of anguish and misery.

I draw my discarded knickers up my thighs, pick up my shoes and purse from the floor, and walk out of his bedroom, knowing that this time I'll be able to leave. And I do. The evident contempt that he feels makes me turn the handle of the door with ease, and I'm on my way down the corridor to the stairwell, my bare feet dragging the floor along with my fallen heart.

"Please don't go. I'm sorry for shouting at you."

His soft voice halts me midstep and rips my breaking heart from my chest. "Don't feel obligated, Miller."

"Obligated?"

"Yes, obligated," I say, starting down the steps again. Miller feeling guilty over his violent reaction isn't what I need, nor is sympathy. I'm not sure what the happy medium is of those two, but acceptance and understanding might help. It'll be more than I allow myself.

"Livy!" I can hear his bare feet coming after me, and when he lands in front of me, I only mildly register that he's wearing only a pair of black boxer shorts. "I'm not sure how many times I have to tell you," he grinds. "When I'm talking to you, you look at me."

He's saying that because he doesn't know what else to say. "And what will you say if I *do* look at you?" I ask, because I don't need to see disgust or guilt or sympathy.

"If you look at me, you'll find out." He hunkers down to get in the field of my dropped vision, prompting me to glance up. I find his beautiful face completely expressionless, and while I usually find this frustrating, right now I'm relieved because with no expression, there is no contempt or any of the other emotions that I don't want to see. "You're still my habit, Livy. Don't ask me to give you up."

"You're disgusted with me," I whisper, forcing my voice to remain steady. I don't want to cry on him again.

"I'm disgusted with myself." He tentatively lifts his hand and seeks out my nape, watching me closely for any signs of denial. I won't deny him. I'll never deny him. I know my face must be as hard to read as his right now, and that is because I'm not sure what I'm feeling. Part of me is relieved; a huge part is still ashamed and another part, the biggest part of all, is acknowledging what Miller Hart means to me.

Comfort.

Refuge.

Love.

I've fallen. This beautiful man fills me with far more comfort and offers far more refuge than my life strategies ever have. When he's not scorning me or reminding me of my manners, he's over-dosing me with adoration, but even the irritating parts of him are stupidly comforting. I'm as much in love with the fake gentleman as I am with the attentive lover. I love him—all of him.

His lips twitch at the corners, but it's nerves. I can tell that much. "I hate the thought of you like that. You should never have been put in that situation."

"I put myself in that situation. I drank to get through it, even if it made me stupid. William sent me away when he realized who I was, but I was determined. I was stupid."

He blinks lazily, trying to absorb being bombarded with my reality. My mother's history. And my history, too. "Please, come back inside."

I nod faintly, and he exhales in relief, putting his arm around my shoulder and tucking me into his chest. We walk slowly and silently back to his apartment.

After sitting me on the couch and placing my purse and shoes under the table, he goes straight to his drinks cabinet and pours some dark liquid into a tumbler, quickly downing it before refilling. His hands are braced on the edge, his head dropped. It's too quiet. Uncomfortable. I need to know what's ticking in that complex mind of his.

After the long, difficult silence, he picks his drink up and makes his way over to my shrinking form, taking a seat on the glass table and placing his drink down, shifting it a tiny bit. He eventually sighs. "Livy, I'm doing a terrible job of pretending that this hasn't knocked me sideways."

"You are," I agree.

"You're so . . . .well, lovely—pure in a healthy way. I love that."

I frown. "Because you get to walk all over me?"

"No, it's just . . ."

"What, Miller? It's just what?"

"You're different. Your beauty starts here." He leans in and runs his palm across my cheek, hypnotizing me with his intense blue gaze. Then he slowly drags it down my throat and onto my chest. "And goes all the way to here. Deep into here. It shines through those sapphire eyes, Olivia Taylor. I saw it the moment I looked at you." My emotions are choking me, the mention of sapphire eyes bringing back fond memories of my granddad. "I want to surrender myself to you completely, Livy. I want to be yours. You are my perfect."

I'm shocked. But I don't voice it. For Miller to say I'm his perfect, given his crazily perfect world, is . . . crazy.

He grabs my hands and kisses my knuckles. "I don't care what happened years ago." His forehead wrinkles and he begins to shake his head. "No, I apologize. I do care, I fucking hate that you did that. I don't understand why."

"I felt lost," I whisper. "Granddad kept things together after my mum vanished. He battled with Nan's grief for years and disguised his own. Then he died. He'd hidden my mother's journal all that time." I draw breath and continue before I lose my flow or Miller loses his mind. He looks more and more shocked by the second. "She wrote about all of these men showering her with gifts and attention. Maybe I could find that, and find her, too."

"Your nan loved you."

"Nan wasn't capable of anything when Granddad died. She

spent every hour of every day crying and praying for answers. She couldn't see me through her grief."

Miller's eyes clench shut but I go on, despite him clearly struggling.

"I left and found William. He was taken by me." Miller's teeth are gritting now. "It didn't take him long to make the connection and he sent me away. But I went back. Now I had an idea of how it worked. I was even more determined to see if I could find out anything about my mum, but I never did. All I felt was shame when I let one of them have me."

"Livy, please." Miller's cheeks puff and release a slow stream of air, an obvious attempt to calm himself.

"William took me home, and I found Nan in a worse state than when I'd left. She was in such a dark place. I felt so guilty and I realized it was my job to take care of her now. We only had each other. I never returned to William and I've never given myself to anyone since. Nan's never known where I went and what I did. She never can."

My clouded vision sees wide blue eyes and a stoic face. It's out there now. No going back.

He seems to shake himself back to life, squeezing my hands in his. "Promise me you won't ever degrade yourself like that again. I beg you."

I don't hesitate. "I promise." It's the easiest promise that I've ever made. That's all he has to say? There's no look of contempt or disgust. "I promise," I affirm. "I promise, I promise, I pro—" I don't get any further. He moves in fast, taking me down to my back, and completely drowns me in his mouth's attention, kissing me until I'm literally seeing stars. He's moaning into my neck, kissing his way over my cheek, thrusting his tongue into my mouth. He's everywhere. "I promise," I moan. "I promise."

He grapples with the shirt I'm wearing, pulling it open to access my body. "You'd better not," he warns seriously, trailing his lips down my neck and onto my chest. His mouth locks around my tingling nipple and sucks hard, and I'm arching my back and throwing my hands into action. They home in on his strong shoulders, my nails scraping at him, and then I feel his fingers between my thighs, separating me, and his head starts moving down. He sends me delirious with a firm, hot lick up my center before he's on his way up my body again and plunging into my mouth. "So ready," he mumbles.

"Inside. I want you inside me." I'm demanding, desperate for him to scrub away the last hour of agonizing confessions and judgments. "Please."

He growls, firming up his kiss. "Condom."

"Get one."

"Shit!" he barks, jumping up and pulling me to my feet. He stoops and throws me onto his shoulder, urgently pacing to the bedroom where he lowers me to the bed and immediately removes his boxers before finding a condom and making quick work of rolling it on.

I'm impatient as I watch him, willing him to hurry up before I lose my screwed up mind. "Miller," I pant, reaching up to stroke down the center of his stomach.

He pushes me to my back and falls to his fists, one on each side of my head. He's breathless, his hair falling forward, his eyes hungry. "This is what it's all about." He rolls his hips and drives into me on a suppressed gasp, holding himself deep while he tries to stabilize his uneven breathing. I cry out. "This is pleasure." He retreats and pushes forward on another burst of air, coaxing another shout of gratification from me. "This is feeling." Back he draws before thrusting forward again. "This is how it'll always be." His pace is meticulous, smooth, and perfectly precise. "This is us."

"I want it to be," I breathe, meeting his advances with constant swivels of my hips. His eyes are smiling, and then like a sun breaking through the gray clouds on an overcast, smoggy day in London, his mouth smiles, too—his perfectly straight, white teeth on full display, his eyes sparkling wildly. He accepts me. All of me.

"I'm glad we've cleared that up, not that you had a choice."

"I don't want a choice."

"You know it makes perfect sense." He drops to his forearms and gets our faces nose to nose, delivering delicious deep grinds over and over. My hands are all over his back, my knees bent and spread, and his shirt a creased up mess, pooling my body. "I have a fascinating habit," he says, scanning my face.

"Me too."

"She's the most beautiful thing."

"My habit is mystifying." I groan and lift my head to capture his lips. "He's in disguise."

"Disguise?" he asks around my mouth, meeting my demanding tongue with his own.

"He's disguised as a gentleman."

A cough of surprise falls past his lips. "If I wasn't enjoying myself so much right now, I'd challenge you for your cheek. I *am* a gentleman." He jerks forward and bites my lip. "Bollocks!"

"A gentleman doesn't swear!" I shout, linking my legs around his waist and tightening them, pushing into his rock-hard arse.

"Fuck!"

"Oh God! Faster!" My hands push into his neck, forcing his lips harder to mine.

"Savored," he argues weakly. "I'll enjoy you slowly."

He might be enjoying me slowly, but I'm losing my mind fast. His control is beyond comprehension. How does he do it? "You want to go faster," I goad him, yanking at his disheveled mop.

"Wrong." He pulls his head away, making me lose my grip. "I didn't before, and I especially don't now."

His harsh reminder of what came before the rightness of this moment halts my tempting tactic in their tracks. "Thank you for keeping me," I whisper.

"Don't thank me. This is happening." He abruptly pulls out and gently turns me over, pulling my hips upward before slowly sliding back into me. My face buries in the pillow, biting at the cotton as he continuously thrusts back and forth, painstakingly slowly. He's wreaking havoc on my senses, and I find my body falling into his momentum, gliding back onto each of his drives. He's moving again, flipping me back onto my back and guiding my legs until they're draped over his shoulders and he's back inside of me, pushing deep.

He's sweating, his waves a delightful mess of wet and his stubble glistening. "I love seeing your body move."

I allow my eyes a glimpse of his chest, finding ripples of muscle riding up his torso with every push forward. I'm on the brink of detonation, but trying to rein it in so I can indulge in him some more. Finding his eyes again, I warm further when he blesses me with another one of his beautiful smiles.

"I guarantee you, Livy. What you're looking at isn't a whisper of the beauty in my view."

"Wrong," I breathe seriously, reaching up to touch him. He exceeds perfection to the point of inflicting pain on my eyes.

"We'll agree to disagree, sweet girl." He grinds with purpose, making it impossible for me to argue with him. "Good?"

"Yes!"

"I concur." He drops a shoulder, letting my leg slide down his arm so he can lower his torso. "Put your hands above your head."

"I want to touch you," I complain, my wandering hands going off on a feeling frenzy.

"Put your hands over your head, Livy." He reinforces his command with a sharp thrust, sending my head flying back, along with my hands. Lowering to his forearms, he rests his palms on the undersides of my arms and strokes to match the tempo of his hips. His blue eyes are wild with passion.

"Are you ready, Livy?"

I nod, then shake my head, then nod again. "Miller!"

He groans, taking his rhythm up a level. "Livy, I'm going to send you crazy with pleasure daily, so you're going to have to learn to control your body."

Now my head is shaking, my body being attacked by persistent shots of pleasure. It's becoming too much. "Please," I beg, looking up into eyes full of triumph. He loves making me crazy. He thrives on it. "You're doing this on purpose."

My other leg is released and he completely cages me in with his body, preventing me from wriggling, moving, or shaking. I can't hold out any longer. I'll pass out.

"Of course I am," he agrees. "If you could see what I'm seeing, you'd drag it out, too."

"Don't torture me," I groan, flicking my hips up.

He dips and kisses me. "I'm not torturing you, Livy. I'm showing you how it should be."

"You're making me crazy," I breathe. He doesn't need to show me. He's done that every time he's worshipped me.

"And it's the most satisfying sight." He bites at my lip. "Would you like to come?"

I nod and lift my arms from my head, and he doesn't stop me. I find his shoulders, my hands slipping everywhere, and kiss the hell out of him. I'm relentless with my tongue as he pushes me higher and higher, and then it happens. He bucks on a yell, I scream on a violent arch of my body, and we both begin to shake and pulse. I'm utterly replete, and once my shakes have subsided, I'm totally limp. Useless. I can't talk, I can't move, and I can't see straight. He's twitching within me, still circling firmly.

"Do you want the good news or the bad news?" he puffs into

my neck, but I can't answer him. I'm breathless, my mind scrambled, and I attempt a shrug that is executed as more of a spasm. "I'll give you the bad news," he says when it becomes obvious that an answer is not forthcoming. "The bad news is I'm paralyzed. I can't bloody move, Livy."

If I had the energy, I'd smile, but I'm a despondent pile of twitching nerve endings. So I hum my response and attempt a little squeeze of him. It's feeble.

"The good news is," he pants, "we haven't got to go anywhere, so we can stay like this forever. Am I heavy?"

He's very heavy but I haven't got the strength or inclination to tell him so. He's all over me, covering every square inch, our sweaty skin rubbing everywhere. I hum my noncommittal reply again, my eyes closing with exhaustion.

"Livy?" he whispers softly.

"Hmmm?"

"No matter what happened, you really are my sweet girl. Nothing will change that."

My eyes open and I find the energy to respond. "I'm a woman, Miller," I say, needing him to realize I'm no girl. I'm a woman and I have needs, and one of those needs—the biggest one—is now Miller Hart.

CHAPTER TWENTY

It was inevitable that he would abandon me. All his actions, reassuring words, and comfort were far too good to be true. I should have known that from the guilt plaguing his face when he stopped me from leaving. I wish he'd never come after me. I wish he'd never let his compassion take over and force him into comforting me. It's made it so much harder to bear. The darkness is constant and the agony relentless. Everything hurts—my brain for thinking too much, my body for missing his touch, and my eyes for not seeing him. I'm not sure how long it has been since he left me. Days. Weeks. Months. It could be longer.

I dare not venture from my silent darkness. I dare not present my injured soul to the world, which puts me further into seclusion than I ever was before I met Miller Hart.

Tears start to pour from my eyes. Visions of my mother's face morph into mine, and my head jerks from the lash of my nan's palm slapping my face.

"Livy?"

"Leave me alone," I sob, pulling my numb body onto my stomach and hiding my tear-drenched face in the pillow.

"Livy." Hands start to pull at my body, and I fight them away, not wanting to face anyone or anything. "Livy, please."

"Get off me!" I scream, thrashing my body aimlessly everywhere.
"Livy!"

I'm suddenly pinned to the mattress, my flailing hands held firmly by my sides.

"Livy, open your eyes."

My head starts shaking and my eyes clench tighter. I'm not ready to face the world yet—probably never will be. My arms are released and my head held still; then the familiar softness of slow-moving lips are on my mouth, and I can hear the low hum that I love so much.

My eyes fly open and I scramble to sit up—shocked, disoriented, and sweating. I'm having heart palpitations and I can't see anything with my wild hair messy and falling all over my face. "Miller?" My hair is pushed from my eyes and he slowly comes into my line of sight, concern etched all over his impossibly beautiful face.

"I'm here, Livy."

Awareness finally hits me and I launch myself onto his kneeling body, knocking him to his back. I'm deranged but relieved, terrified but calm.

It was just a dream.

A dream that made me feel all too vividly how it might be if he's gone. "Promise me you won't abandon me," I mumble. "Promise me you're not going anywhere."

"Hey, whatever's brought this on?"

"Just say it." I sink my face into his neck, unwilling to let him go. I've had dreams before, I've woken up and wondered if they've really happened, but this was different. This was frighteningly real. I can still feel the ache in my chest and the panic engulfing me, even now when he's got me firmly in his arms.

It takes some effort on his part, but he eventually pries my clawed fingers from his back and detaches me from his body. Sitting up and placing me between his thighs, he circles my neck completely with his palms and tilts my head until our gazes lock, mine brimming with tears, his with tenderness. "I'm not your mother," he says firmly.

"It hurt so much." I'm sobbing, trying to reassure myself that it was just a dream—a stupid, stupid dream.

His face falls. "Your mother walked out on you, Livy. Of course it hurt."

"No." I shake my head in his hold. "That doesn't hurt anymore." This new fear has drowned any sense of abandonment that I felt before. "I'm better off without her." He winces, his eyes closing painfully at my harshness. I don't care. "I'm talking about you," I whisper. "You left me." I'm aware that I sound needy and weak, but my desperation is crippling me. Compared to how I'm feeling now, coping with my mother's abandonment seems like a breeze. Miller's shown me comfort. He's accepted me. "I've never felt pain like it."

"Livy—"

"No." I cut him off. He needs to know. I move from his personal space, shifting myself across the bed so I'm out of touching distance.

"Livy, what are you doing?" he asks, reaching for me. "Come here."

"You need to know something," I murmur nervously, refusing to meet his eyes.

"There's more?" he blurts, pulling his reaching hand back, like I might bite him. He's cautious, wary. It doesn't boost my confidence. I've shocked Miller Hart with my dirty little secrets, more than he's ever shocked me with his moods—transforming from domineering to passive and from cold-hearted to loving faster than I can keep up with.

"There's one more thing," I admit, hearing him draw breath, preparing himself for what I might hit him with next. For him, this might be the biggest shock of all.

"I believe we might be conversing, Livy." His tone is clipped and intimidating, the one that makes me take notice, whether I scoff at it or cower. Right now, I'm cowering.

"You still fascinate me," I say, looking up at him. "All of your set ways, your faffing with things when they're already perfect, and the way you have to have things just so."

He's frowning at me, and for a split second I think he might deny it. But he doesn't. "Take me as I am, Livy."

"That's what I'm saying."

"Elaborate," he demands harshly, making me cower further.

"You take command over me," I start nervously, "and it should probably frighten me or perhaps have me telling you to piss off, but..."

"I believe you might have told me to go to hell last night."

"Your fault."

"Probably," he relents on a grunt and a roll of those blistering blue eyes. "Continue."

I smile inwardly. He's doing it right now—being brusque and starched, but it's terribly alluring, even when it's bloody infuriating. I feel so safe with him. "I don't know whether my heart can survive you," I say quietly, watching closely for his reaction, "but I want to take you as you are." I shouldn't be surprised when his expression remains completely blank, and I'm not, but those eyes tell me a little something. They're telling me he knows how I feel already. He'd be pretty stupid not to. "I've fallen."

His blue gaze touches my soul. It's now full of knowing and understanding. "Why are you on the other side of the bed, Livy?" he asks, his voice low and sure.

My eyes travel the distance between our bodies, noting a good meter of mattress between us. Perhaps I did go over the top with my decision to distance myself, but I didn't want to feel his body stiffen when I uttered those words. I've not said it, but Miller is an intelligent man. My cards have been slowly laid, and now they are faceup for all to see.

"I...I...I didn't..."

"Why are you on the other side of the bed, Livy?"

Our eyes connect. He's looking at me sternly, like he really is mad about my distance, but I can still see understanding in them, too. "I..."

"I've already repeated myself." He cuts me off completely. "Don't make me do it again."

I hesitate too long, going to shift toward him but quickly drawing back, wondering what's running through that multilayered mind of his.

"Overthinking, Livy," he warns. "Give me my *thing*."

I inch forward slowly, but he doesn't welcome me with open arms or encourage me forward. He just watches me blackly, following my eyes as they get closer and closer until I'm gently crawling onto his lap and circling his shoulders tentatively with my arms. I feel his palms gently rest on my hips and begin a languid caress of my back while he slowly lowers his face into my hair until we're locked together, completely encasing each other...just holding each other. Miller Hart's *thing* has fast become my *thing*, too. Nothing will ever beat the sense of refuge and solace that I get from a simple cuddle delivered by Miller. His touch soaks up all of the anguish and despair.

"I'm not sure if I can function without you," I say softly. "I feel like you've become a vital part of what keeps me breathing." I'm not exaggerating. That dream was chillingly real, and that feeling alone is enough to make me spill. But he's too quiet. I can feel his heart beating under my chest, and it's steady, not shocked and erratic, but that's all I can feel. I'm very rapidly considering what he must be thinking—probably that I'm stupid and naive. I've never experienced this before, but these feelings are intense, uncontrollable. I'm not sure I'm equipped for them, and I'm even less confident that Miller is. "Please speak," I plead quietly, following up my request with a little squeeze. "Say something."

He accepts my squeeze, reciprocating with his own, and then he withdraws from the sanctuary of my neck and takes a deep breath, letting it stream from his lips slowly and calmly. I take a deep breath, too, except I hold mine.

Smoothing his palms up my spine, his hand finds my hair and starts combing through with his fingers as he watches. Then he slowly brings his eyes to mine. "This beautiful, pure girl has fallen in love with the big bad wolf."

My eyebrows meet in the middle. "You're not a big bad wolf," I argue, not thinking to deny his other conclusion. He's absolutely right, and I'm not ashamed of it. I *am* in love with him. "And I thought we established that I'm not so sweet." I want to feel his hair and his lips, but he looks despondent, almost troubled by the knowledge that someone loves him.

"We established nothing of the sort. You're *my* sweet girl, and we'll be leaving that line of conversation exactly there."

"Okay." I succumb immediately and easily, hating his curt delivery of those words, but secretly loving the words he's used. I'm his.

He sighs and kisses me chastely. "You must be hungry. Let me make you supper." He starts to untangle our bodies and places me on my feet, running his eyes down my body. I'm still wearing his shirt, buttons undone, hanging open, and it's creased beyond creased. "Look at the state of that," he muses on a subtle shake of his head. And just like that, he's switched back to perfect, precise Miller Hart, like I haven't just confessed my love for him.

"Maybe you should invest in non-iron shirts," I say thoughtfully, pulling the two sides together.

"Cheap material." He pushes my hands away and starts buttoning me up, and even straightens the collar before nodding his halfhearted approval and taking my nape.

He's already wearing a pair of shorts, which means only one

thing. While I was having terrible nightmares, my finicky, fine Miller was tidying up.

"Please, sit," he says when we arrive in the kitchen, releasing me from his grasp. "What would you like?"

I park my bum on the chair, the coolness on my bottom reminding me that I have no knickers on. "I'll have what you're having."

"Well, I'm having bruschetta. Will you join me?" He takes numerous containers from the fridge and turns the grill on.

He means tomatoes, I think. "Sure," I reply, placing my hands in my lap in preparation for him to set the eating area. I should offer to help, but I know my consideration won't be appreciated. Nevertheless, I do anyway. I might surprise myself—and Miller—and get it all right. "I'll lay the table." I get up, not missing the tensing of his shoulders as he slowly turns toward me.

"No, please, let me tend to you." He's using his whole worshipping business as an excuse to prevent me from screwing up his perfection.

"I'd like to." I dismiss his worry and make my way over to the cupboard where I know the dishes to be, while Miller reluctantly starts coating some bread with olive oil. "Why didn't you just tell me about your club?" I ask, keen to distract him from the potential of his sweet girl screwing up his perfect table. I slide two plates from the cupboard and make my way back to the table, setting them down neatly.

He's wary, his eyes flicking from the plates to me as he finishes up with the oil. "I told you. I don't like mixing business with pleasure."

"So you'll never talk about work with me?" I ask, heading for the stack of drawers.

"No. It's draining." He slides the tray full of bread under the grill and sets about tidying up the mess that isn't there. "When I'm with you, I want to concentrate on only you."

I falter as I collect two pairs of knives and forks. "I can live with that," I say on a small smile.

"Who said you have a choice?"

My smile widens as I face him. "I don't want a choice."

"Then this is a pointless conversation, wouldn't you agree?"

"Agreed."

"I'm glad we've cleared that up," he says seriously, pulling the lightly toasted bread from under the grill. "Would you like wine with your supper?"

Again, I'm faltering, certain I've not heard him right. After everything I've told him? "I'll have water." I pad back to the island.

"With bruschetta?" He sounds disgusted. "No, you have Chianti with bruschetta. There's a bottle on the drinks cabinet and the glasses are in the left-hand cupboard." He nods toward the lounge while neatly spooning the prepared tomato mixture onto the toast and setting it on a white platter.

After placing the knives and forks as accurately as possible, I make my way to the drinks cabinet, finding dozens of wine bottles, all displayed in tidy rows, labels facing outward. Not daring to touch them, I bend slightly to start reading the labels, getting through every single bottle and finding nothing named Chianti. I straighten and frown, running my eyes over *all* of the bottles gracing the surface of the cabinet, noting them grouped according to the alcoholic drink contained in each one. It's then I see a basket containing a dumpy bottle and as I close in, I see the label says "Chianti." It's also open.

"Bingo." I smile, taking the bottle from the wicker container and opening the left cupboard to pick two glasses. They all sparkle when the artificial light from the room hits the cut glass, and I admire the shards of light ricocheting between them for a few moments, before collecting two and making my way back. "Chianti and two glasses," I declare, holding up my finds, but quickly halting when I see my effort to lay a perfect table has been a complete waste of time. He's just tweaking the freshly laundered napkins into accurate triangles to the left side of each place setting as he looks up.

I'm frowning at him, but he's frowning at me, too. I have no idea why. He studies the bottle, then the glasses, and in total exasperation, strides over and takes it all from my hands. I'm completely dismayed as I watch him take it all back to the cabinet, putting the bottle back in the basket and the glasses back in the cupboard. I saw the label. It said "Chianti," and I may not be a connoisseur of wine, but they were definitely wineglasses.

My frown only deepens when he takes two other glasses from the very same cupboard, and then takes the basket containing the wine and starts back across the room. "Are you going to sit?" he asks, ushering me toward the table when he reaches me.

I answer him by lowering my bum to the chair and watching as he sets the glasses down to the right side above the forks. Then he puts the basket containing the wine between us. Not happy with the items' final resting places, he shifts them all before taking the wine and pouring a few inches into my glass.

"What did I do?" I ask, still frowning.

"Chianti is traditionally kept in a fiasco." He pours himself a few inches, too. "And the glasses you picked are for white wine."

Looking at the glasses, now a fraction full of red wine, I frown even more. "Does it matter?"

He looks at me all shocked, and on a little gape of his luscious mouth. "Yes, of course it matters. Red wine glasses are wider because the increased exposure to air helps the deeper and more multifaceted flavors of red wine to develop fully." He takes a sip and rolls it around his mouth for a few seconds. I half expect him to spit it out, but he doesn't. He swallows and continues. "The greater surface area allows higher air exposure and the wider bowl of a red wine glass allows more wine to be exposed at any one time."

I'm speechless and feeling rather uncultured and intimidated. "I knew that," I grumble, picking up my own glass. "You're such a smart arse."

He's fighting a smile, I know it. I wish he'd just loosen up with the sophistication and uptight manners—that being at a dinner table especially brings—and flash me that heart-stopping smile. "I'm a smart arse because I appreciate beautiful things?" He raises his perfect eyebrows as he raises his perfect glass containing the perfect wine, taking a perfectly slow and suggestive sip with those perfect lips.

"Appreciate or obsess about?" I put the word out there because if there's one thing about Miller Hart that I'm absolutely certain of, it's that he's obsessive, and he's obsessive about most things in his life. And I hope that one of those things is me.

"I'm more inclined to appreciate."

"I'm more inclined to obsess."

He cocks his head, amused. "Are you talking in code, sweet girl?"

"Are you good at cracking codes?"

"The master," he utters lowly, licking his lips, making me squirm on my chair. "I've cracked you." He tips his glass toward me. "I've also conquered you."

I can't argue with him; he has, so I reach over and take some bruschetta. "This looks delicious."

"I concur," he says, taking a piece for himself. I sink my teeth in on a satisfied hum, quickly noting that I'm being looked at in disapproval again. My chewing slows, wondering what I've done now. I soon find out. He picks up his knife and fork and makes a stupidly slow display of slicing his way through the bread before slowly taking the piece from the fork and setting his cutlery down neatly. He starts to chew as he watches me heating with embarrassment. I need to take some lessons in refinement.

"Do I annoy you?" I ask, setting down my bruschetta and following his lead.

"Annoy me?"

"Yes."

"Far from it, Livy. Except when you're being a little reckless." He hits me with a disapproving look, which I choose to sidestep. "You fascinate me."

"With my common ways?" I ask quietly.

"You're not common."

"No, you're right. *You're* a snob..." I pause briefly as he coughs his surprise. "Sometimes," I add. My beautiful man in disguise is generally a gentleman, except when he's being an arrogant twat.

"I don't think well mannered classifies as snobbery."

"You're more than well mannered, Miller." I sigh, resisting the urge to put my elbows on the table. "I quite like it, though."

"Like I've said before, Livy. Take me as I am."

"I have."

"As I have you."

I recoil on the inside, a little injured by his remark. He means that he's accepted my shameful history and lack of manners, that's what he means—I've accepted him for being a part-time gentleman with a fascinating compulsion to have everything in his life perfect, while he's accepted me for being a careless tart, who doesn't know her white wine glass from her red. He's right, though, and I'm glad he's accepted me, but he doesn't need to remind me of my shortcomings.

"Overthinking, Livy," he says quietly, snapping me from my mental deliberation.

"I'm sorry. I just don't understand..."

"You're being silly."

"I don't think—"

"Stop it!" he shouts, shifting his recently placed wineglass at the same time. "Just accept that it's happening, like I said it would." I retreat in my chair cautiously, keeping quiet. "I've already told you that I don't necessarily understand, but it's happening and there is nothing neither I nor you can, or should, do about it." He swipes his glass up, making his action of a second ago completely pointless, and takes a violent swig—not a sip, he doesn't savor the taste; he swigs it.

He's really mad.

"Shit," he spits, slamming his glass down and grabbing his head. "Livy, I..." He sighs and pushes himself out on his chair, holding his hands out to me. "Please, come here."

I sigh, too, getting up from the table on a frustrated shake of my head and making my way around to him, quickly climbing onto his lap and letting him apologize with his *thing*.

"I apologize," he whispers, kissing my hair. "It upsets me when you talk like that, like you're not worthy. I'm the unworthy one."

"Not true," I say, pulling back so I can get his lovely face in my sight. And it really is lovely, his signature shadow holding fort and his light blue eyes glistening. Reaching up I take a wave of his hair and twist it gently between my fingers.

"We'll agree to disagree." He drops his mouth to mine and reinforces his apology with a lazy dance of his tongue with mine. The world is right again, but the flashes of that temper he's warned me of are becoming a concern. He always looks momentarily feral and I can see with clarity his battle to rein it in.

After apologizing thoroughly, he turns me around on his lap and feeds me some bruschetta, and then takes some for himself. We eat in a comfortable silence, but I'm a bit bemused that Miller's table manners accept me on his lap, but it won't accept the bottle of wine slightly off position.

It's all calm and lovely until the sound of his iPhone breaks our peaceful supper, ringing persistently from somewhere behind me. "Excuse me," he says, lifting me from his lap and pacing over to a set of shelves by the fridge. I definitely see a look of irritation when he glances at the screen before answering. "Miller Hart." He walks from the kitchen, leaving me to settle back on my chair. "It's no problem," he assures whoever's on the other end of the line, his bare back disappearing from view.

I take the opportunity while he's away from the table to study the setup, again trying to work out if there's a theory to his madness. I reach over and pick up the platter in a silly test to see if there is an outline that marks its place. Of course there isn't, but it doesn't stop me from picking up my plate to check under there, too. Nothing. Smiling, I reach the swift conclusion that there *are* outlines for everything, but only Miller can see them. Then I take my red wine glass and snick my nose in the top before sipping cautiously.

My attention is pulled to Miller when he reenters the kitchen and pops his phone back where it belongs in the docking station. "That was the manager of Ice."

"The manager?"

"Yes, Tony. He takes care of things in my absence."

"Oh."

"I have an interview tomorrow. He was just confirming times."

"An interview for a newspaper?"

"Yes, about the opening of London's new elite club." He starts loading the dishwasher. "Six tomorrow evening. Would you like to come with me?"

My spirits lift to stupid heights. "I thought you didn't mix business with pleasure." I arch an eyebrow at him, and he arches one right back, making me grin.

"Would you like to come?" he repeats.

I'm smiling properly now. "Where is it?"

"At Ice. I'll take you for dinner after." He casts me a sideways glance. "It's rude not to accept a gentleman's offer to wine and dine you," he says seriously. "Ask your grandmother."

I laugh and start to collect the dishes from the table. "Offer accepted."

"Jolly good, Miss Taylor." There's humor in his tone, too, and it widens my smile. "May I suggest you call your grandmother?"

"You may." I slide the last of the dishes on the counter, leaving Miller to reshuffle and load. "Which drawer will I find my things in?"

"Second from bottom. And be quick. I have a habit that I want to lose myself with under the sheets." He's serious and stern . . . and I couldn't care less.

Chapter Twenty-one

I drifted off to the calming tone of Miller humming sweetly in my ear, kissing my hair repeatedly and surrounding me in his *thing*. I know he got out of bed to pick up his boxers and shirt that I left strewn on the floor, but he was soon back, cuddling up behind me.

When I woke, Miller was already up, showered and suited with his side of the bed made. I lay there for a few moments, thinking how me entering his life has played havoc with his perfectly assembled and organized world before I was ordered to get up and get dressed. With a lack of other clothes, I was delivered home in my freshly laundered dress, much to Nan's delight.

After showering, texting Gregory to advise him that I'm alive, and readying myself for work, I dart down the stairs with only twenty minutes to get my happy arse to the bistro. Nan's waiting for me at the bottom of the stairs, her cheerful face a pleasure to see, but the diary in her hand, not so much.

"Ask Miller about dinner," she orders as I slip my denim jacket on. She flicks the pages of her diary and runs her wrinkled finger down the dates. "I can do tonight, but I can't do tomorrow or Wednesday. Tonight's cutting it a little fine, but I have time to pop to Harrods. Or we could do Saturday...oh, no, we can't. I have a tea and cakes meeting."

"Miller has an interview this evening."

Her old navy blues fly up in surprise. "An interview?"

"Yes, for the new bar he's opened."

"Miller owns a bar? Goodness me!" She snaps her diary shut. "You mean to say he'll be in the paper?"

"Yes." I swing my satchel across my body. "He's picking me up from work so I won't be here for tea."

"How exciting! How about Saturday for dinner? I can rearrange my diary."

It staggers me how my grandmother's social life is more active than mine...or it was until recently. "I'll ask him." I pacify her, opening the front door.

"Call him now."

I turn on a frown. "I'll be seeing him later."

"No, no." She points to my satchel. "I need to know now. I'll have to go shopping and call the community center to rearrange the tea and cakes meeting. I can't just fall into line with you and Miller."

I inwardly laugh. "Let's have dinner next week, then," I suggest, solving the problem immediately.

Her old, thin lips purse. "Make the call!" she insists, prompting me to immediately dive into my bag for my phone. I can't deny her the excitement, not now Miller and I seem to be on the same page.

"Okay," I soothe, dialing Miller under her watchful eyes.

He answers in an instant. "Miller Hart," he says, all formal and businesslike.

I frown down the line. "Do you have my number stored?"

"Of course."

"Then why are you answering like you don't know who it is?"

"Habit."

I shake my head and glance up to see Nan frowning, too. "Are you available Saturday evening?" I ask, feeling incredibly awkward under my grandmother's observation. It's times like now, when he's reserved and clipped, that he defies the tender man who I'm faced with when he's out of those suits and has me to himself.

"Are you asking me on a date?" I can hear a hint of amusement in his tone.

"No, my nan is. She'd like you to come for dinner again." I feel like such a juvenile.

"It would be my pleasure," he says. "I'll bring my buns."

I can't help the burst of laughter that slips out, making Nan look offended. "Nan will be pleased."

"Who wouldn't?" he asks cockily. "See you after work, sweet girl."

I disconnect the call and leave Nan in the hallway as I practically skip down the path from the house.

"Well?" she calls as she follows me out.

"You have a date!"

"What was so funny?"

"Miller's bringing his buns!" I shout back.

"But I was going to make my pineapple upside-down cake!"

I laugh to myself, all the way to work.

* * *

"I might need you on Sunday night, Livy," Del says toward the end of my shift. "Do you think you could help me out? Big event. I need as many hands as I can get."

"Sure."

"Sylvie?" he asks, nodding toward her as she works her way out of the bistro with the mop.

She pivots on her biker books and smiles sickeningly sweetly. "No," she says simply.

Our boss leaves grumbling something about "help these days," while Paul laughs and I try not to.

"So," Sylvie begins, after Paul has also said his good-byes. "I'm hoping your good mood is because Friday night with Mr. Wide Eyes went exceptionally well."

I cringe. "He was nice."

"Is that it?" she asks incredulously.

"Yes."

"Fucking hell, Livy. If you're going to nab a decent bloke, then you need to be a little more enthusiastic." She's glaring at me, and I'm doing everything to avoid it. "So what's made you so chirpy?"

"I think you already know." I'm not looking at her, but I know she has just tried to disguise an eye roll and an exhale of worried breath. "Miller's picking me up," I tell her, glancing down the road. "He'll be here in a minute."

"Right," she says, short and clipped. "I'm not sure—"

"Sylvie." I stop and turn, placing a hand gently on her arm. "Your concern is appreciated, but please don't try to stop me from seeing him."

"It's just..."

"A nice girl like me?"

She smiles mildly. "You're too nice. That's my worry."

"This is right, Sylvie. I can't walk away. If you had led the life I have, you might see this for what it is."

I can see her face drift into thought, trying to surmise what I mean. "What is 'this'?"

"A chance for me to feel alive," I admit. "He's a chance for me to live and feel."

She nods slowly and leans in to kiss my cheek, then wraps me in her arms. "I'm here," she says simply. "I hope he's everything you want and need."

"I know he is." I take a deep breath and break free from Sylvie's hold. "Here he is." I leave Sylvie and make my way over to the black Mercedes, sliding in and giving her a quick wave. She returns it as she slowly backs away.

"Good evening, Olivia Taylor."

"Good evening, Miller Hart," I counter, pulling my belt on, smiling when I hear Crystal Waters's "Gypsy Woman." "Have you had a nice day?"

He pulls into the traffic swiftly. "I've had a very *busy* day. And you?"

"Busy."

"Are you hungry?" He looks over to me, face straight, no expression.

"A little," I reply, feeling a little chilly in the air-conditioned car. Looking at the digital display on the dashboard, I note masses of switches and dials. There are two temperature displays and a dial next to each, both reading sixteen degrees. "Why are there two temperature gauges?"

"One for the passenger side, one for the driver's side." He keeps his eyes on the road.

"So you can set two different temperatures?"

"Yes."

"So my side can be twenty degrees, and your side can be sixteen degrees?"

"Yes."

I reach forward, thinking it's such a ridiculously stupid piece of gadgetry, and turn my dial up, making my side of the car twenty degrees.

"What are you doing?" he asks, starting to twitch in his seat.

"I'm chilly."

He reaches for the dial and turns it back until the display reads sixteen degrees again. "It's not chilly."

Looking across the car to him, I begin to work out the issue.

"But isn't that the point of having duel temperatures? So both passenger and driver can set their own comfort level?"

"In this car, they stay the same."

"How about if I turn them *both* up to twenty degrees?"

"Then I'd be too warm," he answers quickly, replacing his hand on the wheel. "The temperature is suitable as it is."

"Or the matching digits are suitable," I say to myself, sitting back in the seat. I can't imagine how stressful it would be to live in a world where the desire to have everything a particular way is so compulsory, it pretty much takes over your life. I smile to myself. Actually, I can, because not only has my life been turned upside down by this confounding, fraudulent gentleman sitting next to me, but his particular ways are having a funny effect on me, too. I'm becoming very aware of how things should be, even if I'm not quite sure how to get them there. But I'll learn, and then I can help make Miller's life as stress-free as possible.

* * *

The club looks entirely different, all lit by natural daylight, the blues that illuminated it by night absent, leaving frosted glass everywhere I look. Now the space is empty, only the bar staff scattered here and there stocking the bars or buffing a section of the large expanse of glass. And it's so much quieter, with only Lana Del Rey humming softly in the background about video games. It's a million miles away from the hard beats of the club on Saturday night.

A well-built, stocky guy, all suited and booted, is waiting just beyond the dance floor, sitting on a Perspex stool sipping from a bottle of beer. As we approach, he lifts his bald head from the paperwork he's perusing and signals the barman, who immediately prepares a drink for Miller, placing it on the glass surface of the bar in time for our arrival.

"Miller." The guy stands, holding his hand out.

My neck is released and Miller gives him a firm, manly shake before indicating for me to sit, which I do without delay. "Tony, this is Olivia. Livy, Tony." He waves his hand between us before wasting no time taking his drink and knocking it back, immediately signaling for another.

"Nice to meet you, Olivia?" He says my name as a question, clearly wondering which version to use.

"Livy." I take his hand and let him do all the shaking while he regards me thoughtfully.

"Would you like a drink?" Miller asks, accepting his second from the barman.

"No, thank you."

"As you wish." He gives Tony his full attention.

"Cassie will be here shortly," Tony says, flicking a cautionary look in my direction. It makes me sit up and pay attention.

"She needn't have bothered," Miller replies, ensuring he keeps his eyes on me. "I told her not to."

Tony laughs. "Since when has she listened to anything you say, son?"

Miller returns his steel stare to Tony but ignores his question, leaving me wondering who the hell Cassie is and why she never listens to Miller. Now is quite obviously not the time to ask, but by Tony's look and Miller's response, I think I already know who Cassie is. Why is she coming here? She never listens to him? What about? Everything? What's everything? I mentally yell at myself and in an attempt to rein in my wandering thoughts until it's an appropriate time to press on it, I take in the cutting-edge décor of the club. It feels cold now, with the absence of crowds and darkness, the light and glass at every turn making me feel like I'm stuck in a gigantic piece of . . . well, ice.

As I watch Miller looking over the papers being held by Tony, I wonder if he would be at all different right now if he was wearing a pair of jeans and a T-shirt, rather than the gray three-piece suit and blue shirt, which make his eyes look shockingly blue, but hold the usual mask in place whenever he's suited—which is ninety-nine percent of the time.

"My office." Miller's voice pulls my eyes from the blue shirt at his neck to the blue of his intense stare.

"Sorry?"

"Make your way down to my office." He tugs me gently down from the stool and turns me in the direction that I should be headed. "Do you remember where?"

"I think so." I remember being taken toward the front of the club and down some stairs, but I was well on my way to a total drunken stupor.

"I'll catch up to you."

I glance back as I leave Miller at the bar with Tony, both men blatantly waiting for me to be out of earshot before they speak. Miller is impassive and Tony is thoughtful. I take all of the awkward vibes from Tony and conclude that they're either talking business and it's not for my ears, or they're talking about me. A funny feeling, plus Tony's discomfort, makes me conclude it's the latter, and when I reach the other side of the club and turn to round the corner, I see Tony waving his hands at Miller, which only confirms my thoughts. I stop and watch through the glass of the stairwell, seeing Tony drop to his arse and put his round face in his palms. It's a sign of despair. Then Miller shows a rare display of aggravation, flashing that temper I've been warned about, throwing his hands up and cursing as he storms off toward me. I hurry down the stairs quickly, weaving my way through the corridors aimlessly, until I spot the metal keypad that I vaguely remember Miller punching some numbers into.

It's mere seconds before he rounds the corner, clearly pissed and running his hand through his waves, pulling back the loose curl that's fallen onto his forehead. Striding toward me with purpose, the aggravation is still so very obvious, even more so when he punches the code in aggressively and pushes the door open a little too hard, making it hit the plaster behind it.

I jump at the loud crash, and Miller drops his head. "Shit," he curses quietly, making no attempt to enter his office.

"Are you okay?" I ask, keeping my distance. I'm constantly willing emotion from him, but not if it's going to be like this.

"I apologize," he murmurs, keeping his eyes to the ground, defying his own rule of looking at someone when you're speaking to them. I don't remind him, though. The words that have just been exchanged between Miller and his bar manager were about me; I have no doubt. And now he's mad. "Livy?"

I feel my spine stretch out, making me stand up straight. "Yes?"

His shoulders rise and fall on a heavy sigh. "Give me my *thing*," he says, turning pleading blue eyes onto me. "Please."

My shoulders drop, seeing a side of Miller Hart that I never have. He wants comfort. I reach up over his broad shoulders, lifting on my tiptoes to get my face in his neck.

"Thank you," he mumbles, wrapping his arms around my waist and lifting me from my feet. The force of his hold compresses on my rib cage, making it a little tricky to breathe, but I'm not about to stop him. I wrap my legs around his waist as he shuts the door and walks us to his empty desk. He rests his arse on the edge, which allows us to maintain our hold, and he shows no sign of letting up. I'm surprised. His suit will be a crumpled mess and he has an interview.

"I'm creasing you," I say quietly.

"I have an iron." He squeezes harder.

"Of course you do." I pull away from him so we're staring into each other's eyes. He doesn't give me anything. His annoyance seems to have faded, his face as expressionless as ever. "What has upset you?"

"Life." He doesn't hesitate. "People overthinking things and interfering."

"Interfering with what?" I ask, but I suspect I already know.

"Everything," he breathes.

"Who's Cassie?" I also know the answer to this question.

He stands, lowers me to my feet, and grabs my cheeks. "The woman you thought was my girlfriend." He hits me with a long, moist kiss, sending me dizzy.

"Why is she coming here?" I ask around his lips.

He doesn't break our kiss. "Because she's a pain in the arse." He pecks up my cheek to my ear. "And because she thinks that holding shares in my club gives her a right to dictate what happens here."

I gasp and pull away. "So she really is a business associate?"

He almost scowls before yanking me back to his chest. "Yes. How many times do I need to tell you? I said trust me."

This knowledge doesn't make me feel any better. I'm not completely stupid and I've seen the way she looks at him. And me, for that matter.

"I've had a terrible day." Miller kisses my cheek softly, distracting me with those soft lips. "But you're going to de-stress me when I get you home."

I let him take my hand and lead me around his desk. "What are we doing?"

He sits me in his chair and turns me to face his desk, and then takes a remote control from the top drawer and crouches beside me, resting his elbow on the arm of the chair. "I want to show you something."

"What?" I ask, noting Miller's desk is as empty as the last time I saw it, the phone its only adornment.

"This." He presses a button and I jump back in my chair on a gasp when his desk starts to shift in front of me.

"What the..." I'm openmouthed and gawking like an idiot as five flat screens start to rise from the back section of Miller's desk. "Bloody hell!"

"Impressed?"

I might be a little stunned, but there is no denying the proud edge to his tone. "So you just watch TV in here?"

"No, Livy," he sighs, pressing another button, which prompts the screens to jump to life, revealing image after image of his club.

"It's CCTV?" I ask, letting my eyes travel over the screens, each one sectioned into six images, except the middle screen. That screen is just one large image.

And I'm on it.

I lean forward, seeing myself on Ice's launch night drinking with Gregory; then the image changes to us walking up the stairs, me looking around in awe. Then I'm on the dance floor. And Miller is on the prowl behind me. I see Gregory whisper in my ear, and me going to turn, and then I watch as he homes in, giving me a thorough inspection before he has his hands on me. The footage is clear, but when Miller reaches forward and touches the center of the screen, it gets bigger, clearer, and the look on his face makes me instantly wet. I'm tingling, too, and it's right now I wonder why the hell I'm staring at a screen when the real thing is crouched next to me.

I slowly turn to face him. "You sat here and watched me." I don't ask it as a question because it's obvious. I knew it, but I didn't consider a club littered with cameras.

He regards me thoughtfully and cocks his head a little. "My gorgeous, sweet girl, are you turned on?"

I don't want to, but I squirm in his big office chair, my cheeks flushing terribly. "You're here. Of course I am." I need to try and meet his poise—*try* being the operative word. I could never match Miller in the intensity stakes or the brooding stakes or the hot stakes or the sexy stakes. I might in the sass stakes, though.

My chair is slowly turned to face him, the remote control placed neatly on the table, and his palms slide under my thighs, pulling me toward him until there are only a few inches between our faces. "When I watched you on Saturday night," he whispers in my face, "I was turned on, too."

An image of Miller reclined in this chair, his tumbler of scotch held to his lips, watching quietly as I drank, chatted, and wandered around his club, invades my lust-filled mind. The mental visual makes the heat drop from my face, straight into my groin. I'm saturated, and he knows it. "Are you turned on now?" I breathe, moving my face a little closer so our noses meet.

"Find out for yourself." He pushes his lips to mine and rises, forcing my head to drop back to accommodate our kiss. His hands are braced on the arms of his office chair, caging me in, and the satisfied moan that seeps from his mouth into mine is the most pleasurable sound I've ever heard.

I waste no time getting my hands on him. I blindly yank his belt undone while our mouths work each other frantically, the softly-softly approach a distant memory in this moment in time. He seems harassed and if I can fix it, then I will.

"Just your hand," he mumbles desperately.

I unzip his fly, unbutton him, and slide my hand into his trousers, finding hard heat immediately.

I grasp it loosely, and he gasps, prompting me to flick my eyes up. I'm looking into blinding blues as I pull a slow, smooth stroke, his parted lips letting his shallow pants warm my face. "Did you do this to yourself when you watched me?" I ask quietly, his desperation powering me on, boosting my confidence.

"I never do this to myself."

His response shocks me, making my rhythm falter. "Never?"

"Never." His hips gently push forward.

"Why not?" I'm shocked to the core, and even though it sounds unbelievable, I believe him.

"It doesn't matter." He swoops down and takes my lips, halting any further questioning. I'm focusing on working him gently, but with his mouth action getting unusually firm, it seems to influence my hands, too, the thrusts of my fist speeding up, coaxing continuous groans from him. "Keep it steady," he almost begs.

Following his guidance, I slow my pace until I'm evenly gliding up and down his length.

"Hmmmm, oh God." He tenses from top to toe, like he's cautious, but he's enjoying it. I can feel him pulsing under my palm, the heat building, his breath hitching further. Maintaining our deep kiss is easy. Holding back from pumping harder with my fist isn't. My awareness of his building climax is driving my confidence, making my clenched hand ache from tensing to prevent the instinct to fly up and down his shaft.

He bites my lip and pulls away, giving me a perfect view of his perfect face as I continue to work him. His hips are starting to thrust with my hand, and I can see the tensing of his arms braced on the chair. But his face is poker straight.

"Good?" I ask, wanting something more than his bodily reactions. I want the words he's so good at during these moments.

"You'll never know." His head drops a little and small wheezing breaths start to puff from his lips. I take my spare hand and find the hem of his shirt, sliding my hand onto his stomach and feeling the contractions of his muscled abs. "Shit!" he curses.

I take his cue and squeeze harder, but then a loud knock at the door makes me jump, and I'm suddenly dropping him and flying back in my chair.

He gasps. "Fucking hell, Livy!"

"I'm sorry!" I blurt, not knowing whether to resume my attention of Miller or hide under the desk.

I can see the pain on his face as he pushes himself up from the chair and tries to get his labored breathing under control. "Well, that's just fucking perfect, isn't it?"

I press my lips together as I watch him quickly tuck himself away and refasten his trousers and belt. "I'm sorry," I repeat, not knowing what else to say. He's still rock solid and it's obvious through his trousers.

"So you should be," he grumbles, and I lose my attempts to hold back my smile. "Look." He points to his groin and cocks his eyebrow when he catches my amusement. "I have a bit of a problem."

"You do," I agree, looking to one of his screens and seeing two people standing outside his office door, just as a knock sounds again. "Should I let them in?"

"This is going to be agony." He adjusts himself on a groan. "Yes, please."

I jump up and leave Miller settling in his chair, finding my own hyped-up state easy to control with the distraction of Miller's clear discomfort. Swinging the door open, I come face-to-face with a lovely looking woman, who immediately gives me the once-over on a frown.

"You are?" she says, waving to a man behind her with a camera.

I step back to give her access before I'm barged from her path. "Livy," I say to myself because she has already passed me and is on her way to Miller's desk, all smiley and gushy. I'm delighted when I see his mask slip right into place, his cool, business persona replacing his despairing pre-climax state.

"Hi!" she sings in his face, practically throwing herself over his desk to get to him. "Diana Low." She puts her hand out, but I can tell she's dying to kiss him. "Wow, this place is just amazing!"

"Thank you." Miller is as formal as ever, shaking her hand before indicating a chair opposite his desk and discreetly adjusting his groin area. "Can I get you a drink?"

She parks her tight arse on the chair and lays her notepad on the table. I'm immediately picking up on the unease emanating from Miller as he looks at the pad. "Oooh, I'm not supposed to drink on the job, but you're my last call of the day. I'll have a martini on the rocks."

The photographer passes me, clearly exhausted.

It's only now I wonder if Miller actually wants me here for this, so I look over to him and gesture to the door, but he starts shaking his head, then nods toward the sofa as he takes Miss Low's pad and hands it to her. He wants me to stay.

I shut the door and watch the photographer take a seat beside the gregarious woman, dumping his camera on his lap.

"Drink?" Miller looks to the man, but I see his head shake from behind.

"Nah, I'm cool."

"I'll get the drinks," I pipe up, opening the door. "Martini and a scotch?"

"On the rocks!" The woman swings around, giving me another once-over. "Make sure it's on the rocks."

"Rocks," I confirm, looking to Miller, who nods his thanks. "I'll be back." I slip out, grateful to be free from Diana Low's irritating voice.

I find the lights have been dimmed and the blue illuminations activated, restoring the bar to the glow I remember. With more than one bar to choose from, I finally plump for the one where Miller met Tony, making my way over and finding a young guy crouched behind, restocking the glass front fridges.

"Hello," I say to get his attention. "Can I get a martini on the rocks and a scotch straight?"

"For Mr. Hart?"

I nod and he flies into action, pulling down a tumbler and giving it an extra polish before pouring a few inches and sliding it across the bar. "And a martini?"

"Please."

While the barman prepares the drink, I stand feeling a little self-conscious, knowing I'm being regarded with interest by Tony.

I look over and receive a small smile, but it's a poor attempt to make me feel comfortable. His round face is thoughtful.

"How's it going down there?" he asks, breaking the difficult silence.

"I just left them to it," I answer politely, and accept the martini.

"Miller doesn't appreciate fuss and attention."

I try to detect a double meaning to Tony's abrupt declaration. "I know," I answer, because I suspect he's implying that I don't.

"He's happy in his own little organized world."

"I know," I repeat, turning to leave the discomfort of the conversation. He's not being particularly unfriendly, but I don't like where this chat is heading.

"He's emotionally unavailable."

I stop and turn, watching the thoughtful look on his face for a few moments before I speak. "Is there a purpose to this?" I ask outright, finding my annoyance advancing my poise. Miller has told me the very same thing, but I'm finding emotions in him. Maybe not the regular way, but they're there.

He smiles, and it's a sincere smile, but it's also a smile that suggests I'm blind, naive, and way out of my depth. "A sweet thing like you shouldn't be getting caught up in this world."

"What gives you the impression that I'm sweet?" I ask, my annoyance growing. And what does he mean by "this world"? Clubs? Drinking? He shakes his head and returns to his paperwork, not giving me an answer to my question. "Tony, what do you mean?"

"I mean..." He pauses and sighs, looking up. "You're a distraction that he could do without."

"A distraction?"

"Yes. He needs to focus."

"On what?" I ask.

Tony lifts his stocky body from the barstool and gathers his papers, slipping his pen behind his ear and taking his bottle of beer. "This world," he says simply, turning and wandering across the club.

I stand motionless as I watch the distance between us grow, feeling completely perplexed. Maybe distraction is exactly what Miller needs. He works hard, he's stressed, and he needs me to de-stress at the end of the day. I want to do that. I want to help him.

Looking down into the two glasses I'm holding, I notice the heat of my palm around the martini glass has melted the ice somewhat, but I don't replace it. Diana Low can have a martini on melted rocks. I head back to Miller's office.

His eyes are on the door as I enter, and Diana is pacing his office, doing an amazing job of swaying her arse, while the photographer just looks plain bored, slumped in his chair.

I take Miller his scotch, placing it in his hand, rather than on the desk, because I have no clue where on his desk I should put it. "Thank you," he almost sighs, patting his lap for me to take a seat. I'm a little stunned by his casual demand in a business meeting, but I don't protest.

I follow his cue and lower my bum to his knee and watch in silent amusement as Diana Low takes in the situation. I can't help a little power play of my own, holding her martini out so she has to come to me to get it.

As soon as the glass leaves my hand, Miller has his arm around my waist and tugs me back against his chest.

Diana Low makes a terrible job of smiling warmly at me as she composes herself. "I guess I'll need to change the title of my article."

"What was the title of your article, Miss Low?" Miller asks coolly.

"Well, it was 'London's most eligible bachelor opens London's most prestigious club.'"

Miller stiffens beneath me. "Yes." He downs the rest of his

drink and positions the glass on his desk with utter accuracy. "Change it."

She gets all flustered and sits back down in the chair opposite Miller's desk. London's most eligible bachelor? Miller has confirmed, but it's still nice to hear someone else acknowledge that he's single. Or was.

She frowns as she places her glass on Miller's desk, making him stiffen and me stiffen as a result of Miller's stiffness.

"Would you mind?" I move forward and reclaim the glass, pushing it back in her hand. "No coaster and the desk is very expensive."

She flicks her confusion to Miller's empty tumbler that *is* on the desk without a coaster...but it's in the right place. "Sorry," she replies, taking the glass.

"No problem." I smile, making it as insincere as hers, feeling Miller squeeze his thanks.

"So let's finish up," she says, struggling to hold her glass while attempting to make notes on her pad. "On what basis do you approve membership to your club?"

"Payment," Miller answers, short and tiredly, making me smile.

"And how do potential members apply?"

"They don't."

She looks up again, confused. "So how do you obtain membership?"

"You have to be nominated by an existing member."

"Doesn't that limit your clientele?" she asks.

"Not at all. I already have over two thousand members and we opened less than a week ago. Now we have a waiting list."

"Oh." She looks disappointed, but then smiles suggestively and crosses her legs slowly. "And what would one need to do to skip the waiting list?"

I screw my face up in disgust at her brashness, the shameless hussy. "Yes, what would one need to do, Miller?" I ask, turning to look at him and pouting my lips.

His eyes sparkle, the corners of his mouth lifting ever so slightly as he directs his gaze back to Diana Low. "Do you know any members, Miss Low?"

She smiles brighter. "I know *you*."

I have to force the cough of shock back down my throat. Can she see me?

"You don't know me, Miss Low," Miller states, low and harsh. "Not many people do."

The photographer shifts uncomfortably in his seat and Diana Low reddens with embarrassment. I'm guessing she doesn't get knocked back very often, and I'm wondering whether Miller should be so hostile when she's going to be writing a piece on him and his new club. His words don't have the same effect on me, though, because I *do* know him.

"Photo!" Diana shrieks, jumping up from her chair and placing her drink down again, obviously forgetting my previous request in her fluster.

I quickly scoop it up before Miller starts twitching and stand to the side so the photographer can get what he needs. I watch as Miller stands and starts brushing down the creases in his suit, huffing and puffing to himself as he does. That's my fault, distracting him from dragging out the ironing board so he can perfect his appearance, even though he really doesn't need to. He always looks perfect.

He casts an accusing gaze in my direction and mouths, "Your fault."

I break out in a big smile, shrugging and mouthing "sorry" back.

"Don't be," he says aloud, "I'm not." He winks, nearly knocking me from my feet, before repositioning himself in his big chair, unfastening the button of his jacket, and nodding to the photographer. "Ready when you are."

"Great." He prepares his camera and takes a few steps back.

"We'll leave the TV screens in place. I was thinking a few more things on your desk, though."

"Like what?" Miller asks, horror beginning to surface at the potential of someone messing with his clear surface.

"Some paperwork," he replies, taking Diana's pad and positioning it to the left of Miller. "Perfect."

It's not perfect at all. Even I can see it's wonky, the edge of the paper not parallel to the edge of the desk, and Miller's swift rearrangement of the pad confirms it. "Get on with it, then," he grunts, trying to relax back in his chair and failing. He's fidgety.

It seems like the photographer spends forever aiming and clicking at my poor Miller, who looks ready to explode with stress. He's directed from one position to another, the guy rounds his desk and gets a shot of the TV monitors with Miller casually observing the screens, and then he asks him to sit on the edge of the desk, all casual with his ankles and arms crossed. It's killing him, and the final straw comes when he's asked to smile.

He looks over at me in disbelief, like *how dare they ask such a thing.* "We're done," he snaps irritably, buttoning up his jacket and collecting the pad that's been poisoning the perfection of his desk for too long. "Thank you for your time." He shoves the pad at Diana Low and strides over to the door, swinging it open and gesturing for them to leave.

Neither the journalist nor the photographer hangs around, both moving quickly across Miller's office toward the door. "Thank you." Diana stops short of the door and gazes up at Miller. "Hope to see you around."

I'm stunned and wondering if this is normal behavior. She's incorrigible. "Good-bye," Miller retorts with utter finality, sending the brash journalist on her way, just as another woman strides into his office.

Miller's business associate.

Cassie.

She appears to be in a fluster and out of breath, but it diminishes the second she claps eyes on Diana Low within touching distance of Miller. Cassie's eyes narrow on the brash journalist. "I said he wasn't available for interviews."

"Yes, I know." Diana isn't perturbed by the hostility pouring from Cassie's designer-adorned figure. "But you were clearly mistaken because a few further calls revealed that he was." She turns back toward Miller and smiles seductively. "Bye for now." Her hand raises and waves before she turns a snide look on Cassie as she sashays out of Miller's office, and once she has disappeared, I know Cassie's cattish mood is about to be turned on me.

She swings around and for the first time seems to register my presence. "What's she doing here?" she spits, looking to Miller for an answer. I recoil in shock, as does Miller.

"Keep your nose out," Miller says calmly, taking her arm and leading her to the door.

"I care about you," she argues, not putting up much of a fight, her words confirming my suspicions.

"Don't waste your energy, Cassie." He pushes her out gently and the door to his office slams shut, sending me a few centimeters back on a frightened jump. He said to trust him and I should have. He really has sent her on her way. He swings to face me, looking grumpy and harassed. "I'm stressed out," he proclaims on a bark, stating the obvious and sending me on another little jump across the carpet.

"Would you like me to get you another drink?" I ask, for the first time thinking that perhaps Miller drinks too much. Or has that just been since he met me?

"I don't need a drink, Livy." His tone has taken on a throaty edge, and his eyes have landed on me with a bang. "I think you know what I need."

My blood reheats under his primal stare, my whole sexual being becoming aware and responsive. God help me when he touches me. "De-stressing," I whisper, looking up through my lashes as he stalks slowly toward me.

"You're like therapy to me." He reaches me and swoops down, kissing me with purpose and meaning, moaning and mumbling into my mouth as his tongue works mine fluidly. My mind immediately scrambles. "I love kissing you."

We're in his office. I don't want to be in his office. I want to be in his bed. "Take me home."

"It'll take too long. I need de-stressing now."

"Please." I rest my hands on his shoulders and pull away. "You make *me* feel stressed when you're all uptight."

He sighs deeply and drops his head, letting loose the wayward curl. It calls for me to push it back from his forehead, so I do, taking the chance while I'm in the vicinity of his hair to feel all of it. I feel privileged that this complex man has designated me the role of de-stressing him, and I'll relish doing it whenever need be, but I can see there are ways in which he can do this for himself.

"I apologize," he murmurs. "Your request has been noted."

"Thank you. Take me to your bed."

"As you wish." He looks down at his suit, scowling at the few creases as he tries to smooth them out. He gives up on an exasperated sigh and cocks his head when he catches me smiling.

"What's so amusing?"

"Nothing." I shrug nonchalantly and set about smoothing myself down. It's a terribly sarcastic act, but when I glance up and see that Miller has pulled an ironing board from a concealed cupboard in the wall and is busy setting it up, my amusement soon abates. "You're not?"

He pauses and casts his eyes over to my bulging ones. "What?"

"You're going to iron your suit?"

"It's all creased." He's horrified that I'm clearly stunned by this. "Someone distracted me before, so I'm going to look like a sack of potatoes in my picture."

"What about bed?" I sigh, seeing a long stretch ahead while I wait for Miller to perfect on perfect.

"As soon as I'm done." He turns and takes an iron out.

"Miller..." I halt when I detect the very subtle jumping of his shoulders, and totally intrigued, I pace quickly over and round him, finding the biggest boyish grin I've ever had the pleasure of seeing. My mouth drops open. I'm stunned and can't even remember what I was going to say.

"Your face!" he laughs, folding the board and putting it back. Miller Hart, Mr. Serious, my confounding, complex creature, is winding me up? Playing a joke? I think I might pass out.

"It's not even that funny," I mutter, pushing the cupboard door shut in a childish act of stroppiness.

"I beg to differ," he laughs, straightening and knocking me sideways with that cheeky grin again. I've never seen anything quite like it.

"Beg all you like," I retort, then yelp when he picks me up and spins me around. "Miller!"

"I'm not going to iron my suit because getting you into my bed is of paramount importance."

"More important than ironing your suit back to perfection?" I ask, threading my fingers through his waves. "And more important than fixing your hair?"

"Considerably." He drops me to my feet. "Ready?"

"I was looking forward to you taking me for dinner."

"Dinner or bed?" he scoffs. "Now you're just being silly."

I smile. "What would one have to do to skip the club's waiting list?"

His eyes lose a little sparkle when they narrow, his lips straightening. He's trying not to laugh. "One would need to know a member."

"I know the *owner*," I declare confidently, but very quickly remember his comment to Miss Low. Will he say the same to me? I know Miller, but does he agree?

He nods thoughtfully and paces over to his desk, opening the drawer and pulling something out. Whatever it is gets swiped, bleeped, and scanned on a section of the flat-screen monitors on Miller's desk before they disappear into the depths of white.

"Here." He hands me a transparent credit card with one word engraved in small block capital letters through the center.

ICE

Turning it over, I see a silver strip, but that's all—nothing else. No details of the club or the member. I look up suspiciously. "This is a fake, isn't it?"

He laughs lightly and leads me out of the room and back up to the main club, but he doesn't take his usual hold of my neck, instead draping his strong arm over my petite shoulders and hugging me into him. "It's very real, Olivia."

CHAPTER TWENTY-TWO

As soon as he's carried me up the stairs to his apartment and let us in, he runs a bath and strips us both down before cradling me in his arms, carrying me up the steps, and lowering us into the hot, bubbly water. It's not his bed, but I don't argue. I'm wrapped in his arms where I'm happiest. It's more than good enough.

I sigh, completely content, while he devotes our bath time to smothering me in his body, feeling me everywhere and squeezing me tightly. He's humming that soft tune. It's becoming very familiar to me now. I know when he's going to draw breath and when the tone changes, and I know when a small pause is approaching, when he's sure to take the brief silence as an opportunity to press his lips to the top of my head.

My cheek is resting on his wet chest as I slowly circle his nipple with my fingertip and stare across the vast expanse of his skin. Relaxed and tranquil go nowhere near to describing how I'm feeling. It's these moments when I feel like I'm experiencing the real Miller Hart, not the man who's hiding behind fine three-piece suits and an impassive face. The serious Miller Hart, the man disguised as a gentleman, hides his inside beauty from the world, leaving it facing a man who seems hell-bent on repelling any friendliness he encounters or confusing people with his impeccable manners, which are always delivered with such aloofness, they snuff the fact that he is, in fact, well mannered.

"Tell me about your family." I break the silence with my quiet question, almost certain he'll brush my inquiry aside.

"I don't have any," he whispers simply and softly, kissing the top of my head again as my brow wrinkles into his chest.

"None at all?" I try not to sound disbelieving, but I fail. I haven't a family, so to speak, just my nan, but the value of at least one family member is . . . well, invaluable.

"Just me," he confirms, leaving me silently sympathetic and pondering the loneliness his admission signifies.

"Just you?"

"It doesn't matter what way you say it, Livy. It'll still just be me."

"You've got no one?"

My body lifts and falls with his chest when he sighs. "That's three. Shall we go for four?" he asks gently. He's not displaying exasperation or impatience, although I can tell if I try for that fourth he might do.

I shouldn't find it so hard to believe, given my own sparse family, but at least I have someone. I have Gregory, too, and George, but only one blood relative. One is more than none, and one is a piece of history. "Not a living soul?" I wince as soon as the fourth slips from my lips and immediately apologize for it. "I'm sorry."

"You've no need to apologize."

"But no one?"

"And we have number five." There's humor in his voice, and hoping I might catch a glimpse of that rare smile, I lift from his chest, but all I find is his wet, impassive beauty.

"Sorry." I smile.

"Accepted." He maneuvers me, taking me to the other end of the bath, and lays me on my back. My thighs are spread and he kneels between them, taking one of my legs and lifting my foot until my sole is resting on the middle of his chest. My tiny size five looks lost in the vast expanse of muscle, even smaller when his manly hand starts stroking over the top as he watches me thoughtfully.

"What?" My voice has been reduced to nothing more than a breath of air under the piercing passion of his blue gaze. Miller Hart has passion seeping from every pore of his striking body and even more through that purposeful blue stare. I'm hoping it's special and kept only for me, but I know I'm hoping in vain. Perhaps Miller Hart only ever expresses himself and removes that mask when he has a woman to indulge in.

"I'm just thinking how lovely you look in my bath," he muses, lifting my foot to his mouth and slowly, painfully slowly, licking from my toes, over the top of my foot until he's at my shin, my knee...my thigh.

The water ripples around me from my mild shift, and my hands splatter against the sides of the tub, slipping on the shiny porcelain. My skin is warm from the heat of the water and the steam in the bathroom, but with the heat of his tongue burning through my already heated flesh, I'm on fire. I'm quietly gasping. I'm closing my eyes and preparing myself to be worshipped, and when he reaches a point where my thigh meets the water, he slips his forearm under my lower back and lifts effortlessly, bringing me to his mouth, making the need to shift my hands essential if I'm going to stop myself from slipping under the water. I find the rim of the bath and grip as best I can, being gently guided into his realm of utter rapture—a place where the throes of passion are intense and where I fall deeper and deeper into the curious world of Miller Hart.

His light nips over my clitoris are difficult to deal with. The light dashes of his tongue that follow each one of those nips are torturous. But when he slowly slips two fingers inside of me and thrusts lazily in time to his nips and tongue dashes, I lose any hope that there was of maintaining the silent serenity surrounding us.

I whimper and bow my back, the muscles of my arms that are holding me up instantly aching and my stomach muscles tensing in an attempt to control the sharp twinges sparking in my groin. My mounting desperation only encourages him, his thrusting fingers upholding his desired pace, but the strokes becoming firmer, more determined.

"I don't know how you do this to me," I mumble to my darkness, my head slowly shaking from side to side.

"Do what?" he whispers, blowing a cool stream of air across my pulsing core, the chill of his breath mixed with my flaming skin making me shudder.

"This." I gasp, mindlessly grappling at the side of the bath and crying out when he punishes me with a precise set of soft nips with his teeth, slow rotations with his tongue, and firm drives of his fingers. "And that!" The power of the spasms bolting through me is sending my body into muscle meltdown as I try my hardest to remain relatively still in the water.

My eyes open and I take a few moments to allow my vision to clear until my sight is distorted again, simply because of what I'm faced with: indescribable flawlessness—a pureness in his eyes that I only ever see when he's worshipping me and his dark hair that's on the verge of being too long, the soft flicks curling out from behind his ears.

Despite my restrained fever, he's cool, calm, and collected as he gazes back at me, never ceasing the motions that bring me so much pleasure. "You mean like if this was forever," he murmurs, "then you'd be happy with that."

I nod, hoping he's agreeing with me and not just trying to vocalize my thoughts.

He doesn't confirm my silent wondering with words, instead returning his attention to the screaming nerves between my thighs. His face buried there and his eyes looking up at me is the most sensual vision I'm ever likely to see. Yet I can't help closing my eyes as I prepare for the onslaught of pressure that's set to blow my mind.

"Don't stop," I breathe, begging for more insane, torturous pleasure. He's moving all of a sudden, the water splashing crazily around us as he crawls up my body and seals our mouths, his tongue caressing me in time to the wicked thrusts of his fingers, his thumb working firm circles on my throbbing clitoris.

My hands grip his wet shoulders, holding on for dear life, his strength the only thing preventing me from slipping under the water. I'm a little fevered, but Miller keeps things steady and controlled, despite my moans of desperation.

And then it happens.

The explosion.

The release of a million lightning bolts that force me to break our kiss and hide my face in his neck as my body tries to deal with the blitz of pleasure. He's quiet as he helps my trembling body settle. His only movements are of his fingers circling deeply and his thumb resting lightly on my twitching mass of nerves, easing the persistent, sharp throbs.

"I thought that I was supposed to de-stress you," I wheeze, not willing to release my hold—not ever.

"Livy, you have."

"By you worshipping me?"

"Yes, a little, but mostly by just letting me be with you." He sits up, taking me with him, and pulls me onto his lap. My heavy, wet hair is arranged just so, and his palms wrap around the tops of my arms, holding me firmly. "You're so beautiful."

I feel my skin heat, and I drop my eyes, a little embarrassed.

"I'm paying you a compliment, Livy," he whispers, pulling my eyes back up.

"Thank you."

He smiles a little and shifts his hands to my waist, his eyes journeying over every visible part of my body. I watch him closely as he slowly drops his lips to my breast and kisses it tenderly, and then he starts trailing his finger over every part of me, so lightly I sometimes can't feel it. He inhales a deep, thoughtful breath and lets it out, his head tilting a little to the side, adding to his thoughtfulness. "Every time I touch you," he whispers, "I feel I need to do it with the utmost care."

"Why?" I ask quietly, a little perplexed.

He takes another long pull of air and turns his eyes to me, blinking slowly. "Because I'm frightened you might turn to dust."

His admission chokes me. "I won't turn to dust."

"You might," he murmurs. "What would I do?" His eyes scan my face, and I'm shocked to see nothing but complete seriousness, maybe even a little fear.

Guilt tells me I shouldn't, but I can't help feeling quietly happy by his question. He's falling, too, just as hard as I am. I embrace his uncertainty and cuddle him tightly, locking my arms around his neck and my legs around his hips, like I'm trying to squeeze some reassurance into him. "I'm only going away if you send me," I say, because I think that's what he means. I couldn't possibly turn to dust.

"There's something I'd like to share with you."

"What?" I ask, remaining where I am with my face stuck to his neck.

"Let's get washed and I'll show you." He reaches behind his neck and pulls my arms away, forcing me to vacate my comfort zone. "You'll be the first."

"First?"

"The first person to see." He's turning me in his arms, therefore turning my inquisitive face away, too.

"See?"

His chin rests on my shoulder. "I love your curiosity."

"You make me curious," I accuse, pushing my cheek onto his lips. "What are you going to show me?"

"You'll see," he teases, releasing me.

I turn around and face him again, seeing him sliding down, dunking his head and rubbing some shampoo through it, before rinsing and following it up with some conditioner.

I make myself comfortable at the other end of the bath and watch as he works the conditioner through his waves. "You use conditioner?"

He pauses with his massaging hands and studies me carefully for a few moments before he speaks. "I have very untamed hair."

"Me too."

"Then you must feel my pain." He slides back down the bath and rinses his untamed waves, while I grin like an idiot. He's embarrassed.

When he surfaces, I'm still grinning, and he rolls his eyes at me as he pushes himself up, my gaze lifting with him forever until he's towering over me and I'm staring at his soaking, naked perfection.

"I'll leave you to wash your untamed mane." He's not smiling, but I can tell he wants to.

"Thank you, kind sir." I continue to admire his wet nakedness as he takes the steps from the bath, his butt cheeks tensing and swelling delightfully. "Nice buns," I say quietly to myself, slipping farther into the bubbles.

He turns slowly and cocks his head to the side. "I beg you don't adopt your grandmother's terminology."

I burn bright red, and with nowhere else to escape my embarrassment, I disappear under the water.

* * *

When I'm finished taming my own wild locks with conditioner, I reluctantly leave the warm serenity of Miller's colossal bath and dry off. Ensuring I've emptied the tub, rinsed the bubbles away, and tidied up the bathroom after me, I pad into his bedroom and find a pair of black boxer shorts and a gray T-shirt spread neatly on the bed. I smile to myself as I dress, his boxer shorts barely staying up on my waist, his T-shirt completely swamping me, but they smell of Miller so I tolerate the annoying need to hold the shorts up as I go in search of him.

I find him in the kitchen, looking breathtaking in his own pair of black boxers and a T-shirt to match the one he has picked for me. Seeing Miller without a perfect suit adorning his perfect body is a rarity, but the casual edge that his casual attire puts on him whenever I do is always welcome. I'm beginning to resent his suits, seeing them as a mask that he hides behind.

"We match," I say, pulling up my boxers.

"So we do." He approaches me and runs his fingers through my wet tendrils before bringing them to his nose and inhaling deeply.

"I should call my grandmother," I say, closing my eyes and absorbing his closeness—his scent, his heat . . . his everything. "I don't want her to worry."

He releases me and arranges my hair, staring at me thoughtfully.

"Are you okay?" I ask.

"Yes, I apologize." He shakes himself from his daydream. "I was just thinking how lovely you look in my clothes."

"They're a bit big," I point out, glancing down at the material swamping me.

"They're perfect on you. Call your grandmother."

Once I'm done checking in with Nan, my nape is taken lightly and I'm led over to the docking station where his iPhone is kept. He presses a few buttons before leading me from the kitchen without a word. The xx's "Angels" joins us, soft and hypnotizing in the background, seeping quietly through the integrated speakers. We pass Miller's bedroom and turn left; then he unlocks a door and pushes me gently into a large room.

"Wow!" I gasp, stumbling to a stop on the threshold. "Oh wow!"

"Come in." He encourages me in and flicks a switch that floods the room with powerful, artificial light. I shield my eyes, annoyed my view has been spoiled for a few seconds while my eyes readjust.

Once I've stopped squinting, I drop one hand, keeping his boxers up with the other, and stare in complete wonder at my surroundings. I'm in awe. I'm in heaven . . . I'm shocked.

I turn toward him and give him a confused look. "This is yours?"

He looks almost embarrassed when his shoulders jump up a little on a mild shrug. "This is my home, so I guess so."

I slowly turn back toward the source of my shock and start to take it all in. The walls are covered, they're propped up on the floor, and they're stacked on wire racking systems. There are dozens, possibly hundreds, and they are all of my beloved London, whether of architecture or landscapes.

"You paint?"

He's up against my back and resting his arms over my shoulders. "Do you think you could say something without it sounding like a question?" He nips at my ear, which would usually make my breath falter, but I still haven't caught it yet. This can't be right.

"You did all of these?" I wave my arm in the general direction of the whole studio, casting my eyes around again.

"Another question." He bites my cheek this time. "This was my habit before I found you."

"This isn't a habit; this is a hobby." I look at the paintings on the wall again, thinking that such excellence couldn't really be classed as a hobby. These belong in a gallery.

"Well, now *you're* my hobby."

I have a moment of comprehension, and I'm suddenly on the move, breaking free from Miller's hold and making my way out of his painting studio, heading for the lounge area until I'm standing before one of the oil canvases gracing his wall. This one is of the

London Eye, blurred but clear. "You did this?" I'm speaking in sodding questions again. "I'm sorry."

He approaches from my left and stands next to me, observing his own creation. "I did."

"And that one?" I point to the opposite wall, where London Bridge is holding court, still keeping the damn boxers up.

"Yes," he confirms, and I'm on the move again, back to his studio. I walk farther into the room this time, surrounding myself with Miller's art.

There are five easels, all holding white canvases with partially finished works. The giant wooden table running the length of the side wall is cluttered with pots of brushes, paints in every color on God's earth, and photographs scattered everywhere, some pinned on corkboards among the art. An old squidgy sofa is sitting in front of the floor-to-ceiling windows, facing the glass so you can sit and admire the view across the city, which nearly matches the magnificence of the paintings around me. It's a typical artist's studio . . . and it completely defies everything that Miller Hart stands for.

It's expressive, but even more shocking, it's an awful mess. I feel like I'm in a bit of a trance, an Alice in Wonderland kind of moment, and in a really silly fit of curiosity, I begin assessing everything more closely to try and establish whether there is some sort of method to his arrangement of things in here. It doesn't look like it; it all looks very random and haphazard, but to be sure, I walk over to the table and pick up a pot of brushes, turning it casually in my hand. Then I put it down aimlessly before turning to see his reaction.

He isn't twitching, he isn't looking at the pot of brushes like it could bite, and he hasn't come over to move it. He's just considering me with interest, and after absorbing his gaze for a few moments, I break out in a smile. My shock has transformed into happiness because what I'm seeing in this room is a different man.

This almost humanizes him. Before me, he expressed himself and de-stressed by painting, and it doesn't matter that he has to be super-duper precise in every other element of his life, because in here, he's chaotic.

"I love it," I say, taking another slow gaze around the room, not even the beauty of Miller keeping me from it. "I just love it."

"I knew you would."

It's suddenly dark again, except for the glow of London by night pouring in from the window, and he walks slowly over and takes my hand, leading me to the old worn couch in front of the window. He sits and encourages me down beside him.

"I fall asleep here most nights," he says wistfully, pulling me a little closer. "It's hypnotic, don't you think?"

"Incredible," I agree, but I'm more in awe of what's behind me. "Have you always painted?"

"On and off."

"Just landscapes and architecture?"

"Mainly."

"You're very gifted," I say quietly, tucking my feet under my bum. "You should exhibit them."

He laughs a little, and I'm soon looking up at him, annoyed that he always chooses to do this when I can't see him. He's not laughing anymore, but he's smiling at me. It's good enough. "Livy, it's just a hobby. I have the club and plenty of stress. Turning a hobby into something more makes it stressful."

I frown, not seeing his logic at all, at the same time hoping his theory doesn't apply to me. I'm a hobby. "I was paying you a compliment." I raise my eyebrows cheekily, making him smile more, eyes sparkling and all.

"So you were. I apologize." He kisses me tenderly and tucks me back under his arm. "Thank you."

"You're welcome," I reply, letting my body mold into the sharp edges of his frame and my hand slip up the hem of his T-shirt.

This Miller Hart I *really* adore—laid-back, carefree, and expressive. I'm tucked snugly under his arm, relishing in his tender kisses on my head and soft strokes of my arm. But then he starts to move me, positioning me on my back so I'm spread down the couch with my head on his lap. My hair is stroked away from my face and he gazes down at me for a few moments before he sighs and lets his head drop back. He continues feeling me as he stares up at the ceiling silently while the wistful tones of the track float in the peaceful air around us. Everything is just lovely—the calmness spacing out my serene mind and Miller's touch lazily skimming my cheek. But then the sound of his phone ringing from the kitchen interrupts our peace.

"Excuse me." He shifts me and exits the room, leaving me feeling bitter and now resentful of the view, so I get up and follow him.

When I enter the kitchen, he's removing his iPhone from the docking station on the shelf, bringing the lovely song to an abrupt halt. "Miller Hart," he greets, making his way back out of the kitchen.

I don't want to follow him when he's on the phone, he'd definitely think that rude, so I sit at the empty table and twiddle my ring, wishing us back into his studio.

When Miller reenters the room, he's still on his phone. He walks with purpose to a stack of drawers and pulls the top one open, removing a leather-bound organizer before flicking through the pages. "Short notice, yes, but like I said, it's not a problem." He takes a pen from the drawer and starts writing across the page. "Look forward to it." He hangs up and quickly flips his organizer shut, placing it back in the drawer. He doesn't sound like he's looking forward to it at all.

It's a few moments before he faces me, but when he does, I see immediately that he's not happy, even if his face is completely straight. "I'll take you home."

My back lengthens as I sit up. "Now?" I ask, slighted and annoyed.

"Yes, I apologize." He strides out of the kitchen. "Last-minute meeting at the club," he mutters, and then he's gone.

Upset, irritated, and wounded, I return to face the perfectly empty table, but then curiosity makes me stand and before I can stop myself, I'm by the drawers, pulling the top one open. The leather-bound organizer is tucked in the bottom right-hand corner, screaming for me to peek, so I study its exact positioning before lifting it out and glancing over my shoulder. I shouldn't be doing this. I'm snooping when I have no right to...but I can't help it. Damn curiosity. And damn Miller Hart for spiking it.

I flick the pages, seeing various notes, but conscious that Miller could rumble me prying at any moment I hastily skip them all until I reach today's date. And there, in that perfect handwriting, is a note.

Quaglino's 9:00.
C.
Black suit. Black tie.

I frown and jump all at once, hearing the shutting of a door. Panicked and with a thundering heart, I make a terrible attempt of putting Miller's organizer back just right. I don't have time. I dart to the table and sit back down, using every modicum of strength to stop shaking and look normal. C? Cassie?

"Your clothes are on the bed."

I turn and find Miller standing in just his boxer shorts, but my mind is too busy racing to appreciate the view. "Thank you."

"You're welcome," he says as he leaves me again. "Chop-chop."

Something isn't right. He's turned back into the masked gentleman, being all formal and clipped, which is an insult after our time together, especially the past few days. He's shared something very private and special, and now he's treating me like a business deal again. Or a hooker. I wince at my own thoughts, knocking the flat of my balled fist on my forehead. What's Quaglino's, and why has he lied about it? Uncertainty and mistrust plague me as I fail to prevent my mind from wandering.

I find my phone and pray it hasn't died. I have two bars, and I also have two missed calls . . . from Luke. He's called me? Whatever for? He didn't reply to my text, and that was days ago. I don't have time to think about it. I clear them and load Google, typing in "Quaglino's" as I make my way back to the kitchen. When my Internet connection finally decides to give me the information I want, I don't like what I see: a fancy restaurant in Mayfair, with a cocktail bar to boot. I'm even more wary when Miller strides into the room wearing a black suit and a black tie.

"Livy, I need to go," he says shortly, standing in the mirror and messing with his pesky tie. It was perfect already.

I leave him behind, perfecting on perfect, and hurry to his room, throwing on my jeans and Converse. I'm suspicious, and I've never been suspicious because I've never had anything to be suspicious about. I don't like it.

"Ready?"

I look up and bitterly register how spectacular he looks. He always does, but a three-piece black suit for a meeting at the club? "Great," I mutter.

"Are you okay?" He takes his customary hold of my nape and directs me from the room.

"I'll come with you," I say, confidence oozing in my tone.

"Olivia, you'll be bored to tears." He's not in the least bit fazed by my demand.

"I won't be bored."

"Trust me, you will." He leans down and kisses my forehead. "I'll be drained by the time I'm done. I'll need you to cuddle, so I'll come get you and you can stay with me tonight."

"I may as well wait here."

"No, you can pack some clothes and I'll take you straight to work in the morning."

I scowl to myself. "What time will you be done?"

"I'm not sure. I'll call you."

I give up and let him push me onward, down the masses of stairs until we arrive at his car in the underground car park. The silence is deathly the whole way home, and when he pulls up outside Nan's, he undoes his belt and shifts in his seat so he's facing me.

"You're upset," he says, reaching over and giving my cheek a gentle brush with his thumb. "I have to work, Livy."

"I'm not upset," I argue, but it's plainly obvious that I am, although for different reasons than Miller thinks.

"I beg to differ."

"I'll speak to you later."

"You will." He leans over and spends a few moments refreshing my memory on what I'll be missing for the next few hours. It doesn't improve my mood.

I get out and walk up the path to my house, mind racing, quickly letting myself in and shutting the door behind me. As I knew she would be, Nan's standing at the bottom of the stairs with the biggest smile on her face.

"Have you had a nice time?" she asks. "With Miller, I mean."

"Great." I try to match her smile, but suspicion and uneasiness are crippling me. If it's work, then why is he meeting her at a fancy restaurant?

"I thought you were staying the night."

"I'm going back out." The words fall from my mouth, my subconscious seeming to make the decision for me

"With Miller?" she calls hopefully.

"Yes," I reply. Her happiness at the potential news tugs painfully at my fallen heart.

CHAPTER TWENTY-THREE

I slide from the taxi as elegantly as I can, exactly how Gregory showed me. I was torn by how to dress, but having checked Google, it would seem you don't wear Converse at Quaglino's, nor do you turn up without making a reservation, but I'm not planning on eating. The cocktail bar, that's where I'm heading.

The doorman nods and pulls open the glass door by the giant Q-shaped door handle. "Good evening."

"Hello." I straighten my back and pass him, and then go about brushing down the short, pale blue silk dress that Gregory made me buy. Miller may have disdained my hair and makeup, but I specifically remember him saying he liked the dress. And now my hair is back to golden waves and my makeup is natural again, he should be fairly pleased. If he's with that woman, then I hope he takes one look at me and chokes.

I wince as I take the stairs down to the maître d', my new nude stilettos pinching my toes. She smiles brightly. "Good evening, madam."

"Hello." I pull a confident tone from nowhere, appearing to be a regular in these types of swanky places.

"Reservation for?" She looks down at her list.

"I'm going to settle at the bar for a cocktail and wait for my date." The words roll off my tongue with ease, surprising me.

"Of course, madam. Please, this way." She gestures toward the bar and leads on, taking me around a corner where I have to refrain from letting out an audible gasp.

A marble staircase comes into view, with polished gold handrails and black Q's linking together to form a balustrade on either side, leading down to the huge restaurant, all light and airy, with a stunning glass vaulted ceiling running down the center of the dining space. It's bustling, busy for a Monday night, with groups of people making happy chatter at every table. I'm relieved when I see the cocktail bar is on this level, the glass panels making it easy for me to see below into the restaurant. My eyes are darting around, scanning every corner, but I can't see him. Have I made a colossal error?

"May I recommend the Cherry and Orange Bellini?" the maître d' says, indicating a stool at the bar.

I decline her offer of a stool near the back of the bar and take one closer to the end so I can see down below. "Thank you. Maybe I'll try." I smile, wondering if I could get away with drinking a glass of water when I'm in such a fancy place wearing a fancy dress.

She nods and leaves me with the barman, who hands me a cocktail menu on a smile. "The Lavender and Lychee Martini is so much better."

"Thank you." I return his smile, feeling more comfortable and at ease now that my body is being supported by the stool.

I cross my legs, keeping my back straight, as I peruse the menu, noting the barman's suggestion has London Dry Gin in the mix, putting it right out of the contest. I smile as I remember my granddad constantly battling with my nan over her gin drinking habits. He always said that if you wanted a woman to break down on you, feed her gin. Then my smile fades as I recall the last time I drank gin myself.

The Cherry and Orange Bellini has champagne in it, a clear winner by a mile. I point and glance up at the waiting barman. "Thank you, but I'll have the Bellini."

"A man can try." He winks and sets about making my drink, while I swivel on my stool and start searching the space below again. A quick scan produces no results, so I begin working my way over each and every table, studying the faces and the backs of heads. It's silly. I'd spot Miller's head in a flash mob of a thousand people in Trafalgar Square. He's not here.

"Madam?" The barman pulls my attention back to the bar and hands me a flute, garnished with mint and a maraschino cherry.

"Thank you." I take the glass delicately and take an equally delicate sip under the watchful eye of the barman. "Lovely." I smile my approval, and he winks again before going to tend to a couple at the other end of the bar.

Turning my back on the bar, I sip the delicious cocktail while considering what on earth I'm going to do. It's nine thirty. His meeting was at nine. He'd still be here, surely? And like my phone's heard my thoughts, it starts ringing from my bag. I panic, quickly setting my drink down and rummaging through my little purse, cringing when I see his name flashing up on my screen. My shoulders meet my ears and every possible muscle in my body tenses as I answer. "Hello."

"I'm wrapping up shortly. I'll be with you in an hour."

I puddle at the bar in relief. I can get my overactive imagination and my overdressed body home within an hour. I'm safe and feeling rather silly. "Okay," I breathe, taking my drink and having a much needed slurp. Was I looking at the wrong day in his organizer? In my frantic, rushed state, it's possible.

"It's noisy. Where are you?"

"Television," I blurt. "Nan's going deaf."

"Evidently," he says dryly. "Are you ready to de-stress me, my sweet girl?"

I smile. "So ready."

"I'm glad we've cleared that up. Be ready in an hour." He hangs up, and I sigh all dreamy and loved up at the bar, quickly necking the rest of my Bellini.

I wave the barman over. "Can I settle the bill, please?"

"Only the one?" he says, nodding at my empty.

"I'm meeting someone."

"Shame," he muses, passing over a tiny black plate with my bill. I hand over a twenty on a smile. "Have a lovely evening, madam."

"Thank you." I drop elegantly to my feet and pivot, making my way to the exit, hoping I can flag a cab quickly.

But I barely make it two paces before I'm skidding to halt. My stomach twists and my skin turns stone cold, sending every fine hair on my body standing upright. He *is* here. And he's with her. She's just settling back in her seat at the table, her back to me, but I can see Miller's face just fine, and it's straight, as usual, yet I can see the boredom plain and clear. Cassie is animated, chucking hand gestures everywhere, throwing her head back on continuous laughs and also throwing champagne down her throat. Her hair's coiled into a tight bun on her nape and she's wearing black satin, not your average business meeting attire. There are oysters on the table. And she keeps reaching over and touching him.

"Decided to stay for another?" the barman asks, but I don't answer. I keep my eyes on Miller and back up until my bum meets the stool. Then I lift myself slowly.

"Yes, please," I murmur, placing my purse back on the bar. I'm not sure how I missed him. His table is directly below, in perfect sight. Maybe I was looking too hard. I think carefully, trying to figure out my next move. Good God, I'm beginning to feel the rage burning in my gut.

I accept the Bellini that's handed to me; then I find my phone, calling him and holding it calmly to my ear. It starts to ring. I watch as he shifts in his seat and holds his finger up to Cassie in a gesture to be excused, but when he glances down at his screen, he shows no emotion or shock at seeing my name. He slips it back in his pocket and shakes his head. It's a motion to suggest that the caller is of no importance. His actions inflame the hurt, but worst of all, it inflames the anger.

I drop my phone back in my purse and turn to the barman. "I'm just going to use the washroom."

"Down the stairs. I'll watch your drink."

"Thank you." I take in a long, confidence-boosting lungful of air and start toward the stairs, taking a firm hold of the gold handrail when I reach it while praying to the stair gods that I don't make a complete fool of myself and stumble to my arse. I'm shaking like a leaf, but I need to remain composed and poised. How the heck did I find myself amidst this hideousness?

Because I put myself here, that's how.

My steps are precise and accurate, my body swaying seductively. I find it too easy. I'm being watched by numerous men. Coming down these stairs is like the parting of the waves. I'm alone, and I'm purposely drawing attention to myself. I'm not looking anywhere, though, except right at my heart's nemesis, willing him to glance up and see me. He's listening to Cassie, nodding and saying the odd word, but he's taking slow sips of his scotch more often than anything else. The resentment cripples me—resentment that another woman is getting a close-up of his perfect lips latching onto the glass.

I quickly divert my stare downward when he casts his eyes toward the stairs. He's seen me, I'm certain of it. I can feel glacial blues freezing my skin, but I refuse to stop, and as I reach the toilets, I glance over my shoulder. He's coming after me. I said I'd make him choke, and I think I have. His face is cut with too many emotions—anger, shock... worry.

I escape into the ladies' and study myself in the mirror. There's no getting away from it; I look ruffled and a little distressed, and the light brushing of my cheeks with my palms turns into light smacks as I try to slap some feeling back into me. I'm in unknown territory. I don't know how to handle this situation, but instinct seems to be guiding me pretty well. He knows I'm here. He knows that I know he's lied to me. What is he going to say?

Deciding that I really want to know, I quickly wash my clammy hands, straighten my dress, and brace myself to face him. I'm a nervous wreck when I open the door to exit, but seeing him standing with his back leaning against the wall, looking all pissed off, soon sucks up all of those nerves. Now I'm just mad.

I meet his clear eyes with equal contempt. "How were the oysters?" I ask evenly.

"Salty," he replies, the hollows of his cheeks pulsing from his ticking jaw.

"That's a shame, but I wouldn't be concerned. Your date's probably too drunk to notice."

His eyes narrow as he steps forward. "She's not my date."

"What is she, then?"

"Business."

I laugh. It's condescending and rude, but I couldn't give a toss. Business meetings don't happen on Monday night in Quaglino's. And you don't wear satin dresses. "You lied to me."

"You've been snooping."

I can't deny it, so I don't. I'm feeling emotion take hold. It's racing through me now, making up for Miller's lack of it.

"Just business." He takes another step toward me, closing the distance. I want to move back, distance myself, but my heels are cemented in place, my muscles refusing to work.

"I don't believe you."

"You should."

"You've given me no reason to, Miller." I fight against my useless limbs and pass him. "Enjoy your evening."

"I will once I can de-stress," he counters softly, taking hold of my neck to stop me escaping. The heat of his touch immediately rids my body of the goose bumps and heats me...everywhere. "Go home, Livy. I'll pick you up soon. We'll have a chat before we start with the de-stressing."

Disgusted and fighting my way from his hold, I swing around and stab at his impassive face with furious eyes. "You'll get nothing more from me."

"I beg to differ."

I flinch at his arrogance and confidence. I've never slapped a man in my life. I've never slapped anyone.

Until now.

The power of my small palm across his face creates the most piercing sound, the smack echoing in the noisy air around us. My hand is on fire and judging by the instant red mark on Miller's tanned skin, so is his cheek. I'm shocked by my actions, and my frozen body and stunned face are proof of it.

He clasps his chin, seeming to click his jaw back into place. Miller Hart doesn't give much away, but there's no denying his surprise. "You have a vicious swipe, sweet girl."

"I'm not your sweet girl," I retort nastily, leaving Miller rubbing some life back into his cheek. Taking the stairs fast, I don't veer left for the exit, the enticement of my Bellini too much to resist. I land at the bar and knock it back quickly, gasping and slamming the empty down, drawing the attention of the barman.

"Another?" he asks, swinging straight into action when I nod.

"Livy." Miller's whisper in my ear makes me jump. "Please go home and wait for me there."

"No."

"Livy, I'm asking you nicely." There's an edge of desperation in his tone that makes me swivel on my stool to face him. His face is straight, but his eyes are pleading. "Let me fix this."

He *is* begging, but he's just confirmed that there is, indeed, something to be fixed. "What needs fixing?" I ask.

"Us." His one-word answer is spoken quietly. "Because there's no me or you anymore, Livy. It's us."

"Then why lie? If you've nothing to hide, why lie to me?"

He closes his eyes, obviously trying to keep his cool, and then reopens them slowly. "Believe me. It's simply business." His eyes and tone are full of sincerity as he leans down and kisses me gently on the lips. "Don't make me go without you tonight. I need you in my arms."

"I'll wait here for you."

"Business and pleasure, Olivia. You know my rules." He pulls me gently down from the stool.

"So you've never mixed business and pleasure with Cassie?"

He frowns. "No."

I'm frowning now, too. "Why the meal in a posh restaurant, then? And the oysters and touching across the table?"

Our furrowed brows are matching, but before Miller has a chance to clear up the obvious confusion, we're confronted with Cassie.

At least who I thought was Cassie. This woman, while stunning and in possession of an amazing figure from behind, is older—by fifteen years, at least. She's obviously wealthy and very exuberant. "Miller, darling!" she sings at him. She's drunk, waving a champagne flute in my face.

"Crystal." He starts twitching, pushing into my back. "Please excuse me for a moment."

"Of course!" She dumps her backside on my recently vacated stool. "Shall I order more drinks?"

"No," Miller replies, pushing me onward. C? Crystal? I'm confused, but my poor, overloaded mind won't allow me to voice it or ask questions.

"There's no need for your friend to leave," she purrs, and I look back, seeing her smiling at me. No, she's not smiling; she's smirking. "The more the merrier."

I frown and look up at Miller, who looks like he's gone into shock. He speaks up, but his jaw is tight, making his words seem threatening. "I told you this was just dinner."

"Yes, yes." She rolls her eyes dramatically and pours the rest of the champagne down her throat. "And would this sweet little thing be the reason for our change in etiquette?"

"That's none of your business." He tries to remove me from the bar, but I'm as stiff as him now, hindering his attempts.

"What's she talking about, Miller?" I ask more calmly than I'm feeling.

"Nothing. Let's go."

"No!" I twist out of his hold and face the woman.

She seems oblivious to the tension bouncing between Miller and myself as she demands more champagne from the barman before handing me a card. "Here. Doesn't look like I'll need this anymore. Keep it safe."

I take the card without thought and glance down at the ivory embossed business card, seeing only Miller's name, telephone number, and e-mail. "What's this?"

Miller goes to snatch it, but my nimble hands move faster, pulling it from his reach. "It's nothing, Livy. Please, give it to me."

The woman laughs. "Put it on speed dial, sweetheart."

"Crystal!" Miller shouts, shutting her up in an instant. "It's time for you to leave."

Her eyes widen and turn slowly to me. "Oh my," she breathes, dragging her smug stare down my frozen body. "Has London's most notorious male escort gone and fallen in love?"

Her words knock all of the air from my lungs and my knees give out a little, causing me to reach out and grab Miller's jacket. Escort? I slowly turn the card over, seeing "Hart Services" in an elegant scrolled font.

"Shut up, Crystal," he snarls, clenching my hand.

"She doesn't know?" She laughs some more, looking at me in

pity. "And there's me thinking she was paying like the rest of us." She downs her fresh champagne, while I'm fighting down the bile that's rising in my throat. "Think yourself lucky, sweetheart. A night with Miller Hart will set you back thousands."

"Stop," I whisper, shaking my head. "Please stop." I want to run away, but my thumping heart won't allow the instructions from my brain to pass through to my legs. It's bouncing them straight back up to my head, making me dizzy and confused.

"Livy." He appears in my downcast view, his face not the usual expressionless beauty that I've fast become used to. "She's drunk. Please don't listen to her."

"You accept money for sex." The words stab at me repeatedly. "You listened to me spill everything—about my mother, about me. You acted all shocked, when you're just like she was. How I . . ."

"No." He shakes his head adamantly.

"Yes," I counter, my motionless body coming back to life and beginning to shake. "You sell yourself."

"No, Livy."

In my peripheral vision, I see Crystal lower from the stool. "I love drama, but I have a fat, balding, bastard of a husband who'll have to suffice for this evening."

Miller swings violently toward her. "You'll keep this to yourself."

She smiles and rubs his arm. "I'm not a gossip, Miller."

He scoffs and she laughs as she sashays out of the bar, taking the fur coat that's held out by the cloakroom attendant on her way.

Miller yanks a wallet from his pocket and throws a pile of notes onto the bar, and then takes my neck. "We're leaving."

I don't fight him off. I'm in shock, I feel sick, and my head is ringing. I can't even think clearly to comprehend what's happening. I feel my legs moving beneath me, but I don't seem to be going anywhere. I can feel my heart beating wildly, but I don't seem to be able to breathe. My eyes are open, but all I can see is my mother.

"Livy?"

I look up at him blankly, finding sorrow, anguish, and torment. "Tell me I'm dreaming this," I murmur quietly. It'll be the worst dream ever, but as long as it's not real, I don't care. Please let me wake up.

His face screws up in defeat as he stops walking, bringing me to a halt by the giant glass doors. He looks totally beaten. "Olivia, I wish I could say yes."

I'm pulled into his arms and compressed against his chest violently, but I don't return his *thing*. I'm numb.

"We're going home." He tucks me into his side and leads me onto the street. We walk some distance, neither one of us saying anything, me because I physically can't and Miller because I know he doesn't know what to say. I might've been rendered useless by shock, but my brain is working better than ever before, and it's making me relive memories that I've already spent too much time on recently. My mother. Me. And now Miller.

I'm bundled into his car carefully, like he's worried I might break. I might—if I'm not broken already. I want to rewind the evening, change so many things, but where would I be then, apart from unaware and completely in the dark?

"Would you like me to take you home?" he asks quietly, settling cautiously in his seat.

I turn my blank face to his. The roles are reversed. It's him showing all of the emotion now, not me. "Where else would I want to go?" I ask.

His eyes drop, he starts the engine, and I'm driven home with Snow Patrol reminding me to open my eyes.

The journey is slow, like he's dragging it out, making it last for the longest time, and when he slowly pulls up outside Nan's house, I open the door to get out without delay.

"Livy." He sounds desperate as he seizes my arm and stops me from getting any farther, but he says no more. I'm not sure what he *can* say, and he clearly doesn't either.

"What?" I ask, hoping I'm going to wake at any moment and find myself wrapped in his thing, safe in his bed away from the cold harshness of the reality that I've found myself in—a reality that is all too familiar.

The silence is disturbed by Miller's phone, and he stabs at the reject button on a curse, but it soon rings again. "Fuck!" he yells, tossing it onto the dashboard. It stops and chimes again.

"You'd better get that." I pull my arm from his grip. "I expect they are all prepared to hand over their thousands for a night with London's most notorious male escort. You may as well make some extra cash while you fuck a woman. I must owe you thousands."

I ignore his wince and leave him in the car with a face full of hurt, set on throwing all my energy into getting over the second prostitute I've been landed with in my short life. Except this one accepted and comforted me. This one will be harder to get over. No, this one will be impossible to get over. I can feel a darker solitude awaiting me.

CHAPTER TWENTY-FOUR

When dawn breaks, I'm still staring blankly up at the ceiling of my bedroom. It was a catch-22 situation—fall asleep and have nightmares, or stay awake and live them. My decision was made for me. I couldn't sleep. My poor mind isn't being given any respite and my eyes are being bombarded with flashbacks of his face. I'm in no fit state to face the world. Just as I feared, I'm further in solitary than I ever was before I met Miller Hart.

My mobile chimes from my bedside table and I reach over, knowing it could be only one of two people, but going by the defeated look on Miller's face last night, I'm opting for Gregory. He'll want the lowdown from the rest of my weekend with the coffee hater. I'm right. I feel no guilt as I reject his call and let the voice mail pick it up. I can't speak to anyone. I fire him a quick text.

Late 4 work. Call u later. Hope u r ok xx

I might be late, I'm not sure, but it doesn't matter because I'm not going anywhere, except farther under my covers where it's dark and silent. I hear the creaking of floorboards, and then the chirpy singing of Nan. It makes my eyes swell with tears again, but I brush them determinedly away when she barrels into my room and hits me with delighted navy eyes.

"Morning!" she chirps, making her way to my curtains and flinging them open. The morning light attacks my eyes.

"Nan! Shut the curtains!" I burrow under my covers, escaping the brightness but mostly escaping the look of her cheerful face. It's eating me up inside.

"But you'll be late."

"I don't have to work today." I'm on auto-pilot as I blurt an excuse to keep me in bed and hopefully Nan away. "I'm working Friday night so Del gave me today off. I'm going to catch up on some sleep." I keep my face hidden under the covers and even though I can't see her, I know she's smiling.

"Didn't get much sleep at Miller's over the weekend, then?" The delight in her tone cripples me.

"No." This is a ridiculously inappropriate conversation to be having with my grandmother, but I know it'll pacify her and give me some peace...for now. I have no room to accept any guilt for lying to her.

"Wonderful!" she cries. "I'm going shopping with George." I feel her hand rub my back over the bed covers briefly before her footsteps get quieter and the door to my room closes.

Finding the strength to break my split with Miller to Nan will have to wait until I can think of a plausible reason. She won't settle for anything less than a full explanation. She doesn't love Miller Hart; she loves the idea of me being happy and in a stable relationship. But if I'm mistaken and she does love Miller, then I can soon remedy that...but I won't. My recent revelation will only stir ghosts for Nan, too. She might be spunky, but she's still an old lady. I'll suffer this darkness alone.

I relax into my mattress and attempt to find sleep, hoping my dreams don't bring more nightmares.

* * *

I was hoping in vain. My sleep was restless, seeing me waking regularly, sweating, breathless, and mad. I give up come evening. After forcing myself to shower, I lie wrapped in a towel on the bed, trying to rid my mind of Miller and desperately trying to seek something else to focus on. Anything other than him.

I should join a gym. I bolt upright in bed. I *have* joined a gym. "Bollocks!" I grab my phone and note that I have forty minutes to get myself to my induction. I can do it, and it's the perfect distraction. They say working out alleviates stress and gets the feel good pheromones pumping. It's just what I need. I swing into a rushed frenzy, stuffing some leggings, an oversized T-shirt, and my white Converse into a bag. I'll look like a complete amateur, with no sporty looking getup in sight, but it'll do for now. I'll go shopping. I bundle my heavy hair up with a hair tie as I scurry down the landing, coming to a stop at the top of the stairs when my phone declares the arrival of a text message. Walking slowly down the stairs, my heart drops with each step I take when I see it's him.

I'll be at Langan's Brasserie on Stratton St at 8. I want my four hours.

My arse hits the step halfway down the stairs, and I stare at the message, reading it over and over. He's had far more than his four hours already. What point is he trying to make here? He's holding me to a deal that was made weeks ago, and has since been quashed by feelings and too many encounters to list. He even said himself that it was a stupid deal. It really *was* a stupid deal. It still is a stupid deal.

His unreasonable demand stirs years of anger until it's fizzing uncontrollably in my gut. I've battled years of self-torture. I've beat myself up trying to understand what my mother found that was more important than me and my grandparents. I've watched the agony she caused affect my dear nan and gramps, and I've tinkered too close to causing more agony myself. I still could, if Nan ever discovered where I really was during my disappearing spell. He's listened to me spill my heart to him, he drowned me in compassion, and all the while he was the king of debasement? I glance back down at his message. He thinks by reverting back to the clipped, arrogant arsehole he'll have me falling at his feet again? A red mist falls, blocking the questions I want to ask and the answers I need to find. I can see nothing except resentment, hurt, and burning anger. I'm not going to the gym to lash out my hurt on a treadmill or punching bag. Miller can take it all.

I jump up and dash to my bedroom, snatching down the third and final dress from my shopping trip with Gregory. Giving it a good inspection, I conclude very quickly that he'll disintegrate before my eyes. Holy shit, it's lethal. I have no idea what possessed me to allow Gregory to talk me into buying it, but I'm so glad I did. It's red, it's backless, it's short, it's . . . reckless.

Once I've taken my time to shower again, shaving everywhere and creaming from top to toe, I wriggle into the dress. The design won't allow for a bra, which, begrudgingly, isn't a problem for me and my sparse chest. I flip my head upside down and blast my masses of blond into perfect waves that tumble freely; then I apply some makeup, concentrating on keeping it natural, just how he likes it. My new black stilettos and purse finish me off and deciding a jacket will spoil the effect, I'm soon darting down the stairs faster than is safe.

The door swings open before I make it there, Nan and George halting all conversation when they clock me flying toward them.

"Wowzers!" George blurts, then apologizes profusely when Nan scowls at him. "Sorry. Bit of a shock, that's all."

"Are you going out with Miller?" Nan looks like she's just hit the jackpot at bingo.

"Yes." I rush past them.

"Jolly good!" she sings. "See how she rocks the red, George?"

I don't hear George's reply, although I gather from his reaction to my red-clad body that it was a resounding yes.

By the time I've run halfway down the street toward the main road, I'm verging on breaking out in a sweat, so I slow my pace, also thinking that I should be fashionably late—make *him* sweat. I hover on the corner for a few minutes, ironically feeling like a hooker, before I flag down a cab and tell him my destination.

I check my makeup in the reflection of the window, make a fuss of my hair and brush my dress down, making certain that it won't be creased. I'm being as precise as Miller, but I bet he hasn't got butterflies in his stomach, and I'm damning myself to hell for having a whole farm of them fluttering around in my tummy.

When the cabbie turns onto Piccadilly toward Stratton Street, I glance at the dashboard clock. It's five past eight. I'm not late enough, and I need a cash machine, too. "This will do," I say, rummaging through my purse and passing over my only twenty. "Thank you." I slide out as elegantly as possible and stride down a busy Piccadilly, where on a weeknight I look ridiculously over-dressed. This only heightens my self-consciousness, but remembering what Gregory told me, I try my very hardest to appear confident—like I always make this much effort. Once I've found a cashpoint, I withdraw some money and round the corner onto Stratton Street. It's eight fifteen, making me a perfect quarter of an hour late. The door is opened for me and I take a deep breath of confidence, entering looking cool and self-assured, when on the inside I'm wondering what the frigging hell I'm doing.

"Are you meeting someone, madam?" the maître d' asks, giving me the once-over, looking both impressed and a little disapproving. It makes me pull my hem down, which I immediately mentally chastise myself for.

"Miller Hart," I inform him with the utmost confidence, making up for the little slipup of adjusting my hem.

"Ah, Mr. Hart." He clearly knows him. It makes me feel like crap. Does he know what Miller does? Does he think I'm a client? My anger burns the nerves away.

He smiles brightly at me and indicates for me to follow, which I do while struggling not to look around the restaurant for Miller.

As we pass through the randomly placed tables, I begin to feel the deep burn on my skin that my heart's nemesis spikes, just from looking at me. Wherever he is, he's seen me, and as I slowly cast my eyes forward, I see him, too. There would be nothing that I could ever do to stop the increase of my heart rate, nor the hitching of my breath. He may be the male equivalent of a high-class prostitute, but he's still Miller and he's still stunning and he's still . . . perfect. He rises from his chair and fastens the button of his jacket, his dark stubble gracing his inconceivably gifted face, his blue eyes blistering me as I approach. I don't falter. I meet his gaze with equal resolve, noting immediately what I'm about to encounter. He has an air of determination surrounding him. He's going to try and seduce me again, which is fine, but he won't be getting his sweet girl.

He nods at the maître d', a signal that he'll take it from here, then rounds the table and pulls my chair out for me. "Please." He swoops his hand toward the seat.

"Thank you." I sit and place my purse on the table, almost relaxed until Miller lays his hand on my shoulder and pushes his mouth to my ear.

"You look unimaginably beautiful." He pulls my hair to the side and skims his lips across the tender hollow below my ear. He can't see me, so it doesn't matter that I close my eyes, but my neck tilting to give him space is a dead giveaway of what he does to me. "Exquisite," he murmurs, sending a wave of tingles down my spine.

Relieving me of his touch, he appears in front of me again, unbuttoning his jacket and taking his seat. He glances down at his expensive watch and raises his eyebrows, silently observing my lateness.

"I've taken the liberty of ordering for us."

I match his raised brow. "You were obviously confident that I would be here."

"You are, aren't you?" He collects a bottle of white wine from the floor standing wine bucket that's positioned next to the table and starts to pour. The glasses are smaller than the red ones that we used yesterday, and I'm wondering how Miller will cope with the placing of things on the restaurant table. Nothing is positioned as it would be at home, but he doesn't seem too bothered by it. He's not twitchy, and weirdly that is making me *very* twitchy. I almost want to put the wine on the table where it belongs.

Pulling my wandering mind back to the man sitting opposite me, I observe his cool persona for a few moments; then I speak. "Why did you ask me to come?"

He lifts his glass and swirls the wine slowly before taking it to those devastating lips and drinking slowly, all the time ensuring his eyes never stray from mine. He knows what he's doing. "I don't recall asking you to come."

For a split second, I nearly lose my composure. "You don't want me here?" I ask cockily.

"As I recall, I sent you a message telling you that I would be here at eight. I also expressed my desire for something. I didn't demand it." He takes another slow sip. "But by you being here, I'm assuming you would like to give me what I desire."

His arrogance has returned full force. It spikes my own sass, and I know Miller is now wary of my sass. He likes his sweet girl. I reach into my purse and gather the cash I've loaded myself with. Then I toss it on the plate in front of him and relax back in my chair, all brash and calm. "I'd like to be entertained for four hours."

His wineglass is floating between his mouth and the table as he stares down at the pile of money, which I've diabolically used my savings account to obtain, the savings account that contains every penny that my mother left me, the savings account that I have never dipped into out of principle. How ironic that I'm now using some of the money to have myself... *entertained*. I've drawn a reaction, just like I planned, and the words he once said are dancing at the front of my mind, egging me on. *Promise me you won't ever degrade yourself like that again.* Me? What about him?

He's speechless. His eyes are fixed on the money, and I can definitely see his suspended hand begin to shake, the wine rippling as evidence. "What's this?" he asks tightly, settling his glass down. I'm not shocked when I see him reposition the glass before he raises incensed blues to me.

"A thousand," I reply, completely unruffled by his obvious anger. "I know the notorious Miller Hart demands more, but as we're brokering a deal on just four hours and you know what you're getting, I figured a thousand was fair." I take my glass and sip lazily, making an exaggerated display of swallowing and licking my lips. His blue eyes are wider than usual. His shock probably wouldn't be noticeable to anyone else, but I know those eyes, and I know that most of his emotion comes from them.

He breathes in deeply and slowly scrapes the money from his plate, tidying it into a neat pile before reaching for my purse and stuffing it back inside. "Don't insult me, Olivia."

"You're insulted?" I actually laugh. "How much money have you made from giving yourself to those women?"

He leans forward, his jaw ticking. Oh, I'm drawing emotion all right. "Enough to buy an exclusive club," he says coldly, "and I don't give *myself* to those women, Olivia. I give them my body, nothing else."

I wince, and I know he catches it, but listening to him speaking like that is turning my stomach. "You hardly give me anything else, either," I state unfairly. He absolutely has given me something other than his body, and his barely noticeable recoil tells me he knows it, too. He's hurt by my claim. "Buy yourself a new tie." I take the money out and throw it on his side of the table, shocked by my own harshness, but his reactions are egging me on, feeding my unreasonable need to prove something, even though I'm not entirely sure what the purpose of my coldness is achieving. I can't stop, though. I'm on auto-pilot.

The hollows of his cheeks begin to pulse. "And how was it different when you did it?" he grinds the question out.

I try to conceal my choked breath. "I put myself in that world for a reason," I seethe. "I didn't relish in the extravagance. I didn't make a living from selling myself."

His mouth snaps shut and he lets his eyes fall to the table briefly before he stands and buttons his jacket. "What's happened to you?"

"I've told you before, Miller Hart. You've happened to me."

"I don't like this person. I like the girl who I . . ."

"Then.You.Should.Have.Left.Me.Alone." I speak slowly and clearly, yanking yet more feeling from this apparently emotionless man. He's barely containing himself. I'm not sure whether he wants to shout or cry.

We're briefly interrupted when the waiter places a platter of ice and oysters on the table. He doesn't speak or ask if we require anything else. He skulks off quickly and quietly, aware of the obvious tension, leaving me staring at the platter in disbelief.

"Oysters," I breathe.

"Yes, enjoy. I'm leaving," he says, clearly forcing his body to turn away from me.

"I'm a paying client," I remind him, reaching for one of the shells and dislodging the meat with my fork.

He turns slowly back toward me. "You make me feel cheap."

Good, I think to myself. Expensive suits and luxury living

doesn't make this acceptable. "And the other women don't?" I ask. "Should I have bought you a Rolex?" I slowly raise the oyster to my lips and tip it down my throat, wiping the back of my hand across my mouth and holding his gaze while I lick my lips seductively.

"Don't push me, Livy."

"Fuck me," I mouth, leaning forward in my chair, getting a strange thrill from seeing him struggle to know what to do with me. He didn't bargain on this when he set this up. I'm turning this around on him.

He takes a few moments to gather himself before leaning across the table. "You want me to fuck you?" he asks, not bothered about his gentlemanly manners in the presence of nearby diners.

I manage to contain my recoil at his returned confidence, even if I don't utter any words.

He leans in farther, his face deadly serious, all hurt, anger, and shock seeming to have disappeared. "I asked you a question. You know how I feel about repeating myself."

For reasons I'll probably never know, I don't hesitate. "Yes." My voice is a breathy murmur and, despite fighting it, my body is flying into full-on responsive mode.

His eyes are burning through me. "Get up."

CHAPTER TWENTY-FIVE

I stand immediately and wait for him to round the table and collect me, taking a firm grip of my neck and pushing me out of the restaurant urgently. When we hit the fresh evening air, I'm directed across the road toward a hotel where I expect his car is parked, except we don't head toward the car park. The doorman opens the glass door to the regal, grand hotel and I'm pushed through, suddenly surrounded by exceptionally traditional décor, with a stone fountain in the center of the foyer and old worn leather couches scattered everywhere. Character is bursting from every corner. It's classically stately, like the Queen herself might appear at any moment.

Miller drops his hold of my neck. "Wait," he instructs shortly, approaching the reception area. He speaks quietly to the woman behind the large, curved counter for a few moments, before taking a key that's quickly handed to him. He turns and cocks his head toward the stairs, but with his lack of hold on my neck, I'm feeling a little unstable. "Livy," he grinds, his impatience kicking me into action.

He leaves me free from his grip as we take the stairs, the tension bouncing between us almost unbearable, but I'm not sure whether it's sexual tension or nervous tension.

It's both.

I'm nervous now, while Miller is overflowing with sexual craving. He stares blankly forward, displaying nothing, which isn't unusual, except now it's making me uneasy. He's shut down completely, and even though I'm sizzling with desire, I'm a little apprehensive, too.

I'm reclaimed by his hold on my neck when we reach the fourth floor and I'm being guided down the extravagant corridor until he's inserting a card into the door and pushing me into the room. I should be overwhelmed by the gigantic four-poster bed and the gushing luxury, but I'm too busy trying to balance my senses. I'm standing in the middle of the room, feeling exposed and vulnerable, while Miller looks poised and powerful.

He reaches up and starts unraveling his tie slowly. "Let's see what a grand gets you with the notorious Miller Hart, shall we?" His tone indicates complete detachment. "Strip, sweet girl." His endearment for me is rife with sarcasm.

I search everywhere for my earlier brashness, but I'm struggling to find it.

"You're hesitating, Livy. The women I fuck don't waste time when they have me."

His words tear at my heart a little, but also inject some courage and reignite my anger. I can't let him see me wavering. I instigated this, but why I have is now forgotten. I firm up my movements and pull my dress from my body, letting it fall to the ground, the red material pooling at my feet.

"No bra," he muses, shrugging his jacket off and unbuttoning his waistcoat. His eyes are dragging slowly down my body, drinking me in. "Take your knickers off." His commanding tone has been used plenty before, but the soft edge has long gone. I don't want to be turned on by it. I don't want the throb between my thighs to intensify. I don't want to find the conceited arsehole before me attractive. Yet I can't prevent my body from responding to him. I'm shaking with anticipation. I'm a foregone conclusion. Even now.

I slowly push my underwear down my thighs and step out, then kick my shoes off. I'm naked, and when I return my eyes to Miller and see he's now barechested, I forget any reluctance, being blinded by the pure extravagance of his torso. There really are no words, but when his trousers and boxers are slowly removed, I find one.

"Ohhh...," I breathe, my lips parting in an attempt to get some air into my lungs. His clothes are cast aside carelessly and he's staring at me through his dark lashes as he slides a condom on.

"Impressed?"

I don't know why he's asked. It's nothing that I haven't seen before, but it improves every time I'm confronted with it. Miller's perfect cock, his perfect body, and his perfect face. It all screams hazard. It did before. I knew it then and I most definitely know it now.

"Are you going to make me ask you again?"

I return my eyes to his and form some words. "Not a thousand pounds impressed." My cockiness shocks me.

His jaw tightens and he starts to approach, taking slow, even strides until he's pushed up against my front, breathing down on me. "Let's see what we can do about that."

I don't have time to respond. I'm pushed back toward the bed until the edge meets the back of my thighs and I can go no farther. I'm desperate to feel him, so I lift my hands and push my fingers into his hair, messing up his dark waves with a few circling caresses.

"Get your hands off me," he growls. I can't hide my shock at his severe order, my hands instantly falling away from his head to my sides. "You don't get to touch me, Livy." He reaches forward and takes my nipple between his thumb and forefinger, squeezing hard.

I hiss in pain and cry out, but the shot of pain surprises me and falls into my groin, mixing with the pleasure. It's a heady cocktail of feelings, and I have not the first idea of how to deal with them.

"I'm going to drive you insane," he declares, producing a belt from behind his back. The sight of the brown leather makes my eyes widen and fly to his, finding an element of uncertainty. He's unsure; I can see it.

"You're going to hurt me?" I ask, the potential of the belt sending a shock wave of fear coursing through me.

"I don't hurt women, Olivia. Lift your hands to the bar."

I look up, seeing the brown wooden bar stretching from one post to another, and relieved his intentions seem to be different from my thoughts, I lift willingly. But I can't reach. "I can't . . ."

"Get on the bed." He's brusque, impatient.

Negotiating the soft mattress is a task, but I eventually steady myself, without any offer of assistance, and hold my wrists to the bar. He's going to bind me, restrain me, and while it's a more appealing option than the thought of being whipped, I'm not entirely happy about it. I thought he'd fuck me. I didn't expect the introduction of restraints, and I certainly thought I would be able to touch him.

His tallness allows him to reach the bar with ease, and he sets about weaving the leather between my wrists and around the bar effortlessly and confidently. He's done this before. "Don't fidget," he snaps when I start to wriggle, the leather cutting into the bone of my wrists.

"Miller, it—"

"Bailing on me?" He raises a challenging eyebrow, victory gushing from his blues. He thinks I will. He thinks that I'm going to call a halt to this.

He's wrong.

"No." I raise my chin in confidence, my sureness strengthening when he loses the smugness.

"As you wish." He pulls my legs down from the bed so I'm suspended, the leather instantly becoming taut and sharp around my wrists. "Hold on to the bar to ease the pressure."

I manage to follow through on his command, linking my fingers over the bar. It alleviates the cutting of the leather into my flesh, making me more comfortable, but Miller's severe words and harsh face do not. He's only ever made love to me. He's only ever worshipped me. I can see clearly that I'm going to get neither now.

He starts running his eyes over my naked, suspended body, clearly trying to decide where to start, then after staring at the apex of my thighs for a few moments, he places his hand on my thigh and starts stroking his way up until he's brushing lightly over my clitoris. I draw in a long breath and hold it. This action is quite tender, but I'm under no illusion that I'm about to be worshipped.

"I have rules," he says slowly, thrusting his fingers into me, pushing all of the air from my lungs. "You don't get to touch me." He withdraws and wipes his fingers across my bottom lip, spreading my wetness everywhere before leaning in, getting as close as possible. "And I don't kiss."

I absorb his hard stare and his hard words. My restrained hands are preventing me from touching him, but his lips are close, so I lean forward to try and capture them. He pulls back, shaking his head, and then curls his hands around the tops of my thighs and grabs harshly, lifting me to his body. Like a man possessed, he yanks me onto him on a guttural bark, impaling me fully, no easing in and no soft words to accompany his taking of me. I scream in shock at his ruthless move, my legs hanging limply around his hips, but he doesn't give me time to adjust. He lifts my body up and yanks me back down again. He's completely merciless. He falls into an unforgivingly fast and brutal pace, hitting me repeatedly, over and over, shouting and barking on each and every strike. My head is limp, my screams loud, and my body in shock. It's painful, but as he pounds on, the discomfort starts to break and pleasure begins to push its way forward, sending my delirious mind into despair.

"Miller!" I cry, yanking and pulling at my wrists in a vain attempt to free myself. I need to feel him, but I'm ignored, his grip increasing further, his hips hitting me harder. "Miller!"

"Shut the fuck up, Livy!" he shouts, following through his cold order with a powerful smash of his body into mine.

I force every useless muscle in my neck to solidify my droopy head, pulling it up and finding clear blue eyes full of purpose. He looks crazed and completely detached, like he's not present in mind and his body is acting on instinct. There's nothing in those eyes. I don't like it. "Kiss me!" I yell, wanting to draw the feelings that I know are there. This is unbearable, and not because of the ruthlessness of him smashing into me, but because of the absence of our usual connection. It's completely gone, and I need it, especially when he's taking me so aggressively. "Kiss me!" I'm screaming in his face now, but he just squeezes my thighs further and pounds harder, the sweat dripping from his face. My pleasure has gone. I'm getting nothing from this, except the earlier pain returning, but it's hurting physically *and* emotionally now. I've lost my grip of the bar above me, leaving the leather of the belt cutting into my skin, and his hold on the backs of my thighs is pinching my flesh. But my heart is hurting the most. I'm not feeling my usual comforted bliss or safety, and his denial to let me kiss him is killing me. He knows exactly what he's doing. And I asked him to do it.

My eyes close and I drop my head back, not wanting to look at his face anymore. I don't recognize it. This isn't the man I've fallen in love with, but I don't stop this because in a screwed-up kind of way, this will help me get over Miller Hart, and the fact that he doesn't chastise me for depriving him of my face only inflames the hurt further. The reasons for my stupid decision to do this are suddenly all I can think of as I blank out and accept his brutality.

I think of all of the loving words he's said to me, all of the tender touches he's given me.

"I'll never do anything less than worship you. I'll never be a drunken fumble. Every time I take you, Livy, you'll remember it. Each and every moment will be etched on that beautiful mind of yours forever. Every kiss. Every touch. Every word."

Miller's loud roar pulls me straight back into a room that's cold and unwelcoming, despite the warmth and luxury of the surroundings. And something strange happens—something out of my control. I'm shocked, my body taking on a mind of its own and responding to his vicious strikes. I orgasm. But it passes with no element of pleasure attached. I'm attacked by one last round of thundering strikes before he raises me slightly to gain more leverage, then finishes on an ear-piercing bellow that resounds around the room. He holds himself inside of me and drops his head back, his chest expanding at a crazy rate and sweat pouring down his neck. I'm numb. I can't feel the pain of the leather or the agony in my heart.

"Any man who's done anything less than worship you should be fucking shot!"

My legs are pushed down from his waist, and he pulls out of me quickly, but he doesn't start to release me. He leaves me on a quiet curse and goes into the bathroom, slamming the door viciously behind him.

All of the missing emotion from that encounter is made up for when I begin to weep. My head goes limp, my chin hitting my chest, and I can't even find the strength to relieve the pain in my wrists by getting myself back on the bed. I'm just hanging lifelessly, my body jerking from my sobs.

Destroyed.

Empty.

I hear the door open, but I keep my head down. I can't look at him and I can't let him see that I've fallen apart. I goaded him, pushed his boundaries. He's hidden this man from me. He's fought his control the whole time.

"Fuck!" he roars, and I drag my heavy head up to see his face pointed toward the ceiling. His features are distorted . . . disturbed. He lets out another ear-piercing bellow and swings around, sending his fist crashing into the bathroom door and splintered wood crashing to the floor.

A suppressed sob escapes my mouth and my chin falls back to my chest.

"Livy?" His voice is softer but doesn't ease my wretched state as I feel his hands working around my wrists. He wraps an arm around my stomach to hold me up while he unravels the belt, and I hiss in pain when my arms drop lifelessly to my side. "Livy, you let go of the fucking bar!" He sits me on the end of the bed and kneels on the floor before me, pushing my hair away so he can see me. I pull my eyes up to meet his. My face is soaked with tears and Miller is just a blur through my glazed eyes, but the horror on his face is clear, even through my distorted vision. "Oh Jesus." He grabs my wrists, lifting my hands to his mouth, and kisses my knuckles repeatedly, but I flinch, pain searing my flesh from his hold, making his face fall further. Shifting his grip to my forearms, he studies the angry welts silently until I pull my arms away from him and stand on shaky legs. "Livy?"

I ignore the anxiety in his voice and pick up my knickers, pulling them on as fast as my wobbly limbs will allow.

"Livy, what are you doing?" he asks, moving in front of me to get in the field of my vision.

I glance up, seeing panic and uncertainty. "I'm going."

"No." He shakes his head and rests his hands on my waist.

"Don't touch me!" I shout, jumping back to escape him. I can't bear it.

"Oh God, no!" He swipes my dress up from the floor and holds it behind his back. "You can't go."

He's wrong. For once I will find it very easy to walk away from him. "Can I have my dress?"

"No!" He chucks it across the room and takes my waist again. "Livy, that man isn't who I am."

"Get off!" I pull out of his hold and start toward the spot where my dress has landed, but he beats me to it. "Please, give me my dress."

"No, Livy. I'm not letting you leave."

"I never want to see you again!" I shout in his face, making him wince.

"Please don't say that," he begs as I try to win my dress back. "Livy, I'm not letting that be your last memory of me."

I snatch my dress, collect my purse and heels, and run half naked from the room, leaving Miller fighting his way into his boxer shorts. My head is spinning and my body trembling as I dive into the elevator and smash my fist on every button in sight, not prepared to take the time to find the one I need.

"Livy!" His thumping footsteps come charging down the hotel corridor as I continue to hit the buttons.

"Come on!" I shout. "Shut!"

"Livy, please!"

I sag against the back wall when the doors begin to shut, but they don't close fully. Miller's arm appears, forcing them open again. "No!" I shout, backing into a corner of the elevator.

He's heaving, sweating, panic clear on that perfect, usually expressionless face. "Olivia, please, get out of the lift."

I wait for him to step in and seize me, but he doesn't. He's just hovering on the threshold, persistently cursing and forcing the doors open each time they try to close.

"Livy, get out."

"No." I shake my head, clutching my belongings to my chest.

He reaches in, but there's at least two feet between his outstretched hand and me. "Give me your hand."

Why isn't he getting in to pull me out? He's looks afraid, and I'm beginning to realize that it's not just because I'm running away from him. He's scared of something else. The horrible realization slams into my frantic mind, accompanied by countless flashbacks of him carrying me up endless stairs. He's scared of the lift.

He takes a slow look around the inside of the lift until his eyes slowly fall back to mine. "Livy, I beg you. Please, give me your hand." He thrusts his hand forward again, but I'm too stunned to take it. He's truly petrified. "Livy!"

"No," I say quietly, pressing the buttons again. "I'm not getting out." My clouded eyes release the pools of tears that have been building and they begin to trickle down my cheeks.

"Fuck!" His hold of the door releases and his hands delve into his dark waves.

Then the doors start to close again.

And this time he doesn't stop them.

We stare at each other for the short time it takes for them to meet in the middle, and the very last image I see of Miller Hart is what I have come to expect. A straight face. Nothing to tell me what he's thinking. But I don't need expressions from him to tell me how he's feeling anymore.

I stare at the door in silence, my mind awash with so many thoughts to process, but a chime from the lift makes me jump and the doors begin to open. It's only now I realize that I'm standing in my underwear with my dress, shoes, and purse still clutched to my chest.

I hurry to dress myself as a corridor comes into view, relieved that there's no one awaiting the lift's arrival. Then I stop at every floor on the way down until the doors open onto the lobby. My strained heart is working overtime, smashing against my breastbone as I dart out of the lift, desperate to escape this hotel. Images of Miller escorting many women through this foyer engulf my mind and the woman on reception catches my eye as I hurry across the affluent lobby. She knows Miller, she knew the drill, handing him a room key without question or payment, and now she's looking at me with a knowing look. I can't bear it.

"Oh!" I yelp, dropping my purse as I lose my footing, tumbling to my knees and sending an expensive leather briefcase skidding across the marble floor. Pain shoots up my arm when my palm smacks the marble in an attempt to stop my head from hitting the hard surface, my tears beyond my control now. Shocked gasps ring out through the air as I stare at the flecked marble floor. Then it falls silent. Everyone is looking at me.

"Are you okay, darling?" A big hand appears in my downcast vision, the deep, grainy voice pulling my eyes up to the crouching form in front of me. I find a mature man in an expensive suit.

I gasp.

He recoils.

I scramble from my knees and fall back, landing on my backside. My heart rate has lost control. We both stare at each other.

"Olivia?"

I scoop up my purse and struggle to my feet, not knowing how much more shock I can take. It's only been seven years, but his salt-and-pepper-flecked temples have grayed completely, as has the rest of his hair. He's shocked to see me, too, but his face still holds that softness and his gray eyes are still sparkling.

"William." His name falls from my lips on a shocked rush of breath.

His tall body rises, his eyes roaming all over my face. "What are you doing here?"

"I—"

"Olivia!"

I swing around and see Miller come flying down the stairs, fighting his way into his suit jacket. He looks disheveled and untidy, a complete about-face from my usual finicky, fine Miller. The lobby is silent, everyone looking at the girl who's just taken a tumble and now at the man who's pelting down the stairs while dressing himself. He hits the bottom and halts dead in his tracks, his stare cast over my shoulder, his eyes wide. It prompts me to slowly turn until I find William staring as intently at Miller. The men are in a staring standoff, me in the middle.

They know each other.

My simple little world has been turned upside down and has now just exploded on me. I need to escape. My legs kick into action, leaving behind the only two men I have ever loved.

William is a ghost to me and should stay that way.

But Miller is the heart beating in my chest.

Every pound of my feet on the steps jolts an image of him. Every inhale of breath spurs a memory of his words. Every thump of my heart spikes the absent feel of his touch. But nothing is worse than the imprint of his beautiful face on my mind's eye as I run away.

Escape from him.

Hide from him.

Protect myself from him.

This is unquestionably the right thing to do. Everything indicates that I'm being wise—my head, my body . . . everything.

Except my fallen heart.

Don't miss the next book in #1 *New York Times* bestselling author Jodi Ellen Malpas's erotic romance series

ONE NIGHT: DENIED

Available November 2014

For an excerpt right now, "like" Jodi's page at Facebook.com/Jodi Ellen Malpas.

★ ★ ★

Still can't get enough? Read the This Man Trilogy!

  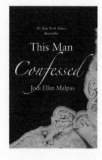

About the Author

Jodi Ellen Malpas was born and raised in the Midlands town of Northampton, England, where she lives with her two boys. Working for her father's construction business full-time, she tried to ignore the lingering idea of writing until it became impossible. She wrote in secret for a long time before finally finding the courage to unleash her creative streak, and in October 2012 she released *This Man*. She took a chance on a story with some intense characters and sparked incredible reactions from women all over the world. Writing powerful love stories and creating addictive characters have become her passion, a passion she now shares with her devoted readers.

You can learn more at:
JodiEllenMalpas.co.uk
Twitter@JodiEllenMalpas
Facebook.com/JodiEllenMalpas